Gang

A Small Town Police Force
Sarcastic, irreverent and crude to each other
Yet loyal to the best interests of its citizens.

M.J. BIERSBACH

outskirts
press

The Gang
A Small Town Police Force
Sarcastic, irreverent, and crude to each other
Yet loyal to the best interests of its citizens
All Rights Reserved.
Copyright © 2018 M.J. Biersbach
v2.0

Outskirts Press, Inc.
http://www.outskirtspress.com

ISBN: 978-1-4787-7973-5

Library of Congress Control Number: 2018902775

Cover Photo © 2018 thinkstockphotos.com. All rights reserved - used with permission.

Outskirts Press and the "OP" logo are trademarks belonging to Outskirts Press, Inc.

PRINTED IN THE UNITED STATES OF AMERICA

*Dedicated to all those in law enforcement who,
even in a small way, made a positive difference
in someone's life without the use of written rules,
policies, recommendations, or the judicial system.*

Acknowledgments

This book is about family--not the conventional type that most people think of when that word is mentioned. It's the story of a family of police officers in a small East Coast tourist town. I think of them as family, because most of the co-workers actually spent more time together in the average twenty-five-year employment than a lot of them did with their own personal family members.

Working with this family was an experience which encompassed some of the better years of my life. After twenty-five years in law enforcement, I retain some unfortunate and unpleasant recollections but also many fond as well as comical memories.

My thanks to the various retired family members who regularly remarked that a book should be written about the number of peculiar people and the unusual events which took place through the early years of the department.

My appreciation to those who knowingly and unknowingly contributed remembrances and ideas for this book, some in which they participated, or after hearing about them, wished they had participated in.

The Police

Small-town police departments used to be a lot like high school gym classes or college fraternities. In addition to dealing with the good guys and the bad guys, there would from time to time be hours of no serious incidents taking place, and sometimes there would be hours of no incidents at all.

During these periods of boredom and lack of animated or physical stimulation, many officers were prone to voice their opinions concerning the boredom and declare, "Something has to be done!" The most popular idea for dealing with the time would be the numerous challenges of how best to ridicule other members of the department for almost any reason.

Individual personality traits of those whose peculiarities were, well... peculiar, would be unceremoniously mocked and scorned for no other reason but for the enjoyment of those doing the mocking.

It was well known that prior to people being concerned about everyone's conduct being culturally, politically, and verbally correct with every word, step, and action, within small-town police departments, the patrolmen could--and would at any opportunity--make fun of as well as insult each other at the first hint of misery and misfortune. That misery and misfortune would always be compensated for with more misery and more torment from fellow employees.

Daily debates would also take place about which unusual experience that may have occurred at a call would be worthy of either admiration or scorn. The more outrageous the circumstance was, the better the chance was of approval and appreciation. That is, as long as blame for the circumstance could not lead to an unfavorable reflection on the department. Whenever unwanted notice would fall upon the department, those involved could be guaranteed official scorn from the administrators, along with an excess of unofficial ridicule from the other officers.

Long before the high visibility of any misjudgments that take place involving law enforcement personnel, police in small towns were normally well known, well liked and generally respected by its citizens. They were allowed and encouraged to solve problems in the best interest of the people involved and usually tried to do so without the involvement of the judicial system getting in the way.

When utilizing problem-solving methods that were more creative than just the black and white of written laws, the participants involved in the situations would tend to become more appreciative, truthful, and candid, concerning their particular dilemmas, and everyone knows the truth is usually much more outrageous and amusing.

The following are some of the accounts of police officers and the residents of one small East Coast town during the 1950s, 1960s, 1970s, and 1980s.

Prologue

Seventeen degrees, with 35-mile-an-hour steady winds put the index figure at six degrees below zero. The damp February winter salt-filled gusts blowing off the nearby ocean added to the misery of a patrolman answering calls while on duty.

The marked patrol car slowly pulled into the covered carport in the rear area of the police department building at 2:02 a.m. The station was equipped with the attached carport so that a patrol car could pull to within a few feet of the electronically operated rear door when bringing in either witnesses or arrested persons, without the disadvantage of walking through a parking lot or through a crowd of people. Many patrolmen would come to the station after responding to a call, in order to give additional information to the dispatchers for their complaint cards. It became customary to leave their car parked in the carport area while that information was being passed.

Since the public access entrance to the station was on the front street side of the building, the carport area was fairly safe from the public eye and also from public mischief. Patrolman Joe Cornwell, like most department members, carried an extra key to his car so that he could leave the car's engine and heater running at a call but lock the car at the same time. Because of the extra keys, many times patrolmen would lock their regular keys in the car at the station even if they did not leave the engine running. Of course, there were also times when they would just assume that the car would be fine for a few minutes while they were inside and leave the keys in the car and fail to lock the doors.

This particular morning, Joe parked his car and left the car running to preserve the heat, and entered the station without locking the vehicle doors. The town was quiet at two in the morning, and he figured he would be out again in a few minutes. Eleven minutes later, at 2:13 a.m., Joe exited the building, and within a few seconds his brain had gone through at least three different scenarios concerning his now-missing patrol car.

First was the remote possibility that maybe he didn't park it in the carport where he thought. Joe jogged to the adjoining parking lot and looked briefly at some of the parked unused patrol vehicles, trying to mentally will one of them into becoming his, but without success.

Secondly, his thoughts rolled through the possibility that some-one had stolen the vehicle, which was a possibility and one that Joe dreaded the thought of for seemingly hundreds of different reasons. Then almost simultaneously he remembered that he left it running and secretly hoped that maybe he didn't park in the carport and that the howling winds had just drowned out the sound of the idling motor. He silently hoped that it was parked just on the other side of one of the extra cars. However, after another longer and agonizing look, that too did not produce the acceptable results.

Lastly reverting to the stolen vehicle scenario, he realized that par-ticular scenario itself had three possibilities--the first being that it was stolen by a neighborhood kid passing by who could easily be famil-iar with the routine of the police leaving their vehicles in the carport. Almost certainly, they would in due course wreck it, which would in all probability result in either a very long or a very permanent suspension and one he did not want to take the time to consider.

Second, the vehicle was taken as a prank by another squad mem-ber, which would result in weeks of ridicule--which he didn't want to consider either, but was much better than the former.

Lastly, and most disheartening of all was that the vehicle had been taken by "The Rude," the Chief of Police.

In the Sixties and Seventies, one of The Rude's favorite pursuits was to show up at the police station unannounced just to see what was going on. Most times he would enter the building, take a quick look around and not say a word to anyone. If you happened to be in the station, you never knew if "the look" was directed at you or not. There were also times that instead of entering the building, he had been known to *borrow* patrol vehicles that were left running and unlocked with the keys in them.

This was also a scenario Joe didn't want to consider, as it could also result in a very long suspension, weeks of ridicule, or both. The only good thing about The Rude taking it was that he probably wouldn't wreck it...he hoped.

By 2:25 a.m., Joe had re-entered the station and notified the dispatcher, Harriet Slater, of his now-missing vehicle. Listening intently while making every attempt to appear sympathetic, Harriet, a seventeen-year veteran of the department who had been witness to many similar situations in the past, slowly shook her head and skillfully suppressed a grin while softly uttering: "You're toast!"

She then quickly radioed the shift commander to stop in at the station for information. Sergeant Billy Durrant arrived at the station and was advised of the missing patrol vehicle. Trying to appear considerate, yet irritated that his otherwise quiet night had been disturbed, he indicated that Joe should take one of the other spare vehicles and start checking the area to try to locate it.

Billy said, "Chances are, if it was stolen by a kid, it won't be far away and probably driven into the woods or one of the area lakes, or if the chief got it, he should be calling the station pretty soon."

After forty-five minutes of frantically searching for the missing car, Harriet radioed Joe and advised him to return to the station to speak with the sergeant.

Upon returning to the station, Joe saw his patrol car parked neatly in the carport in the same spot in which he left it, lights on, engine running, and doors secure. Only there, taped on the steering wheel, was a handwritten note.

"Police cars have door locks! Patrolmen have door lock keys! Patrolmen need to lock patrol car doors so that the patrol cars remain where they are parked! Then you will not have to spend your time looking for them, and I won't have to explain why my knuckleheaded patrolmen can't keep track of the taxpayer's vehicles! Make sure that it doesn't happen again"!
Signed: JRD.

The relief of knowing his car was not stolen and driven into a tree or a lake was short lived, thanks to the knowledge that the chief was indeed the culprit. The absolute worst thing about the entire situation was the uncertainty of what might happen in the near future. Was the note by the chief a sufficient warning against future mistakes or simply a prerequisite to a more severe reprimand the next time he was on day work?

As usual, the entire department had become aware of the missing patrol car within 24 hours. Beginning around the 25th hour, numerous fictitious stolen car reports, along with pictures of wrecked police cars, and short stories and badly written poems concerning the incident began to appear in Joe's work mailbox and on walls, chairs, and of course the bathroom toilets and urinals.

This internal harassment continued for about two weeks until it appeared it no longer had any humiliating effect. By this time, Joe had stopped trying to make excuses and began to smile and laugh whenever it was brought up, which unquestionably meant that it was time for the other patrolmen to move on to the next victim.

Thankfully, at least as far as Joe was concerned, there were also no formal requests for him to visit with the chief. Rumor had it that The Rude had decided that the two- week public in-house humiliation was good enough.

CHAPTER 1

"To Protect and To Serve"

Most people have heard that phrase at one time or another. Popularized by television shows, books, magazines, and movies, it has come to be known as the mantra of the American Police Department.

Larger police departments in urban areas consist of patrolmen, investigators, supervisory officers, administrative officers, communication personnel, and clerical workers plus personnel who specialize in specific areas of enforcement or investigation.

The norm for most small community police departments is street patrol, consisting of motor vehicle patrols and sometimes walking or bicycle patrols, maybe a couple of detectives, one or two supervisors, and if they're lucky, a secretary or two. Basically, it usually amounts to as many employees as the municipal budget will allow.

Police are the men and women who do some of the most boring, monotonous, repetitive, and time-consuming as well as heroic and courageous deeds on a daily basis. This is also usually done without thinking twice about the possible and the sometimes probable aggravating and/or dire consequences of their actions.

Statistically, most people have one or two possible life-changing incidents take place in their lifetime. Many police officers have dozens, and even hundreds or more during their relatively short careers.

The added benefit of being a cop is the expectation and probability of some excitement and amusement, and of course having a decent pension to show for putting their life, family, and reputation on the line. Statistically, the average life expectancy of a police officer after retirement is only around five years. A pension is not a lot to ask for after twenty-five to thirty years of solving other people's problems while working shift work, weekends, and holidays and the countless missed opportunities to be with loved ones.

It also comes in handy when child and spousal support payments are ordered by the Domestic Relations Courts, also due to the twenty-five to thirty years of solving other people's problems while working shift work, weekends, and holidays and the countless missed opportunities to be with loved ones.

The true reality is that day in and day out, police officers rarely transact business with calm, kind, pleasant, well-mannered people. The vast majority of the people they encounter have no desire to have any type of contact with the police or to share any reliable information about themselves or others which would aid in investigating criminal matters.

Generally, the police are limited to listening to perpetual as well as vivid rants, pleas, demands, and threats from those who know or care little about laws, the legal system, or common decency, and have absolutely little or no respect for other people's feelings or their property.

Those same rant-spewing people do, however, believe that they should be afforded a full complement of retaliatory protection and assistance whenever they think their lifestyle or their routine has been disrupted. The vast majority of "calls for service" involve speaking with displeased people who bear strong resemblances to spoiled ten-year-olds who have just been told "*NO*."

On a daily basis, police are faced with the challenging attempt to enlighten the public in the most simplistic terms possible. When these explanations are not done correctly, with the right amount of finesse, the encounter can easily develop into a lot of unnecessary anguish and/or violence.

Some of the more common incidents that are difficult to explain are domestic disputes and why parties are being either arrested or forced to leave their homes simply because their spouse, or even a neighbor, may have been witness to a simple physical demonstration of displeasure which involved throwing a badly cooked dinner across the kitchen--or more impressively, through a previously closed window and out into the yard or driveway.

By far the most difficult explanation to express to anyone who has not been involved in law enforcement is that there is nothing that can be done to help at that particular time, because their particular problem doesn't fall into a particular regulated or "helpable" category.

These types of incidents and their explanations generally always develop into the speaking with the spoiled ten-year-old who has been told "*NO*" category.

In every city, town, borough, or village, members of police departments prowl the streets twenty-four hours a day. They look for any suspicious activity, and keep people and their property safe while awaiting dispatched calls where they are then:

1. Expected to arrive instantaneously but without breaking any traffic laws.
2. Asked for and expected to deliver expert advice on any and all subjects.
3. Expected to solve everyone's personal problems in as little time as possible.
4. Expected to find any and all lost people and property before the end of their shift.
5. Expected to break up arguments and fights without getting hurt or hurting anyone else.
6. Asked to listen intently to all complaints, even though they know they will not be able to give any answer that will satisfy the complaint.
7. Expected to enter unoccupied and unlighted dilapidated buildings and homes whenever open doors or windows are found, just to see who or what's inside.
8. Expected to catch the bad guys at all costs but at little or no cost to the taxpayer.
9. Expected to never, ever make a mistake.

And, the big one;

10. Expected never to get upset or offended when called pigs, assholes, pricks, cocksuckers, or motherfuckers.

There are undoubtedly many more, but these are usually the top ten.

For every situation that is handled in a "by the book," legal, white-washed, purely methodical and analytical manner, by some straight-laced, criminal justice graduate Sgt. Friday- type cop, there is a single, duo, or group of cops that evolved from the troublemakers, petty thugs, thieves, practical joker's, and just plain sarcastic individuals who somehow found their way into law enforcement.

It is generally believed, at least by the latter individuals, that the sarcastic, petty thieving, troublemaking, practical jokers make the best cops. Intuition, gut feeling, and investigative procedures generally come easier for the "been there, done that" individual. The criminal justice graduate Sgt. Friday types usually end up as administrators and many times are the backstabbing SOB's that make the job more stressful and a lot less fun.

The truth is that most cops are just regular people who for some reason chose a sometimes dangerous, sometimes boring, sometimes exciting, sometimes depressing, and sometimes even fun occupation.

That's the theory, anyway.

CHAPTER 2

A Little History of Our Town; Cedar Springs.

Cedar Springs was a somewhat typical small-town which had its share of normal as well as some unusual and quirky police officers. On the other hand, for its size, it had more than its share of peculiar citizens and unusual occurrences.

It was commonly known as and once advertised in a popular tourist magazine as a small seedy little inland East Coast area with sections bordering the Atlantic Ocean and the Delaware Bay. Not exactly a stunning endorsement, but by the 1980s, it was the most populated community in the county.

Historically, the general area was first populated by the Lenape Native Americans, and was initially explored by outsiders in the early 1600s and then established as a claim for the New Englanders from the colony which is now the State of Massachusetts. By the 1700s, the Lenape were being treated unfavorably by the newcomers, and not unlike most Native Americans, they were eventually driven out and moved via the government to a reservation.

The area began to attract settlers searching for whales and safe ship landing areas, some of which were reportedly used by legendary pirates such as Captain Kidd. Some local churches and their graveyards date back as far as 1718. Railroads and steamships finally made their way to the area, and a lighthouse was built in the late 1850s. In the early 1900s, the US Navy established an official base in the region, converting an old amusement park area into a base for ship support and coastal defense.

After WWI, that base was adapted to house dirigibles. A hangar--at the time, the largest in the world, at over 700 feet long and 100 feet tall--was built to house the airship *The R-38*. However, after it crashed on its maiden test flight, the government, with an unusually intelligent and sensible resolution, decided lighter-than-air craft were not suitable for their use.

Around 1924, the coast guard began to occupy the base, and also added a small air strip a few miles inland. The air strip and a few small planes, along with wooden patrol boats or "cutters," supported the US Customs Service, in keeping watch on the rumrunners that were notoriously operating off the area's coast.

During WWII, army engineers dug a canal through Cedar Springs, connecting the bay with the ocean in order to make coastal patrols more efficient. Several submarine watch towers, each over 100 feet high, were built along the ocean shore area shortly after the Pearl Harbor attack. The last remaining tower still stands in Cedar Springs.

Following the war, the canal opened up commercial fishing industries due to the large harbors at the end of the canal.

Through all the additions and improvements, the area's permanent population began to grow. Because of its many miles of ocean and bay shoreline and wide sandy beaches, the tourist trade flourished, which also contributed to the population growth.

The region which would eventually become Cedar Springs was two hours southeast of Philadelphia, and within three hours of New York City. Because the location was toward the southern end of a peninsula, there was nowhere to go but north, making most viable industry virtually non-existent. Consequently, the area relied heavily on the tourist trade during the summer months. The only industries to speak of were hotels, motels, restaurants, commercial and pleasure fishing, and numerous neighborhood convenience stores, taverns, and nightclubs.

Besides the home-grown residents, there were transplants from northern areas who were hard-working blue collar types that worked and saved and made an investment in a summer bungalow on small 40 x 100 foot lots on dirt roads at the shore. When originally built in the

1940s and 1950s, the one-or two-bedroom bungalows sold for around six hundred dollars each.

These vacationers came down to their small unheated, uninsulated getaway retreats on spring weekends and stayed for a few weeks during the summer months. Most houses had fifteen- to twenty-foot shallow water wells, septic tanks, and just big enough electric services for lights, radios, well pumps, and refrigerators. September came, and most owners closed and boarded the houses up for the winter months.

Eventually the soon-to-be transplants from the north made the permanent move south, either because of their retirement from their jobs or because the old neighborhoods in the cities were changing and they just couldn't or wouldn't adjust to the changes.

As the influx of people continued at *The Shore*, and more vacationers were becoming permanent residents, the farmlands and wooded areas continued to be sold off and subdivided into hundreds of buildable lots.

The summer bungalows began to expand with additions. Sun porches were turned into extra bedrooms. Triple-track storm windows were installed, along with gas floor heaters or electric baseboard heat.

Propane gas dealers sprouted up in the area offering free storage tanks, gas appliances and home delivery services. Fiberglass insulation was added in walls, crawlspaces and attics and electric service and deeper wells were updated to handle the new demands.

Collectively, toward the late 1950s, the immediate neighboring communities featured summer populations that would sometimes reach six to seven figures. By the 1960s, the tiny community of Cedar Springs had approximately 15,000 permanent residents, twelve banks, and more than twenty-five licensed alcohol serving establishments.

As a general rule, alcohol causes problems, and Cedar Springs was no exception. The community had their hands full. It was not unusual for a patrolman to be sent to a reported argument at one of the taverns and find as many as fifteen to twenty patrons engaged in a fist fight.

At times, it seemed as though families from Philadelphia and New York were moving to the area en masse, and with them came many new situations and many new problems.

Concerning the large influx of new, year-round residents and the big-city troubles they brought with them, it was routinely expressed, although never entirely proven as factual, and certainly objected to by many, that Cedar Springs was where Philadelphia and New York dumped their garbage.

CHAPTER 3

The Fishing Industry

The commercial fishing industry of the community expanded as the canal was created and dredged on a regular basis. The local harbor's water depth was increased significantly, which allowed bigger boats to dock and helped the local harbor to become one of the busiest on the eastern seaboard. This expansion also brought its share of problems with it.

In the 1960s and 1970s, most of the commercial fishing boats in the harbors were wooden 40- to 60-foot clam and scallop boats. As the years passed and the old wooden boats wore out, the owners changed over to new 70- to 100-foot or more steel-hulled vessels, capable of staying out for days at a time. Additionally, even larger processing boats were built, capable of staying out for weeks at a time to take the transferred catches from the smaller boats. Most catches would be cleaned, processed, and packaged all prior to bringing them to the harbor for shipping.

Fishing is a hard and dangerous business. The boats go out in all kinds of weather and their deck hands are required to work in that weather. It is not uncommon that deck hands sometimes are required to work 16- to 20-hour days with no guarantee of a paycheck at the end of the day, as they are paid only if they catch fish. Conversely, when the fishing is good, the money is good. When the money is good, the fishermen want to spend it.

Commercial fishing boats travel up and down the East Coast fishing in different areas, depending on what product is "in season." As boats fish along the eastern seaboard, they dock and unload in many different ports. Boats from as far away as Bangor Maine to Miami

Florida could be found docked in Cedar Springs at any given time.

Most of the boat owners and boat captains generally reinvested their earnings into their boats, and the majority of them were productive members of their communities. The crew generally were not, and could be problems when the boats were in port for any length of time.

Many of the deck hands on commercial fishing boats were from many different areas. Some were just transient types. If the boat they were working on needed repairs or was not due to go out for a few days, many deckhands would try to "catch on" with another boat working their way from Maine to Florida and back. Hence, there were many people around dock areas that had very few or no ties to the community and little or no interest in whether or not they respected the police, the laws, or the desires of the communities they happened to be in.

Many of these deck hands, some of whom were local residents and some who were transient workers, spent their earnings just as quickly as they earned them--usually on alcohol, drugs and women or what they called and considered "having a good time after work." Needless to say, from time to time, this type of behavior resulted in problematic consequences for the community and the police.

Pleasure boat ownership also grew in leaps and bounds in the 1950s and 1960s. Hundreds of docking spaces were constructed in the area, which also attracted burglaries and thefts during the summer and in the winter months while dry-docked.

With the expansion of the area's year-round population and the increase of the commercial as well as pleasure fishing industry, the community soon was in dire need of more infrastructure security. Following much debate, the town fathers decided that a bonafide police department was the clear and logical answer.

CHAPTER 4

The Official Start

T he Rude didn't like to be called "The Rude."

His real name was Jonathan, and he liked to be called Jon, but virtually everyone called him "Chief" to his face and referred to him as The Rude or "Big Jon Rude" when talking about him to anyone else. At 6 feet 5 inches tall and a lean 220 pounds, Jonathan R. Denahee looked every bit the part of being the Chief of Police. Straight-faced and somber-looking, Jon was rarely seen smiling. He was also rarely seen in uniform or without the ever-present cigarette dangling from his mouth or in his hand.

When dealing with members of the department, or the public, or even the town council, most questions asked of him were answered with curt "yes," "no," or "I'll look into it," and he was able to get away with it because of his stature and "in charge" demeanor. Apparently, the town council's concerns were satisfied, or they were genuinely afraid of him, as they rarely interfered with the operation of the department.

The chief had received his nickname The Rude, because he happened to have a middle name that was easy to make fun of: "Rudolph." No one really knew how or why he received the name, as he rarely talked about himself. The nickname didn't really mean anything derogatory aside from the obligatory Santa Claus and reindeer expected comments. The department members just thought it was a more clever way to describe their boss's usual mood, plus utilizing his middle name, which they knew he hated.

Rarely dressing in a uniform, he instead preferred to wear polyester trousers and golf-type polo shirts. A .45 automatic and later a .9 mm was worn high on his hip, and a gold "Chief" badge was worn clipped to his belt, partially covered by his signature green sports jacket.

It was rumored that he had once taken up golf as a hobby and had aspirations of being a professional golfer and winning The Masters. He went out and bought a green sports coat in order to acclimate himself to the award. Due to the fact that he rarely finished a round without breaking one of his clubs in frustration or running out of balls, the hobby was soon forgotten, and the remaining clubs sold in a yard sale. The green coat, however, remained a permanent part of his wardrobe and his persona.

The Rude was the first official Chief of the Cedar Springs Police Department. He had been one of the three full-time officers working in town before the actual establishment of the department. There was Jon, Henry Jensen, and Thomas Buck Morningston. Along with them were Billy Durant, Ben Bailey, and Robert "Lead Legs" Roberts, who all worked part time and would eventually be hired as full-time employees.

Henry Jensen was probably the first man hired as a patrolman and had been a landmark in the community for at least fifteen years before The Rude, Buck and the others were hired.

Henry had been raised in the community and was initially hired as a part-time crossing guard at the local grammar school. Henry had suffered a broken leg in his teens that was not properly set. He always claimed he had taken a tumble when saving a boy while working as a deck hand on a party fishing boat.

Party boats were 30- to 40-foot, four-hour deep-sea fishing boats rented out by tourists in the summer months. Henry's version of events was that the boy had been attempting to jump from the boat onto the dock. The boy stumbled and was heroically grabbed just prior to going into the water. Both Henry and the boy landed safely on the dock, but Henry's knee buckled upon impact. The true version came from the boat's captain years later. He stated Henry just plain tripped as he stepped onto the dock. The captain carried no insurance, and while a local doctor examined Henry for free, he couldn't set the bone in his office. The leg was bandaged and taped, with instructions to go to the hospital for further procedures. Henry's family couldn't afford a hospital visit. Henry told his mom that it felt pretty good and the leg healed as it was. This left him with a distinct limp, or what appeared to be more of a hop when he walked.

As a crossing guard, Henry was the only person in town who wore any type of uniform. He was appointed by the town as a full-time police officer following the tragic death of a ten-year-old boy who was struck by a 1946 Buick driven by George "BB" Leaming, a local man who had too much to drink at 11:00 in the morning.

George received his nickname as a result of his stuttering. It seems that he had difficulty pronouncing the letter "B" without repeating it several times prior to finally getting the word of choice out. He had troubles with some other letters, but the "B" was the one that earned him his nickname. There were times when it was reported to have been both frustrating and agonizing to listen to how many times he would repeat the letter "B" before the actual word was pronounced, and because of this, his nickname was born.

The accident took the state police, who at that time covered much of the county, three hours to respond to, and by the time they spoke with "BB," he had all but sobered up. Since there were no eyewitnesses to the accident, "BB's" version was that while he was driving very slowly down the road, under the speed limit and obeying all traffic laws, the boy had suddenly just run out in front of him. "BB" marginally passed the visual and physical examinations of the state trooper, and ultimately the incident was recorded as an unfortunate but devastating accident.

Most people in town who knew "BB" believed him to be a fairly harmless drunk. They also knew there were very few days--and none that anyone could remember--that he was even remotely sober, let alone able to properly drive a car by 11:00 a.m. Most citizens had strong beliefs concerning the truth of his testimony, but no one, with the exception of the deceased boy, was actually witness to the accident, and they found that there wasn't much they could do about it.

After receiving numerous complaints from the boy's family as well as many civic- minded citizens, the town fathers decided that the community was in need of a safer and quicker form of protection other than the state police, who could be and usually were hours away. They decided they needed some form of police on a local level. Henry Jensen became the immediate answer.

For several years the town was happy with Henry, also known as "Hop-a-Long Henry." With one bad leg, Henry was fine as a crossing guard but was lacking as a police officer, as any type of foot chases were out of the question. Jon and Buck were added as part-time officers and handled most of the physical complaints.

As the population slowly began to increase, the people asked for more. After much consideration, by the mid-1950s, and with the promotion of Jon and Buck also as full-timers, the town council decided to formally create a police department.

Henry Jensen certainly had seniority over the others, but never referred to himself as the chief or even the senior officer, and never showed an interest in being responsible for anyone's actions other than his own.

After the incorporation of the department, Henry said that he had decided that he was going to step down--or in his case, hop down--and become a part-time employee again rather than take on the responsibilities, stress, and pressure of leading an entire three-man department.

Next in line was Jonathan R. Denahee who had been hired two months before Buck Morningston. By township decree, Jonathan R. Denahee became the first police chief of Cedar Springs.

CHAPTER 5

The Department Gets Organized

The Rude, after becoming the chief of police, recognized that Cedar Springs was going to continue to grow, as a large influx of people had been steadily moving into the area. The population had almost doubled in the few short years he had worked there, and more and more people were beginning to make their summer bungalows into year-round residences.

With the town growing, The Rude's first order of business was to expand the police department as soon as possible. Within six years, he had convinced town council of his beliefs and the department had a dozen patrolmen, two secretaries, their own radio communication system, and four dispatchers to answer phone calls and dispatch calls for service to the men.

The Rude was determined that he had to formulate a group with a mission statement that would have instant recognition as well as respect in the growing neighborhoods. Using his military background and borrowing a few ideas from the state police, The Rude decided that his department would look and act a bit differently from the neighboring departments.

He had decided that residents and visitors to Cedar Springs should not only feel safe but also have confidence that the members of the police department could protect as well as assist them. In addition, he believed those who caused problems in town should retain vivid memories of a professional group of officers that could be very proactive toward physical activity, should the need arise.

For looks, The Rude chose standard dark-blue uniforms, but trimmed in a bright royal blue, with long-sleeved shirts, ties, and state police-style exterior thigh-length jackets complete with royal-blue epaulets and Sam Brown-type utility belts, with holsters and guns worn outside the jackets. These "blouses," as they were known, were extremely uncomfortable and difficult to move in, but The Rude thought, and correctly so, that they made a patrolman look like he was in charge before he said anything. Actually, they somewhat resembled the Gestapo uniforms of WWII Germany, making the patrolmen look significantly expressive, but with much better attitudes.

In the summer months, the men changed over into light-gray shirts and pants trimmed in black. Summer uniforms came complete with gray straw cowboy or deputy-style hats. Many rumors and theories were offered and debated concerning the hats, but no one other than The Rude ever knew the reason for the choice. Truth be told, they did look unique, and with a coat or two of spray lacquer, they worked well in the rain and also came in handy for Western Halloween costumes.

Standard-issue side arms were fierce-looking army surplus .45-caliber automatics, long before automatic hand guns became vogue and in style. When ninety percent of police were using .38-caliber revolvers, the sight of a rather large holstered .45-caliber automatic, trigger safety on, but fully cocked and holding seven rounds of ammunition, would cause many people to think they were in trouble before a question was asked or a word was spoken.

Not everything was perfect, though. The Rude required all officers to carry their guns on the right side, regardless of whether they were right-handed or left-handed. All new hires were told this was because The Rude had decided that if members of the department were ever in a full-blown gun battle and had to retrieve an extra magazine of ammunition from their dead partner's utility belt, they would always know the magazines were kept on the left side of the bloodied, bullet-riddled body.

It was always said that it would be more likely that the dead naturally left-handed partner was dead because he had been a lousy shot right-handed or had quickly drawn left- handed and had aimed a replacement magazine at the suspect instead of a gun.

The other notion, and probably the correct one, was that only right-handed holsters had been available when they were purchased.

Another area The Rude considered was the look of the patrol vehicles. For nearly twenty-five years, prior to the fire departments lobbying for exclusive use of blue emergency lighting, Cedar Springs had the distinction of being the only police department in the area that used only blue lights on its patrol cars, as compared to other departments' use of red or a combination of blue and red. Residents of Cedar Springs, as well as neighboring towns, knew *All Blue* meant that The Rude's men were en route, and there was a good possibility that someone was going to be leaving under arrest in the back of a patrol car or quite possibly in an ambulance.

The Rude had very definite ideas about how the patrolmen were supposed to conduct themselves, which was basically to treat people the way they treated you. They were told emphatically, "Don't act like bullies, but if it's bullies the people want, it will be bullies they'll get." His simple rule concerning any physical contact was to make sure any actions taken were justified, not overdone, and when necessary, they should only be a direct response to an initial physical attack on a patrolman by the soon to be arrested individual.

The Rude's department could be an unruly horde, but basically they were a bunch of guys who knew right from wrong, arrested the people who needed to be arrested, and frequently used creative ways to enforce a change of heart to those local and non-local people who may have used poor judgment in a situation where an arrest would serve no useful purpose.

CHAPTER 6

Locals & Non-Locals

With as many as twenty-five alcohol-serving establishments, several handfuls of BYOB restaurants, tourists from virtually all fifty states and Canada, a well-established drug availability at the nightclubs and dock areas, the influx of people from Philadelphia and New York, and the hard-drinking, hard-living commercial fishermen working the clam and scallop boats, there were a good number of brawl calls that involved anywhere from two to twenty or more people involved. Thankfully back in that era, fights were just that. Very seldom were guns or knives involved, as it was usually a matter of ego vs. ego where the toughest guy, or gal, or group would prevail.

There were also some established methods of handling certain types of calls, which kept situations simple with a minimum amount of determination as to the cause and the cure for the problem.

The accepted method of the police dealing with fight calls was to answer the call with as many patrolmen as possible. After arriving, they would cautiously approach and slowly enter the establishment, as one never knew if someone was lurking just inside the door waiting to ambush you as you came in. Once safely inside, you had to promptly determine if the incident involved any flying objects such as bottles, ashtrays, chairs, or people, and if so, determine where the lift-off point was and swiftly cease the unauthorized flights as quickly as possible--especially if people were being thrown, as flying people tended to cause distinctive damages and injuries.

The second thing was to determine who was the loudest individual there, or who was the one most people were staring at or pointing to. Then it became time to determine whether that individual was a local or a non-local. Not much else mattered. Either you were local, or you were not. Being local meant that the officer who showed up at the call personally knew you. If they didn't, then you were considered a non-local until or unless another officer indicated otherwise.

Somehow, if the individual was determined to be a local, all it took was The Rude or Buck or Henry or any of the men hired for the next ten years or so to approach the local and tell him that you needed to speak with them outside.

It was an unwritten assumption that once outside, the local would be questioned about their involvement, and if the circumstances were not too serious, they would then usually be offered a ride home, regardless of whether they had started or even ended the fight. It was also assumed and explained that they would return on the following day to retrieve their automobile, if they had one, and take care of any damage to the establishment.

If anyone wanted to sign complaints against anyone, they were also told to come in the following day. This gave everyone a chance to forget most of what the argument was about and time for the liquored-up egos to calm down. The establishment owners and the locals understood this, and for the most part it seemed to work very well.

Hence, the call would be recorded as a verbal disagreement--no complaint, and of course, no pesky written report. If complaints were signed the following day, the call would be upgraded, and a short report would have to be written, but more often than not, the item of disagreement would be forgotten, damages paid for, and life went on.

If the boisterous individual whom everyone was pointing at was found to be an outsider or non-local, they were also asked to step outside to discuss the situation. Identifications were recorded, and again if the circumstances were not too serious or if they were not injured too badly and the damages not too excessive, they were advised to immediately leave. If any arguments or complaints continued, the ole' "I'll count to three and you better be gone" rule came into effect.

This rule was used when an arrest was not really preferred. There were times that the numbers one and two would be repeated several times, to benefit the individual. If they were still there at the count of three, an arrest would ensue. Depending on the temperament of the individual, and which officer was initiating the request, there were also times that the count to three went very quickly.

If injuries were involved, they were looked at in two categories. Cuts, bruises, abrasions, bloody noses or lips, severe limping, and broken or dislocated fingers were regarded as *no* injuries. These were considered personal problems and explained to be expected collateral damages for getting into an argument in the first place. If the then determined to be non-injured party disagreed with the decision, then the ole' "I'll count to three" rule would then come into play.

Injuries that involved broken big bones (arms, legs, etc.), lacerations of three inches or more, (either long or deep), loss of eyesight, teeth, fingers, or toes, and disappearances of testicles due to blunt force trauma were considered reason enough to summon the local volunteer rescue squad.

The individuals that were considered to have legitimate injuries were treated professionally and without delay. Subsequent or necessary arrests were made accordingly due to those injuries, and investigation reports would be filed for future court appearances.

CHAPTER 7

Divorce and the Annual Barbeques

The Rude was married, had a couple of kids, lived in the neighborhood, and every year had a summer barbecue at his house for the members of the department.

Beside the fact that The Rude was the boss, having an in-ground pool certainly helped with attendance. However, the certainty that some type of domestic quarrel would occur during the barbecue that all the members of the department could talk and joke about for several weeks after the affair was a more powerful or at least an easily equal draw for attendance.

The Rude happened to be married to what most of the department members referred to cautiously and only as "the chief's wife." Being the wife of the chief of police had many advantages. If so inclined, the wife could conduct her affairs pretty much anyway she wanted. She could be quiet, polite, and discreet in the life she led, or not so quiet, not so polite, and unfortunately for the other spouse, not so discreet.

Following several years of an apparent rocky marriage, The Rude's wife decided to choose the latter, and routinely took advantage of the fact that she was for the most part untouchable. When it came to the possibility of her actions being an embarrassment to another family member, she made former President Jimmy Carter's brother Billy Carter look like an amateur.

Her actions and lifestyle certainly did not go unnoticed by the patrolmen or by The Rude, who was trying desperately to keep an air of respectability within the department. Some of her actions and

the consequences of those actions led to the numerous domestic arguments and problems at the home and at the police station. Of course,
to be fair, there were those who speculated that The Rude's sparkling
personality may have been a contributing factor in some of those
disagreements.

Luckily, these arguments took place prior to the current legislation
where some type of police action must take place following a domestic
quarrel. Currently, if any type of violence or even a threat of violence
is reported or actually takes place, one of the actors is required to leave
the residence, either by choice or by an arrest.

Back in the day, it was common knowledge that should a call come
in from the chief's home or from any of his neighbors, only the shift
supervisor would respond and respond very nonchalantly, acting like
he was just in the neighborhood and had decided to drop by for a visit.
It was also well known that no written reports concerning the calls or
the visits would ever be filed.

In spite of the problems, the summer barbecues were always a special event. They all started out with the best intentions much like any
annual family reunion. Everyone who attended brought some type of
food and drink to share. The barbecues were an event where everybody
could just relax, and very little "shop" talk took place. There were always plenty of games, and of course the pool for the kids, and usually
some very non-competitive volleyball, horseshoes, or touch football
games for the adults.

However, every year toward the end of the marriage, after a few
hours and a few drinks, the guaranteed domestic quarrel between The
Rude and "the chief's wife" would take place. They were complete with
plenty of yelling, cursing, verbal threats, and of course the obligatory
finger-pointing, usually followed by flying utensils, paper cups, plates,
beer bottles (some that were empty, some that were full), and the pin-
nacle of the day, trashcans and food being thrown into the pool. What
greater entertainment and future conversation material could one ask
for?

The barbecues were like watching an old John McEnroe ten-
nis match. Expectations of a grand event were anticipated. You also
knew that sometime before the end of the day, there was going to be a

difference of opinion, then an argument, then some flying debris, and finally some first-rate fodder for future gossiping stories to share that would last for the next few weeks within the department.

Everyone always looked forward to the barbecues, because they knew that for several weeks following the event, the chief would stay in his office and would not want to speak to anyone, and they were pretty sure that their patrol cars would not go missing from the station's carport.

As said in the Bible's book of Mathew, as well as on George Harrison's iconic triple album, "All things must pass," well...all things did pass. The marriage between The Rude and his wife deteriorated, and the idea of get-togethers for the department members and their families also passed. Unfortunately, for several years they became something that used to take place and were ultimately considered to be unnecessary.

It became a standing rule after The Rude moved out of the marital home that "the chief's wife" should not be allowed to enter the station, and that if for some reason she forced her way in, which happened from time to time, no one should interfere with, nor hear, nor see whatever took place. More times than not, it was known that she was a possible show, when after hearing the yelling emitting from the chief's office while he was discussing some details of the divorce settlement on the phone, the chief would almost run out of the station, get in his car, and disappear for hours.

Sometimes she would, without notice, decide to discuss the settlement in person. Since the doors were electronically locked, it was not uncommon for her to stand and wait until someone was entering the station--usually a Town Hall employee--and simply follow them in. When she was successful in gaining entry to the station, she would discreetly walk down the hallway to the chief's office. This would result in The Rude walking very quickly out of his office and out of the building, closely followed by a screaming wild banshee.

In time, usually several hours, the chief would return, saying nothing, and retreat to his office. A quick phone call to the dispatcher ensured that no reports were filed and that to the best of everyone's knowledge, she had never been there. These types of encounters continued throughout the divorce and for several years after, which made for many good stories that were enjoyed by everyone. Everyone, that is, except The Rude.

Through all the years of marital difficulties, family history problems, and constant ridicule by all members of the department behind his back, The Rude was basically a person who cared about his community and tried his best and in fact succeeded in creating a department that assisted and helped the people in the community.

For almost thirty years after he was named chief, whenever a patrolman did something good, they could bet that The Rude would never mention it, because it was simply what he expected and what the job was all about.

When it was something they did that was not so acceptable, they could also be assured that very soon, they would be summoned to the chief's office. No matter how well tracks may have been covered, somehow The Rude had found out what had happened, and he was about to ruin their day.

When in his office, one was never invited to sit. The Rude, never smiling and always sitting behind his sparsely outfitted desk smoking a cigarette, would ask what had taken place. Knowing that he already knew all the circumstances of the event, but secretly hoping he didn't, the summoned patrolman would offer whatever justification for his actions that they thought sounded best.

The Rude would sit patiently smoking his ever-present cigarette, listening to the explanation with a silent, bored, yet menacing gaze, never indicating whether the explanation was acceptable. His finishing statement to the officer would be, "Don't let it happen again, or you will soon be driving down this road and telling people you used to work here."

The worst thing about it was that since The Rude always looked like he was mad about something, you were never sure how long he was going to hold a grudge and whether his look was still directed at you or at someone else. Years later, a patrolman would realize that the trivial attempt by the chief at some form of verbal reprimand was the entire amount of reprimand that usually ever took place. However, because of his usual disposition, The Rude had an uncanny ability to make one think that they had been admonished and put on a tight rein.

Following one of these admonishments, whether talking to himself or privately discussing some of the more questionable decisions made by the patrolmen with the captain or one of the sergeants, The Rude's favorite saying was:

"This isn't a police department, it's a damn gang!"

CHAPTER 8

Tourette's

As in many small towns prior to their infrastructures being developed, the homes in Cedar Springs utilized wells for drinking water and septic systems for wastewater disposal.

We mention that only because Cedar Springs seemed to have a vast array of quirky and unusual characters. It was rumored and stated as fact by some of the second- and third-generation citizenry that the particular quirks of some of the characters existed solely because many of the water wells had been dug far too close to the septic systems. That statement, of course, could also be relevant by stating it the other way around.

The local Board of Health would never confirm or deny this as having anything to do with the peculiarities of some of the citizens. However, the future regulated construction requirements of septic systems and water wells were vastly modified and revised during the late 1960s. The distances required between the two were also amended, with the gap increased to at least twice the older accepted guidelines. These regulations evolved into some of the most strictly enforced guidelines in the county.

There were two young men who lived in the area who certainly fit the criteria of unusual and quirky. They were reportedly distant relatives of a prominent family in town; however, the family members never confirmed or denied that rumor. The brothers were known affectionately around the department as the main argument for (and could probably have been poster children for) the development of a municipal water treatment system and supply.

The family lived on what remained of an old dairy farm property complete with farm house, barn, septic system, well for water, and an old fifty-foot-tall farm grain silo. The two boys, after reaching their teen years, lived in a detached garage apartment which had been built just in front of the old grain silo. Not unlike most teenagers, they apparently wanted some freedom from their parents, and it was reported that their parents had no qualms or arguments about them moving into the garage apartment.

The oldest boy, Harold, in his mid-twenties in the late 1970s, was simply known as Harry. With his usual three- to four-day-old beard and stringy greased-down hair, he stood approximately 6 foot 5 inches and generally always dressed in black: black jeans, black shirts, and sometimes a wrinkled dark navy-blue jacket. He wore combat boots and walked wherever he went. It was generally accepted and assumed to be factual that the state would have been remiss if they had ever agreed to let Harry have a driver's license and operate a motor vehicle.

It was also a fact that Harry talked to himself. It's true that a lot of people do it, but not quite the way Harry did. At least, most folks that he encountered assumed he talked to himself, because it sounded as though questions were being asked and then answered. Because of his appearance and mannerisms, no one really wanted to stop and ask him if he was directing what he asked or what he answered toward them or simply having a conversation with himself. Harry also seemed to have arguments with himself, as angry shouts and physical movements of foot-stomping and shadow-punching would sometimes occur as he walked down the street.

In today's world he would probably be diagnosed as bipolar or schizophrenic. Back then, it was believed there was the possibility that he had taken some type of psychedelic drugs in the late 1960s and had not yet returned from his "trip," or that he was psychic and was conversing with the dead, or some combination of the two. Both notions were guesses, and no one ever submitted any factual evidence proving either of these possibilities. It was easier and safer just to assume that he was just having extended conversations with…himself.

Long before Tourette's Syndrome became well known and somewhat fashionable, Harry was yelling curse words at an alarming rate wherever he went and for no apparent reason. Some have even said that Harry may have invented Tourette's Syndrome although there was again no factual proof of that and it probably didn't happen.

The older he became the fiercer looking and angrier sounding Harry grew to be. Every now and then, a citizen would call the police and report a "Harry sighting." Sometimes people would just call to report Harry was walking down the street talking and yelling and foot stomping while others would be convinced that the conversations and yelling were directed toward them.

Some callers would state that they believed that Harry had actually personally threatened them and whenever that happened, the police had to actually investigate the complaint. Harry had never seemed very fond of the police even though several members of his mystery family had reportedly been police officers, firemen and correctional officers at the state prison. It was also rumored that perhaps that bit of information was instrumental in Harry's true feelings toward any authority but that was never proven either.

Sometimes when investigating a "Harry sighting," a patrolman would pull up alongside Harry while he was walking. Whenever he would be fairly calm and not doing the yelling, cursing "Tourette's" thing there were times the officer would offer him a ride. On rare occasions, Harry would let some of the older members of the department that he recognized give him a ride home but most times after being asked where he was going, he would just walk away screaming in what became known in the department as "Harry Tourette's" language. More times than not, he would usually head straight home and not be heard from for the next few days.

Now Harry had a younger brother, Johnny, who apparently idolized his older sibling, or he was drinking the same bad water from the same bad well. Except for the fact that Johnny was a bit younger and shorter than Harry, they certainly shared the same physical mannerisms and gene pool, and both were consistent in wearing identical wardrobes. The most notable difference between the two brothers was that Johnny had never been seen or heard doing the Tourette's thing.

Now Harry and Johnny had grown up with a specific quirk that was a great deal more interesting than most. They not only were thought to have had an unshielded septic system and a closely located

contaminated well; they also had their very own old farm grain silo that was later found to contain many, many years of the family's trash. This was courtesy of Harry and Johnny, who either just didn't feel like putting it out to be picked up by the town, or they just couldn't bear to part with it. They had been piling it into the silo like farmer's corn for years. It was thought that quite possibly, like some people filling an old fruit jar or milk container with pennies, they just wanted to find out how much it would hold.

The Rude's unwritten orders on matters concerning Harry and his brother Johnny were that the police had to do what they had to do should the time come when they had to do something because of what they did.

Which, when you think about it, compared with the bureaucratic, politically correct "spin doctor" statements and decisions the police have to make nowadays, what The Rude said was actually pretty straightforward and covered pretty much anything that may or may not happen.

Unless Harry really did something dangerous other than just look and sound dangerous, the police couldn't do much other than offer him a ride home—which, when he accepted, was quite entertaining in itself.

Being six-foot-five or so, Harry, as would be the case for anyone his size, always had trouble getting into the police cars, especially after they started using the Plexiglas and steel shields. The shields were installed behind the front seats to protect the patrolmen from injuries inflicted by some rear-seat passengers.

The shields also made the rear seat area about six to eight inches smaller than they already were. The actual factory-installed rear seats were removed and replaced with fiberglass one-piece units that were designed to thwart arrestees hiding drugs and/or weapons after they were put into the car, and also to make it easier to clean when passengers decided to leave undigested meals and other unpleasant and nauseating bodily treats after becoming car sick or just plain sick. The most entertaining thing about the seats was that the original designs did not come equipped with seat belts.

No seatbelts meant that if you happen to have been transporting a handcuffed, obnoxious, or unruly individual who was busy promising immediate retaliation for his arrest upon you or members of your family, there was always a chance, and a good one at that, that a dog or some other type of animal would dart across the roadway, making it immediately necessary to slam on the brakes without warning.

The consequence of this action would be the detainee coming face to face with the steel and Plexiglas shield at an alarming rate of speed. This usually resulted in the arrestee becoming much calmer and quieter. However, there were times that several animals would dart into the road before the passenger calmed down.

Back in the day, it was an unwritten rule that no one was supposed to be transported in the front seat of a patrol vehicle unless it was one of your immediate family members, a close friend, or an attractive woman in a short skirt.

Nobody ever really wanted to let Harry or Johnny in the rear seat, let alone the front seat. Nobody, that is, with the exception of The Rude.

Many times, The Rude, who always monitored calls either from his office, his car, or at home, would arrive at the scene of a "Harry sighting," get out of his car, and in an intimidating, stern yet loving gravelly voice, yell at Harry or Johnny, "Get in the fucking car!"

The boys would hang their heads, slide into the front seat, and they and The Rude would drive off into the sunset and straight to the grain silo.

Something about animals always being able to recognize and be subservient to their elders always came to mind whenever that happened.

Eventually, Harry started to become more and more troublesome. When he would enter neighborhood stores, people would stare. Harry would begin to grumble and mumble, causing the people to stare even more. Whispered comments from the onlookers would cause Harry to begin some foot-stomping and uncontrolled finger-pointing. With paranoia now settling in, Harry would then begin to curse, old ladies would cringe, dogs would bark, and children would cry.

Harry, after years of never getting the hugs he needed or being able to buy Girl Scout cookies without a problem, eventually tired of trying to mind his own business and usually resorted to "Harry Tourette's" language. At least that seemed to get people's attention. Whenever he started his rants, people would scatter, dogs would bark louder, children would continue to cry, and store managers would call the police.

After being charged and brought in front of the judge several times for being a "Disorderly Person," Harry gave a celebrated live audition of "Harry Tourette's" in the courtroom for the judge and was finally sent away for a mental evaluation. The first time was an overnighter in the quiet room at the local hospital. After another repeat of Tourette's in court came the fourteen-day mandatory stay at the mental hospital about an hour away. Following his third episode, which actually caused the judge to abruptly leave his chair and retreat to his chambers, Harry was finally referred to the Hospital of Mental Illness and Education Correction Facility Building, or "HOMECFB." It was affectionately referred to by most law enforcement personnel simply as "Home Ec."

The Home Ec building was a State mental facilities hospital where people who have shown the potential to be a danger to the State or the people by their criminal behavior are sent.

The secured facility was run a lot like a prison, because all of its patients had committed some type of crime. Judges and/or doctors were the only ones who decided who could be patients. The staff was unique, as they had to contend with the type of people that humanity likes to forget exists.

The facility greeters seemed to be consistently all well over 6 feet tall and weighed an average of about 200 to 300 pounds. Not surprisingly, there were not too many patients that ever gave the staff a hard time once they arrived--at least, not more than once.

The police and sheriff's department personnel who transported people there always enjoyed it when they had a particularly unruly or rowdy individual. The security guards, or what was referred to as the acceptance personnel, upon hearing a new arrival was on the way, would meet the transportation car at the fenced-in entry gate and evaluate the situation.

If the new arriving guest gave even the faintest impression that they would be a problem of any kind, the staff greeters would ever so gently escort the patient into the building.

The "ever so gently" usually meant the patient was lifted off the ground and was literally carried into the building with both their little legs kicking and thrashing in the air. Once inside and through the electronic and airtight doors, an eerie silence followed. Most were not seen again for many months, and some were never heard from again.

Harry was practicing his Tourette's on the way to the Home Ec and began to get a little anxious after entering the fenced-in reception area. Harry was no exception to the house rules, and with legs kicking and thrashing in the air, he was taken inside to become a captive member of the facility alumni. He was not heard from for many years.

Rumors spread that Harry had become a vegged-out permanent resident thanks to massive doses of "US Prime Government approved, calm way the hell down" daily medications.

It wasn't until ten-plus years later that Harry was seen on rare visitation passes at the old dairy farm home, standing still in the front yard for long periods of time, staring at traffic, looking a little gray and twice his age, extremely subdued and no longer very fierce.

The police, after noticing Harry in his yard staring at traffic on numerous occasions, would later say that if Harry had been three feet shorter, they could have given him a pair of knickers to wear, and a lantern to hold, and he would have been a great-looking lawn ornament.

CHAPTER 9

The Back Route

The Cedar Springs Rescue Squad was almost exclusively made up of volunteers, except for Tony Smart, the rescue squad departmental chief. Tony was a rather large man at six foot four inches and 350 pounds, and as these things sometimes happen, was also known as "Smalls."

"Smalls" was a very dedicated first responder and was capable of providing the best care one could expect in an emergency situation. He also had a cynical and sarcastic side and could be short on patience when the person in medical need was unappreciative of his or his squad's efforts to be caring and/or professional.

Patrolmen could always count on "Smalls" to treat obnoxious individuals in a way that mirrored the way they treated him. If and when they complained about the sometimes appropriate curt and physical type of service, patrolmen would back up the subsequent actions of "Smalls" as necessary medical assistance--as far as they were concerned, anyway.

Additionally, because the rescue squad was always understaffed and underappreciated, the police were almost always sent to assist the squad, usually by helping carry patients from homes to the ambulance and calming excited, injured, and/or intoxicated persons so that they could be treated.

Since the police knew they were understaffed, the rescue members also knew that the police would not call them to a scene to give treatment unless there was a serious injury, or the patient was either a personal friend or a belligerent, demanding individual who insisted on being checked out by medical personnel upon threat of legal action against the officer or the department.

Legitimate ailments and injuries were treated professionally and either released at the scene or transported to the local hospital. If the ill or injured person was not placed under arrest, the call was considered a rescue assist and did not require a written report.

It was not unusual for an unruly patient to be strapped down onto a stretcher either for their safety, the safety of others, or because they gave "Smalls," the police, or any of the rescue squad personnel a hard time. It was also not unusual for an intoxicated and/or belligerent individual to sustain additional injuries (purely unintentional and unrecorded, of course), while being strapped down and transported. "Smalls" was especially talented at utilizing his entire 350 pounds to convince patients to calm down.

If the belligerence continued and the illness or injury the individual had sustained was one which would cause a great deal of discomfort by any sudden movements, no great care went into the placing and strapping down of the individual onto the stretcher. Additionally, a decision was usually made for the transport to go to the hospital via "The Back Route."

There were two distinct routes to the hospital, one via a smooth four-lane expressway, and the second via an old two-lane concrete roadway full of dips, cracks, pot holes, and some rather large bumps.

Heavy ambulances--known for not having the best suspensions in vehicles--could become some very uncomfortable vehicles for an injured person to be strapped down in on a bumpy roadway. Transgressions against an officer or rescue squad members would be sorely regretted by the patient for the entire 20-to-30-minute ride over these dips, bumps, and pot holes.

A lot of troublemaking people who were transported the back way to the hospital soon forgot all about the cause of their injuries or who caused them. Most just wanted to be out of the ambulance and out of pain and to forget whatever incident they had been involved in, whether they were the victim or the agitator.

CHAPTER 10

Civil Service Promotions

The Rude ran a tight ship, but as the town and the department grew, he couldn't be around all the time. The number of calls for service required 24-hour patrols and supervision to oversee them. After several years of being the only administrator above the sergeants, he reluctantly decided the department needed a captain and lieutenant to help run things.

By the early 1960s, Cedar Springs had joined most of the other neighboring communities by agreeing to hire new employees through the procedures of Civil Service examinations. Citizens interested in positions now were required to take and pass written and physical State-sponsored examinations prior to promises of employment.

Of course, because these exams were given and graded by the State, municipal employment immediately took on the process, matching the federal and state government's formula of "hurry up and wait." Waits of up to three years for a test to occur were not unusual, and receiving the results of testing could take up to six months. In addition to initial hiring, promotional positions would also be subject to additional written tests, in order to be considered for the particular post.

No longer would promotions be based upon merit, assertive production, the personal knowledge and understanding of one's community, and knowing which procedures to use that would result in peaceful and agreeable conclusions. Promotions were now left to whoever scored highest on tests consisting of questions concerning situations that may never happen in one's particular community.

Civil service believed that everyone should know procedures that were largely based on populations that lived in urban areas, even if your particular community's tallest building was a two-story hardware store or its population consisted of more livestock than people.

Ahhh, the wisdom of government.

CHAPTER 11

Patrick Benjamin

At 5 foot 10 and a slim and fit 170 pounds; Patrick Benjamin was an exceedingly anal, consistently all spit and polish, well-educated and well-spoken man. Pat was also a bona fide weekend warrior in the National Guard, complete with the military "high-n-tight" haircut fashionably accented by the unfortunate misfortune of having been born with rather large "Dumbo"-type ears.

Patrick Benjamin, a test-passing sanctioned civil service sergeant, was acquired from a smaller neighboring department. Pat had taken a state lieutenant/captain promotional exam, but after passing it found that the department he worked for had decided that another administrative position was not necessary at that time, and they cancelled their decision to create the promotion.

Sergeant Benjamin wanted desperately to be in charge and thought he had a better chance of climbing the ladder in a department that was sure to grow--and Cedar Springs was certainly growing. With a bit of hometown political subterfuge, a special inter-county lateral transfer was approved, and Patrick Benjamin soon became a member of the Cedar Springs Police Department.

Pat was immediately dubbed "Sergeant Benny" by the patrolmen, and then soon after his next promotion, "Captain Benny." Closely following his personal mantra, Benny always wanted to do things by the book and considered the Civil Service exams the best thing since sliced bread. If there were books available that were supposed to help in the training of police, Benny either owned them or had read them and could recite quotes from all of them. It was rumored and later confirmed that Benny had books about the books he had.

"Benny," in today's world, would have been diagnosed as ADD, ECD, SAD, or any of those other psychological problems identified by three letters. Aside from his personality plights, he did, however, always look the part of what most people thought of when they thought of a police officer. Slow and precise enunciation, perfect posture, razor-straight seams in both pants and shirt with chrome, brass, leather, and shoes always polished, and never seen in public without his strategically placed hat. He was a walking testament to what an old Sears catalog portrayed what a police officer should look like.

Benny was already cognizant of the changes taking place in society and had dedicated his life and career to doing things perceptibly correctly and professionally by the book, whether any of the old-timers agreed with him or not.

After joining Cedar Springs and prior to his promotion to captain, Benny was assigned to a squad as a sergeant and decided right from the start that the members of the Cedar Springs Police Department needed, in his opinion, to look and act more professional and to become more proficient in effectively dealing with the members of the public.

Benny had two flaws. One was that he desperately wanted to be respected because he was sure that he was perfect, and because he was so sure, he wanted to begin training everyone else to be perfect. The second was the unfortunate misfortune of having the large ears which turned a bright crimson shade of red whenever he was under any type of stress. From day one in Cedar Springs, Benny could do absolutely nothing to improve either one.

Benny's role of procedure perfectionist was constantly critiqued by the older patrolmen, who knew from years of actual experience on the street that "by the book" seldom works the way it's written when applied to a real-life situation. Book instruction can never include the many different aspects or levels that a situation can escalate to. Nothing but experience and knowing the people you're dealing with can assist in a successful conclusion to the particular problem one may cope with.

Benny had come from a significantly quieter and less populated town than Cedar Springs. It was mostly an older Victorian tourist town with tourists for three to four months in the summer. Once the tourists and visitors left, it was also well known for removing the then-unnecessary parking meters and traffic signals from the roadways for the remainder of the year. Residents and visitors were generally older, affluent types more interested in the Victorian architecture of the bed and breakfast rental units than making problems for the police. Unfortunately and predictably, Benny's books and the stories they conveyed were the source of most of his real police experience.

CHAPTER 12

A Lesson Learned

A call to the station to report a typical barroom brawl in the fishing dock area of town resulted in a celebrated and predictable account concerning the newly appointed Sergeant Benny's by-the-book procedures.

The brawl in question involved a couple of local men well known to the older patrolmen as good, hard-working men who were also good, hard-drinking men who could be a handful should they be treated in what their minds was the wrong way.

These were men, typical at that time, who could have an old-fashioned fist fight, get bloody, break a few tables, chairs or windows, go home, sleep it off, and return the following day and take care of any damage, apologize to the owners, and be the best of friends to each other that same day.

Getting them home without getting them involved in the legal system took a certain amount of finesse that only people who grew up with them, worked with them, or had dealt with them in the past could possess. Benny had done none of the above.

A couple of the older patrolmen, Danny Green and Bruce Daily, had been dispatched to the call and had arrived at the bar known as Neptune's Galley. The Neptune was a dockside tavern whose customers were almost exclusively locals and was well known for its occasional brawls involving fishermen with outsiders who happened to have entered the establishment and were overheard making disparaging remarks concerning the local area or clientele.

After cautiously entering, Danny and Bruce quickly picked out the two main combatants. This was fairly easy to do, as the other customers had scattered and we're either standing in the parking lot or were still inside glued to the exterior walls trying their best to stay out of the way. The obvious problem was John Wilkinson and Ted Mason. Both were local commercial fishermen.

John was a scallop boat captain and boat owner. He was forty-five years old, with twenty-one years of fishing experience. A somewhat typical brawler in his late teens and early twenties, John stood 6 foot 5 and weighed in around 290 pounds. After a brief encounter with a charge of aggravated assault following a fight with three other individuals (which John reportedly won), he decided to settle down. Charges were eventually dropped after it was found that the other three had started the fight, and John retaliated only after being struck with a beer bottle and baseball bat several times. Ted, a local clam boat owner and captain with twenty-four years on the water, was a few years older, almost two inches taller, and fifty pounds heavier than John. Ted was known on the docks as having a "clean" boat, insisting that no drugs or drug users would ever be employed as hands. If found that any of them did, Ted had no problem throwing them off the boat as soon as he returned to port. More times than not, the throwing off would be comprised of the offensive employee being thrown into the harbor's waters. It was also well known that no such employee ever complained, as they reportedly were happy that the short swim to the dock was better than being thrown overboard several hundred miles at sea.

Both men, who had known each other for almost thirty years, were known to be perfect gentlemen and good husbands and fathers…unless they were drinking. Today they were drinking.

Most of the body and property damage had already been done and both men were leaning against the bar about three feet apart, breathing heavily and in the process of taking a break while loudly discussing who had insulted whose boat first.

John looked to have a broken nose, with blood dripping down his face onto the floor. Ted's face was red and his left eye was beginning to swell and close. Both men's shirts were torn and remnants of three tables, several chairs, and numerous bottles and glasses were strewn about the tavern floor, having been flattened at some notable and significant part of the disagreement.

Experience told the two patrolmen that both men had several more rounds in reserve, and most anything could trigger more fighting and a lot more damage. As good- natured as John and Ted were sober, it would take many more than the two patrolmen present to separate them if they went at each other again.

John and Ted both looked up as the two patrolmen cautiously came in to the bar. As they slowly approached the men, John and Ted both recognized Danny and Bruce as two of the "old guys" and seemed somewhat relieved and to relax a bit.

Danny, who sometimes worked part time on the docks, said, "John... Ted...it looks like you two are having some type of disagreement."

Both John and Ted wearily nodded their heads. While looking around at some of the obviously still-petrified clientele hugging the walls, Danny added, "I'm also getting the feeling that your disagreement has some of the other customers just a wee bit on edge."

Ted, now able to see out of only one eye, seemed surprised to see a small group of people huddled in the far corner.

Bruce asked, "How about you guys relax for a spell and tell us what happened, and we'll see if there's anything that we can do to help take care of this."

Both men looked at each other, and then explained that the argument was about their boats being insulted. After patiently listening to both sides of the argument, John and Ted were told that they both had valid points, but they should probably finish the discussion the following day before anyone really got hurt. With blood dripping on the floor and Ted's eye now completely closed, both men slowly nodded their heads.

Ted said with a slight smile on his face, "Yeah, you're probably right. We probably need to go home."

Just as the men were beginning to walk away from the bar and toward the door, Sergeant Benny, after hearing the call of a fight, arrived in a freshly laundered uniform with crisp seams and polished shoes. He had made sure to don his hat to just the right angle prior to entering the establishment. When he saw that the two patrolmen were standing fairly relaxed talking to a bloody John and Ted with the barroom in total disarray, he was unsure what was taking place.

Sergeant Benny immediately walked up toward the two fishermen and withdrew his departmental issued and highly polished riot baton, a 24-inch plastic pole, which when used properly is intended to be used as leverage on a wrist, arm, or even a leg to persuade people to do what you want.

When John saw an unfamiliar face holding a police baton, his bloodied nostrils flared and both hands clenched into massive fists. Ted saw the baton at the same time and while looking straight at Benny, said, "I don't know who you are or who you think you are, but if you don't get that nightstick out of my face, I'm gonna shove it up your ass!"

Benny started to respond when Danny stepped in front of Ted, turning his back to the two fishermen, and advised Benny, "We got this one, Sarge. We're just getting some information for the report, and we'll be clear in a few minutes."

Benny's ears were turning a bright shade of red, and while stepping back, he put his baton back in its polished holder. He took another look at John and Ted and stated that he would be right outside if any further assistance was needed.

After about ten minutes of calming John and Ted down for the second time and explaining to the owner of the bar that all damages would be taken care of the following day, both John and Ted were given rides home with apologies and handshakes to Danny and Bruce with assurances that they didn't mean to get the police involved.

Back at the station, Benny called the two patrolmen into the squad room and stated that although the situation had been taken care of, he thought the threatening statements made by Ted were detrimental to his authority and that he was considering charging him with threats against a police officer.

Danny advised Benny, as candidly and as sarcastically as he could, that he could do what he thought was right but added that if Ted had wanted to shove the baton up Benny's ass, he probably would have done so, and in order to stop him from doing so, he would have had to have been shot many, many times to prevent it, and he wasn't sure they had enough ammunition among the three of them to do that.

After a slight hesitation, Benny took the hint and dropped the subject but indicated that it would be more appropriate in the future if the patrolmen wore their hats when answering calls.

The incident didn't seem to deter Benny from his perfectionist goals, but in the future, whenever he made an appearance at a bar fight or any type of disturbance, he purposely left his baton in its holder, preferring to administrate the situation from the rear while closely checking the appearance of the troops and making mental notes of ill-fitting uniforms and un-shined shoes.

CHAPTER 13

Another Nickname

Always wanting to be accepted by the troops, there were many times Benny continued to offer information about himself that he felt would help to solidify his standing that as a supervisor, he was not only an administrator but still just a regular guy. Unfortunately for "Benny," this too was unsuccessful.

During a rather cold and damp evening shift in mid-January when northeastern ocean and bay winds were adding an additional 20-degree wind chill factor to an already sub zero temperature, a few of the patrolmen had gathered in the squad room discussing just how cold and miserable it really was outside. Talk of double insulated socks, long cotton underwear, and wool vs. nylon was discussed in detail and which combination worked best.

Benny just happened to have been walking down the hallway and overheard some of the conversation. He joined the group, and after listening for a few more minutes decided to volunteer his thoughts on the subject. Benny stated that his method of staying warm was to wear a pair of his wife's nylon stockings under his uniform pants. This was immediately followed by about five seconds of complete silence.

Now if this statement had come from another patrolman, he would have been ridiculed right out the back door. However, not wanting to sound crass or to openly ridicule a ranking officer, this information was met with enthusiastic agreements of such a novel and clever idea. Naturally, the absence of outright mockery toward his statements gave Benny the illusion that the patrolmen considered his wearing his wife's lingerie was completely acceptable and perfectly normal. It took no more than 24 hours for everyone in the department to learn of Benny's somewhat confidential disclosure.

Almost understandably and predictably, shortly after the 25th hour following the revelation, Benny's account led to the deliverance of his other un-complementary nickname: "Pantyhose."

For the next several weeks, no more than a day or two went by without Benny finding a used pair of women's stockings draped over his office chair, his desk, his car antenna, the car bumpers, and even the hedges in front of his home. Benny tried to ride out the affront to his perfection but was betrayed by the crimson red of his ears each time a member of the department came into the station stating how cold it was outside.

Benny was never quite sure whether these standard weather comments were in fact just standard weather comments or if they were "Pantyhose" comments. After several months of anguish, the *hosing* finally subsided. However, to be fair, this was mostly due to the change in weather and the lack of discussion about the cold rather than lack of interest in the disclosure about Benny's choice of questionable attire.

Benny was certainly relieved, but the legend of the nickname lived on, and the history and the account of it were faithfully passed down to each and every new employee for many years to come.

Like quirks that occur in nature, along with the wisdom of the civil service promotional process, and the fact that his test score was higher than the other sergeants who had taken the exam, in due time, Benny became the first captain of the Cedar Springs Police Department.

CHAPTER 14

Almost Assuming Command

O n a crisp spring day in May, a call was received at the station, reporting that a shooting had just taken place on or near one of the commercial fishing boats tied up at the docks on the south end of the community. It was initially unclear as to whether any injuries had occurred, but the shooter, reported to be a fisherman on one of the boats, was supposedly still on the boat and had reportedly indicated that he would shoot anyone who tried to take him to jail.

Of course, the last statement would sometimes be added to a report by an excited citizen to ensure that the police would respond quickly. It would normally turn out to be not the case and not even said, but one could never be 100% certain.

When the fishing boats were in port, many times they would be tied up two and occasionally three abreast, and the only way to get to the farthest one from the dock was to climb onto the first, jump to the second and then jump to the third. It seemed that every time some type of problem or emergency took place on a fishing boat, it was always at a time when numerous boats were in, and the emergency and/or suspect was located on the farthest boat out from the dock.

This particular incident was no different. A northeastern--or *nor'easter*--storm, as they are called, was due to hit the region within a day and had caused a number of boats to return to the safety of the harbor. The boats were tied up three abreast, up and down the entire length of the docks.

Information relayed from the dispatcher to the responding three cars was that the suspect--apparently highly intoxicated or just plain high--had gotten tired of ranting and raving around on the deck of the boat and had taken a gun, reportedly a rifle of some type, fired off a round into the air and had gone below to the lower quarters of the boat.

Several patrolmen responding to the scene received reports from observers that the suspect had just recently appeared on the deck of the boat holding a rifle. After staggering around, yelling and appearing intoxicated, the suspect fired off another round into the air, hollered more gibberish, and then had gone below deck.

Captain Benny happened to be working this day. After monitoring the call from his office and checking to make sure all his ribbons, pins, and badges were straight, and his hat sitting at just the right angle, he responded to the scene. His first act after his arrival was to don his spotlessly cleaned and pressed tactical jump suit and army surplus flak jacket from his vehicle's trunk. He then announced, and not unexpectedly, that he would be the officer in charge of the situation. The patrolmen at the scene, with a slight bit of eye-rolling and heavy sighs, advised Benny of what information they had received.

The boat in question was moored toward the western end of the dock in the vicinity of the dockside restaurant, the Lobster Shanty, and their floating wooden schooner that doubled as a secondary bar in the summer months. The harbor area was approximately 200 feet wide. On the one side was the restaurant, its outdoor dockside raw bar, the schooner, a fish-packing plant, ice house, and several warehouse buildings.

On the opposite side of the harbor were several waterfront houses and apartments, and also the entryway to a pleasure-boat docking area. The commercial fishing boats would dock and unload east of the restaurant in the area of the fish packing facility and ice house, then move into a lay-over position west of the restaurant.

When several boats were in port, the dock area resembled taxi cabs at an airport. They would be double and triple parked. The dock area was a tourist attraction when the boats were in; many visitors who had never seen a *real* fishing boat would spend time inspecting them, while hoping to also experience the possibility of witnessing a *real* fisherman.

On this particular day, a lot of tourists got to see more than they bargained for. Several made the ole' "God, if you get me out of this situation, I'll never do whatever they should not have been doing in the first place" promises, after being in the area when a incapacitated *real* fisherman went on a tangent and fired off a couple of rifle shots into the air.

The boat in question, the *Josephine Mary*, was tied three out from the dock and offered the suspect a fairly open view to the general public on the dock as well as the houses and apartments to the south, which could be very bad should he decide to take pot shots at people from the deck of the boat.

Benny set up his command post safely behind one of the restaurant's storage sheds located on the dock but also out of view of any possible random stray bullets. While cautiously sneaking up to and peeking around a large wood piling, he took a long look at the boat and indicated to everyone there that this was going to be a tough situation to handle because of the logistics and lack of manpower to evacuate the entire area.

With this thought in mind, Benny radioed to the dispatcher that he was requesting assistance from the two neighboring police departments and the county prosecutor's office and also the US Coast Guard, apparently just in case the suspect turned out to be an ex swimming champion and attempted a water escape. He also wanted the county's SWAT team activated so that they could report to the dock area should an armed assault on the boat be called for.

Benny was being careful and was conducting the operation of this situation using as much reference as he could relate to with the documented book cases he had read about and the similar previous intoxicated commercial fisherman cases that had taken place in the area in the last twenty years. Benny wanted to take down the armed fisherman with absolutely no violence, no injuries, no property damage, and no Monday morning quarterbacking by anyone, especially The Rude.

Benny figured that he could get a megaphone, talk to the suspect and convince him to give up peacefully. If that failed, Benny was prepared and was getting the entire county prepared to wait him out, no matter how long it took or how much it cost.

Now, as usual, The Rude happened to have also heard the original call and decided to wait a while before showing up at the docks just to see how Captain Benny handled the situation.

After Benny had set up his command post, The Rude, in his usual casual attire—light-gray plaid polyester pants and a golf shirt, with his .45 on his hip, gold badge on his belt, and a cigarette in his mouth--arrived at the dock. He couldn't help but notice that Captain Benny, now stationed behind the storage shed, was dressed to the nines. He was peeking around the corner or the shed from time to time, checking out the fishing boat. When The Rude made his way up to the shed, Benny gave him the particulars of what had taken place and what he had ordered to be done.

After hearing Benny's plans to incorporate most of the law enforcement agencies in the entire county, The Rude took a long drag from his ever-present cigarette, breathed heavily, and asked, "Has anyone seen this guy in the last few minutes?"

Benny explained he was waiting for a bullhorn with which to communicate the wishes of the police and also to receive the possible demands of the suspect.

Exasperated, The Rude said, "Damn it, Pat, it's probably a drunken fisherman, not a hostage situation."

Captain Benny, not wanting to face criticism so early in the case, said, "With all due respect, Chief, I believe we should approach this situation with the utmost safety of the suspect and any civilians that may be in the area by assuming that the suspect may be unstable. I think we should be prepared to take as much time as needed to see a peaceful and safe solution to this problem."

The Rude just looked at Benny, took another long drag from his cigarette, looked around, and mumbled, "Humph!"

About twenty minutes later, the department's army surplus megaphone was brought to the scene, and Captain Benny bellowed that he was Captain Patrick Benjamin of the Cedar Springs Police Department. He announced, in perfect diction, to the now- empty boat deck, hoping the sound would drift down into the quarters of the boat, that he was aware that some type of problem had taken place which involved a weapon. Benny roared, with perfect pronunciation, that it was the department's wish that no harm would befall anyone, and that if the subject exited the boat with his hands high in the air, he would be treated fairly until a proper investigation could be completed.

Now all the patrolmen and the chief knew that no self-respecting alcohol or drug induced, probably dead on his feet from working twenty or thirty hours with no sleep fisherman would give two craps about the proper investigation of anything. They also knew that anyone high on drugs or intoxicated on alcohol probably couldn't understand what Captain Benny was saying anyway.

Everyone at the scene, with the exception of Captain Benny, thought it would be easier if the alleged gun-toting law-breaking fisherman would come out on deck with the rifle and take a shot or two at someone or something so that all the patrolmen could pretend the fisherman was a life-sized paper target and they were at the pistol range. After all, the boat was from another port out of state, so the perpetrator was automatically looked upon as a non-local.

The Rude, after listening to what was going on for a few minutes, was probably thinking he didn't want to hang around the docks all day and night and certainly didn't want to have to supply any press releases to the newspapers or explain all the requests for assistance the captain had asked for to the local politicians.

While Captain Benny was adjusting his hat and checking to see that everyone looked professional, The Rude made a decision. He stepped from behind the shed and walked down the dock, tossed his cigarette into the water, climbed onto the nearest boat tied up, made his way onto the second boat, and hopped onto the third just as the suspect opened the cabin door and began to step out onto the deck from below.

The bellowing of Benny on the bullhorn had apparently either woken him up or just plain irritated him, and he was coming up to see what all the commotion was, again holding the rifle.

At the same time that he was clumsily climbing over the bulkhead and stepping onto the deck, and beginning to bring the rifle up into a firing position, The Rude, who was now a step away from the cabin door, walked up close, reached out, and quickly grabbed the gun out of the suspect's hands saying, "Give me that fucking thing!" Followed by, "Now hit the fucking deck!"

The suspect, scared, surprised, humiliated, or a combination of the three, immediately dropped into a prone position and The Rude planted his size-13 shoe on the back of his neck. And just like Chuck Connors used to do on *The Rifleman*, he then checked the rifle and quickly ejected the remaining shells, making sure it was empty, all without removing the size 13 from the suspect's neck.

A swarm of patrolmen hopping from the dock to the boats quickly surrounded the suspect, where he was handcuffed and carried off the boats for a ride to the station.

Upon climbing off the boat onto the dock, The Rude walked up and looked at Captain Benny, handed him the rifle and shells and said, "Now you can do your 'proper investigation.'"

Captain Benny stood with his ears bright red and his mouth open for a few moments before regaining his composure. Without showing his disappointment, he gave orders to search the boat, question any witnesses, and gather information about the ownership of the boat so that the investigation could be completed.

It was later found that the intoxicated fisherman had not injured anyone. The boat had docked the day before, and he had argued with the boat's captain about a raise after consuming an entire liter of some very cheap vodka. It was also learned that he had obviously not verbally convinced the boat captain that he was worth the respect or the extra money he was asking for.

Following the boat captain's refusal to accept any deals, the fisherman decided his best course of action would be to try and forget the confrontation for a while and do some more drinking.

After becoming even more boisterous by even further intoxication, and not realizing that he was by then the only one on board, he grabbed the boat's rifle and decided to fire off a few rounds to try to get the attention of the captain, who was no longer there, to reconsider his requests.

The Rude had probably been lucky, but that was the way things were handled before the guidance counselors and the media informed people that they had the right to be inconsiderate and offensive and that they should expect and demand to be treated with respect by the police as well as everyone else no matter how ignorant, intoxicated and antagonistic they were. These few minutes of The Rude's Law

Enforcement Personality Alteration Therapy, gave everyone something to talk about for a couple of weeks.

Benny made it a point to approach all the patrolmen who had responded to the scene and explained that the procedure that he had instigated would have resulted in much the same outcome. He told everyone, even though everyone knew it never happened, that the chief had requested he explain to them that what had taken place was not necessarily proper police work.

Benny said that those outside of law enforcement would probably have construed it to be politically incorrect and possibly an infringement upon the fisherman's rights, and he asked each and every patrolman who was on the scene to keep the actions of the chief solely within the department and away from the members of the general public.

He also added that if similar situations occurred in the future, he would like to see more patrolmen put their tactical jumpsuits on immediately after arriving at the scene so that everyone looked the same and that the department would be perceived as "Unit Professionals."

CHAPTER 15

Benny's Hat Policy

T here were also times when Benny's ideas and procedures went to the extreme and were met with instant resistance and usually for all the right reasons.

On one of The Rude's infrequent vacations, Benny took it upon himself to make up the following directive that was distributed to each and every patrolman in the department. Benny firmly believed that if it succeeded, the chief would, upon his return, congratulate him for implementing the declaration and doing such a good job.

Instead of just saying "I want everyone to start wearing their hats when answering calls," Benny concocted and distributed the following:

Special order # 80423.

Title:
Head Apparel

Purpose:
To provide a respectable procedure for all officers of the department to follow in the line of duty when approaching any conceivable in-progress meeting or confrontation with the public which result in the public's visual observance of said responding officers.

Concept of Operation:
The emphasis of this plan is directed toward a future routine

containment and covering of all officers' heads with proper uniform attire whenever the departure of their vehicles and contact with the public becomes necessary.

This will ensure that any public observations of said officers will be of a positive nature with the perception of professionalism within the entire department.

Any and all surveillance of the order will be conducted by myself with full documentation of any and all infractions by officers which shall be made a part of their personnel file.

The following shall become effective immediately:

Police Communications Personnel (Dispatchers) will:

a. Identify and assign a minimum of one patrol unit to respond to calls with pertinent information as to whether or not the possibility exists that said officer should personally meet with the complaint, which would then indicate that proper headgear should be worn as soon as possible so that said officer is properly attired when he arrives at the scene.

b. In cases where multiple patrol units are assigned to respond, those units would automatically know that the situation would be one in which some type of contact with the public would be assumed or warranted and headgear would be mandatory for all of the responding units.

c. Upon the notification by the dispatcher that the call to which the officer or officers are responding to is no longer a valid call prior to their arrival, the responding officers should disregard the requirements of the wearing of headgear at that point and resume normal patrol.

d. Any officer at any time may at their discretion, choose to exhibit uniform headgear at all times throughout their shift.

Captain Patrick Benjamin
Patrol Commander

Now virtually everyone in the department agreed on two distinct things. The first was that Benny was a maniac who didn't have a clue, and the second was that this directive or *Special Order* was purely a useless waste of paper. Some, after reading the memo, said, "What the hell is he trying to say?" A few just said, "Hummph," tossed the order in the trash, and went about their daily routines. By far the majority of the department asked one question.

"Why didn't he just tell us to wear hats?"

The other element that was unanimously agreed upon was that the written order had been fabricated and passed out only because The Rude was on vacation for two weeks in Florida.

They also assumed--and assumed correctly--that The Rude would have never allowed Benny to use the title "Patrol Commander" if he was in town, or in fact as long as he was still associated with the department.

Some of the more ingenious and literary inclined members of the department took the order, rewrote it, and then distributed it the following day again to each and every patrolman in the department.

Special Order # 80432 "B"

Title:
Noggin Apparel Instruction Plans

Purpose:
To provide a respectable procedure for all officers of this department to follow while in the line of duty when approaching any "in-progress,"

"out of progress," "may-be- in-progress," "progressing to progress" or any direct contact with the public which results in the public viewing of said officers' heads.

Concept of Operations:
The emphasis of this plan is directed toward uniform containment of all uncovered heads whenever departing operated vehicles becomes necessary.

All surveillance concerning compliance of this order will be conducted personally by myself and documented in triplicate for any future disciplinary actions.

The following shall become effective immediately:

Police Communication Personnel (Dispatchers), will:

a. Identify the type of call and immediately and personally don the appropriate headgear. i.e.; service uniform cap, wool watch cap, fur trooper's cap (flaps up or down optional), straw Western hat, or riot helmet.

b. Assign a minimum of one patrol unit to respond to the call and advise which headgear should probably be worn by the responding patrol officers.

c. Emergency transmissions will only take place in the event of two or more calls at the same time requiring two or more different types of headgear to be worn, in order to clarify which responding unit should wear which particular headgear.

Responding officers shall:

a. Respond to calls exhibiting the initially reported head gear being worn by the dispatcher unless otherwise advised by the shift commander to adjust and change into a more appropriate type of headgear.

b. Communicate and coordinate any action at scene of call to verify the correct headgear to be worn by any and all assisting back-up units if necessary, in order to ensure perfect visual attendance by all parties concerned.

c. Upon notification by the dispatcher that the call to which the officer is responding is no longer a valid call, said officer shall immediately remove all previously applied headgear unless said officer respectfully decides to retain such headgear and return to normal routine patrol.

d. Upon the dispatcher's notification to a patrol unit that a call involving a physical altercation is taking place, is about to take place, or may take place, said officer, upon their discretion, may or may not wear protective headgear or any headgear regardless as to what headgear is being worn by the dispatcher, as it has been shown that this type of situation may or may not result in said headgear being dislodged.

e. All officers shall keep at their disposal several different types of headgear, not only for themselves, but to be distributed to private citizens who may at times become involved in the police action taking place, so that citizens not involved will continue to hold deep regard for the department for making everyone look uniformly correct.

f. Upon the arrest of citizens as a result of their actions at a call, said arresting officers shall remove any headgear worn by them, so as to distinguish the arrested individual as the bad guy, as viewed by the public.

Captain Patrick "Pantyhose" Benjamin
Supreme Commander for Two Weeks.

As usual, there were a few who read the order and said, "What the hell is he trying to say now?" And some who just stated, "Hummph," tossed the order in the trash, and went about their usual routines.

By the end of the day, as expected, all remaining copies of the two Special Orders disappeared from the squad room and mail boxes.

There were absolutely no comments by Captain Benny concerning either order or for that matter, anyone wearing or not wearing hats, for quite some time.

Several patrolmen actually began to wear their hats, not when answering calls, but whenever they would enter the station, in hopes that Captain Benny would be around, as each time he observed a patrolman in the station with a hat, his ears would turn a deep shade of red, which in turn caused him to retreat to his office.

This continued for several weeks until patrolmen found something more interesting to focus their time on.

The Rude, upon his return from vacation, naturally received several copies of both orders. After reading both, he lit another cigarette, took a long drag, and while shaking his head, promptly balled up the papers and threw them in the trash. His only remark was,

"Humph! I swear it's a God damn gang!"

It was rumored that shortly after the hat situation, The Rude had given some serious thought to actually having a real Special Order written and implemented directing that absolutely no Special Orders could be prepared or put into operation without his direct and personal approval, by anyone, for any reason, at any time.

That rumor was never proven. It probably didn't happen--but it probably should have.

CHAPTER 16

Roll Call

Because Benny was so particular about himself, he figured that everyone else in the department should also be particular about themselves. Not a day went by when someone wasn't advised that their shoes weren't shined enough or their badge or name tag wasn't straight enough--and his favorite, being caught not wearing a hat when answering a call.

During the early 1980s, Benny decided that it would be beneficial to consistent performance of the patrolmen by mustering the troops each day for inspection prior to duty. This new procedure was usually conducted on the evening shift after The Rude had left for the day. The Rude, of course, knew what was going on, but decided again to see how long it lasted until some sort of revolt took place. Additionally, it was done at night because if not, The Rude would always make it a point to walk down the hall past the mustering patrolmen, chuckling and shaking his head.

Since coming to Cedar Springs, Benny was always a stickler for everyone to be in proper attire. It soon thereafter became a challenge for everyone to come up with some small part of their uniform that they could alter so that Benny would make some type of comment about it being not quite right.

On a five-man squad, it was customary for each man to pick a night and purposely not wear his name tag or have it pinned on a bit crooked, which would be enough to make Benny cringe, cause his ears to turn bright red, and trigger him to go off on a tangent about the perception of looking professional and the importance of being properly identified by the public.

Following the tangent, each man would then profusely apologize, blaming their wives, girlfriends, or children for the pin not being where it belonged and promise it would never happen again. The next night--a different man, different pin, same crimson ears, same tangent, and the same apology.

Neither Benny nor the patrolmen ever seemed to tire of the inspection routine. In fact, there were times when a particular squad would be disappointed when Benny did not inspect them, because they had decided to present some small indiscretion in their uniform just to see if Benny could identify the proposed recklessness.

Captain Benny wanted to implement into the department as many things as possible that seemed to work in the National Guard. As the older men began to retire or otherwise disappeared and were replaced with new men, it was a challenge for Benny to try to install some of his beliefs in them before, as he believed, they were tarnished by the "good ole boy" attitudes and behaviors of the men who were able to take care of problems without utilizing police theories from a book.

Benny firmly believed that the ideas of how to solve situations that were in his books were there solely because they were tried and true responses to the many recorded public dilemmas that had required police involvement. He thought that if it worked well enough to be in a book, it was good enough to be implemented on a regular basis.

Benny wanted the patrolmen to be ready for anything, just like his guardsmen were advertised to be. With no demand from the chief to terminate the mustering, Benny reveled in the fact that through his inspections, he had successfully come across, and was correcting the many uniform discrepancies of the patrolmen. With this thought in mind, he then decided to expand the inspections to include a weapons inspection.

His well-thought-out "shift transition protocol" would now be extended to include the patrol sergeant to arrive at the station thirty minutes prior to the rest of his squad and obtain any important information from the outgoing patrol sergeant. The incoming sergeant would then meet with his squad and pass along this information.

Following the repetitious passing of what usually amounted to useless information, unless of course someone had done some heroic deed or made some horrendous mistake and had embarrassed themselves to the point of departmental stardom or scorn, the squad members would then bite their tongues and prepare for the possibility of an inspection by the captain.

This new inspection was scheduled to be done only on an average of once per week per shift, to ensure the element of surprise, which Benny believed would guarantee the patrolmen were always ready and that the shift sergeants were doing their jobs as supervisors.

This type of inspection continued for a few months and everyone, with the exception of Benny, was weary of them. It was hoped that The Rude, in his usual way, allowed them to continue just to see how long they would continue before someone did something that would cause Benny to discontinue them.

As these things sometimes happen, on a summer day during the mid-1980s, Sergeant "Big Ben" Bailey's squad had gathered at the station for their briefing and were very unceremoniously advised that there was nothing extraordinary to pass on. At the time, the senior man on the squad, Nicky Harlow, exclaimed that he was tired of these meetings that didn't amount to anything but wasted time.

Another patrolman, Rick Ginessie, said, "All we need now is for Benny to line us up again in the hallway to look at our guns and buttons. Another fucking waste of time!"

Sergeant Bailey indicated to everyone's dismay that he had been advised that the dreaded "Benny Button and Weapon Peek & Point" was to take place in just a few minutes.

Nicky, with what had become his customary clearing of his throat and short snort, advised the group that Benny had gotten way out of line. He added, "We all know he's just an anal clean freak. These things have got to stop."

One of the members of the squad was Dave Smith, who would eventually leave the department a few years later to start a somewhat successful auto detailing business. He left mostly because he was asked to leave. Actually, The Rude, never known as one who would sympathize with anyone's personal weaknesses, suggested to Dave, "Just walk away and don't look back." This advice was suggested mostly due to Dave spending a considerable amount of time with a quite stunning young lady appearing to be mostly blonde and regrettably not his wife. While these things sometimes happen, Dave's biggest mistake was that the considerable amount of time spent with the mostly blonde was mostly while on duty.

At this particular time, Dave had been on the department for a few years and generally went along with whatever happened at or in the department. During the discussion of the absurdity of the inspections, Dave agreed, and then with no suspicion of any immediate malicious actions from his fellow squad members, indicated he had to use the men's room. As was sometimes customary, he removed his gun belt and laid it on one of the desks, and went out the door and down the hall to do his business.

While he was gone, Nicky and Rick decided to try to make this the last Benny inspection that took place. Nicky removed Dave's 9-millimeter automatic from his holster, (the department had changed over to these but still supplied only right-handed holsters), and emptied the shavings from the pencil sharpener into the breach of the gun. He then wadded up a small piece of paper and shoved it in the end of the barrel and returned the gun to the holster. Now relieved and thinking nothing out of the ordinary, Dave returned from the men's room and put his gun belt on once again.

A short time later, Captain Benny arrived and requested the members of the squad all line up in the hallway. Reminiscent of General Patton, Benny slowly made his visual inspection of each man. As he approached each new man, he would conduct his visual inspection of his uniform and then ask for his weapon. He would carefully point the weapon toward the ceiling, extracting the clip (magazine), and hand it to the officer. He would then eject the round in the chamber and look up through the breech and the barrel to observe the interior of the barrel for cleanliness. After this he would reload the weapon and return it to the officer who would then return it to their holster.

All went as expected until he reached Dave. Benny asked for and was given the gun. He pointed the weapon up, ejected the magazine, then as he ejected the round in the chamber to inspect the breech and barrel, all the pencil shavings came out and fell into his face and onto his freshly laundered, starched, and immaculate white shirt.

The entire squad broke into laughter, including Dave, who had no idea of what was going to happen. Benny slowly handed Dave his weapon, never uttering a word, and proceeded to the men's room to clean up. Eventually, he came out of the bathroom wearing his now badly pencil-lead-stained shirt accented by his crimson red ears and silently went to his office and closed the door.

Almost as expected, all mustering and inspections of the troops immediately ceased. Additionally, and probably because of the initial surprised look on Dave's face when the shavings fell, he was never summoned to Benny's office to explain the episode, and it was thought by the rest of the squad that it might be best not to prolong the incident with the usual further examples of artwork and poems around the building.

Years later, after leaving the department, whenever Benny met any of the older patrolmen, he would always comment on whether or not all the games and random acts of cruelty used to antagonize him were done on purpose. He was always assured that yes, they definitely were, but that it was all mischievousness and not done with any real particular malice. Right....

"After all," they would tell him, "it wouldn't have been any fun if you hadn't reacted to them, and you would always react to them."

Benny's ears would once again turn dark red, then subside to pink, and when his blood pressure was back to normal, Benny would say with a nervous tic, "Yeah, well--I knew... I knew. I always knew you guys were just playing around." And as always, Benny really never knew whether they were telling him the truth.

CHAPTER 17

The Yeti

The Rude had always been the kind of man who neither accepted nor gave advice well but could say things in a minimum amount of words that would address the situation, state his opinion concerning it, and also make an impression that would stick with people for years.

One day the town court clerk had come into the station with some paperwork and began speaking to a fairly new patrolman, Tommy Adkinson. He was being chastised for requesting a postponement of a traffic case. The clerk was well known for being an eleven on a scale of one to ten for being abominable. Because she was so abominable, she had earned the fitting nickname of "Yeti."

It was difficult to determine whether she disliked the police, or her job, or just everything in general. Whenever a patrolman would enter the court clerk's office, they were immediately met with a menacing scowl from Yeti. Even legitimate questions concerning court cases first received a distinctive eye roll and heavy sigh before being answered. Most of the department members learned to ignore her angry attitudes and outbursts. They just figured she either had a very high estrogen level and due to her not-so- pleasant personality, was never able to expel any of it in the normal female manner or had way too little estrogen, a big touch of testosterone, and was trapped in a "wanna-be" situation.

She always attempted to admonish the police any chance she could for requesting anything that she thought would make her job the least bit difficult. The fact that her job was not difficult at all made the admonishments that much harder to accept without some sort of insurgency.

To Yeti, a postponement of a case would require that she look for and then actually open a file folder in order to locate a phone number of the defendant and/or witness and then physically call them and advise them that the court date had been postponed and then explain the newly assigned court date and time.

If no phone number existed, then the only course of action was the dreaded post card. The post cards were in fact preprinted, but certain boxes had to be checked and new dates and times filled in by hand. Oh, and of course postage had to be affixed. To Yeti, this was a horrendous task and one that should never have to happen in her world.

After listening for a few minutes to the horror about how backed up her work load was and the difficulties that a postponement would make for the entire town's judiciary process, along with a hindrance to the entire county and state monetary infrastructure, and a probable delay to a national balanced budget and world peace, Tommy settled back on his haunches and let go a litany of retorts.

Being fairly new but not foolish, Tommy decided that it would probably be wise to not go completely postal, as he had learned quickly that one never knew if someone was related to someone who was related to someone else, so excluding any intentional Yeti or estrogen comments, he advised the clerk very calmly yet emphatically that since she was "just the clerk," she should never attempt to tell the police what they can or cannot do, and she should remember that the only reason she had a job was because of the court cases the police brought into her office.

The conversation came to an abrupt and silent end when Tommy, in a clear, decisive, and quite loud voice advised the clerk to take her opinions and complaints, write them down in triplicate, crumple them up, and put them where the sun never shines. Of course, the exact spot he referred to was a bit more explicit.

Up until this point the clerk was really not used to being talked to like that. The older patrolmen knew what she was like and just got back at her lack of personality and charm by leaving the effects of good old-fashioned flatulence in her office as much and as often as possible. Many patrolmen would visit the clerk's office for no other reason other than having gastrointestinal issues from some bad or spicy food the night before.

With a look of surprise, Yeti looked around, and finding no one making an attempt to step up to the plate to defend her, promptly rolled her eyes, mumbled a "Humph" and left the building without a word and returned to her office next door.

The Rude, sitting in his office and easily being able to hear what had taken place, got up, walked down the hallway, put his cigarette in his left hand and extended his right hand to the patrolman, stating, "Way to go, I didn't think you had it in you. I'm surprised you didn't fart," and then abruptly turned and left.

CHAPTER 18

Horrible Hank

U ntil the mid-1970s, Cedar Springs also happened to have the last remaining magistrate in the state instead of a politically appointed judge. Judge Henry Albright, aka "Horrible Hank," had been born and raised in the area and knew most of the department's older members and their families on a first name basis.

His theory on judgeship and the testimony of the police was extremely simple: as long as an officer testified truthfully and was never caught fabricating or embellishing anything about an alleged incident, locals as well as outsiders were usually found guilty of the charged offense solely based upon the testimony of the officer, no matter how many witnesses the arrestee could bring to court to testify to the contrary. His idea of swearing to tell the truth in his courtroom was something he took very seriously, and he had no problem showing his displeasure if he thought someone wasn't.

Locals, after they had either pled or were found guilty, were usually given a stern warning and advised that they should not make another appearance in his court. He would add that if they did, they would face stiff financial penalties or incarceration. Being local and homegrown himself, an added incentive for better behavior by the individual was Hank indicating in court that the subject's mother, father, or even grandmother (calling them by their names), would be ashamed of their alleged behavior. For those who may have thought their court appearance was going to be somewhat confidential, he would add that he would be personally be expressing his regret to the relatives within the next few days.

It was also not unusual to see Hank's typically calm demeanor quickly change after visually examining a defendant whose name had just been called for attendance. If the outcome of the examination was not what he expected, he would request the individual to approach the bench. Many times, he would suggest very rigorously that the defendant go home to get a change of clothes, additionally advising them to be back within the hour, as he believed that they had not respected his courtroom because of the way they were dressed. Those who failed to return properly dressed in the allotted time would find that they now faced additional charges of failure to appear.

While trusting the integrity of an officer's testimony was a major factor concerning his decisions, Hank could also just as easily find someone not guilty based upon that same testimony. If an officer's story was just plain unbelievable or caused certain disbelieving expressions on the face of the arrestee, then Horrible Hank was prone to digging a little more into the circumstances surrounding the case.

There were times when the town prosecutor, who sometimes assisted the officers in disputed cases, or a defense attorney, indicated that they had no more questions for the officer, Hank would have no problem interrupting the proceedings to say, "Well, I do."

Hank himself would publicly grill that officer on the stand about the incident, and if he decided that the officer had been fabricating some part of the story to make a charge seem more serious than it should have been or to cover some type of inappropriate behavior, it didn't bother Hank one bit to publicly tell the officer while he was still on the stand that his testimony was not what he had expected. Many times, he would just state on the record that the testimony of the officer was just not believable and therefore found in favor of the defendant. While a definite aid for the defense, this was instant humiliation to the officer. In addition, he would advise the officer not to show up in his courtroom again unless he did a proper investigation and could testify professionally about it.

In future appearances, those same officers would be grilled several more times until Hank was convinced the officer would base his actions and testimony according to the law statutes and to testify to the whole truth and nothing but the truth for the rest of their career.

New hires that came into the department with a bit of an ego were never told about Horrible Hank, as it was always fun to watch their first attempts to testify in court. Until Hank retired in the late seventies, many officers were taught to conduct their investigations and submit reports that were beyond reproach because of Horrible Hank. Those who didn't learn and practice the proper procedures usually found different employment.

CHAPTER 19

Buck

Now when giving a depiction of the department's supervisory personnel, it's fitting to talk about the first Cedar Springs lieutenant at the same time as the first Cedar Springs captain, not only because they were the number two and number three men in the administration but also because they were such literal and visibly recognizable opposites.

Thomas Buckstrome "Buck" Morningston

Officer Tommy Buck Morningston, one of Cedar Springs' original patrolmen, after several years on the street, had taken a promotional test and had become a sergeant, much like Benny had in his old department. No one knew when Tommy began to be called Buck, but it was assumed that he just didn't like his name Tommy. Patrolmen hired after the late 1960's probably didn't even know that Buck was not his first name or that it was actually "Buckstrome." It was as though he had always just been Buck.

Buck was a true old-school cop with his own set of idiosyncrasies to deal with. Buck and Benny had casually known each other for many years, but their personalities and personal attributes were a lot farther apart than one could imagine. Yin and Yang were more alike than Benny and Buck.

Buck had been hired back in the day with The Rude and for years ruled the streets utilizing discriminating decisions based upon the circumstances of the incident and an iron hand when needed. It was rumored that Buck had actually invented the ole' "If you're not gone by the time I count to three, you're going to jail" routine, but no factual evidence was ever found to prove it. It was also rumored that when Buck instigated the rule, he counted really fast.

Buck took the lieutenant/captain promotional test at the same time Benny did but ultimately ended up with a lower score. As luck would have it, and also because he was the only other eligible member who took and passed the test, Buck became the first lieutenant in Cedar Springs.

Buck, not known by anyone as Tommy, was usually known by and referred to as "Pappy" by most of the members of the department since he had become a sergeant.

Buck got his nickname of Pappy solely because he looked much older than his true age. In the few times when he decided to communicate with other people or was in a good mood and sober, which tended to be very sporadic, he tended to call anyone younger than thirty and all the new hires "son."

Overweight, balding, with a really dreadful-looking comb-over consisting of a few dozen long singular hairs originating from a part slightly above his left ear, Pappy was consistently gruff, grumpy, abrupt, and bad-tempered.

The lieutenants and captains were assigned to wear white shirts instead of blue or gray. As white, starched, and ironed as Captain Benny's shirts were, "Pappy's" were soiled, yellowed and wrinkled. On top of that, Buck seemed to be incapable of having the entire yellowed and wrinkled shirt tail tucked in to his pants at any one time. It was rumored that he may have been trying to set a new styling trend that he could patent and cash in on, but to anyone's knowledge, that was never proven, and no such patent was ever applied for.

Together with one side of the shirt or the other always hanging out, scuffed-up shoes with telltale pushed-in heels from forcing his feet in rather than untying and retying the laces, faded, worn out, drooping elastic white socks, and the ever-present food stains on his tie, Pappy was evidence of and testament to the fact that in reference to the likes of the crisp styling of Patrick Benjamin, everything in the universe does indeed have a direct opposite.

If Benny was the average person's imaginary image of what a police officer should look like, Buck was that same person's image of what they should not look like.

CHAPTER 20

Aromatherapy

Along with his somewhat original imposing physical characteristics and clothing style, it was universally alleged by the members of the department that Buck had the distinct reputation of smelling as bad as or worse than any member of a police department should, or any person, period, for that matter.

Buck's odor was usually described in two ways. The first was that of a wet dog. There is really no way to describe what a wet dog smells like, but virtually everyone who has had a dog has also experienced this phenomenon. As enjoyable and satisfying as a dog can be, when wet, they become the most unbelievably odorously offensive best friend a man can have.

The second description was what one would smell like if he had just put on clothes that had been washed but left in the washer for a few days to sour before being thrown in the dryer. They look and smell all right from a distance, but if you get close enough to them, you know right off that something is not quite right.

The problem with the washer/dryer theory in regard to Buck was the fact that he virtually never washed his clothes. He also had a slight problem with bathing--the slight part being that it didn't happen very often, which then favored the wet dog theory without the dog. Of course, if he had bathed and washed his clothes, the three to four days in the washer to sour before drying scenario would then certainly apply.

He was said to have explained that his way of living wasn't due to any religious or political beliefs, but that he had simply decided that his clothes just didn't need to be regularly cleaned. Rather than launder his clothes, he just occasionally ironed them or bought new ones when they finally wore out. He figured that if his shirts were pressed, they looked good enough and they also looked clean from a distance, and he saved the time and expense of the cleaning, which to him correlated to more beer money.

It was undecided whether the ironed-in sweat or the nicotine from his two pack a day smoking habit contributed more to the yellowing of his shirts, and debates on the subject usually ended in draws. His uniform white shirts were actually more yellow than white.

Absolutely no one who had met Buck or stood downwind of him wanted to be downwind of him again and certainly no one wanted to be required to ride in the same car with him, as Febreze hadn't been invented yet. Patrol vehicles would need several hours' driving around time, with the windows open, in order to release the Buck odors into the atmosphere.

On top of all these traits--or what were more politely described as idiosyncrasies--it was also common knowledge that whenever Pappy was not working, he was drinking. Adding the lingering odor of alcohol spewing sweat pores to clothing saturated with ironed in body odor and nicotine gave Pappy the distinguished honor of where the camaraderie of cops and the *Thick Blue Line* clearly stopped.

There was a striking contrast between the white uniform shirts worn by Captain Benny that were always bright white, starched, and ironed with badges and pins perfectly aligned and those worn by Pappy. His were close to the color of a number two pencil, complete with the underarm stains close to the color of the pencil lead. Badges and pins were also usually haphazardly attached.

Pappy was a gangly old-school street cop who in the old days banged heads with the best of them. Somewhere along the line, and in between divorces and drinking binges, he had altered his personal cleanliness but also managed to take and pass civil service tests to become a sergeant and then a lieutenant. Apparently, the State Civil Service Commission did not include consideration of personal hygiene in the criteria for promotions.

In his earlier years, Pappy was streetwise and observant of the rights and expectations people had to expect reasonable protection from inconsiderate knuckleheads. When people needed assistance, it was provided without question.

With his promotion to lieutenant, Pappy assumed the total persona of one who had paid his dues and was content to end his career as a "Do as I say and don't cause any problems for me" type of supervisor.

CHAPTER 21

Airing out the Laundry

So in one office the department had spit and polish "Felix Unger" Captain Benny, trying to set an example to the rest of the department and the community that the police were someone that you could look up to, if for no other reason than because they looked good. In the other office there was "Oscar Madison" Lieutenant Buck/Pappy who smelled bad, looked bad, and more times than not was hung over from the day before and couldn't care less what the community thought of him or the department.

Benny and Pappy took turns supervising the evening and weekend shifts. Either one being in charge on any given day could be an adventure for all those who happened to be working.

When Pappy would work, or more appropriately described as assigned to come into the workplace, the low man on the totem pole or FNG (fucking new guy) would have to go and pick him up at home, as Pappy rarely drove.

A police vehicle was not issued to him or Captain Benny, mainly because there weren't enough cars to do so until the mid to late 1970s when the town tried to keep some of the well-worn yet still viable patrol cars, minus the overhead lights, as transportation for the administrators. The other reason was that The Rude wanted to be the only one with a personal unmarked police car. Buck had his own personal car, but most times it could be found parked somewhat haphazardly in his driveway or side yard.

When picking up Buck, it was always a guess and sometimes used as the daily wager as to whether or not he was going to come out of the house slightly intoxicated and antagonistic, or hung over, subdued and argumentative. Either or both these scenarios were the probable reason he was not provided a police vehicle to take home even after there were enough to go around. That, and the fact that if an emergency occurred, and Buck was off duty, it was assumed, and assumed correctly, that one; he was drinking, and two; no one wanted to call him in when he had been drinking, and everyone knew that he was not going to be able to, or even want to assist properly with anything even if he was called in.

What was always a sure thing was that if you were chosen to pick him up, he was going to smell really bad. It didn't matter what day it was, what shift it was, or what time of year it was.

If you showed up at his house during the summer with the air conditioning blasting with the windows open, thinking or hoping that the good odors could outweigh the bad, the first thing Pappy did was ask you to close the windows. Pappy didn't have air conditioning at home, and like anyone without it, he enjoyed the full effect of the car's cool air. Within a few short blocks, the recycled air in the car would become soiled, and it wasn't long before the speed limit was being exceeded.

During the winter months, it was even worse. Pappy would not only asked to close the windows but asked that the heat be turned up, which naturally multiplied the odors, which in turn again resulted in excessive speeds.

FNG's selected, or more appropriately ordered, to pick up Buck would drive as fast as possible back to the station and when Buck got out, immediately lower their windows and drive many miles either in the heat or the cold until the odors subsided. It became standard practice for all the patrol vehicles to have a can of air freshener stashed in the glove box or their tote bags.

When Buck entered the station, he would check the call cards, not to see what had taken place or what was taking place, but more to see if there was any chance he may have to make a decision or listen to some complaint about how someone was treated or not treated.

If things looked relatively quiet, Buck could retreat down the hall into his office, put his feet up, and look forward to going home. There were times when Buck would wander down to the dispatch center and watch TV with one of the dispatchers. The only real plus to having Lieutenant Buck work was that he rarely interfered with what patrol did and virtually never showed up on a call.

CHAPTER 22

Taking on the Hulk

In the late 1960s and early 1970s, new hires were allowed to work on the streets for up to six months prior to completing their state-mandated police training. Accordingly, in the mid 1960s, the department hired four new men who were promised a spot in the Academy the following year as long as they didn't get seriously hurt, criminally charged, or be responsible for any undue and unexplainable embarrassment to the chief or to the department.

Pappy was at this time a patrol sergeant, and with the addition of the new hires, he was then responsible for a four-man squad, which included himself. Patrol zones then were basically split into the north area, the south area, and a floater who patrolled everything in between. Pappy, when not hung over or distracted by most anything else, would sometimes back up the patrolmen on calls.

One of the new hires, Angelo Demucchi, a transplanted second-generation Italian city kid from the Philadelphia Irish neighborhood, whose father and uncle were questionable characters' in the deeply rooted Italian part of the city, had been assigned to Pappy's squad. Angelo, raised in Philadelphia, had spent some time in L.A. in the late '60s and was rumored to have extensive knowledge of the drug and alcohol lifestyle. He even claimed to have attended Woodstock and was fond of pointing himself out as the youth in the white tee shirt and jeans in the 27th row of people in the center of the crowd on the cover of the Woodstock album. Admittedly, the picture could have been identified as any of the other several hundred thousand young men at the concert, but Angelo steadfastly insisted that it was him. It was well known that over two million people have claimed to have been a part of the four hundred thousand in attendance, so hey, his claim was just as good as any of the others.

After Angelo's basic training was completed, he would be assigned to the County Narcotics Squad attempting to quell the use of illegal drugs in the area. However, prior to the academy training, he had been assigned to Pappy's squad in order to gain some practical knowledge designed to aid him in the pursuit of his career in law enforcement.

Angelo rode with Pappy for one night. This was an unusual occurrence for new hires. Normally they would ride with the shift sergeant for a week to become acclimated to the areas and how things should be done. Because Buck was so charismatic and really hated to have to do what he considered babysitting, with anyone for any reason, he made a command decision. At the end of the first shift, Pappy stated Angelo was okay to be on his own and was assigned a car and a zone the following night.

It was said that it was difficult to determine who was the more appreciative of and grateful for this decision--Pappy, who didn't like to act like he was in charge for an entire eight-hour shift and certainly didn't want to have to talk to someone for that long, or Angelo, who had Pappy stop at a drug store after the first hour so that he could purchase some chewing gum along with a small jar of Vicks Vapo-Rub, which he immediately put in each nostril.

The next two nights for Angelo by himself were fairly quiet. It was the middle of the week, so there was not a lot of action, and Angelo virtually never even saw Pappy. On his fourth night of duty, he was dispatched to a domestic disturbance call at around 9:00 p.m. The dispatcher referred to the call as ongoing violence in the north area. After accepting the call, it was immediately followed by the south area car indicating he would be responding from the far south area of the town or at least ten to fifteen minutes away, and the floater car indicating he was actually in another jurisdiction getting criminal information from an informant. Not out of the ordinary, absolutely nothing was heard from Pappy.

Assuming that ongoing violence meant someone was in the process of getting assaulted or worse, Angelo lit up the blues and sped to the address, all the while knowing that he would probably be on his own.

The residence was one of the area's retrofitted small bungalows on a small 40 X 100 foot lot. These bungalows consisted of a living room, two small bedrooms, a kitchen, and a bathroom. Having one weather-beaten sedan parked in the grassless front yard littered with trash identified it as a probable rental property. The front door was half open. A storm door minus the glass lay next to the small concrete stoop, along with two battered trash cans.

Angelo pulled up cautiously to the home but saw no one. Once out of the patrol car, he could distinctly hear a woman's screams coming from inside the residence. With intestinal fortitude, or what used to be called youthful guts, and with the belief that the next few minutes could change the course of someone's life—or, much more important-ly, possibly cinch his future in the department as a hero--he entered the partially open front door.

There, just a few feet away, sitting on a well-worn flower-patterned tweed sofa, was a woman uncontrollably sobbing with her head buried in her hands. A sight to be seen, sat this vision of what was in all prob-ability a domestic dispute victim. The woman slowly looked up. She was blue-eyed strawberry blonde dressed only in a sheer, see-through teddy-type negligee reminiscent of Suzanne Somers. With a slight bruise around her left eye and a bit of blood dripping from the corner of her mouth, she exclaimed in a coarse, tired, alcohol-and-nicotine-worn voice, "Get the fuck out of my house, motherfucker!" Suzanne Somers never talked like that!

When she stood up from the couch and upon a more thorough examination, it was found that the lovely "Suzanne" was in fact about a 5-foot-4-inch 200-pound woman who definitely did not resemble the real Suzanne in any way, shape, or form. Even the negligee was several sizes too big. Suddenly Angelo thought that this might in fact be the assaulter and not the assaultee, but with no one else in the room, he decided to go ahead and ask the predictable question as to what had happened.

He asked, "What happened?"

What Angelo didn't realize was that Suzanne's 6-foot-5-inch, 285-pound boyfriend had fled out the back door when he pulled up. He had then circled the house and was at that time entering the front door and approaching Angelo from behind holding a rather large and very sharp butcher knife.

Angelo's police instincts were not yet finely tuned. He was somehow strangely attracted to the Bizarro Suzanne, undoubtedly solely due to the see-though negligee, and at the same time slightly revolted, also undoubtedly solely due to the see-through negligee, and thus was completely unaware of any danger.

Just prior to The Incredible Hulk boyfriend interfering with Angelo's visual interrogation, a slight breeze blew into the room from the still-open front door, filled with the unmistakable and familiar stench of sour, foul air. As Angelo slowly turned around to investigate the Pappy-like odor, he caught a glimpse of the butcher knife being knocked to the floor as Pappy appeared to fly through the air and onto the shoulders and back of the knife-welding boyfriend. The Hulk boyfriend was taken to the floor, pummeled many many times by Pappy during a short scuffle, and was eventually handcuffed.

After intently looking at the distressed yet formidable Suzanne now sitting and sniffling on the couch, Pappy advised Angelo, "Son, take this guy in to the station and put him in the holding cell. I'll stay here and gather the additional information needed."

Angelo, happy to be un-stabbed, and being new, did as he was told. The Hulk was now somewhat subdued and didn't even object when put into a holding cell. It seems that he and Suzanne were discussing the finer details of who would get what following their recent break-up. Things got a bit testy concerning possession of the stereo system after finishing off the better part of a wine in a box container of White Zinfandel.

Somewhat predictably, the Hulk stated that he had never struck Suzanne, whose real name was Rachel. When asked about the bruises on her face, he followed up with the other old predictable statement that she had had a lot to drink and probably got the bruises and cut lip while running into a door.

The night shift ended at midnight, and Pappy had not yet returned to the station. It was later ascertained that Pappy had spent a considerable amount of time and most of the night gathering the information needed while consoling an apparent sense of smell lacking Rachel about her poor choice in domestic partners.

The highly intoxicated and entirely subdued Hulk spent the night in a holding cell and was released by Pappy in the early morning hours, apologetic and somewhat sober, with no charges being filed.

The conflicting parties were separated for the night, the violence quelled, no reportable arrests had been necessary, and a new employee had learned an entirely new way of solving public disputes.

CHAPTER 23

Flaps

Thomas Buck Morningston had three main claims to fame.

One, he openly admitted that he was not fond of bathing or any type of personal hygiene, which was pretty obvious to anyone who met him or talked to him in person for more than a few moments.

The second was that his first marriage to a local woman whose husband had died suddenly was one of the shortest romance stories known to the department. Pappy happened to have been involved with the case and apparently offered some type of personal comfort to the widow that somehow was not offensive or repulsive.

For obvious reasons, he must have tidied up and bathed for a while, as the two ended up getting married in a surprisingly short period of time. The marriage lasted only a few months, after his wife confirmed her suspicions that cleanliness and sobriety were not strong points with her new husband.

The third and perhaps most noteworthy claim was the relationship that budded between Pappy and a part-time radio dispatcher named Abigail but commonly referred to among the troops as "Flaps."

Abigail was a middle-aged woman who at one time had been a bit chubby and fairly attractive but had obviously kind of let herself go and gained an enormous amount of weight.

To the members of the public who came to the information window with questions or complaints, Abigail, while sitting in a chair behind the radio console, appeared from the shoulders up to still be a reasonably attractive-looking woman.

However, her excess weight was centrally located in the stomach, hip, and upper thigh regions, requiring her to wear a wardrobe consisting of a large amount of warm-up type cotton and spandex outfits.

Wearing this stretching material probably helped hold things together while walking, but also when seated created many overhanging slabs of tissue that resembled flaps. The department's patrolmen, being clever creators of descriptive nicknames, decided that what you see is what you get and what it should be. Hence Abigail was dubbed Flaps. It was always said at least by the more straightforward members of the department that Pappy and Abigail would probably make the perfect couple.

Flaps, presumably because of her weight, after walking the seventy-five feet from her car to the dispatch area, had a tendency to profusely sweat. It was speculated that the spandex pants worked somewhat like a skin diver's wet suit and contained the moisture, which in time surely turned pungent and sour. With the just completed seventy-five-foot super-secretion sweat walk in mind, it was deduced that Flaps would also sweat a great deal in her day-to-day activities at home, and as everyone also knows, sweat usually eventually equals odor.

The patrolmen were faced with hours of discussions culminating in numerous theories on what the customary procedure was when removing the spandex when she got home. Most of those theories were expressed in great detail and quickly followed by a hunching of the shoulders, nausea, and vigorous full-body shivers while making a vocal noise reported to be close to that of a trapped animal.

Pappy was also equated with an unpleasant stench even without the sweat, so it seemed to be a match made in the heavens by the aroma gods. It was, however, doubted that even Flaps would be able to rise above the odor that surrounded Pappy long enough to get to *really* know him.

On the flip side, it was decided that Pappy would be the best choice to fill the question mark scenario surrounding the odds betting for the person most likely to be able to, or desire to, attempt the removal of Abigail's spandex other than Abigail herself.

More importantly, at least in the twisted imaginations of the department's personnel, it was doubted they could ever get to know each other in the biological way, as the search for the proverbial grand and regal "magic spot" seemed to be much too great a physical challenge and emotional adventure for the both of them to overcome.

Apparently, miracles do still happen in present-day times, as two visible changes began to occur during the next several months.

Pappy was being observed around the station with almost-white shirts or actually almost-not-yellow shirts with all the tails tucked in. His combover was slicked down to one side and not splayed all over his head. Probably the most unusual thing that happened was that he hardly ever reported to work looking full-blown intoxicated, slightly intoxicated, or for that matter, even hung over.

There was a hint of a hop and a bop in his step and rumors of the occasional aroma of Old Spice were reported when Buck passed in the hallway. Patrolmen obviously had to take carefully executed chances in order to substantiate the Old Spice rumors, as it was standard procedure not to breathe or take a breath while passing Buck, and not to breathe for at least another 10 to 15 feet following the passing.

The other thing was that Flaps appeared to be gaining a vast amount of even more accumulative weight in and around her midsection.

It was hard to tell which miracle was more astonishing or attention-grabbing--the almost-clean, Old Spiced, un-intoxicated Lieutenant Buck, or the uncanny ability Flaps had to gain more weight.

To add to the unusual happenings, it was also worth mentioning the skill and talent of the patrolmen who, even under the stress of day-to-day crime fighting, were able to notice the eerie and mysterious weight gain. Eyes were rolling and speculations flew around the department concerning the changes of Flaps and Pappy, with countless theories abounding.

Some suggested the chief had finally gotten tired of holding his breath while walking down the hallway to pass Buck and just told him to bite the bullet and take a bath and wash his clothes, which were certainly distinct possibilities. Another was that maybe there was a possibility of some large inheritance being left to Buck if he promised to clean himself up, but as far as anyone knew, Buck had no wealthy relatives--or at least none that acknowledged they were related.

Concerning Flaps, it was thought that maybe she had started some mashed potato, butter, and fried food diet or had developed an unusual and yet unheard-of case of bloating gastrointestinal cancer.

It wasn't until about the sixth month of gestation that the truth came out that Pappy and Flaps had somehow figured out a position to consummate their apparent torrid affair and had done the dirty deed.

Apparently Pappy still had some little larva that wasn't alcohol-and/or odor- impaired and who were still able to swim upstream, and Flaps still had some active ovaries with enough magnetism left to attract a little tadpole, along with enough courage to invite him in.

Flaps was going to be Mama Pappy; and Pappy, in his late fifties and ready to retire, was going to be a Pappy Pop-Pop.

To make a long and somehow if you think about it somewhat disgusting and nauseating story about the apparent consummation of fluids between Pappy and Flaps short, Flaps went full term, somehow managed to squeeze out the little pup without smothering him, and Pappy took a couple of weeks off to mask in the glow and glory of fatherhood. Unfortunately for Buck, Flaps, within a month's time, decided that he needed much too much attention to keep him clean and sober and decided to devote her time to keeping the baby clean instead.

Flaps broke off the relationship with Pappy and took a leave of absence from the department and then just never returned. It was reported she moved out of the area, where she would quickly change the subject whenever asked about the baby's father, but continued to keep spandex and warm-up suits as her preferred wardrobe. Pappy quickly reverted to his tried-and-true yellowed somewhat soiled shirt status and off-duty drinking prominence.

Within six months of the birth of the Pappy Puppy, Buck was unceremoniously rewarded for his fatherly efforts with certified mailings of formal paperwork from the county domestic relations courts that mandated him to look forward to paying child support for the next eighteen to twenty-three years.

CHAPTER 24

Better Benny than Buck

The main difference between Benny and Buck was that no matter what you did, or whether you were right or wrong, Benny was the one who would always defend the patrolmen in front of the public. Not only was this probably his most admirable trait in law enforcement, it was the one thing the patrolmen could count on. That and being told that they needed to shine their shoes, straighten their name tags, and wear their hats.

In fact, Benny was well known for coming up with some pretty elaborate stories and excuses for the erratic behavior and actions of some of the troops. It was rumored and probably true that Benny only made up these stories and excuses so that The Rude wouldn't badger him for not teaching the patrolmen to take care of things in ways that would not bring any disrespect or embarrassment to him or the department.

After the fact, you could always count on being summoned to his office to be lectured about proper protocol and procedures. Printed handouts of specific recommendations from the state or federal government, or excerpts from one or several of Benny's training manuals were also given to the offending officer with strict directives to "read it, learn it, and live it." While you were there, you could also count on being subjected to another visual inspection of your uniform and listening to another tangent about more protocol, more procedures, and more professional public perceptions.

Benny, who after calming down from whatever little misdeed that was done and exhausted from telling the patrolman about printed directives and of course imperfections in their uniform, would then suggest ways to cleverly not include certain aspects of what had taken place in any written reports.

This didn't entail covering up anything that could or would have been considered illegal. Despite the vast number of attention-grabbing occurrences that took place in Cedar Springs which directly involved the department, virtually none were regarded as being too far outside the scope of legality. Embarrassing and condescending, yes, but not illegal.

To bring to a close an internal investigation, or what was then referred to as a citizen inquiry concerning the methods utilized to conclude a situation, Benny would also include his own report in the file, which covered the basic events of the particular incident, including any of his meetings with the complaining civilians, which would inevitably indicate that the majority of the incident and the actions of the police and those of the complaining party were for the most part just a large misunderstanding.

On rare occasions the final closure of an incident would require the infrequent explanation that loosely resembled an apology by the patrolman to the complainant. The usual speech to them was about how most civilians were not able to understand the complexities of law enforcement and the far-reaching desires of "community safety" by the department and its patrolmen, who under duress of fear for the loss of that safety in general may have been one reason that they had extended their powers of authority this one time, and were truly apologetic for any inconveniencies caused.

Whew!

With a bit of professional finesse, and Benny looking so visibly professional in the background standing in front of his American flag, this explanation, more times than not, quelled any distress the public had toward the police. The captain was certainly a silver- tongued, spin-doctor problem-solver when it came to communicating with the public, even though he personally may not have been very smooth on the streets.

In contrast, Pappy, after becoming the lieutenant, virtually never talked to the public, and whenever he did, the conversations did not last long, probably due to the negative and destructive quality of the air in the room and the fact that Pappy really wasn't that interested.

Pappy didn't have much patience to listen to anybody and would sometimes side with the public just to get the meeting over with. Unfortunately, the officer or officers in question were then instructed to include the original circumstances as well as a description of the public's complaint in their written report, which would then be subject to possible official reprimands. There was not much fun to be had when Pappy was working.

As they say, ingenuity and/or necessity is the mother of invention. Whenever Pappy was on duty and a civilian complaint concerning some type of indiscretion by a patrolman came to the station, they were advised that no one higher than the rank of patrol sergeant was available. This was advised as long as Pappy wasn't standing next to the dispatcher speaking with the complainant through the safety glass or observing the officer speaking with the complainant.

They would tell the complaining civilian that they could speak with the sergeant or could choose to return and speak with the captain of police the next time he was working, completely overlooking and never mentioning the lieutenant. Most people that wanted their complaint to be heard at a higher level and who had some idea of the degrees of ranking chose to wait for a captain over a sergeant.

On the whole, the patrolmen were also relieved when they chose to wait for the captain. Perceptions, protocols, tangents, and inspections aside, most of the department members realized that they were fortunate to have an administrator who would support their actions. Of the two, patrolmen were more than content to work with Benny.

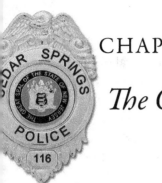

CHAPTER 25

The Chief's Car

P rior to having several spare patrol vehicles, the only two unmarked cars the department owned were a used repainted patrol
car minus the roof mounted emergency lights that was used by the
detectives, and of course the chief's car.

Captain Benny loved it whenever The Rude took any time off.
After his divorce from "the chief's wife", and years of anguish following it, he began to take a yearly vacation out of town. Whenever he
went on vacation, he would leave his car at the station rather than take
a chance on it getting damaged while parked on the street, as it was
pretty obvious it was an unmarked police vehicle. Back in the day, the
four doors, black wall tires, rather large whip antenna and small plain
hubcaps were a surefire clue.

Benny would wait at least 24 hours before touching the car just
in case The Rude changed his mind and didn't go out of town. On
the second day, Benny would drive to the station in his personal car
as usual but then utilize the chief's car whenever leaving the building,
including taking it home so he would be suitably ready to make any
official decisions during the night that should require him to actually
use the car and go to a scene.

In the mornings, he would walk slower from his front door to the
chief's car in hopes that one of his neighbors would be outside and
make a comment about him having an unmarked police car at his disposal. Benny had an entire litany ready about how he was responsible
for the entire town, its people, and their property, and how important
it was to be ready at a moment's notice to spring into action. Sadly, to
the best of anyone's knowledge, he never got to utilize the litany.

He got close one time on a Saturday morning when his neighbor's teenage daughter was in her front yard with several of her friends. Benny came out of his house in his perfectly starched and polished uniform, complete with strategically placed hat, but when the girls began to snicker and whisper, as teenage girls tend to do, he thought better than to start a conversation, as he was uncomfortably distraught--and probably rightly so--that the snickers were aimed at and concerning him.

On this particular second day of The Rude's vacation, Benny was in his glory, returning to the station after eating lunch at a local restaurant where he wrangled a table in the middle of the room, which enabled him to be the center of attention again in hopes that someone would approach him and ask a law enforcement type question. And again, much to his disappointment, it didn't happen.

When returning to the station, he approached an intersection about three blocks from the station. The intersection was a four-way stop, but with no other cars visible, Benny did a California stop, slowing slightly and then proceeding ahead. Suddenly a small dog (and yes, this time it was an actual dog), wandered into the roadway, stopped smack in the middle of the road, and looked at Benny like a deer at night caught in the headlights of a car.

Almost instantaneously, Benny had two thoughts go through his mind. The first was to continue forward and run over the dog, using the justification that he was operating an emergency vehicle, which in his mind should have the right of way for any and all reasons. The second was to make an attempt to avoid hitting the dog, which would probably result in, at the least, a great deal of tire screeching, which would also possibly result in a great number of people stopping, looking, and wondering what had happened. Hummm...decisions, decisions.

Kill the dog and be the goat, or miss the dog and possibly be the hero? As Benny wanted to avoid being the goat as much as possible, it was decided he would try to miss the dog. He secretly hoped that the end result would be many congratulatory pats on the back for his accomplished defensive driving skills, along with the possibility to explain that he was also in charge of the entire town.

In the few split seconds in which all these thoughts went through

Benny's mind, they just as quickly disappeared. After successfully twisting the steering wheel sharply to the right and then to the left and miraculously missing the dog, the chief's car promptly responded poorly to Benny's evasive techniques, slid across the roadway, and struck a parked car with a loud bang followed by the sound of bending sheet metal and breaking glass.

After Benny's heart settled back into his chest, he slowly exited the car, and the first thing he noticed was that the dog had disappeared and there was no one around.

Benny had wrecked the The Rude's car, and there was not even a single witness there to corroborate his story about the dog that was now nonexistent. No one came out of their homes to see what had happened--and what was even worse, he now had to find the owner of the parked car he hit and figure out a way to keep from getting fired for using and wrecking The Rude's car.

The damage to the parked car, a 1962 Oldsmobile, was minimal, as Benny had slid into its rear bumper. The bumper showed a few scratches and one small dent that would probably have to be pointed out to even be noticed.

The damage to the chief's car, however, was substantial, as the better part of the right front fender was bent almost to the point of touching the front tire. The front bumper was also pushed in at an odd angle and the headlight and turn signal lights had been broken. So much for the quality of a new car in the 1970s.

Benny had to go to three different houses before he found that the parked car belonged to an elderly couple, the Flannigan's. They were somewhat intimidated by the starched uniform and perfect diction of the captain and at the same time slick enough to know that this was an opportunity to make an easy buck.

After quietly listening to Benny's story for a few minutes, they both hobbled out to look at their car, each verbally reminiscing about the many memories they shared during their devout ownership of the vehicle.

Upon seeing the small dent and several scratches in their rear bumper, they seemingly reluctantly agreed to take a monetary settlement to cover the damage. It was rumored, and later found to be accurate, that the settlement would probably have been enough to replace both of the bumpers of the car along with a complimentary wash and wax to boot.

Since no one except the dog had actually witnessed the accident, Benny decided not to report the accident, knowing that with a report, it would also come with ridicule and disrespect in the form of homemade pictures and badly written poems in/and around the station. With no dog or eye witnesses, his insurance company would surely assume that some type of operator error had occurred, which would inevitably result in raised rates. In addition to the parked car damage, he decided to also take care of the damage to The Rude's car on his own.

That same day, after dropping off cash to the Flannigan's who decided not to accept a check, Benny took the chief's car to one of the local repair shops and practically begged them to complete the repairs in the next few days in order for it to be completed prior to The Rude's return.

The repairs, a new front fender, bumper, light fixtures and paint were completed in time and Benny parked the car back in the same place The Rude had left it. The Rude returned from his vacation, retrieved his car from the station and life in the department continued.

After several days of not hearing anything unusual from the chief, Benny was sure that he had successfully quelled the distinct possibility of an ugly quagmire by spending well over $1500 of his own money to try and cover up his mistake of saving the life of the mysterious missing dog.

After four days, The Rude finally called Benny into his office to discuss a few mundane and routine matters. While he was there, he also inquired if anything had taken place while he was gone that he may be questioned about in the future to which Benny replied, "No, not really. It was actually a pretty quiet couple of weeks."

The Rude, trying his hardest to look somber and official, lit a cigarette, took a long drag and exhaled the smoke. Then, nodding his head, he said, "Okay...good!"

This was the customary proposition and cue to whoever was in the chief's office, that the meeting was completed, and it was time to leave.

Benny was no exception to this practice.

Just as Benny was turning to leave, the chief very quietly and condescendingly said, "Oh, and by the way, the paint is a pretty good match. I myself probably would have gone through the town's insurance company!"

CHAPTER 26

The Sergeants

Following the promotions and the expansion of the department during the late '60s and early '70s, the department had a "slew" of sergeants to supervise the necessary squads of patrolmen. Originally there were only two sergeants, but with the growth of the town, it was decided that the department needed four squads and a detective division. With the promotions of Benny and Buck to captain and lieutenant, there was then theoretically a need for a total of five sergeants--five being the "slew" number for a small town such as Cedar Springs.

At the time of the civil service testing, almost everyone working in the department had enough time on the streets to be eligible to take the promotional exam. A test was given and the *five* future sergeants were selected from the *four* men who actually passed the test.

Of the five, Dudley Sergeant--whose last name was actually "Sergeant"--thankfully for him, passed. He just about had to pass the test at some point and get the promotion, as "Patrolman Sergeant" just didn't cut it for him and was particularly confusing to the secretaries who typed up reports and the attorneys who had to read them.

Along with a somewhat unclear last name, Dudley was also the holder of a first name surprisingly similar to the Saturday morning cartoon character who was presented as a member of the Royal Canadian Mounted Police. Always present and ready to help but still not quite capable to do so without some type of dilemma.

Following his promotion, it became customary to refer to Dudley simply as "Sarge," which then conveniently covered both his name and his position.

Two more were actually brothers, Robert and Peter Roberts. The

Roberts brothers, nicknamed "Lead Legs" and "Pinochle," were born and bred local boys. Peter or "Pinochle Pete" was obviously, because of his nickname, a big fan of card games. Before police work, he had worked as a laborer, usually in construction or on the fishing docks unloading boats and packing fish on ice. This continued on a part-time basis even after being hired in the department. His working another job helped when dealing with the locals, as he grew up with, went to school with, or had worked with most of the blue-collar people in town.

Robert, "Lead Legs," or usually just Lead was also promoted. Lead got his nickname because of the way he seemed to move. No one could ever recall, including his brother, seeing him moving, driving, or speaking faster than at a very, very slow, deliberate pace.

It was rumored that he had been named Lead Legs in his younger years by his mother after repeatedly having to tell him to hurry up to do most anything. She supposedly told him that it was irritating and just plain painful to watch how sluggish he was and became fond of asking him if he had lead in his feet. Eventually the often-asked question channeled into a nickname. Within a period of time she just began to refer to him as Lead. As things happen, it wasn't long before his brothers and friends also utilized the name.

In spite of his questionable and apparent lack of enthusiasm, Lead was actually a talented and respectable concrete mason who designed and installed brick façades, fireplaces, and patios in the area. In addition to that, he was an amateur photographer who also developed his own photos. This was beneficial, as Lead not only knew the blue-collar types but also got to know many white-collar families who could afford custom masonry or photographic work.

The fourth, Ben Bailey, was another local boy. Nicknamed "Big Ben," he personally knew almost everyone in town and was well liked in the community. A home-grown boy and ex-high school star athlete, Ben was also physically bigger than everybody else, which was an advantage in convincing people to change their behavior and in quelling disturbances. Like Pete, he had worked many jobs in the area and learned many useful trades, eventually even getting an electrician's contractor license. Ben was the proverbial jack of all trades and acquired many side jobs through his contacts with the public. He would also be destined to take over the annual barbecues after The Rude's separation and eventual divorce from his wife.

The last, Billy Durrant, really didn't do so well on the test but had been around long enough to complain and threaten to reveal many dirty little secrets about the other four and was promoted along with the rest. The chief used Billy's time and experience on the street to convince the State to add a few points onto his score, which kept the skeletons in the closet and kept the status quo.

Billy had been a pretty good cop for the first five or six years he was on the street. Sometime in the mid 1960s, well before the outbreak of fashionable PTSD, he had the unfortunate occasion to confront a burglary suspect face to face. The immediate reaction of the suspect was to pull out a handgun, place it point-blank at Billy's chest, and pull the trigger a very quick six times. For whatever reason—fate, if you will--the gun misfired all six times. It seems that the .22-caliber revolver that the suspect had was loaded with rim fire cartridges designed for a .22-caliber rifle. Fortunately for Billy, the handgun only fired center fire cartridges.

The culprit was arrested, and because he happened to be related to an influential individual, (from the northern part of the state,) eventually was given some ridiculous light sentence. The majority of the sentence turned out to be probation, which also added fuel to Billy's fire. The whole incident had a lasting effect on Billy, who from that time on, and probably somewhat understandably, mostly just went through the motions of police work and also understandably never went out of his way to confront people again. He became known as, and was, the moodiest person on the face of the earth, or at least in Cedar Springs.

CHAPTER 27

Pinochle Pete's Crazy Squad

Pete, aka Pinochle, was a pretty reasonable, down-to-earth guy, and when faced with decisions usually dismissed the black and white of the law and ventured into the gray areas to make judgments which would solve the problem with as few legal proceedings as possible. Pete was a believer in second and sometimes third chances but could also be harsh and inflexible to anyone who took advantage of his beliefs.

Although Pete wasn't very big, being about five foot seven, he was never one to ignore or drive slowly to a good bar fight and had an uncanny ability to be in the area of the call and be one of the first cars on the scene. Another thing that Pete never ignored was a really good or even a really bad game of cards. Both of these so-called talents earned him both a nickname and a reputation.

Two things were important to Pete. The first was that if he was involved in a card game, chances were good that he would be coming in late or a sick, or vacation day was in order. Card games that Pete got involved in became legendary. It was not unusual for a game of gin rummy or poker to continue as a tournament and last for several days.

Secondly, if assigned to his squad, you were expected to respond as soon as possible, with no excuses, to any and all bar fights or other officers' calls for assistance. Because of the large number of drinking establishments, low-rent housing, and commercial fishing docks in town, these types of calls were an integral and common occurrence during the 1970s and 1980s.

The only excuses for missing or not showing up for these occasions was the fact that you were out sick, on vacation, or already involved in another matter that you could not break away from. Unexcused absences on potentially physical-type calls were met with aversion, mockery, and ridicule from Pete as well as the rest of the squad. If absences continued, it would generally become justification for Pete to inform other members of the department, which would develop into more ridicule and mockery, culminating in Pete advising the individual to start showing up or ship out.

There was a several-year period when Pete's squad was comprised of patrolmen who reveled in potentially physical-type calls. One regularly arrested local troublemaker making an appearance in court was asked by the judge if the financial fine that he was imposing on him was enough to make him think of the consequences of his actions in the future. Slowly shaking his head, he sheepishly stated, "Your honor, I am definitely through with drinking and fighting in bars. To be honest with you, it's not the fines, it's because the cops that arrested me this time were just plain crazy."

Hence another legendary account of departmental history was indoctrinated, and Pete's squad became well known in the department--and more importantly, in the community--as "The Crazy Squad."

The Crazy Squad regularly utilized Captain Benny's unique art of calming the civilian complainers on a regular basis, as many parents and spouses considered their loved ones had been handled with excess vigor by the "crazies."

It was also rumored that The Crazy Squad was also somewhat instrumental in the eventual departure of Captain Benny from the department. It seems they were responsible for the majority of the "discrepancies in appearance" during Benny's mustering and uniform inspections. Of course, members of the squad denied any and all questionable actions toward the captain and added that their methods of conducting arrests resulted in a substantial reduction of criminal recidivism by their particular arrestees.

Besides being the leader of The Crazy Squad, Pete was noted for a few other things. One was that he was almost never seen without his pipe, usually filled with cherry aroma blended tobacco. The pipe became a sign to the other officers on a call. If a decision was being mulled over as to whether or not to make an arrest, as long as Pete kept smoking his pipe, things were copacetic. When Pete put his pipe in his pocket, it was universally understood that the subject under investigation was to be placed under arrest, restrained, and advised why at a later time.

The second, and probably most important to Pete, was that he also almost never went more than a 48-hour period without being involved in some marathon card game. Marathon because once started, Pete would play cards for hours and hours, usually only stopping to eat, sometimes to grab a few hours' sleep, and sometimes to go to work.

More times than not, when Pete was picked up at home for work, several people could be seen crowded around the kitchen table, immersed in the next hand. Most games were confined to nickel/dime betting, but with the hours and hours played, they soon elevated into some serious wagering.

It became a distinct fact that as much as Pete enjoyed a card game, and as good as he was in leading The Crazy Squad, Pete really sucked at cards and lost a whole bunch of nickels and dimes.

Unfortunately, the loss of the bunch's of nickels and dimes eventually resulted in Pete's having to file bankruptcy, which also resulted in the loss of his home. Pete eventually rebounded and was even promoted to the rank of captain after Benny left the department for a permanent position in the National Guard. When The Rude retired a few years later, Pete would become only the second chief of the department. While governing the troops with his usual common sense procedures, the department continued to advance, adding additional members and new technology. Pete was even instrumental in administrating an upgrade to a new police building, with room for many years of future growth. Pete's retirement a few years after his last promotion brought about the first real change of standards and methods of problem-solving in Cedar Springs.

CHAPTER 28

Timothy O'Doul

There was one beneficial element that the members of Pete's squad had. It enabled them to know which calls they were expected to answer resourcefully and/or in force. This beneficial element was their radio dispatcher.

In those days, each squad had their own radio dispatcher who worked the same shifts and hours as the squad. This was advantageous to both the dispatchers and the patrolmen who would become familiar with each other, and with their individual habits or traits.

Pete's dispatcher was an old Irish retired Philadelphia street cop, Timothy O'Doul, usually referred to as "Dooley," who had worked the rough streets of Philly in the days of Frank Rizzo. After his many years in Philadelphia, Dooley had a knack of knowing which calls were legitimate and also which had the potential for some type of hazardous encounter or violence. Tim had an 85 to 90% success rate on his predictions.

It was said that the members of the squad were able to distinguish which calls had a danger factor just by the way Dooley dispatched the call on the air. If the information was transmitted using a fair amount of sarcasm, it was believed to be one of the town's usual callers, and the call was not considered to be the type to involve any physical trouble. If it was dispatched with a great deal of sarcasm, it was known that it was definitely a regular caller, and a caller Dooley had tried but couldn't talk out of wanting to actually see an officer.

Dooley probably handled half of the complaint calls while talking to the caller on the phone by giving out information and suggestions. Of course, there were the overly irritating complaints that sometimes resulted in threats and promises by Dooley to send some of his boys down if they didn't stop whatever it was they were doing.

The local chronic complainers knew which dispatchers they could push and how far they could push them. They knew that they could not push Dooley very far or they would suffer the consequences of meeting and dealing with The Crazy Squad.

After once dealing with Dooley and his boys, most local callers knew and were cautious when asking for any type of assistance in the future. The possible implications of Dooley sending some of his boys to quell a problem, was a definite deterrent to crime--or at the least the crank calls from drunks who thought it might be amusing if they could cause some type of irritation to the police.

Many wise guys just trying to aggravate the police paid many hundreds and sometimes thousands of dollars in fines for being arrested because they chose to ignore Dooley's suggestions to stop their disruptive behavior before they would be visited by his boys.

Physical arrests at these types of calls were rare unless know-it-all, beer-muscled jug heads, after having too much to drink, thought they could call the police "pigs" or express their opinions concerning an officer's wife, girlfriend, mother--or even dispatcher Dooley. After all, insulting one's dispatcher was viewed as serious as an insult to one's immediate family, providing the particular dispatcher they were referring to was one who in turn was also just as protective of his boys.

However, if Dooley sounded serious and professional in giving out the call, you were prone to believe that something serious had taken place or was about to take place. Additionally, whenever Dooley dispatched two or more cars to a call, you knew that something unlawful definitely had already taken place, was taking place, or was going to take place, and some type of action was called for. These types of calls were categorized as mandatory attendance for all squad members unless specifically advised otherwise by Sergeant Pete.

CHAPTER 29

The Squeeze

The police station had two holding cells located in a side room just inside the back door. These were utilized as temporary confinements for arrested subjects. Arrestees would be placed into the cells while paperwork was completed outlining the particular charge or charges against them. Following the formal presentation of the charges, the subjects were either released on their own recognizance or transferred to the county jail in lieu of bail. Before regulations prevented it, subjects under the influence of alcohol were sometimes kept in the cells until they were reasonably sober, which was usually the following morning.

The front and back doors leading inside the building were electronically operated by the dispatcher or by utilizing a key. The dispatch office had a window facing the public entrance in the front of the building and a door with a smaller window, which faced the station's rear electronic entrance door. All officers had keys for both electronic doors but generally relied on the dispatcher to buzz them in. When returning to the station with someone in custody, an officer didn't have to rely on fumbling with keys to open the door. He would simply radio the station that he was in the carport with a prisoner, ring a doorbell to let the dispatcher know they were ready, and then be buzzed in.

Whenever anyone became a "guest," cell checks were required indicating the condition of the guest at the time of the arrest and at least every half hour thereafter. There were cameras and monitors that allowed the dispatchers to see what the prisoners were doing, but every once in a while a guest would start doing a Bruce Lee imitation by attempting to break the concrete block walls with their fists—or, more impressively, with their heads--or those who would climb up the bars trying to see if there were any escape hatches hidden in the ceilings. Of course, there were always those who just decided to yell and scream and holler as loud as possible, just in case there was anyone around that they could annoy or irritate.

Whenever any of these things happened, the dispatcher would have to call in someone from patrol to physically check on the detainees in order to protect the public's property--not that any concrete blocks were ever broken, but just in case the injuries sustained in the attempts to break them amounted to more than collateral damages, thus requiring a visit by the rescue squad.

Dooley, being a former cop, had no qualms about assisting his squad while they were in the station. Sometimes multiple arrests were made, and one could always rely on Dooley to be handy to hold open the back door and/or assist with a struggling prisoner.

There were times when patrolmen brought particular unruly individuals to the station that refused to comply with the requests of the officer to enter a holding cell. When this occurred on Pete's squad and another officer was not immediately available, that officer would sometimes be assisted by Dooley in getting the individual into one of the holding cells.

One such individual by the name of Walter was brought into the station highly intoxicated and wearing only a tee shirt. No pants, no socks, no shoes--just a tee shirt. During a romantic interlude with his girlfriend, the episode was interrupted and came to an unexpected close when Walter's wife came home from work early because she wasn't feeling well.

The expected domestic argument took place, including a four-minute cat fight between the two women. This was reportedly like a main event, starting in the bedroom, working through the home, and finishing in the front yard with both combatants evenly matched, with the exception that one was clothed and the other was not.

Neighbors who indicated that they were lucky enough to witness the match said it was fairly even until Nancy (the naked girlfriend), roundhouse kicked Cheryl (the wife) on the side of the head, rendering her unconscious. Because Nancy was also intoxicated, it was believed that the outcome would have come much earlier if she had been sober.

With a change of heart, Walter drunkenly decided his wife was in need of assistance and his girlfriend was a bully. Staggering out the front door wearing only his tee shirt, he promptly struck Nancy with a clumsy right cross, luckily hitting her in the temple, rendering her just as unconscious as his wife. Standing unsteadily over his naked prior conquest, he shook his head and reportedly mumbled, "Stupid bitch."

The police had been called and arrived at about the same time both women were coming around. Not quite clear as to what had happened or who was at fault, they initially assumed Walter had assaulted both women. Witnesses supplied them with what they had seen, and Walter was told he was going to be arrested, which caused him to loudly and physically express his displeasure with that decision by wildly swinging at and referring to the police as jerk-offs and assholes. With *Rule Number 10* never really being heeded, Walter was very unceremoniously cuffed and roughly inserted into the back seat of a patrol car.

Curiously, both women apparently decided their man was not worth the neighborhood attraction or aggravation, and expressed to the police that they were in complete agreement with the arrest of Walter.

Because of his demeanor, after arriving at the station, his handcuffs were not initially removed. Even with his arms behind his back, he lashed out and struggled. Dooley assisted the officer in pushing the thrashing and threatening Walter into the cell. Staggering back a couple of steps, Walter immediately rushed forward in an attempt to get back out. Dooley and the officer were able to push him back into the cell and then quickly slid the heavy steel door closed. Unfortunately for the tee-shirt-only-wearing Walter, when he moved forward trying to get out and was pushed back in, his penis didn't quite make it all the way into the cell when the door slid shut.

Now, almost every man eventually gets nipped by a pants zipper at least once in his life and prays that it never happens again. It goes without saying that the sliding steel door was certainly much more of an attention-getter than the nip of a pants zipper. As one can easily envision, the tee-shirt-only-wearing Walter became quite docile for the rest of his stay. Since the slamming of the door resulted in a lot of bruising but no blood, he was given a bag of ice, and the injury was considered to be collateral damage.

Following a few phone calls, relatives came to the station the next morning with clothing to retrieve the now subdued Walter. Making no mention of the sliding door incident to his family, he was also extremely apologetic about his past behavior to both his family and the police.

It was reported, following the anticipated and eventual break-up between Walter and his wife Cheryl--that she and Nancy became friends and regularly joked about the incident. As predicted, Walter paid a small fine and was never again reportedly arrested in Cedar Springs.

Dooley gained recognition and fame for years as causing an unruly, boisterous individual commonly referred to as a "dickhead" to have an even bigger and much more swollen extremity.

CHAPTER 30

Cedargate

D
ooley, being a retired Philadelphia cop, was also an avid Philadelphia Eagles football fan. Quite a few people in town were also Eagles fans, and game days were usually fairly quiet--at least until the games were over.

During Sunday and Monday night games, some people would call the department just to get an update on the games. When scheduled to work, and being an avid fan, this was particularly frustrating to Dooley as all he really wanted was some peace and quiet and to watch the game.

During one particular game, in the course of an exciting play, the telephone rang and Dooley reluctantly answered it, identifying the department. When the caller asked how the Eagles were doing and what the score was, Dooley reportedly replied in desperation, "Ah, shit on that," and promptly hung up the phone, returning his attention to the game.

The same individual called back a few minutes later identifying himself as the tri-county administrative superior court law judge and demanded to know why he was told to go shit in his hat? Dooley, now thinking that one of his squad members was playing a prank on him, which was not uncommon, replied something to the effect of, "Yeah, and I'm Benjamin Franklin" and hung up the phone again.

Expecting several more crank calls from his boys, it was a good thirty minutes later when he realized that he had not received any. The game now over, Dooley began to have second thoughts about the caller and believed it might be wise to re-listen to the two phone calls.

At that time, all calls coming into the station were recorded on an old Dictaphone reel-to-reel tape recorder. After listening to the call a few times, Dooley came to the conclusion that the caller may not have been one of his boys and may well have been the tri-county administrative law judge. He decided that some creative backpedaling into the gray area might just be in order.

Dooley called Sergeant Pete in and explained what had taken place. Pete, in turn, listened to the calls and unhappily came to the same conclusion as Dooley. Pete then called the squad in and the situation was discussed. With the Nixon "Watergate" scandal still fresh in everyone's minds, it was decided the best course of action was to create a scenario in which the department never received the calls and the alleged "Ben Franklin go shit in your hat" incident never took place.

The following day, the somewhat expected phone call from a very insulted tri-county administrative superior court law judge was received by the administration. The also expected apologies were given, even before checking out the allegations, and promises of immediate repercussions were assured. Rumors and accusations flew through the buildings like tornados.

The Rude simply said to get to the bottom of it. Captain Benny worried the department's reputation could be tarnished if what was alleged to have been said had actually been said. Lieutenant Buck, not worried at all, went home and had a drink.

The first order of business was to review the Dictaphone tape. After the initial review, it was believed that either the judge had been mistaken about calling the department, which would mean that he was also mistaken about being told to go shit in his hat by Ben Franklin, or that there was some type of malfunction in the dictaphone, as there seemed to be a blank gap in the tape.

It was not quite the famed 18 ½ minute "Nixon" gap but a respectful 9 ½ minute silence. This gap seemed to make it at least half as important and just as mysterious. Then after many, many hours of repeated listening and careful deliberation, it was determined that there was indeed a third theory that, like its famed predecessor, should never have happened. The Dictaphone machine, which was thought to be tamper-proof, had in fact most definitely been tampered with.

Schedules were checked to know with certainty what personnel were on duty. Dooley was called at home. He indicated that he had no idea what they were talking about. Sgt. Pete was called at home, and he too advised that he had no idea what they were talking about. The following night, the entire squad was questioned by Captain Benny. Every member, all who had the night before agreed to stick with the deny, deny, deny response, assured the captain that they were busy keeping the citizens of the town safe and doing police work and knew nothing about the allegations.

The *Thick Blue Line* held. The Dictaphone machine was immediately retrofitted with hasps and padlocks on its cabinet. No one knew what was ultimately told to the administrative law judge, and no one dared to ask. The Rude once again referred to the department as a "God dammed gang" and Captain Benny's ears turned crimson red with disgust anytime he saw The Crazy Squad members for several weeks.

As word spread throughout the department of this latest Crazy Squad revolt against the establishment The Rude received six patrol transfer requests to be reassigned to The Crazy Squad, and Dooley was once again unofficially declared a legend.

All dispatchers were told that in the future, they would be required to answer all phone calls identifying not only the department but themselves, be polite and answer to the best of their ability any and all questions the callers asked, and finally, to never touch the Dictaphone machine and to turn the volume down on the television, or it was going to be removed.

CHAPTER 31

"Lead Legs"

Pete's brother Robert Roberts, alias "Lead Legs," was also promoted to sergeant. Lead, after his promotion, was assigned to supervise the detective division. The detective division at that time was basically comprised of two patrolmen and a sergeant assigned to work in plain clothes and do further investigations into crimes that were too complex or time-consuming for regular shift patrolmen to handle.

The detective division headquarters was actually a 12 X 12 office at the end of the hall, with three desks and three filing cabinets. Storage for evidence and investigative equipment consisted of a four-foot-wide utility closet located in the hallway.

Robert allegedly was blessed at birth with two identical names because his mother had argued with his father over naming him either Roger or Bertram. After discussing the choice for several days after the birth, they finally in exasperation decided to just use "Robert." His mother always said that she had agreed to this as it was a combination of Roger and Bertram, or at least she thought so.

Along with sloth like movements, Lead's expressions consisted of either a blank stare or at times a slight snicker complete with a small "Humph" which passed as his version of a laugh, and other times as either an expression of concurrence or one of distaste. Speech was usually confined to almost-inaudible mumbles, and all his interviews were routinely witnessed by another detective so that they could document the questions and any outcomes, as Lead rarely wrote anything down or submitted reports.

Without another witness to an interrogation, the conclusion would sometimes result in Lead advising one of the detectives that the interrogated subject had just confessed and should be charged and taken to the county jail.

Interrogations were recorded on cassette tapes, however; rather than attempting to listen to and decipher Lead's mumbles and then try to make out what had been the actual question or answer, it was easier to become a witness to the interrogation, take copious notes, and submit a factual report of what had transpired. The tapes were later transcribed by a secretary who routinely loudly cursed Lead many times while trying to figure out what was being said.

Whoever was assigned to partner with him learned quickly that they always had to watch everything he did or wanted to do, because he also almost never carried his gun. More times than not, it was in his desk drawer at the station or in the glove box of the detective's car. Most would be inclined to believe that this was just another example of Lead's lack of enthusiasm, when in fact it was because he just didn't like the loud noises guns could make.

Lead did have an uncanny ability to read other people and some-how usually knew when someone was lying. During a typical interro-gation by him, he would settle back in his chair, put his feet up on the desk, and ask the perpetrator to tell him everything they knew about the particular situation. After the story was told, with Lead not utter-ing a single word, he would then ask them to tell the story again; and again and again and again.

There were times during difficult interviews when Lead would ap-pear to fall asleep. Some individuals would actually attempt to wake him and ask him if he was all right. At that point, Lead would ask them about the differences in the many stories they had been telling him and would ask them to explain why their stories had changed.

Some, out of pure exasperation or exhaustion of the denial of their involvement, would finally admit their contribution to whatever they had been questioned about just so they wouldn't have to go through it again. For the stubborn ones, particular questions would be asked, and Lead would just wait until the suspect gave some type of an answer, no matter how long it took. The rule was--and the technique is effective when used, if one has the patience for it--when a question is asked, he who speaks first usually loses.

Lead was a peculiar sort, but his techniques were effective and the department became well known for leading the county in successful prosecutions of criminal matters.

CHAPTER 32

The "Real" Roberts Brothers

Lead Legs and Pinochle Pete had a well-known and considerable accumulation of fears and concerns between them. They were known to be apprehensive about being in dark places, being in small spaces, being in high places, immediate and foreboding alarm when hearing loud noises such as thunder or gunshots, witnessing lightning in real time, and a rather strange one, that of a fear of steps, escalators, and elevators which may or may not have been an extension of the dark, small, and high places complex.

It was even rumored, although never proven or admitted, that when they were children, their mother considered them a bit odd and would actually hide them in the attic whenever company stopped by their home. This would of course offer an explanation for the dark, small spaces and steps fixation. There were probably many more little quirks, but it was incredible that men with such fears of everyday occurrences should choose a career that would surely lead to encounters with all of them on a regular basis.

In addition to the fears, Pete of course, had a problem with betting on card games when he was one of the world's worst card players, and Lead Legs was a bit of an old lecher when it came to women in general. In addition to having one of the most noteworthy collections of skin magazines ever seen, he, after speaking to a female witness or complainant or really any female at all, would always critique the physical characteristics of the woman complete with opinions on how he would improve them, in great detail, to whoever he happened to be working with at the time. The official term used to describe him nowadays would be an uncouth, vulgar yet harmless "pervert."

One evening at about 10:00, Lead, who was the detective sergeant at the time, radioed for Pete and Angelo Demucchi, who at the time were an integral part of The Crazy Squad, to meet him in a parking lot toward the southern part of town. When the three met, Lead advised them that he had received information that five or six individuals were in the upstairs portion of an old abandoned farmhouse near the jurisdictional line of Cedar Springs and a neighboring community. He stated that he had confirmation that they were dealing pot and methamphetamines to many of the young people in the area, and quite possibly supplying the drugs to some of the fishermen at the docks.

The old house had been vacant for several years and had recently been condemned by the local building inspector for being structurally unsound. Just as many early 1900s farm houses were built, it had been constructed on brick pillars that were just laid on the ground. Over the years, several of the pillars had collapsed or sunk, causing the two-story house to tilt in an unnatural and unsafe manner.

Lead indicated his informant had advised him that the apparent trespassers were sitting on several pounds of pot and a couple ounces of methamphetamine. When Angelo questioned him about the use of additional manpower, Lead quickly indicated the three of them would be more than enough and that they really didn't have the time to wait for and explain the operation to more people.

Pete initially agreed with his brother concerning a surprise and quick visit. Angelo, not wanting to blemish his so-far respectable reputation and image, thought that a major drug bust would certainly help to solidify it.

The three drove closer to the location and as quietly as possible exited their cars and approached the house. The home's front screen door was completely open and was leaning lopsided against the house, hanging by one hinge. The dried-out and cracked wooden entrance door, still showing portions of red paint, appeared to have been forced open and was partially ajar.

As Angelo climbed the four wooden front steps leading to the porch and front door, being careful not to make noise, he could see what appeared to be flickering candle light in a second-floor window. Peering through the open door, he noticed a stairway straight ahead leading to the second floor. The steps were littered with trash and broken plaster that had fallen from the walls and ceilings. The stairs themselves appeared to be whole and intact.

Prior to entering the house, Angelo stopped and realized that both Lead and Pete were standing by the corner of the house, peeking around to observe what he was doing. Not knowing why they had stayed behind, he motioned for them to follow, but they didn't move and motioned for Angelo to come back to their location.

Thinking they had seen something that he hadn't, he returned to the corner of the house. Pete asked very seriously if it was very dark in the building. Angelo advised him that yes it was but that he had a flashlight. Lead also very seriously asked if there were a lot of steps. Angelo, biting his tongue, advised him that besides the four front steps, there were about fifteen steps in the stairway inside leading to a landing. He said it looked like the landing went right, and then the hallway went toward the rear of the building.

Pete then asked if Angelo was able to hear anything or anyone. Angelo advised him that he hadn't had time to really listen for anything, because they had motioned him back.

Lead Legs then said, "Well why don't you give me your flashlight? You go up first, Pete will be right behind you, and I'll follow with the flashlight."

Angelo once again cautiously got to the front door, entered the house, and started up the steps as quietly as he possibly could. He could hear what sounded like four or five people speaking in hushed tones. He believed it to be at least two females and two or three males. Reaching the halfway point on the staircase, he looked behind him, and neither Pete nor Lead had even started up the steps and were standing together by the front door. A bit annoyed, he waved them up. It seemed that reluctantly and very slowly they began to climb the darkened steps. Lead was pointing the flashlight straight down and directly in front of him, which did no one else any benefit.

At that point, Angelo realized that any assistance to him by the two was going to be pretty much nonexistent because of their homegrown idiosyncrasies. Being in the "gray" and also quite possible in an exigent situation with unknown consequences, he reached the top of the stairs, drew his gun, and quickly stormed through the door where he had seen the light and heard the voices.

Screaming at the top of his voice, Angelo yelled, "Police...don't move!"

As soon as his eyes adjusted to the dim light, he observed two males and two females in sleeping bags, obviously enjoying sexual companionship in the most rigorous terms imaginable. Simply put, they had obviously been humping their brains out.

Finally, after all parties had realized that their private party had been all but cancelled, Pete and Lead finally entered the room. Pete moved close to Angelo while Lead began to direct the beam of the flashlight slowly and methodically over each of the sleeping bags. He never looked for the reported large quantities of pot or meth, nor did he even ask where they might be hidden.

As Angelo looked around the room, he noticed a cardboard box being utilized as a table. On top of the box was a battery-powered lantern, a small votive-type candle, a small plastic bag with what looked to be at the most an eighth of an ounce of pot, and some rolling papers.

Was this a sampling of the mother lode? After a quick check around the rest of the room and finding absolutely nothing other than the sparse camping gear, it appeared that it was.

Lead Legs, now noticing clothing on the floor near the sleeping bags, then told the occupants to get out of them and stand up. None of the recently discovered and now captured lovers wanted to emerge, as they stated that they were all naked. Angelo actually feeling somewhat like a peeper, suggested giving the girls their shirts and pants from the floor and allowing them to slip them on prior to exiting the bags. Lead, looking thwarted, reluctantly agreed.

Once the girls had covered up, they extricated themselves from the bags. The lantern was turned up, and the rest of the camping gear was checked out. Once nothing dangerous was found, they had the guys get out of the bags one at a time and put their pants on--after Pete and Angelo checked the pockets.

As Lead further questioned the girls, Angelo and Pete thoroughly searched the rest of the room and the adjacent rooms without finding any trace of the alleged large quantity of drugs. With the exception of the campers, the abandoned house was empty. After speaking separately with the two guys and then comparing notes, it was found that they had all hitchhiked from Allentown PA to spend some time camping at the Jersey Shore and stumbled upon the vacant building with an opened door. They had thought they had found a nice quiet and abandoned spot and decided to make it their campsite for the weekend.

Lead Legs motioned for his brother and Angelo to come and speak with him quietly. He said he had decided to arrest them all for possession of the eighth ounce of pot because the girls wouldn't say who it belonged to.

Even with his own quirks, Pete also knew that his brother only wanted to spend more time interrogating the girls and had basically wasted his and Angelo's time. Not saying a word, Pete turned around, picked up the bag of vegetation from the cardboard box, walked over to a broken window in the corner of the room, and dumped the contents of the bag out the window. The boys and girls just watched without saying anything.

Without looking at his brother, Pete then told the trespassers in a stern, fatherly voice, "Now get your shit together and get the hell out of this house in ten minutes."

In less than five, the four campers had gathered their belongings and while expressing their gratitude, left the building and headed down the road.

As they were approaching their cars, Pete said to his brother, "Let me guess. You were driving around and happened to see two girls and two guys walking with camping gear and noticed that they had gone into the old house. So you made up a story about drugs, informants, and fishermen and got us involved just so you could get a better look at those girls. You really are a pervert."

Lead, never willing to accept defeat or admit any shortcomings, responded, "Hey, there's been a lot of activity in and out of this house in the last few months. Heck for all we knew, those girls could have been hookers."

Pete rolled his eyes and Angelo simply shook his head and said, "Okay, Lead, whatever. Do what ya gotta do," and looked at the episode as just another experience with the Roberts brothers.

CHAPTER 33

Sarge Sergeant

Even with the required compulsory training offered at the police academy, new employees still had to become accustomed to the people and the areas that they would be required to keep watch over.

Sergeants were assigned to show the rookies what they would be up against and what would be expected of them in the future.

Rick Ginessie was a city kid from Boston who had joined the coast guard, did most of his time at the local base near Cedar Springs, and while doing it, met his wife who lived in the area and decided to stay. Being a MP in the guard, he acquired an interest in law enforcement. He took the civil service exam after his release and was eventually hired by Cedar Springs.

He didn't have much expertise in the way of the "good old boy" extreme southern New Jersey police routine or etiquette. After being hired, he noticed that the members of Cedar Springs PD even wore cowboy hats in the summer, which was something he never envisioned any cop doing in Boston or in the coast guard, so this was a whole new ball game for him.

He was indoctrinated to how things really worked or at least how some things worked after he was assigned to Dudley Sergeant's squad. Sarge Sergeant was a lanky, fairly good-looking man. It was reported that he also idolized Elvis Presley. After first meeting him, Rick confirmed that report, as it appeared that Sarge continued to style his hair reminiscent of the 1958 version of The King, complete with hair styling gel and the small bit of curled hair which dangled down onto his forehead.

Sarge had been uniquely named Dudley Sergeant as his birth name, and because of that it was almost an unwritten requirement for him to enter either the military or law enforcement. One can imagine the time he spent as Patrolman Sergeant was problematic for the obvious reason.

The first night Rick worked; he was advised that he would be riding with Sarge. Within the first two minutes in the patrol car, Rick was quickly advised of two things by Sarge. One was that he would probably never be as good a cop as he was and the only people on the streets after midnight are cops and people who will eventually be arrested by cops. After several years, Rick admitted that at least one of those statements had been fairly accurate.

After driving around the town and listening for about an hour to nonstop narratives of the endless major incidents and arrests that Sarge had allegedly been involved with during his illustrious career, he asked Rick if he had any questions.

Rick asked, "Sergeant....Is that you're real name or just your title here?"

Sarge responded, "Sergeant is my family name. Dudley is the name my mother gave me at birth, and I am a sergeant."

Rick, now fixated on the name "Dudley," was trying hard not to liken his new boss with the Saturday morning Royal Canadian Mounties cartoon character, but there seemed to be an actual visual resemblance to the "Do-Right" character. He also thought it was unlikely that any mother would inherently and deliberately name their child after a military category or a cartoon character unless she was expressing her aversion to the initial pregnancy by a statement made sure to pay back the child in the future for causing her stretch marks. However, Rick was also momentarily somewhat impressed that Sarge had indeed become a sergeant.

Following a few seconds of the cartoon images floating through his head, Rick then quickly stated, "Shame your last name wasn't Lieutenant. You might have risen higher up the ladder in the department."

No retort came from the sergeant. It was always regarded by Rick that Sarge never fully understood the sarcasm in what he said or what he meant.

Sarge was regarded as a fairly polite guy and a good cop, until he spoke, and it was later learned by Rick that it was unilaterally agreed by most of the department members that Sarge was always considered to be a law enforcement legend in his own mind.

After about two hours of being shown the various zones of the thirty-some square miles of Cedar Springs, they came to an area located at the southern edge of the town. Sarge drove the patrol car down a desolate dirt road and continued to drive over bumps, ruts, and ridges for what seemed to be at least two miles. When the vehicle finally came to a stop, he moved the gear shift lever into park and told Rick to get in the back seat.

Not understanding the strange request, Rick asked the sensible and logical question. He asked, "What?...Why?"

Sarge advised him that he wanted to spread out on the front seat for a nap and suggested that Rick do the same in the back seat.

Being the rookie and concerned not only about his future in law enforcement but his personal safety being alone with someone who had a gun, and whom he had just met a couple of hours ago, who also happened to be his boss, in a desolate area at the end of a dirt road, he decided he would be safer in the rear seat than in the front.

After about an hour and a half of lying in the back seat, eyes wide open and wondering about his employment choices, he noticed that Sarge sat up, got out of the vehicle, opened the rear door and said, "Alright, youngster--let's get to work."

Now wondering what was to come, Rick hesitated a moment before slowly getting out of the car, and with lingering suspicions of what "work" might include, began inching his right hand toward his duty weapon when Sarge said, "Come on. Let's go. Get around there and get back in."

Thinking that he may have--and at the same time hoping that he hadn't--just dodged the proverbial bullet, Rick relocated back to the front passenger's seat.

Sarge then drove to another area and another dirt road until they came to a wooden fence. Turning off the headlights, they drove down the fence line for about 500 feet until they came to a stop in front of a wooden gate. Sarge turned on the car's loudspeaker, grabbed the microphone, and began to make sounds that he advised Rick were comparable to a bull looking to get laid.

Now completely convinced he had made a serious mistake in employment choices, Rick was wondering if he could find his way out of the area if he took off running through the woods. It took less than thirty seconds for Rick to then hear what sounded like a stampede of charging animals taking place. Surprisingly, there in front of the gate, stood a dozen or more cows.

Sarge, with a slight chuckle and a wink of an eye said, "Yep, it works every time. These cows think they are gonna get laid."

Rick, quickly thinking that his last sarcastic comment went unnoticed, and now unsure if he would survive his first night, asked, "Did you ever screw any of them?"

Sarge laughed. Rick was sure that Sarge hadn't realized that he wasn't kidding.

After watching the cows for a while, they then left the area and drove to the dock area in the south end of town, where Sarge told Rick to get out and walk the docks. He stated that he would return in a half hour or so to pick him up. He told him to check the doors and also to look for drunken fisherman as you never knew what they might be up to.

Being new, Rick did as he was told and after twenty minutes of walking the dock, he noticed the patrol car parked in front of the dock area café. A look in the window revealed Sarge having his morning coffee and breakfast while jawing with the two waitresses.

Rick then realized that he had been indoctrinated into law enforcement and Cedar Springs PD with his assignment to Sarge's squad. In addition, he had the distinction of having been honored with the privilege of being able to be trained by the legend himself, Sergeant Dudley Sergeant.

It also made him a firm believer, at least he hoped, that any future training officers or sergeants would certainly have to provide more useful insights into the law enforcement profession. If not, it was going to be a very, very, long twenty-five years.

CHAPTER 34

Another Dudley Sarge Sergeant Tale

Shortly after being promoted to a sergeant, and now overly confident because his name now matched his profession, Sarge was becoming well known to his assigned squad members that as unpredictable as he had been as a patrolman, he was just as, or more so challenged as a supervisor.

He had become well known for having favorites, even though he was confident that he was his own favorite. It became legendary that any newly assigned member of his squad could look forward to being sent by the dispatcher, Raymond Burry, through a directive from Sarge, to answer the vast majority of crap calls, which consisted of barking dogs, loud music, suspicious people or suspicious vehicles, etc. This would continue until the new member asked for a transfer, threatened the other squad members, or figured out how to somehow, someway get on Sarge's good side and be accepted as an equal.

Raymond Burry was the perfect match of a dispatcher to Sarge, as Dooley was to Pete Roberts. Ray was an old navy man who still wore a high and tight crew cut straight from the 1950s. His forte consisted of having an extremely professional-sounding speaking voice with a combination of an Oklahoma/Texas accent, which sounded extremely accurate and factual when on the air. It was said that Ray sounded like a cross between Humphrey Bogart and the late actor and former Tennessee senator Fred Thompson.

His downfall was that along with each piece of factual information he transmitted, one could be assured that there were at least one or more non-factual--or what Ray construed to be "possibly connected bits of information"--transmitted with them.

His report of an ongoing situation would usually be found to be that the situation had occurred at least twice in "any" amount of time. Minutes, hours, days, or weeks. His retort to an accusation of his over-zealous imagination would be, "Well, I thought that was what they were trying to tell me."

After his promotion, Sarge had convinced Ray that all new patrol-men, or FNG's, "fucking new guys," should answer the majority of all calls as a training exercise.

Tommy Sutliff, who had joined the department after working for several years at the county jail, was assigned to Sarge's squad in the late 1970s. Tommy had grown up in the area and had been told many times that Dudley Sergeant was possibly a bit distinctively, out of the ordi-nary, but had decided to keep his opinions to himself until he could personally vouch for the fact that he was or was not indeed "special." In keeping with the usual Sarge's squad procedure, he routinely was given the garbage calls and advised that the zone car was busy elsewhere.

The scenario continued throughout most of the summer months. In mid-September, when the majority of the vacationers had gone home, Tommy was working a midnight shift in the north end of the town and was dispatched to a call of an unruly person causing prob-lems in front of one of the hotels in the south zone, about six miles away. Even though radio transmissions had been almost nonexistent, he was advised that the zone car was tied up and the others were too far away to respond in a timely manner.

Knowing this was another classic example of being rewarded for being the FNG, Tommy responded to the call and eventually found a man obviously intoxicated and mostly asleep near the front door of the hotel that had made the complaint.

Tommy got out of his car and carefully shook the man's shoulder. As intoxicated as he was, he was also polite and co-operative, indicat-ing that he had simply asked someone at the hotel to call him a cab. After a few minutes of conversation with the subject, it was ascertained that he had been drinking at a neighborhood bar, decided he had too much to drink and drive, and had left his car at the bar. After walking several blocks, he got tired and tried to have someone at the nearby hotel call him a cab. Tommy ended up giving him a ride to his home several blocks away.

During the thirty-five minutes it took from the start of the call to the completion of the call, Tommy never heard a single transmission from any of the other cars, and absolutely nothing from Sarge.

Tommy decided his being given all the garbage calls was getting old, and he wanted it to stop. Driving by the station and seeing no patrol cars there, he decided to speak with Sarge directly about it. Determined to bring an end to being the fall guy, Tommy decided to drive by Sarge's house to see if he was there. When he arrived in the area, he was quite surprised to see all three patrol cars parked in the double-wide driveway.

Partly confused and partly irritated to finally confirm the fact that there really was no valid reason he was given all the crap calls, he circled around the block. As he approached the house for the second time, Tommy turned off his lights, killed the engine, and slowly and silently rolled into the driveway. Getting out of his car as quietly as possible, he proceeded to walk as softly as he could to the back of the house, where he observed light and heard conversations coming through a screen door. Tommy peeked in, and there, at the kitchen table sat Sarge and the other two patrolmen of the squad, leisurely having coffee and eating bacon and eggs that Sarge had just cooked for them.

Tommy, now fully aware of being duped throughout the last few weeks, cursed and mumbled to himself, "Fucking Dudley Do-Wrong motherfucker!"

After just a moment of hesitation, and hoping that he wouldn't be shot by accident, he walked up and stood at the center of the screen door and loudly yelled, "Hey!!!"

He then quickly threw open the screen door and immediately entered the kitchen jolting the nerves and the crap out of all three.

He then nonchalantly asked, "Do you think I could get a fried egg sandwich on toast to go, as I seem to be responsible to answer all the calls in the entire town?"

After the three had regained their composure, Sarge chuckled and told him to sit down and cooked him breakfast. They all finished their meals and eventually returned to their zones. Tommy had made his point and calls were mysteriously equally divided in the future.

CHAPTER 35

African Queen Adventure Tales

Along with a vivid and descriptive imagination, Sarge's radio dispatcher Raymond Burry had a couple of other little quirks that he was well known for.

Every day of his shift, Ray would arrive at the station at least fifteen minutes early driving a rather large four-door, full-sized, king cab, dual-rear-axle pickup truck with an eight-foot bed and a fifth-wheel towing hitch attached in the bed to tow his travel trailer. Due to his voice sounding a bit like Bogart, Ray's somewhat behemoth-looking pickup truck was affectionately called "The African Queen" by the imaginative members of the department.

Ray always dressed in a uniform similar to the patrolmen but always wore long- sleeved shirts with the sleeves one-fourth rolled up, and a clip-on tie hanging from an unbuttoned collar. Additionally, he always carried a black briefcase. Although looking quite professional, the case contained nothing but sandwiches, cookies, fruit, and two thermos bottles of hot black coffee. It was said he would present himself this way because he liked to look like he was always in the middle of something and always working.

One of his more irritating quirks, at least to those wishing for a healthy environment, was that he was a one to two pack a shift cigarette smoker, making him what was probably a three to four pack a day smoker. What was worse was that he smoked an unfiltered popular brand that had the tendency to linger and pollute any nonsmoker's senses in a very short period of time. Additionally, Ray drank the contents of both thermos bottles, and what amounted to about seven to ten cups, of strong black coffee per shift.

Ray also had some curious and unusual eating habits. If you have ever been witness to an individual who ate and smoked at the same time, you can imagine what it was like to watch Ray take a long, hard drag from his unfiltered cigarette, hold in the smoke while taking a big bite of an otherwise ordinary sandwich, exhale, and while chewing at the same time, immediately take another long drag of the cigarette and immediately take a sip of hot black coffee.

It was difficult to comprehend whether Ray enjoyed the nicotine, the food, or the caffeine more or had simply grown accustomed to mixing them together for years. It was discussed by members of the department that the inside of Ray's trailer (yes, he lived in a trailer park), must be a deep rich brown color and very sticky due to the number of cigarettes he smoked.

Ray's other peculiarity was his habit of telling tall tales involving his supposed personal expertise and experiences in whatever anyone was discussing or watching on TV at the time. If a movie was being shown about people climbing Mt. Everest, he would state that he had done that or was part of a rescue team that had saved climbers. If the program involved the FBI or Secret Service, he had worked closely with both as an advisor. If it was a medical show, he had suffered and survived each and every disease and now advised other medical establishments on how to combat and cure these diseases.

Ray had supposedly ridden with the Hells Angels, given advice to Howard Hughes to invest in air lines and Las Vegas, and warned both President Eisenhower and Kennedy about sending advisors to Viet Nam. It became a challenge to the members of his squad to start a discussion about a topic and bet how long it would take for Ray to offer his advice or at least his personal history of involvement concerning the topic.

It was always an anticipated day when Ray returned from a week's vacation. Ray and his wife Rita would hook up the African Queen to his travel trailer that he kept in the driveway at the trailer park where he lived. (Yes, Ray lived in a trailer and vacationed utilizing another trailer.)

It didn't really matter if Ray only went to a local campground for a few days; he would always return with stories of doom, gloom, and glory with him as the main focus of attention.

Speculations regarding Ray's adventures on the road would begin on his first day of vacation and accelerate quickly depending on local or tri-state news stories involving acts of heroism or widespread carnage, as it was a sure bet that Ray, upon his return, would advise the department that he had somehow been involved in the stories.

It was not unusual for Ray to return to work with stories of him and Rita charging through hurricane and tornado-ridden small towns in the African Queen with Ray shouting, "Hang on Rita…we're going through!"

Rescuing displaced citizens or stopping in at police stations across the states and assisting with emergency situations that the towns just couldn't seem to handle without Ray's help became the norm.

During a fairly routine conversation between patrolmen about their adventures while on their days off or on their vacations, these talks would sometimes be overheard by Ray. No matter where that adventure may have taken place, Ray was sure to inject his own tale of some bizarre adventure that he had gotten involved in, not unsurprisingly in the very same location.

Some stories were eerily similar to nationally reported events in papers and magazines. It was rumored and believed by some that Ray and Rita were actually secret government agency employees on duty while on their trips, but no factual proof of that ever surfaced. It was more likely that Ray had been telling stories for so many years that he was at a point in his life that he actually believed he was involved with what he heard or read about.

It became a challenge at least once a week or so to concoct some fictional story about some fictional occurrence that had occurred, along with just enough factual-sounding fictional evidence to entice Ray into joining the conversation. Ray never disappointed, as he soon would add that he somehow had done what was being discussed, either while he was in the military or on one of his vacations.

If one chose to believe what Ray said to be factual, then according to Ray, he had been to virtually every city in every country in the entire world and had done such deeds as meeting with England's queen, crab fished in the North Atlantic where he of course saved several fishermen from drowning, visited with the Dalai Lama, participated in the space program, and fought in each war from WWII, where he battled both the Germans and the Japanese seemingly at the same time, Korea, providing security to the MASH units, and in Vietnam, historically, and according to Jim, referred to as a defeat, only because the administration failed to listen to his suggestions.

The most ironic thing about Ray was that he was also responsible to gather vital information from callers concerning possible life and death situations that he was sending patrolmen to investigate. It became universally accepted that any information given by Ray should automatically be reduced in truth by 50%. Because of this, in addition to working with Sarge and his book of idiosyncrasies, one had to be overly cautious when answering any type of call dispatched by Ray.

Ray was unique, but the most overwhelming as well as exasperating bit of information concerning him was that Sergeant Dudley Sergeant was convinced there was absolutely nothing wrong with him.

CHAPTER 36

A Billy Durrant Story

Sergeant Billy Durrant was well known as being the moodiest person in the Cedar Springs Police Department but was also usually the easiest to work for. It was a long- established rule that if you left him alone, he would normally pay little attention to you or whatever it was you were doing. He didn't like to have any problems to solve and thoroughly enjoyed it most if he never had to talk to anyone on his squad.

Most often when you did have contact with him, he was reasonably pleasant but definitely did not like anything to ruin his quiet shift. Basically, Billy didn't like to hear any calls that would possibly require his attention. Eerily comparable with the likes of Lieutenant Buck, the main difference was Billy did have normal personal hygiene habits.

Not unlike a lot of people, one of his most annoying shortcomings was that he was always more interested in his private life than his professional life.

Billy owned a few acres of land and farmed most of them. Farming, meaning not really farming but rather that he had a very large home garden. In addition to the garden, he had also started a small chain saw and lawn mower business which flourished more than he or anyone would have guessed.

Billy had started the business about the time Franklin and airtight wood stoves developed into popularity and wood became a big feature for heating fuel. The lawn mowers and other related yard maintenance machines rounded out the business during the warmer months.

The business lasted about ten years until most of his customers finally realized that Billy would sell them anything but really didn't have a clue as to how to fix the products when they broke. But by that time, the wood stove craze had diminished.

Most of his time on patrol was spent listening to Country-Western music or local weather reports in regard to his garden, as he constantly worried about his crops--in particular, his tomatoes. If not listening to the radio, he would be reading up on new chain saws and lawn mowers and which ones had the biggest profit margins when sold. If that wasn't enough, he also had a boat which took up quite a bit of time to get ready for fishing season each year. Police work came in a distant fourth, except of course around pay day.

Every few years, The Rude would switch patrolmen around to different squads so no one could get too comfortable. Charlie Donaldson had been with the department for a couple of years and had never worked with Billy. He had heard most of the rumors but had a hard time believing that Billy could be as disinterested in being a cop as was reported. After about a month on the squad and speaking with Billy a total of three times, the rumors began to be more believable.

On a particular midnight shift, Billy and Charlie happened to be in the station at the same time. Billy was in an exceptional mood, no doubt due to some escalating lawn mower sales now that the summer weather had finally taken over.

Talking with Charlie like they had been best friends for years, he was explaining to Charlie that his tomato plants were growing like wildflowers and were getting to the point that he was going to have to install taller support poles before they fell down.

Charlie, just trying to be a part of the conversation, advised him that he had heard on the television weather channel just before he had been picked up that the area was in store for some high winds from the northeast.

Billy's face seemed to grow pale, and with a curt explanation of having something to check, he immediately left the room and went to his patrol vehicle. Charlie figured that he was probably going out to listen to the latest weather forecast to double check what he had been told.

About an hour later, Charlie was asked to meet with the senior patrolman of the squad, Bruce Dailey, who advised him that if he should get involved in anything, that he should call him for assistance, as Billy was busy and out of service for a while.

Curiosity certainly got the best of Charlie, and he couldn't wait to drive by Billy's home to see what he was up to. There was a fire access road at the rear of Billy's property which bordered a large parcel of woods. Charlie drove as quietly as possible down the road with lights off until he was within walking distance of Billy's house. The first thing he noticed was that Billy had parked his marked patrol car neatly behind his garage and out of sight.

As Charlie got closer, he spotted Billy hurrying among his tomato plants, dressed in his uniform shirt, a baggy, worn pair of dungaree or blue denim bib overalls, and bright orange rubber boots. He was installing longer poles next to each tomato plant and tying them off with twine to keep them in place. As he crept closer, he distinctly heard Billy talking to each and every plant, explaining the latest weather reports and assuring them that they would be safe.

Thinking this a bit unusual but also realizing that many people talk to their plants, he made a decision to let Billy know that he knew. Walking quietly toward the garden, he paused just before coming into view. As he quickly stepped into the garden about six feet away, Charlie lit him up with the beam of his flashlight. Billy jumped about six inches off the ground and looked like he might have soiled himself.

Charlie nonchalantly looking at Billy said, "Nice pants…. And the boots…. Wow."

Looking a bit sheepish, Billy said, "Ahhh, it's like you said, a big storm is coming."

Charlie said, "Yeah, well--I'll help you if you give me some tomatoes when they get ripe."

The two went to work, and new taller support poles were installed in a couple of hours. Both Charlie and Billy, after changing back into his full uniform, returned to work with Billy comforted by the fact that his beloved tomato plants would now survive the up and coming winds.

After that night Billy and Charlie became good friends. When August rolled around, Billy made it a point to invite Charlie over to get a bushel of nice ripe tomatoes.

CHAPTER 37

Are You in Trouble If You Run Into a Police Car?

B illy was reluctant to interact with the public. His ideal day at work was one in which he was not asked any questions or required to make any decisions. Of course, being a shift-supervising sergeant, there were times when he was forced to supervise.

Shift change times were 8 a.m., 4 p.m., and 12 midnight, with the sergeants coming in one half-hour earlier. On a summer night at around 11:45, there was a traffic accident reportedly involving a car and a motorcycle. The accident had taken place in a residential area but on one of the main roadways. Mike Harding, a fairly new hire, was assigned to the call. When he arrived, he observed that a sedan driven by a middle-aged woman had struck a motorcycle ridden by an individual who had been thrown from the bike and was presently lying in the middle of the roadway. The sedan was still in the middle of the roadway with extensive damage to the front, making it inoperable.

The driver of the sedan was crouching near the motorcycle driver, checking on his well-being. The woman was extremely distraught and was tearfully asking him if he was all right. The man simply stated that he could hardly breathe.

Mike parked his patrol car with emergency lights on in the middle of the roadway to protect the injured motorcyclist. Upon checking the downed man, Mike recognized him as a business owner named Brian whom he had worked part time for a few years earlier. Brian, who had managed to remove his badly cracked helmet, recognizing Mike, attempted to tell him that he could not breathe and that he wanted to sit up. Mike saw some cuts and scrapes on Brian's arms and legs, but even with minimal medical training, he was knowledgeable enough to know an injured person, especially one with probable internal injuries, should not be moved. At least not by him. From the location of the damaged motorcycle, it was clear that Brian had been thrown almost 100 feet from the point of impact and was sure to be a bit scrambled inside.

A backup unit driven by Dave Smith, from the oncoming squad, arrived to assist at the scene. Additionally, the rescue squad arrived and tended to Brian. A quick look by "Smalls" established that he had most assuredly suffered massive internal injuries. As quickly and as gingerly as possible, he was transported from the scene to the local airstrip, where a medical helicopter had been summoned to transfer him to a larger hospital better equipped to deal with his apparent injuries.

Unfortunately for Brian, shortly after the helicopter departed, he went into full cardiac arrest and could not be revived. The autopsy revealed that most if not all of his internal organs had been damaged and dislodged from their original places. The cardiac arrest was the direct result of damage to the heart and internal bleeding. It was said Brian's flight from the motorcycle after impact was equivalent of a 3-to-4 story freefall.

Because the accident was now considered a fatal motor vehicle accident, a specific type of accident report complete with diagrams, photos, and measurements was required. Mike, being new, had not yet done one. Billy Durant, the on-coming sergeant, arrived at the scene and advised Dave Smith, who had been on the street for a few years, to assist Mike with the report to make sure it was done correctly. Billy helped direct traffic around the scene for a few minutes and left as soon as he possibly could.

Normally, accident scenes are cleaned up with vehicles removed as soon as possible. Due to the fact that the accident involved a death and measurements were needed to show the correct locations of the vehicles and the deceased, neither the woman's car nor the motorcycle had been removed. Nearing one o'clock in the morning, traffic was light. Vehicles approaching were diverted around a block in either direction. Measurements and photos were collected, and the vehicles were finally removed from the area at around two am.

Dave had parked his patrol car next to Mike's, also with the emergency lights flashing. Traffic was almost nonexistent, and Mike and Dave were both sitting in Mike's car making sure they had what they needed and getting ready to return to the station to complete the report.

Suddenly and without warning their vehicle was violently struck from behind by another car. The rear end of the patrol car folded up like an accordion as the car was pushed forward about 20 feet. Mike's chest and legs were pushed into the steering wheel and column and Dave was thrown into the dash and windshield.

With papers, reports, tape measures, and camera now scattered about the car, both Dave and Mike slowly looked at each other and said, "What the fuck?"

Looking behind them, they could make out a vehicle now parked pretty much in the trunk of the patrol car. Not entirely sure that what just happened really had just happened, Mike got out of the car and found that his left knee had been cut by something on the steering column. It was bleeding and extremely painful. Dave sat in the car and moaned and mumbled something about his back. The passenger door had been pushed forward and Dave was unable to open it.

Dave, now looking pale and realizing he couldn't get out said, "I can't get out."

Mike said, "Well then, don't go anywhere. I'm gonna go beat the crap out of whoever is driving that car."

Dave said, "Drag his ass up here so I can at least beat him with the clipboard."

"You got it, brother," said Mike as he limped back to the now smoldering car.

Since terrorism hadn't become fashionable yet, Mike went to the car that had struck the patrol vehicle with the firm belief that the driver was simply an underprivileged member of society who after a few cocktails had somehow failed to observe the two police cars with flashing lights parked in the middle of the road. He was also sure that the driver would have sufficient reasons for the slight mishap. Of course, they would be profusely apologetic and, while weeping freely, promise that all damages would be taken care of and that life would be filled with sunshine and rainbows once again.

Of course, because the driver had symbolically struck the officers first, it was in Mike's mind sufficient grounds for retaliation and he was prepared to cause great anguish upon his or her body and soul. The sunshine and rainbows could be discussed later. Mike found the driver, a male in his forties, either passed out, knocked out, or possibly dead sitting behind the wheel.

Disappointed that a confrontation was not going to take place, he did a quick check of his condition. A weak pulse and visual acknowledgement that he was breathing by his chest moving in and out, added to Mike's immediate anger and pain. Even with his back and knee hurting, he had hoped that the driver would give him any reason to conduct an immediate attitude adjustment.

After a minute or two, and knowing retaliatory satisfaction was not going to take place, Mike returned to his car and checked on Dave. Dave moaned and said his back was really hurting. Mike said, "That's because you were just in a car accident, dumbass. The jerk-off back there is passed out and smells like a brewery."

Dave, with a cross between a grin and a painful ache, said, "That fucker. Guess we can't adjust his attitude, can we?" After thinking for a few seconds, Dave said, "Hummm…of course on the up side…two patrolmen in an accident. That means that the sergeant would then be required to do the report."

Knowing how much the sergeant liked to be left alone while working, he said with some satisfaction, "Billy's gonna be pissed."

Thankfully, the car's radio still worked, and Mike advised that his car had been involved in an accident. Dispatcher Harriet Slater asked if he was injured. He replied, "Pissed off but fine."

Sergeant Billy Durrant, hearing the transmission, then asked where the accident had taken place, as he assumed that the original accident had been cleared up and that Mike had screwed up and been involved in another one. Mike advised that the accident had taken place at the site of the motorcycle accident and that another car had driven into the back of the patrol car. Mike was going to add that the patrol car was probably totaled but decided to let Billy see for himself.

Billy called Dave on the radio and asked his location, probably trying to come up with some way to avoid going to the scene. Dave answered, "I'm in the accident with Mike, and I'm stuck in the passenger's seat. The door on my side is pushed in and won't open." After a moment of silence, Billy stated that he would be right there.

Now, it's not every day that someone plows into the rear of a police car. Especially when there are two of them that are parked next to one another in the middle of the road, with both cars' emergency lights and flashers going at full speed. Someone would have to be blind, asleep, or so inebriated that they were next to blind or asleep to miss the fact that some type of emergency was taking place and they needed to stop.

As unusual as the incident was, the actions of Billy when he arrived at the scene were even more unusual. Seeming a bit upset that a police vehicle was involved in the accident, probably because he would be required to submit the report, he reluctantly went to check the driver of the striking vehicle.

Billy recognized the driver. He was one of his friends who coincidentally had purchased a chain saw, riding lawn mower, weed whacker, and snow blower in the past several months. He now seemed to be dreading what he was probably going to have to do. The driver had regained consciousness and was slurringly attempting to explain to Billy that he did not see the cars parked in the middle of the roadway.

Billy initially advised Mike and Dave, who was still trapped in the car, that he was going to give the driver a ride home, have his car towed, and explain the accident as a case of failure to see the police car. He stated that he would probably end up giving him a ticket for speeding or careless driving to cover the damage to the police car.

Dave, awaiting the rescue squad's return from the airport, had been unable to take a deep breath without pain. As sarcastically as he could, he told Billy that the first thing he should probably do was arrest the driver for drunk driving. He said, "How the fuck can you agree that he didn't see two police cars with overhead lights flashing, sitting in the middle of the road? Let me guess. It's one of your friends or someone you just sold a fucking chain saw to."

Knowing that his night was ruined and hoping that Mike and Dave weren't really hurt that bad, he said, "Well actually--he bought a bunch of stuff and I've known him for a long time."

Mike simply looked at him and said, "Really?"

Dave, who had known Billy for years, said, "If you don't run him on the breathalyzer, I'm gonna spray vegetation killer on your garden, burn down your garage, and then sue him and you."

With that information, Billy reluctantly advised his friend that he would have to go to the station with him. The driver was found to be almost three times the legal limit to drive. The patrol car was totaled, and both Mike and Dave were transported to the hospital to be examined.

While Smalls and the rescue squad took great care to make them both comfortable on the ride to the hospital, (they took the smooth four-lane expressway), they regretted having to turn them over to the hospital staff. The hospital was well known to provide somewhat substandard and questionable treatment and promptly advised both men to have seats on the hard, plastic chairs in the waiting room until a doctor could see them.

Almost three hours later, a nurse took their temperature and checked their blood pressure. The ER doctor quickly checked the men, ordering two sutures in Mike's knee and ibuprofen for the both of them, for back pain. With a failed attempt to act the competent professional while shifting future responsibilities to others, he additionally advised them to see their family doctor should any pain continue for more than 48 hours.

Mike's knee swelled up to twice its size the following day. He was out of work for two weeks and the injury bothered him for the remainder of his career. Dave went out on workman's compensation for two months and wore an elastic back brace for the remainder of his time in the department.

Billy was pissed that his quiet night was ruined and that he had to do an accident and drunken driving report, but never once called the hospital to check the well-being of the two patrolmen. Billy's *blue line* had definitely faded.

The driver of the car hired an attorney who, after speaking with Mike and Dave, quickly advised his client to plead guilty.

When advised of the accident, The Rude at least asked if Mike and Dave were okay. His next question was, "How's the car?"

CHAPTER 38

Big Ben Bailey

Ben, all of 6 feet 5 and 1/4 inches as he used to constantly remind everyone, was a local boy and a genuine high school sports hero. Proficient at football, baseball, basketball, and track/field events because of his agility and his size, he unfortunately did not continue on to college due to a lack of two things: an obtainable scholarship and accessible income.

Ben worked a number of jobs in the area, including packing fish on the local docks, construction, as an electrician's helper, and finally decided he missed some of the physical contact that he had encountered in sports. Ben thought that a job as a cop might just fit the bill of a profession with benefits for himself and his family and also provide some physical confrontations in which he could take out some of his youthful aggressions. With that in mind, he took a civil service exam, which he passed, and was eventually hired by the Cedar Springs Police Department.

With the likable personality of a gentle giant, Ben was immediately accepted with open arms in the department. Married, with three daughters, his fast and hard rule was that no comments concerning them were acceptable. Because of Ben's size, none were even contemplated, at least not within hearing distance.

Most problems with the public would come to an end quickly when Ben got out of his car. Through the years, Ben generally had no problems when telling people they needed to stop doing whatever it was they were not supposed to be doing. Whenever he did have a problem, his reaction, which he became fairly well known and famous for, was reaching out with either one of his very large hands, affectionately known as "Cease and Desist,"and grabbing the neck of the disgruntled individual. Then with little effort, he would lift them off the ground and repeat the request very politely to stop whatever it was they were doing. Ben had said that this was his way of "makin um do the ole John Barleycorn"

Now John Barleycorn was actually an old British folksong from the 1600s about the importance of the cereal crop barley and the alcoholic beverages made from it. The lyrics were also made memorable in a song of the same name by the British rock band Traffic in the '60s.

The song supposedly represented the growths, attacks, death, and indignities the crop must go through during the stages of cultivation and manufacture of alcohol, which really had nothing to do with Ben's method of attention-getting.

One of the patrolmen, Nicky Harlow, heard Ben describe his actions concerning one young gentleman who had refused to leave the scene of a bar fight but then quickly had a change of heart once his dangling feet returned to the ground having been made to "do the ole John Barleycorn." Nicky, after explaining the actual meaning to Ben, asked why he called it that. Ben's only remark was, "Oh…well, I just thought it sounded cool…and I liked the song."

The other patrolmen always agreed with Ben for two reasons. The first was that they also thought it sounded cool, and the second was because he did it so well, they figured he could call it whatever he wanted.

Ben was probably the most appreciated back-up officer in the department. However, being committed and agreeable to the actions of whoever he worked with could sometimes be detrimental and entertaining at the same time. When a loud and obnoxious individual was under arrest but refusing to calm down and listen to reason, there were times a squad member would use Ben's sense of allegiance for their own amusement.

At the pivotal time when Ben would arrive at the scene to assist, thought-provoking patrolmen, with genuine sincerity and natural deception in their hearts, would sometimes say loud enough for Ben to hear, "No that's my partner, and I don't appreciate what you just said!"

Naturally Ben's curiosity would take over and he would ask what was said. And naturally the patrolman would indicate that the individual had made some disparaging remark about Ben's wife or one of his daughters.

If the performance was pulled off with enough conviction and the subject was still promising retaliation upon the arresting officer and/or his family, Ben would invariably ask the individual to clarify what they had said about *his* family, even though they had not said anything. If the individual did not immediately apologize, Ben would help the subject to begin to "do the ole John Barleycorn" while convincing him to never threaten the police again.

The patrolman would always wait a few days before telling Ben that the story had been made up. When his anger or frustration subsided, Ben's comment would be, "You guys are killing me!"

Within several years Ben tested again and became one of the men promoted to the rank of sergeant.

It should be noted that after his promotion, Ben kept his loyalty to anyone who worked on his squad, and squad members also continued to utilize Ben's gullibility when dealing with obnoxious individuals occasionally advising him that they had disrespected his family.

CHAPTER 39

Big Ben and Stuart

A new hire, Stuart Tarrantino, another transplant originally from South Philadelphia with a strong Italian heritage, had just completed his training at the State Police Academy where it was reported he lived mostly on beef jerky, cookies, and ice cream sandwiches from the vending machines. It was well known that the cooks at the academy were on loan from the state prison system and didn't cook anything "true" Italian. Stuart's whole family was Italian. His grand-parents were first-generation immigrants, and his parents still spoke broken English and Italian to one another. Stuart's theory was, if it didn't come with gravy (sauce), it wasn't real food and he didn't want to eat it. For some reason, that didn't apply to the beef jerky, cookies, and ice cream.

Stuart reportedly had somewhat of a sordid past growing up in the city, including a number of run-ins with the police while associating with some of his friends who were of the juvenile criminal persuasion. Stuart's friends, as they grew older, seemed to choose full-time criminal-type occupations or full-time municipal-type work. The illegal occupations included theft, drugs, extortion, and other similar branch-offs of those choices. Some chose the municipal laborer jobs, fire departments, and police departments. After several of his friends were sent to prison, Stuart decided it would be wiser to choose either the municipal, firefighting, or law enforcement field. Stuart decided that he wasn't crazy about collecting garbage or running into burning buildings, but after being pursued by the police many times in his teens, he figured he wouldn't mind trying to be the pursuer for a change.

Stuart's family vacationed yearly at the shore and made the permanent move there shortly after Stuart graduated from high school. After marrying his childhood sweetheart, and with a bit of political influence from a family member, which included no mention of any teenage transgressions, Stuart was hired as a part-time officer during the summer months in one of the neighboring departments. Relishing the work, he took a civil service test and eventually was hired in Cedar Springs as a full-time officer.

Shortly before being hired in Cedar Springs, Stuart had developed a fondness toward religion following a spiritual awakening rumored, but never admitted to or proven, to have included certain promises to God and also to his wife regarding never again drinking, or at least not drinking to excess or seeing several other women who apparently were not his wife. Whatever the actual reason, it seemed to work for him. However, through the years it seemed to sometimes mysteriously come and go.

A day out of the academy and ten pounds heavier thanks to the ice cream and cookies, he was assigned to Big Ben's squad. As was the custom, Stuart was advised he would be riding with the sergeant for a few days until he became acclimated to the town and the manner in which the police handled matters in the town.

On the second day of working, Ben and Stuart were driving north on one of the main roads. Stuart noticed some movement in a passing vehicle and advised Ben that the male driver of the vehicle had just passed a "joint" or marijuana cigarette to the passenger. Ben immediately made a u-turn, flipped on the overhead lights, and called in the stop to the dispatch center.

Ben approached the driver's side of the vehicle while Stuart cautiously approached on the passenger's side. While Ben was asking for a driver's license, registration, and proof of insurance from the driver, ever ready to influence his request with a demonstration of how to do the "ole John Barleycorn," Stuart motioned for the passenger to lower his window. When the window was lowered, he advised the passenger to step out of the car. Stuart had witnessed the passenger drop the joint between the seat and the car door.

As he got out of the car, Stuart saw the joint now lying on the door jamb and advised him that he was under arrest and made him stand beside the front of the car. During a pat-down, a glassine bag containing what appeared to be a "dime bag" of marijuana was found haphazardly stuffed in his sock. Ben, by this time, having watched Stuart pat down the passenger, had advised the driver to also get out and also found another small bag of pot concealed in his sock. Both men were cuffed and advised to stand at the rear of the car.

During the pat-downs, Ben and Stuart were joined at the scene by two of the town's detectives, Lead Roberts and Anthony, (Tony) Sergeant, who happened to be Dudley Sergeant's brother who would eventually leave to join another department.

It was rumored that the two brothers, Dudley and Tony, as brothers can be, had always been fiercely competitive and that competitiveness carried over into police work. The competition finally came to a head when after a heated argument, the two decided that one of them should leave the department.

It was decided that they would have a good old-fashioned fist fight and that the winner would stay and the loser would resign. Once again, rumored but never fully proven, but at the same time very believable, the story went that the fight was ended quickly when Sarge, most assuredly in a loving, brotherly fashion, promptly kicked Tony in the groin and followed up with a quick sucker punch uppercut to the jaw, rendering Tony incapacitated. It was also rumored and probably also true that if Sarge hadn't kicked and sucker-punched Tony first, that Tony had planned to do the exact same thing to Sarge.

Lead and Tony, both in plain clothes, were always ready to help with a drug-related incident on the street, especially one in which they could worm their way into and partially or wholly take credit for. Lead sauntered over to ask Ben what he had. In his just barely discernible mumble Lead said, "Ben, whaddya got?"

Ben started to explain what had taken place while Stuart began to search the inside of the car. After several minutes, when it was obvious that Stuart had not found anything else in the car, he innocently asked the driver "Hey, does this thing have the big V-8 and 4 barrel carburetor? Can I take a look?"

The driver, momentarily forgetting his dilemma and flaunting his ownership of the muscle car, stated, "Sure does."

Hearing no refusal, he pulled a lever under the dash and then went to the front of the car and started to open the hood.

Tony, having several years of street experience and knowing that Stuart was a rookie who had just started, didn't know why he wanted to look at an engine. Shaking his head, he stated in the most condescending tone that he could muster, "You're just wasting your time there, young man."

Ben, not knowing why Stuart was looking either, quickly intervened and advised Tony, "Hey! Leave him alone. It's his stop."

Stuart opened the hood and quickly took the wing nut off of the carburetor breather, and when the top was removed, he found two plastic bags filled with vegetation in place of the air filter. He held them up so that the group could see.

Ben, smiling, then said to Lead, "While you're here, why not make yourself useful and take some photos of Tarantino's pot find? It looks to me like about a quarter pound."

Neither Lead nor Tony seemed too happy about a rookie getting a substantial drug arrest on his second day on the street or being all but dismissed about getting involved with the case, but they did as they were asked. Ben and Stuart transported the two men back to the station and did the paperwork.

Both Lead and Tony approached Stuart in the station and introduced themselves and asked how he had known to search the air breather. They asked if he had an informant that had contacted him with the information.

Stuart answered sheepishly, saying, "It's only my second day on the job. I haven't done this long enough to have any informants yet"

Ben had been listening, and with a grin that he knew would add fuel to the fire of jealousy stated, "Well...we weighed the pot you got. It's just a smidgeon over one quarter pound."

He then said with a chuckle, "Hey, Tony, when's the last time you detectives got that much pot?" Tony didn't bother to answer. Lead made an unintelligible grunt and mumble, and then they both left the room.

Ben, after a few minutes looked at Stuart and asked, "Okay, tell me, how did you know about looking in the air breather?"

Stuart very seriously replied, "That's where my friends and I always hid our stash when we were going on short trips."

Ben laughed again and said, "We'll just keep that to ourselves, but if you keep this shit up, you'll be in plain clothes in no time."

CHAPTER 40

Harriet and Millie

Just as Pete and The Crazy Squad had dispatcher Dooley and Dudley Sergeant had Ray Burry and his African Queen Adventure stories, Harriet Slater and Millie Townson were assigned to Billy Durrant and Big Ben Bailey's squads, respectively.

Both of these fine women were originally hired shortly after The Rude took over as chief, and as the saying goes, "They'd seen them come and they'd seen them go." Working closely with men for many years, they were also both case-hardened to flattery, rudeness, and/or ridicule and could usually hold their own with any of the employees, consistently coming out on top of debates, arguments, or insults.

Because of the number of years employed, they had worked for and with just about everyone in the department; however, they primarily had been assigned to Billy and Ben.

Harriet:

Harriet was often described as the epitome of what a well-kept but aging retired Las Vegas show girl probably would look like. Behind the silver hair, liver spots, and aging facial lines was a woman still proud to and able to wear a tight skirt and form-fitting blouse with ease and respectability. Without the silver hair, from behind Harriet could easily pass for a woman in her forties. The respectability, however, ended if and when anyone got on her wrong side, when she would retreat into a tirade of language that could make any fisherman or truck driver blush. Verbal threats by Harriet were taken somewhat seriously, as she had the persona of someone who could and would deliver on her promises.

Not willing to take any grief from the patrolmen or the public, tough as nails Harriet did have one or two small weak points. One was that she had a sweet tooth and routinely brought in desserts to share with the men, and in turn they routinely brought her treats such as cakes and candy to keep her happy. The other was that she was deathly afraid of bugs or anything that crawled or slithered.

Now in each squad, there was usually one person who was designated either by choice or demand as the snake wrangler. Cedar Springs had very few poisonous snakes but had an abundance of "black" or "rat" snakes, because much of the acreage in the area used to be or continued to be woods or cleared fields utilized for farming corn, lima beans, and tomatoes.

It was not unusual for callers to indicate that they had opened a door to their basements, crawl spaces, closets or garages and found a 4-to-6 foot black snake. Black snakes are usually harmless and more afraid of people than people are of them, but for snake-fearing people, any 4-to-6 foot snake is exactly 4-to-6 feet too much of a snake.

One patrolman on Harriet's squad happened to be Jan McCord, who would become something of a legend after singlehandedly killing a three-day-old four-wheel-drive patrol vehicle by drowning. Jan didn't really love snakes but just happened to be able to tolerate them from the experience of having owned one when he was growing up. As things usually happen, Jan had made mention of this at some point in a conversation either with or overheard by Harriet and was then assigned to all snake calls, whether or not he wanted them. After about a half dozen snake-corralling calls, he mentioned to Harriet that maybe she should give some thought to sending *all* the patrolmen to these calls and not just him. Harriet replied very sweetly, "Oh yeah, sweetie, not a problem."

Just two weeks later Jan received another call about a five-footer that had crawled into a baseboard heater--not surprisingly, located in another patrolman's area. Jan reluctantly answered the call and after dutifully capturing and releasing the slithering beast back into the wild, promptly drove to the station and questioned Harriet about the call. Harriet said that she had forgotten and just resorted to habit. Knowing her fear of reptiles, Jan decided to break the habit by telling Harriet that the next time, instead of releasing the snake into the woods, he would be making a personal gift of it to her.

Sure enough, as things sometimes happen, just a few months later, another snake call was received and another dispatched call to Jan to handle it. Without debate or any sign of despair or disappointment, Jan responded to the call and found a rather small four- foot black snake again, which had crawled into a baseboard electric heater. After removing the snake from the heater, and as they usually do when grabbed by or near the head, the snake immediately wrapped itself around Jan's arm, awaiting the next move.

Jan decided to make good on his promise, and after clearing the call, indicated on the radio that he would be coming to the station with further information, all the while holding the snake still wrapped tightly around his arm.

As Jan pulled into the carport area and got out of his car, Harriet was able to see him through the glass doorway approaching the entrance and became aware of the serpent wrapped on Jan's arm and immediately jumped from her chair, dropping the phone, abruptly causing a conversation with a citizen to come to an hasty end, and began to run screaming uncontrollably down the hallway toward the chief's office.

The Rude, not knowing what was happening, had gotten up from his desk and was just at his doorway when Harriet ran into his arms in near hysteria. Following several attempts to express to The Rude what was happening, and cowering behind him in the corner, Jan appeared in the doorway still holding the curled snake and calmly looked at Harriet and the chief and said, "I got your friend. Where would you like me to put him?"

With a screaming dispatcher now in full-blown alarm and terror, The Rude, with a cross between a heavy sigh and a slight chuckle, along with a long drag on his cigarette, calmly told Jan to take the monster outside.

It was close to an hour before Harriet was able to return to the dispatch room, and Billy had to come in off the street to answer the phone in her absence. Later that day, Jan asked Harriet if she could now try to divide the snake calls up to the other patrolmen instead of giving them just to him. With a small tic still in one eye, Harriet agreed, then added with a calm but forceful tone that if Jan ever tried that again, she would cut his balls off very slowly with a dull knife. As much as Jan knew the snake had done its job, he also had no doubt that Harriet could and probably would follow through with her very personal threat if needed.

Now it wasn't only snakes that Harriet disliked. She made it known that any type of crawling animal was on her hit list. Knowing what had transpired between Jan and Harriet and realizing that individual testicles might be at risk, the squad decided that in the future, should they decide to play a trick on Harriet, they would have to act as a whole because they thought it would be safer to their futures as manly men if they worked as a team.

One night around 8:00 on a rather busy Saturday, and coincidentally only two days before Halloween, Billy, in an unusually good mood after selling six new chain saws that day, met with a few of his squad members and while recalling the snake escapade, indicated that maybe it was time for "Trick or Treat" at the station and to round up another critter for Harriet.

In a short period of search time, one of the patrolmen happened to capture a small tree frog and placed it into an ordinary brown lunch-type paper bag. As frogs do, it would sit still for a while and then attempt to hop around and escape the bag, causing the bag to move and appear somewhat possessed.

Sometime during the night, a couple of the patrolmen, neither of which was Jan, who had indicated he wanted to hang on to his testicles for future use, entered the station to relay some additional information to Harriet. While her attention was busy with one patrolman, the other casually placed the bag containing the frog on the dispatch counter. It was thought that even if Harriet noticed the bag, she might assume that someone had brought her a dessert.

A short time later, the patrolmen left the station. Harriet, while taking a complaint call about a noisy party that the caller indicated was getting out of hand and needed to be shut down, Harriet noticed the brown bag and also thought she noticed that the bag might have moved a bit.

Now, not really listening to the caller and focusing all her attention on the bag, it then appeared to momentarily rise off the table in a hopping motion. When a throaty croaking noise accompanied the next hop, Harriet took the phone away from her ear and began striking the bag furiously while screaming at the top of her lungs that she was going to cut the balls off each and every member of the squad.

Two minutes later, the bag had been flattened, with a large brown and red stain appearing through the paper.

Approximately fifteen minutes later, Billy received a request from Harriet to come to the station for information. Twenty minutes after his arrival, Billy advised the squad members to meet with him in the parking lot. A short impromptu meeting took place starting with a few chuckles, grins, and laughter from the patrolmen. These were quickly quelled and admonished by Billy.

He explained that Harriet had advised him that should another incident like the hopping bag ever happen again, she was prepared to divulge each and every discrepancy and questionable behavior both professional and personal of each member of the squad to the chief, the town fathers, the county prosecutor's office, the state police, the press, wives, children, girlfriends, and whoever else wanted to listen.

All members, not unlike little boys who had just been caught with their hands in the cookie jar, one by one made their apologies to Harriet, mostly to ensure that accounts of their own discrepancies remained undisclosed. Once again, Harriet came out on top and for the remainder of her career was routinely brought deserts and treats, but no more tricks.

And Millie:

Millie Townson was similar to Harriet in that she had somehow managed to stay in excellent physical shape for her age. The main difference between the two was that Harriet, at around five feet ten inches tall, resembled a woman who could have been and actually was at one point in her life a professional dancer, while Millie was only about five feet tall but blessed with great legs, a slim waist, and an ample bosom. She was inclined to wear skirts cut above the knees, form-fitting blouses with the first two or three buttons open, and like Harriet, was feisty as a teenager.

Millie had a professional air about her while speaking to the public and could remain calm under extreme circumstances. She also had a quick wit and broad sense of humor. In short, she was usually fun to work with, as she understood that sometimes bad things happen to people. She also knew that in order to cope with that, one had to learn to not take things too seriously or too personally.

Millie was known to take the position of "I see nothing, I saw nothing, I know nothing" when members of the department arranged certain pranks toward other members of the department, some of which took place while she worked. Millie was, for the most part, an associate member of the *Thick Blue Line*.

Her Achilles heel was that when taking a complaint call, she had the bad habit of not asking additional questions that would certainly be helpful to the responding officers. A typical call to a patrolman from Millie would go something like:

Dispatch: Dispatch to car #12.

Car #12: Car #12, go ahead.

Dispatch: I have a report of a fight taking place at 245 Main Street.

Car #12: Okay--who's involved, what's involved, and how many are involved?

Dispatch: That's unknown.

Now, there were times and probably still are that this type of short and curt description is sometimes received this way, with the caller quickly hanging up with no further information given. This sometimes happened because the caller did not want to get involved and sometimes it happened because the caller actually was involved and an integral part of the mêlée that was taking place.

However, more times than not, if they were asked, a caller would volunteer much more information about who was involved and what the argument was about--or, at least, what the caller believed the argument was about. It was the responsibility of the dispatchers to attempt to pry as much information from callers as possible for the safety of the responding officers. Many times, callers would be grilled for information solely because of the dispatcher's own curiosity. Millie apparently was never overly curious, as she routinely failed to ask additional questions.

It was not unusual for the dispatched officer to tell Millie to call the party back and ask more questions. As aggravating as this sometimes was, Millie had the type of bubbly personality that made these little idiosyncrasies somewhat acceptable.

There was also one other quality attribute that Millie had perfected which made her stand out among the other dispatchers.

During the summer months, especially weekends, it was not unusual to have several overnight guests or prisoners in the holding cells awaiting either morning transport to the county jail or to be released to family members after sobering up for a few hours.

At around 7 a.m., Millie would take great care in entering the holding cell area, usually with the top two or three buttons of her blouse unbuttoned, and announce to everyone that it was a beautiful new day and good to be alive. She would then advise all detainees that she would be taking orders for breakfast.

When asked what was available, she would respond with a great big smile that she would provide anything their little hearts desired. Usually one prisoner would slowly ask if bacon and eggs were available, and Millie would answer "Of course" and then ask how they wanted them cooked and what type of toast they would like, and even what type of jelly to go with it. Additionally, coffee or tea was offered and a choice of three or four different fruit juices. Millie would dutifully write down everyone's name and their order complete with a smile or a showing of cleavage and empathy toward their particular predicament.

State requirements to feed prisoners held for more than six hours were routinely satisfied in Cedar Springs through a call to a local restaurant for fried egg sandwiches on untoasted, usually stale white bread and a cup of semi-warm black coffee.

The majority of the visitors that had just given their breakfast orders to Millie were now believing that being arrested and locked up was not as bad as what it was reported to be, due to the friendly waitress/employee taking orders and promising better meals than most had had in days.

About an hour later on those same mornings it was just as much as a shock finding out the whole ordering process was a charade. When receiving their dried-out fried egg sandwich in brown paper bags, the delivering patrolmen, trying to keep a straight face, would exclaim that they had no idea what the prisoners were talking about.

Officers assigned to transport or release prisoners on the following shift shortly after Millie had left the building, many times encountered angry, loud, and abusive individuals because of the deceptions.

Millie never seemed to tire of the deception and continued the act until it became mandatory that people be transported to another facility or released as soon as possible after an arrest.

CHAPTER 41

Another Ben and Stuart Story

O n the third day of Stuart Tarrentino's Cedar Springs law enforcement career, while still riding with Big Ben, they received a report of a traffic accident on one of the main roads in the vicinity of the fishing docks and fish markets. When they arrived at the scene, they found that an open-top Jeep had somehow lost control and overturned, sliding across approximately 80 feet of roadway.

The Jeep was equipped with seat belts and a roll bar to protect the driver in just such an event. The visually obvious glitch involving these safety devices was that the driver had failed to wear his seat belt and when the vehicle flipped, forward force and then gravity came into effect. The driver's head had been located between the roadway and the roll bar, which had the effect of crushing and scraping the man's head to the point of what then resembled a very messy strawberry and whipped cream pancake.

The driver apparently had been fishing, as he had about two dozen large bluefish and weakfish iced down in two big ice coolers in the back of the Jeep. During the crash, the coolers had been thrown out and opened, resulting in fish all over the highway.

Ben, following a quick visual check of the driver also quickly decided that Stuart should be indoctrinated into *real* police work by checking out a *real* dead driver. He advised Stuart to check the condition and welfare of the driver. Stuart, after a short and nauseating check of the semi-headless driver who was obviously deceased, reported back to Ben and said, "I'm pretty sure he's not gonna make it any further than where he's at right now."

Ben, satisfied with Stuart's literal, yet sarcastic, yet still somewhat compassionate rationalization of the driver's condition, advised Stuart that he should begin directing traffic around the accident scene. Ben stated that he would help coordinate the rescue squad, medical examiner, all necessary photographs, and measurements and would also later show him how a fatal motor vehicle accident report was to be done.

As the traffic unhurriedly crept by Stuart, complete with each and every driver slowing down to gaze at the grisly scene, one particularly interested-looking man driving an old beat-up pickup truck came to a complete stop and asked if he could have the fish lying all over the highway. Stuart, wondering and hoping this would be the only idiot who would ask that question, told him no and advised him to keep moving.

Stuart then turned around to direct and allow traffic to flow from the other direction. Unknown to him, the fish fancier had pulled off the roadway, stopped, gotten out and was beginning to pick up the fish and was putting them in a garbage bag he had taken from his truck.

Ben, who was assisting the rescue squad and coroner finding the various pieces of skull and brain matter, noticed the man running in the roadway gathering the fish. With a look that could kill, he hurried from the overturned vehicle, crossed the roadway, and then hollered, "Hey, asshole! What the hell do you think you're doing?"

Stuart turned when he heard Ben yell. Seeing what the man was doing he quickly hollered, "Sarge, he just asked me if he could have the fish and I told him no and to keep going. Apparently he doesn't hear very well or just doesn't care."

Ben in his now trademark "Ole John Barleycorn" move, approached the man and grabbed him by the throat, lifting him off the ground with one hand. He walked him and then threw him on the hood of the truck he had driven and cuffed him all in one swift, beautiful, flowing movement. As the now somewhat surprised driver was escorted across the roadway toward the marked patrol car, he was told he was under arrest for impeding traffic, failure to obey a lawful police order, and for being an asshole. Ben literally threw him into the rear of the police vehicle and then for good measure reached in closed all the windows and turned the air conditioning off.

Approximately an hour later when all agencies were clear, and the fish collector was getting the distinct impression his actions had not been appreciated, Ben and Stuart returned to the patrol car. Ben said to Stuart clearly, loud enough for the man to hear, "It's bad enough we got a fucking body in the road with a flat head and brains all over the place; this shithead drives up with no brains in his head and wants the fucking fish. What's this world coming to?"

The fish collector was brought to the station, charged and released and told to walk back to his car, which now was about eight miles away.

The additional reports were finished and Ben said, "Come on, we gotta go down to the fish market."

The market was across the street from the scene of the accident. Stuart, thinking they were possibly going to speak with a witness, asked, "Did somebody call in about the accident?"

Ben didn't answer. When they reached the market, they went inside and one of the employees said to Ben, "Right over there, Benny."

Ben said, "Thanks, Al."

Looking at Stuart, he said, "That Al was the meanest linebacker I ever saw playing high school football."

Along the wall near a refrigerated display case were the salvageable fish from the accident, recently headed, gutted, cleaned, and neatly packed with ice in waxed fish boxes.

Ben again said, "Thanks again, Al," and asked Stuart if he wanted any fish.

Stuart declined, saying he didn't feel like cooking them because the whole house would smell like fish. As they loaded the boxes in the trunk, Ben looked at Stuart very seriously and said, "I can get them cooked by Bobby at the Lobster Shanty if you want."

The Lobster Shanty was a popular and frequented restaurant in the dock area.

Ben seemed to know everybody.

On the ride back to the station, Ben shook his head and turning to Stuart, said, "I still can't get over that guy driving by, seeing a dead body and brains lying all over the road, and he tries to take the fucking fish. What is the matter with people?"

Stuart looked at him and laughed.

Ben then said, "Well, he sure as hell didn't deserve um and we sure as hell do."

At the station, Ben called in the rest of the squad and handed out fish to whoever wanted any.

Ben also seemed to take care of everybody.

CHAPTER 42

The Land Yacht

I n the 1970s and 1980s, one of the areas of the town that was routinely patrolled was a strip of ocean front acreage where several motels and nightclubs were located. The beach itself was comprised of approximately 200 feet of sand during low tide and half that during a normal high tide. During low tide it was not unusual for a patrolman in a four-wheel- drive vehicle, to drive onto the sand and drive close to the water's edge where the sand was packed hard.

In the summer months, one could drive north along the hard-packed beach for several miles into other jurisdictions just for something different to do and also to observe beachgoers, mostly of the female persuasion, who would show their skin to the sun gods while not really minding being gawked at by other beach people or the occasional passing patrol vehicle.

The Cedar Springs highly developed beachfront motel and night-club region covered about one half mile of ocean coastal beach acreage. There was another area about one half miles south of the motel's that was mostly undeveloped sand dunes and high dune grass.

The Army Corps of Engineers had decided, in the early years before WWII, that the best way to stop beach erosion on the coast was to build rock jetties that extended from the beach out into and past the low waterline to disrupt the natural erosion of sand by the ocean waves and tides. The rocks were supposed to help in retaining the sand during the changing of tides and during storms. The towns also incorporated rain outfall pipes from their streets along these jetties, utilizing them as a natural support for the pipes. The jetties, constructed from large granite boulders strategically placed on top of one another and having a somewhat flat top, also made them a convenient spot for surf fishermen to use.

The undeveloped area was privately owned, not completely fenced in, and also not guarded by lifeguards and was usually used as a place for people to quietly walk and for patrol to capture a glimpse of an occasional surf fisherman, a pair of lovers, and the occasional female topless sun worshiper. Night time was no exception, although the main events in this area were limited to the occasional lovers or for a patrolman to catch up on some reading or studying for the next promotional test.

During low tide, it was easy enough to drive around the ends of the granite jetties, as the damp sand was highly compacted and hard. During high tide, it was impossible to go around the jetties, as there was as much as three to five feet of water at their end. It was equally impossible to drive over them, as they were basically a two-to-three-foot wall of rock sticking out of the sand.

One particular patrolman, Jan McCord, happened to have been assigned to the area in question on a quiet midnight shift. It was fall, and most of the restaurants and bars had closed for the season. The motels were vacant except for weekends, and the beach human activities dwindled to an occasional call every few hours, and those assigned to that area generally had a lot of down time.

Jan, after meticulously and professionally scanning for trouble spots in the sector without finding anything out of the ordinary, had decided that the undeveloped dunes and high grass area needed to be carefully checked for any signs of unlawful activity. As luck would have it, that midnight shift at that particular time was during the "convenient to drive around the jetty time frame" of a low tide.

With dedication in his heart and the safety of the dunes and high dune grass undoubtedly primarily in mind, Jan drove the "newly acquired, only a few days old," four- wheel-drive Chevrolet Suburban onto the beach and around the jetty and began his diligent patrol of the area.

After making what was surely a thorough examination of the entire region for an extended period of time, Jan decided that his visual efforts of the conservation of nature was a success, and that it was probably time to head back to the more populated areas of the town.

At the completion of his task and feeling very patriotic about his part in keeping the East Coast protected from possible foreign invasion and the dune grass safe from vegetation killing off road vehicles, with the exception of his own, Jan drove back to the end of the jetty, which had now accumulated what appeared to be a few inches of water around it.

At that point Jan had two choices. He could wait up to twelve hours for low tide to come around again or take a chance that the water was in fact only a few inches deep. With full confidence in his super nautical X-ray vision of the depth of the water and driving a new four-wheel-drive vehicle, Jan decided the twelve-hour wait would be difficult to explain to his relief, who was scheduled to be picked up in a couple of hours.

As luck would have it, just as he passed the end point of the jetty, the Suburban's back tire sunk into a small rut hole, which quickly transformed into what people who spend a lot of time on beaches digging holes near moving water and to what desert- stationed solders call a "tank trap."

A gallant effort was made to escape the trap utilizing the four-wheel drive, but the wheel base on the Suburban was so long that once it bottomed out onto its frame, it became something resembling a giant white steel woolly mammoth caught in a tar pit and began to sink a little deeper and deeper and deeper and deeper into the sandy salt water and sand.

Now there were never any oral directives, or written policies in the department to actually require any patrol to take place on the south side of the jetty. The land was undeveloped and unless there was some type of rescue needed during the summer, there really was no reason to go there.

The area further south of the high grass area was owned by the US Coast Guard. For their security, they had constructed a 15-foot-high chain-link and barbed-wire fence buried two feet in the ground and running right down to the water's edge. The fence made access to the coast guard area inaccessible, and it also made it impossible to get to the town's area from the coast guard's base.

The majority of the dunes themselves were made up of very soft sand which when dry was inoperable by any motor vehicle except dune buggies, which Cedar Springs did not have. A four-wheel-drive vehicle could maneuver fairly well when close to the water or where the dune grass was particularly thick. The only practical way to get a motor vehicle into this area was to drive around the jetty during low tide, and whoever chose to do so was taking a chance to feel the wrath of The Rude should their timing or something else go wrong.

East Coast ocean tides tend to come in rather quickly and Jan knew he had less than an hour to get the vehicle out of the tank trap before the water reached the door jambs.

This particular incident happened well before cell phones, and Jan knew that a patrol radio transmission to the station would not only bring some type of assistance but would also bring embarrassment to him and ridicule from every member of the department for weeks to come.

It would also mean facing The Rude after doing something foolish as well as having to listen to Captain Benny, lecture about how the public perception of a patrolman getting stuck in the sand would look. Jan figured--and probably figured right--that Captain Benny's first question would probably be whether he had been wearing his hat.

With this in mind, Jan tried time and again to dislodge the Suburban from the ever- growing sand trap and succeeded in doing nothing more than sinking the vehicle deeper into the water. The ocean waves were now beginning to seep into the lower doorways of the less than a week old shiny new Suburban sport utility vehicle. After another few tries, with salt water now half way up the seats inside and approaching the police radio attached to its bracket bolted to the floor, Jan decided that he would just have to take whatever punishment and humiliation came his way and radioed to his dispatcher Harriet that his vehicle was stuck in the sand.

Historically, because the town was located around beaches, police vehicles would get stuck in the sand from time to time. Beach sand can be deceptive. One day it may be firmly packed, and you would have no trouble driving on it. The next day it may be the equivalent of a giant soft sandbox that would sink the tires of a vehicle in a matter of a few feet so a call to dispatch of a stuck vehicle was not necessarily something to get overly anxious or concerned about.

Harriet, still holding a slight grudge against Jan for bringing her the black snake, answered as sarcastically and condescendingly as possible that she had received the massage and would advise the shift sergeant. The supervising sergeant on duty, Billy Durrant, upon hearing Jan's transmission, inquired as to whether a tow truck would be needed. He hoped that Jan had gotten stuck in the sand where another patrol car could pull the stuck car out with a rope rather than having a tow truck winch the vehicle out with the usual fanfare and elaborate, unflattering advertisement of the department's patrol procedures. His experience and gut, along with the fact that there had been virtually no calls to answer for the last few hours, told him, however, that Jan had probably gotten stuck in the dunes on the south side of the jetty. During low tide, this usually meant that another four-wheel-drive vehicle would drive around the jetty, hook a chain or rope from one vehicle to the other, pull the stuck vehicle out of a hole, and no one would be the wiser.

When Jan started to explain that the vehicle was stuck in the sand with the tide approaching, the sergeant was still holding out hope for a clean beach rescue of the vehicle. He thought he would ask Jan the logical next question, which was how close was the tide water to the vehicle?

He said, "How close is the tide water to the vehicle?"

The question was met with silence.... Not necessarily a good sign. After the second request from the sergeant, Jan indicated that the sergeant should probably report to his location as soon as possible.

This was certainly not a good sign.

With this said, or in fact not said, everyone on duty at the time now knew that Jan had done something stupid. With those thoughts in mind, they all wanted to see just how dumb Jan had been, and as luck would have it, the town was quiet enough to allow the entire shift to personally be able to respond to the area.

With anticipation of being witness to headline-making blunders by a fellow employee, the remaining squad members were indeed fortunate enough to observe the recently acquired, less than a thousand mile, brand-new, four-wheel-drive Chevy Suburban sitting on the beach in the area of the jetty with water almost up to the windows of the car and Jan sitting cross-legged on the top, holding his briefcase and portable radio, awaiting help.

Talk about fuel for the fire of future humiliation of a fellow member of the department. This was, without a doubt, one of the most momentous and historic events in the history of Cedar Springs. Those in attendance knew that stories of the sinking of a police cruiser would be circulating for months, and maybe even years.

A tow truck complete with driver/diver eventually managed to hook up and winch the vehicle out. It was rumored that one of the other patrolmen had taken some Polaroid pictures of Jan perched on top trying to keep his balance until he could safely jump to dry land. Talk circulated that the pictures would be posted around the station on a monthly basis as long as Jan was employed, but no known copies ever surfaced. It was also rumored that Jan had paid a substantial sum for the original prints, which he allegedly destroyed.

The new truck was brought up to dry land, visually inspected for contraband or endangered sea life and then towed, sprinkling droplets of salt water the entire way, to the town's municipal garage, thankfully under cover of darkness. The following day after a thorough walk around and many speculations about what the real story was, the town's mechanics removed the interior and police electronics. The entire vehicle was then power washed. The engine and transmission, as well as the entire drive train and brake system, were drained of fluids. The gasoline tank and radiator were removed and cleaned, and all dash gauges and switches were thoroughly dried and re-lubricated.

Somehow, after many man hours of drying, cursing, drying, cleaning, drying, adjustments, more cursing, and of course more drying, the truck managed to run again. Many new electronic modules and sensors, along with a new police radio, were replaced, but it was never quite right again. There were some days it would run like the new vehicle that it was, and other days it resembled a vehicle with an eight-cylinder engine running on only 3-to-4 cylinders.

After many months and problematic hours and days in the town's garage for a variety of different ailments, it was mercifully traded in the following year at a substantial loss to the taxpayers, who undoubtedly were informed that the department had suffered the unfortunate purchase of a Detroit lemon.

Jan was the subject of days, weeks, and months of constant motor vehicle and fishing ridicule, complete with poetry, pictures, and displays made by the more artistic members of the department.

Daily tributes to the sinking of the Chevy land yacht would appear on the walls of the department as well as the toilets, urinals, and drinking fountains. Die cast and plastic models of Chevy Suburban's with added periscopes, dirty waterlines and small fake cans of tuna inside would appear in Jan's mailbox at the station. Signs indicating *SS Cedar Springs Titanic* were constantly taped to any patrol vehicle that Jan was assigned to drive, and on special occasions a dead fish or two would be jammed into the bumpers.

The badgering continued on what was usually a daily basis. It was also sometimes skipped for a day or two and then continued to make Jan think it was over when in fact it was not really over. This stop and start strategy caused the hoped-for reaction of newfound irritation. All in all, Jan was the brunt of ridicule for the better part of three months, plus the occasional "high tide" anniversary taunts until such time as it didn't appear that the flack he was receiving was having any effect anymore.

The Rude pulled Jan into his office for an extended closed-door talk of which the contents were never made public, but Jan was very subdued and quiet for several months and most certainly had been taken off the chief's Christmas card list.

Jan was also informed that he had to speak with Captain Benny about the possibility of the real story becoming public. As predicted, Benny's first question was whether Jan had been wearing his hat while sitting on top of the vehicle, just in case he had been seen by any members of the public.

After being assured that Jan had taken all possible precautions about not being seen by the public out of proper attire, Benny gave Jan an extended lecture about the importance of defensive driving, vehicle maintenance, and proper patrol procedures, all the time visually checking Jan's uniform for crooked badges, missing buttons, or uneven seams.

CHAPTER 43

Recon

After the annual family barbecues at The Rude's home came to an end, one of the sergeants, Big Ben Bailey, began having the annual event at his house. Basically they were eerily similar to The Rude's. There were the same people, same games, and always the expectation of one of the couples having a public domestic argument that could be talked about for weeks.

Big Ben didn't have an in-ground pool, but he did have a large above-ground one. He lived at the end of a cul-de-sac and had a huge back yard that backed up to a wooded area with only a neighbor to one side. The other neighbors were across the street, making his location fairly shielded from complaints about noise, etc. during the events.

Ben had three daughters, two of which were teenagers, so the yard was basically Ben's man cave area. Besides the pool, he also had a regulation horseshoe pit, volleyball net, brick barbecue, and stone-lined fire pit. In support of the annual barbecues, everyone who attended brought lounge chairs, folding tables, and of course food and drink.

The only drawback in any of these get-togethers was Big Ben's next-door neighbor, Roberta Hensley. Mrs. Hensley was a 72-year-old widow who had no children, no known relatives, no known friends or even known acquaintances. Barely five feet tall, she was rarely seen in anything but a red-and-white plaid long-sleeved shirt, khaki pants, and a wide-brimmed straw hat covering her close-cropped gray hair.

What she did have was a well-known disdain for the fact that Ben was a police officer with teenage children. In addition to her dislike of police and teenagers, she immensely detested the yearly barbecue affairs--or any type of entertainment affairs, for that matter.

She also had flowers. Lots of flowers. Beds and beds of flowers that she absolutely cherished. It seems that the only thing that Mrs. Hensley had besides her intense dislike for the police and the annual barbecues was a knack for growing, and expertly so, many types and strains of beautiful flowers.

In the weeks leading up to the annual event, Mrs. Hensley would spend large amounts of time weeding and preening the flower beds as the party date coincided with the peak blooming period of some of her most prominent plants, and those which she was the most proud of.

During this time, whenever Ben happened to be in the yard, she would waddle over and ask about the planned party. Reminiscent of the personas of the stern and harsh '50s Catholic school nuns that taught her in grade school, she substituted a hand-held metal weeding hoe for the nun's infamous wooden pointers. While shaking the tool, she would continually remind Ben that her prized plants were preparing to bloom and insist that each and every one of his visitors be instructed to stay off her property and away from her flowers.

Mrs. Hensley would say, "As you should be aware, I will not be intimidated. I insist that you guarantee that no people, footballs, volleyballs, or shuttlecocks intentionally or unintentionally invade my yard or my flower beds. I am well aware of my rights, and I have the right to absolute privacy. If they are violated by any of your guests or their shenanigans, I will not hesitate to notify the state police."

It seemed that Mrs. Hensley always thought that the governor and the state police actually ran all of the municipal governments and police departments. In her mind, small departments like Cedar Springs were merely sub stations and personally answerable to the state police. She figured that a threat of state involvement would ensure that Ben would bend to her wishes and be in fear of having to suffer the consequences of being called on the carpet by the governor or the superintendent of the state police.

Ben, not wanting to have any problems and not willing to explain the protocol of law enforcement to his neighbor, would agree that they would all be advised, all the while with Mrs. Hensley shaking her weeding tool menacingly in his face.

It was not unusual that when Ben and his wife would have family or friends over, Mrs. Hensley would actually call the police station and lodge a noise or trespassing complaint and demand that the get-together be shut down.

It was rumored that she also demanded that all the participants be removed, arrested, or subsequently executed should they not immediately comply--but no one was ever able to prove that, and it was probably just a rumor. At least the part about the demands for execution.

One particularly memorable police barbecue party started out much like any other with lots of laughter, drinking, relaxation, drinking, games for the kids, drinking for the adults, and of course the much-anticipated touch football game for those still able to function enough to play.

The barbecue was on a Saturday. It was well attended, and as promised, Ben advised everyone when they arrived that Mrs. Hensley was still alive, still annoying, and still, as they spoke, probably actively watching the property line for trespassers and potential violators of her rights.

Many jokes were made, and all were met with calm looks from Ben and his wife Karen, who reiterated that everyone should just stay away from her property. They both knew that sooner or later during the day they would probably have to confront their neighbor and apologize to her about the noise, the occasional windblown shuttlecock, an overthrown volleyball, and of course all the laughter and all the people having a good time.

One of the guests and a member of Ben's squad was Lenny Brisco. Lenny, a Vietnam veteran, was generally quiet and reserved and well looked up to as someone you could count on if ever in a serious situation. Lenny had done four tours in Vietnam while serving in the army. Rumors abounded concerning exactly what Lenny did in the army, as whenever asked, the standard answer would be, "Most of the stuff is still classified."

However, after several drinks, Lenny would sometimes entertain the other men with declassified stories from his days where he worked in reconnaissance missions with the mountain people in areas where the army was not supposed to be, and doing things that the army was not supposed to be doing. Lenny would always refrain from explicit details of the war, with his only reference to combat as, "Bullets kill."

When advised of the Hensley situation, Lenny said he was surprised that she was still alive and equally surprised that any flowers would actually bloom for such a miserable specimen of whining, complaining, and horrific female that the world and especially the neighborhood would be better off without.

Ben sarcastically said, "Lenny, don't sugarcoat it; tell me how you really feel!"

Despite the threats from the neighborhood's 72-year-old, weeding-tool-wielding, trespassing-death-penalty advocate, the party was beginning to look like a success. The children had a pool to swim and play in, and the women had husbands and boyfriends to talk about. The men had wives and girlfriends to complain about concerning their complaints about them. Of course, there was also an almost constant volleyball or badminton game in progress, as well as the yearly horseshoe tournament, which went on all day in singles and doubles matches. Equally important was the fact that there was plenty of alcohol to consume and the much-anticipated up-and-coming touch football game.

Mid afternoon came, and it became time for the football game, which would start out as a friendly touch game that inevitably would turn into a full-blown tackle game complete with torn, dirty clothing, bloody lips and noses, and the occasional sprained ankle or dislocated finger.

The captains were chosen, and teams were picked one by one. There was really no advantage for either side. Most of the younger guys were of course quicker and in better shape than the older guys, but the exception was the older guys all cheated and cared little for any real rules. The only thing each team had in common was that most everyone was fairly intoxicated. Tempers flared, and arguments were many but were also soon forgotten.

Scores between the two teams stayed close, mostly due to the constant cheating, until late in the second hour of play when two consecutive long bombs resulted in two quick touchdowns. One of the players on the now-behind team grabbed the ball and kicked it, attempting to show his disgust concerning his team's deficient secondary coverage.

It turned out to be the defining moment of the game, as the ball gained altitude and distance far beyond the expectations of the kicker or any of the players. Reminiscent of a movie scripted event, all fourteen players watched transfixed as the ball's flight took a slight curve in the wind and ended its voyage by promptly landing in Mrs. Hensley's side flower garden. Almost in unison, a murmur of joined voices was heard to exclaim,

"Ohhhhhhhhhhh…shiiitttttt!"

As shrewdly and cunningly as possible, Ben went over to retrieve the ball, optimistically hoping that no damage had occurred and praying that his neighbor had somehow missed the unauthorized flight.

Unfortunately, this was not to be, as the moment he journeyed onto her property, she simultaneously exited her back door, armed with her weeding tool, and let go a plethora of rants concerning her rights, Ben's wrongs, and of course an overabundance of "I told you so's."

After careful examination of the flowers, it was determined that one stem had been bent and two buds had been dislodged. That, and of course the divot the ball had made in the earth, were cause for additional rants about how long it took to construct the beds and the skill it took to ensure that the surrounding topsoil was level.

After several bouts of accusations vs. apologies, it was somewhat agreed that Ben would pay for a replacement plant. Mrs. Hensley was also assured that the ball-kicking assailant would be severely dealt with and probably drawn and quartered, or at least caned until the welts were clearly visible, and never again be invited to another event.

Mrs. Hensley, probably in flower shock and not quite realizing the sarcasm Ben had used in explaining how he would deal with the kicker, merely said, "Very well, then," and promptly returned to her house, all the while mumbling and shaking her weeding tool.

The players had returned to the volleyball area awaiting the outcome of the meeting. Ben had wisely taken his wife with him when he had gone to see Mrs. Hensley. He stated that she had a better relationship--or at least a less dramatic one--with the woman, but everyone knew she was there as more of a back-up for protection from the dreaded weeding tool.

It was even odds as to whether or not Ben would ever make Mrs.

Hensley "do the ole John Barleycorn" with his neck-grabbing scenario in a fit of exasperation, but it was also well known that Karen, Ben's wife, would take only so much abuse, and everyone wanted to be a witness to the possibility of an old-fashioned cat fight, no matter the ages of the participants.

As expected, upon the return of Ben and Karen to the group, there were many snide yet comical remarks regarding Mrs. Hensley's flowers. It was unilaterally agreed by the intoxicated partiers that Ben would probably have had fewer problems with her if he had been a bit more personal with their relationship.

It seems it was alleged by the more imaginative members of the department that Mrs. Hensley had large amounts of hormones not being utilized in a productive manner and that she was simply annoyed that Ben had not made an attempt to assist with her hormonal urges--probably more adequately described as her annoyances.

It was also unilaterally agreed that everyone would chip in and contribute to the costs of the replacement plants. Karen was delighted with the gestures, even though Ben knew that those monetary contributions would never happen.

It seemed that everyone was taking the neighborly quarrel in stride, with the exception of Lenny. Lenny sat quietly intoxicated with a look of deep contemplation concerning the situation. It was on this particular day that Lenny took it upon himself and for the good of all mankind, to once again revert to his army training and expertise in an attempt to bring an end to the turmoil between Ben and Mrs. Hensley.

As the afternoon progressed, most of the guests had forgotten about the complaint, the damages and the promises of restitution when someone noticed that Lenny had been missing from the group for quite a while.

His wife stated, "Hey, he's had a few drinks; I can't keep up with everything he does. He's probably swimming naked in the pool," which was another passion that Lenny generally performed after a few drinks.

About an hour following his disappearance from the party, Lenny reappeared at the grouping with a noticeable smug and sneering-type grin on his face. He clearly announced to Ben that he could now relax and enjoy the rest of the barbecue because the problem with his neighbor was taken care of. Ben had seen this mischievous yet serious look in the past and asked Lenny what had happened and what exactly had he done to "take care of" the problem.

Lenny drunkenly waved Ben over and motioned for him to follow him to the side of the house which faced the complaining and possibly sexually frustrated Mrs. Hensley's home. He motioned toward the evergreen bushes planted in front of Ben's house and pointed to a rather large pile of freshly picked flowers lying behind them.

Stumbling up close to Ben, Lenny whispered in a slow, alcohol-induced slur, "Recon!"

As surprised and angry as Ben was, the first thing he did after mumbling to himself, "You guys are killing me," was to thank Lenny for all the hard work that he had done and then very seriously asked if his neighbor was still breathing. It was common knowledge that Lenny could probably do "recon" whenever and to whomever he wanted without getting caught or much less even being considered a suspect. It was better to always thank Lenny for his efforts, even though they may have been a bit misguided, because nobody wanted Lenny doing "recon" on them or their property.

Lenny assured Ben that unfortunately she probably was still alive, because he had not seen her and she had not seen him. Ultimately Ben, with heavy heart, knew that he had to once again confront his fears and his neighbor about the new damages and hope that they could somehow convince her that these too could be repaired without a cat fight or legal litigation.

Unfortunately, Lenny's reconnaissance mission proved to be the end of the yearly barbecues at Big Ben's but also made it the most memorable. Lenny became another department hero and idol, with stories of the recon mission being repeated at almost every get-together that included more than two members of the department, for the next several years.

CHAPTER 44

Gypsy Moths Can
Make You Sterile

The gypsy moth, officially known as *Lymantria dispar* is a moth that was brought into to the United States around 1869 in a failed attempt to start a silkworm industry. Prior to molting and emerging as a moth, the larvae, or caterpillars, damage trees by eating the leaves, mostly at night.

They have a preference for the leaves of hardwood trees such as maple, elm, and particularly oak all which were in abundant supply in and around Cedar Springs. Through modern chemistry, the worst of the gypsy moth epidemic has now passed, but it was widespread during the 1970s and 1980s.

Pete Roberts and Angelo Demucchi, both of whom would become members of the famed Crazy Squad in later years, were working in the detective division in the mid-1970s. One evening they were riding around engrossed in the investigative technique and in the process of performing follow up exploratory ride-bys of suspected drug and criminal activity locations, or what they adeptly and in these particular instances often described as "basically doing absolutely nothing."

While gripped in their exploratory and investigative approach to law enforcement, they overheard dispatcher Ray Burry transmit a call to the north area car of what was reported to be a B&E in progress--or a breaking and entering taking place.

Both immediately thought that Ray had probably greatly enhanced the importance of the call, but with the slim chance that the reported incident was legitimate, Pete said he thought their assistance could be instrumental. In actuality, Pete said that if they were lucky, maybe they could catch somebody inside the house and beat the crap out of them. As usual, Angelo added, "Yeah, whatever"

Being about a mile away, they headed toward the location.

They arrived shortly after the marked unit. The owner of the property, Mr. Sanitos, met them in the front yard. As suspected, he indicated that there had been no burglary. He explained that his daughter, home from college, had told him she had seen someone standing by one of the trees in the back yard, staring at the house.

Mr. Sanitos said that when he went to the kitchen, he saw what he described as a tall, heavy-set, long-haired kid standing very still, looking at his house. When he opened the door and went outside, the kid quickly turned and ran into the wooded area behind the yard.

The group walked to the back yard with Mr. Sanitos, who indicated the area where the subject had been seen. Angelo asked if his daughter was having any difficulties with boyfriends or knew anyone who may want to be in the yard for any reason. Mr. Sanitos said that he had no idea and that they should ask his daughter. He then called to his wife and asked her to tell his daughter to come out to the back yard.

It immediately became obvious as to the reason anyone would be staring at the house when Mr. Sanitos' daughter came out of the house. Darlene Sanitos, a nineteen-year-old blonde, hazel-eyed, incredibly gorgeous young lady dressed in not much more than a very sheer nightgown emerged from the house and sashayed over to her father, the patrolman, and the two now somewhat dumbstruck detectives. When asked if she was having any problems with anyone, she innocently stated she had no idea who or why anyone would be in her yard or why anyone would be staring at her.

Both Pete and Angelo thought to themselves, *Aahhh, the naïve, young, and foolish.*

Pete asked the dispatcher to check the Sanitos' address for any prior incidents. Upon checking, it seemed that the department had recorded a few minor property damage reports in the general area, along with a few Peeping Tom reports, most of which took place at night or on weekends. It wasn't difficult to figure that this particular report was probably related to a lot of the others.

Pete and Angelo advised the marked patrol unit to get the information needed for a report and leave the area, thinking that if the subject was still in the woods, he would think the police had gotten no detailed description and would not be looking for him.

Pete and Angelo drove about two blocks away, parked their car, and hiked into the woods, believing that they would have a better chance of finding the perpetrator in plain clothes than as uniformed officers.

Slowly and methodically, they searched around the area, and as they had predicted, found a subject quietly sitting on the ground, leaning against a tree, smoking a cigarette and probably thinking no one was looking for him.

Approached from two sides, the subject was quite surprised to find he was soon staring at two men with very large handguns pointing at him, politely asking him to stay seated and remain very still.

The subject turned out to be a fourteen-year-old harebrained kid who lived in the area. He was almost six feet tall but probably well over 250 pounds, with the typical (for the times) long, stringy, dirty-looking hair and a terrible case of teenage acne. Judging from the appearance of Mr. Sanitos' daughter, it was also assumed the young man had an understandable yet unhealthy approach in dealing with his teenage testosterone levels.

He was patted down and handcuffed and was advised of the recent Peeping Tom reports. He was then questioned about his being at that particular wooded location. Not unlike someone who just got caught, he denied everything and said he was doing nothing other than taking a walk through the woods.

Knowing that the only thing that they possibly had on the boy was a juvenile complaint for trespassing, Pete advised Angelo that they had to do some canvassing of the area for any possible witnesses pertaining to the boy's recent activities. Angelo didn't know exactly what Pete had in mind but went along with it.

Pete removed one cuff from the boy and told him to place his arms around the oak tree he had been leaning against. He then re-cuffed him and advised him to stay where he was until they returned from speaking to witnesses who had earlier reported him to be a Peeping Tom. He was told that they would be back as soon as possible to finish up the investigation.

As Pete and Angelo were walking away, the boy, now looking a bit more concerned and not quite sure of his future, asked, "You guys are coming back, right?"

After receiving no immediate answer from the two detectives, he then asked, "What are these bugs that keep falling out of the trees?"

Pete said, "Those are gypsy moths. There all over the woods this time of year." He added very seriously, "Don't let them land on you, because if they bite you, you'll end up sterile"

Unexpectedly the boy's face somewhat scrunched up and he then asked, "What does sterile mean?"

Pete told him that meant his future girlfriend and baby-making days would never happen. Angelo, trying not to laugh, just nodded in agreement.

Pete told him, "Just be quiet and relax. I want you to take this time to think about what you *really* did this evening." He added in a menacing voice, "And if you start screaming and hollering, you'll just attract more gypsy moths and find yourself cuffed to that tree for a very long time."

It was just starting to get dark when they left him. They drove around for about two hours, eventually believing that the oak tree probably needed to be rescued and returned to the young man in the woods. When they got to him, it was apparent that he had been crying, and he immediately thanked them for coming back. He quickly also advised them that he had never screamed or hollered. It was also quite obvious that the mosquitoes had proficiently feasted on him, as he was covered with numerous telltale red bumps.

Pete asked, "Are any of those bites from gypsy moths?"

The boy answered, "I don't think so. I tried to be as quiet as I could, and I did my best to shake them off whenever any landed on me."

Both Pete and Angelo then read him the riot act concerning his hormonal urges, his peeping, and his general history of causing problems for the police. They told him that if he solemnly promised to keep his nose clean, they would release him with no charges, because he had been so cooperative.

Pete advised the boy in his best authoritative yet fatherly tone that they had utilized what was known in law enforcement as the "Diversionary Detainment Procedure." He advised that this well-known but seldom-used procedure allowed them to handcuff him to the tree until they had spoken to the many possible witnesses to his offense.

As an afterthought--but then again, possibly one which he had already planned--Pete advised the boy that the only remedy for gypsy moth bites was to wipe rubbing alcohol or witch hazel all over any possibly affected areas, which in the boy's case unfortunately was most of his mosquito-bitten body. The three then walked out of the woods with the boy profusely and repeatedly thanking them for giving him a break.

Knowing the stinging effects the alcohol or witch hazel was going to have on the mosquito bites caused both Pete and Angelo to chuckle. Not surprisingly, the department never received another report of the boy involved in any type of problem.

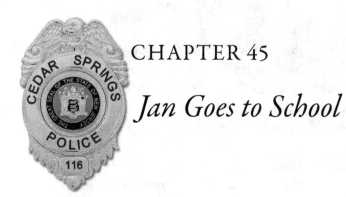

CHAPTER 45

Jan Goes to School

Acouple of years after sinking the new Suburban in the ocean, and after most of the other patrolmen pretended to have forgotten the incident but merely decided that more important issues needed their attention, Jan decided that he needed to go in a different direction to possibly gain some respect in the department.

Jan had been personally interested in cars and aviation, owning several classic cars over the years, and was taking helicopter-flying lessons at the airstrip in town. The Cedar Springs area did not have a PAL league or Boys and Girls Club. Jan thought that the area needed something for the youth. He decided to start a juvenile club for youth who were also interested in cars, aviation, and police work. The group was called--utilizing the obvious interests--the police-auto-aviation cadets. The club concentrated on grade-school-aged students who wanted to become involved in some type of law enforcement careers and were also interested in cars and planes.

The club was sponsored by the department, but in name only, and with no financial backing. The Rude gave his blessing to Jan to create the organization--providing no bad publicity be shone upon the department.

Using his own money, plus donations from community businesses, Jan provided uniforms for the youth and had bi-weekly or monthly meetings or outings, mostly at the airport, where the members were given information about what police do and also what planes and pilots do. The cadets were utilized during town events such as fairs, running races, and car shows to assist with parking, hand out pamphlets, and help clean up following the events. Slowly over the years, the club began to catch on and become a recognizable part of the department and the community.

The '80s arrived, and with them came state and federally funded programs for the youths of communities. One such program was the drug awareness for children program called D.A.R.E., or Drug Abuse Resistance Education. The program was designed for fifth- and sixth-grade students, who would receive instruction from police officers who had been trained to teach lessons on how to avoid and resist drug and alcohol usage. The thinking was that by presenting these lessons to youth, they could reduce the growing number of teenage and adult drug and alcohol abuse cases.

Seeing a chance to do something different, Jan submitted his request to The Rude to be able to attend training and be certified to teach the lessons. The main attention-getter for the chief was the fact that the state would pay the fees involved for attending the classes, and if the department and schools accepted the program, they would also provide matching funds in order to purchase a new or used vehicle decorated with D.A.R.E. emblems that the patrolmen instructors would exclusively operate. Truthfully, The Rude probably figured that it would be the only way to replace the Suburban that Jan had destroyed years earlier.

Now The Rude didn't exactly agree with the program across the board. He stated that he would allow Jan to attend the classes only if the local school would agree to accept the instruction classes into their curriculum. By luck, Jan was friends with the superintendent of the elementary school system, who happened to be fairly ahead of his time and was universally in favor of the drug awareness program. He basically advised the school principal to work the weekly classes into the teaching schedule.

Cedar Springs was the first community in the county to conduct the D.A.R.E. program, and Jan had found an area of police work that he enjoyed and also one which kept him off patrol duties and away from barking dog and snake wrangling calls a couple of days per week.

Within three years of working with the community youth and the schools, Jan became the first school resource officer in the elementary schools and was assigned a daily schedule matching that of the students and teachers of the schools. His role was to introduce law enforcement personnel to youth as people that they should think of as helpful and someone that they could go to for advice. The plus for the schools was that he also became something of a truant officer and handled school-related complaints.

Now all of this information was presented solely to re-introduce Jan as more than the snake-charming, car-drowning patrolman that he was known to be. It became apparent in the eighties and nineties that Jan also possessed something of a distorted sense of humor, which was so important in establishing a legacy in police work in Cedar Springs.

Hey, who knew?

The only problem was that the majority of shenanigans conducted by Jan at the schools went largely unnoticed by other department members, and in keeping with equal and fair representation, it seemed somewhat important to include some of his acts of cynicism, sarcasm, and mayhem.

Being a role model and confidant for the young adults, much like a school counselor, meant that conversations taking place between him and the youths would for the most part remain private and not to be disclosed.

The school did have a drug and alcohol counselor, named Timothy Cassello, who was a trained and certified psychologist. Tim was a down-to-earth second-generation Italian whose family had arrived straight from Sicily and settled in Philadelphia. It was rumored but never proven that his mother gave him the Irish name Timothy in order to separate him from the old family business. After all, it would be difficult to be an "old- school Italian tough guy" growing up with a name like Timmy. It must have worked, as Tim went through college, got his master's degree, and was well on his way to a doctorate and reportedly had no ties with the trucking, trash, construction, or high-interest short- term loan so-called "family industries."

Tim's first concern was the welfare of the youth, but his interest in police work helped him to quickly bond with Jan. The two were close in age, and both had similar senses of humor, with the exception that Tim was so gullible, he would think that almost everything Jan stated was factual, because he couldn't believe that a police officer would fabricate a story that wasn't truthful. Sort of like how the internet started out.

Following each and every story or episode where Tim was found to be the goat, Jan would apologize for the fabrication and promise that nothing like it would happen in the future. Days or sometimes even hours later, with Tim being so sincere and serious, there would be another trumped-up story, another potentially embarrassing incident, another laugh, and another promise that it would never happen again.

While the students and their problems and personalities were looked at as strictly business, the personalities of the school's teachers, administrators, and support staff were fair game for consideration of their particular quirks, conduct, qualities, and behavior.

Jan took great pride in advising Tim, usually on a daily basis, of some small detail that was overly embellished or just a plain big lie, solely to get his frustrated reaction to it when the truth became evident. In time, Tim began to finally catch on to the charades and began to advise Jan of situations that didn't exist to try and get his reaction. Like Jan, Tim soon found that it was somewhat enjoyable to irritate the gullible.

The principal of the school soon learned that unexpected visits from either Jan or Tim were usually a result of one advising the other that they were needed immediately in the office to discuss some type of incident that never happened. The main office secretaries and the loudspeakers were also utilized on occasion to solidify the requests, so that neither was ever quite sure that the requests to see the principal were actually valid.

It was during Jan's time at the school that so-called security cameras were being brought into public buildings. Employees were advised that camera installations would protect them from false accusations from students and other employees, or they would be used to investigate instances of vandalism or thefts.

The school had cameras installed on the outside of the buildings and in some of the hallways, group areas, and the main offices. Memos were sent home to parents stating that the school district's insurance adjusters had suggested the installations to protect the schools from false claims in and around the buildings.

Many conversations concerning the installation and use of cameras took place between Tim and Jan and the direction society was moving, involving video proof of everyone's every move. As with most discussions concerning changes, there were pros and cons debated, with the final consensus being that they were stuck with them. Both agreed, with hopes that at the least, they would be utilized properly.

Tim, being a student psychologist, was confident that his office and line of employment were secure from a video invasion because of the confidentiality aspect of what took place there.

Jan, seeing that Tim was so certain he would be safe from the prying eyes of the cameras, which was absolutely true, began to formulate another opportunity to exploit an exploitable situation. He sent away for and acquired a simulated security camera that looked identical to the cameras being installed around the school. These replicas were manufactured for people or businesses that could not afford the real thing, but to the passerby, they appeared to be genuine and functional.

On the very next weekend, Jan brought the bogus camera into the school and carefully installed it in Tim's office, attaching it to a ceiling tile in the corner of the room and directing the lens to face Tim's desk.

On Monday morning, as Jan predicted, Tim called a mere ten minutes after arriving, asking in a somewhat subdued voice for him to report to his office as soon as possible. When Jan got to his office, Tim was pacing the floor and seemed as distraught as one who had just lost his dog or a winning lottery ticket. Turning his back to the room's corner, he motioned with his thumb, quickly pointing in the direction of the camera. Not knowing if the device could also record sound, he exclaimed in a hushed whisper, "Do you see that? How can they do this? I have confidential meetings in here with students and parents. I can't believe they can do this. Why did they do this? How can they do this?"

Tim rambled on for about five minutes about how confidential his work was, with Jan just looking calm and nodding in agreement from time to time. After a pause, Jan looked at the camera and began to explain how the world was changing, how they had talked about these changes in the past few weeks, and that everyone had to acknowledge the changes and accept new things and do the best they could with what was available.

Tim listened intently to Jan's little speech and realized that Jan was not jumping onto the bandwagon with him. Now knowing that he was not going to get any sympathy, he began to hyperventilate.

Shaking his head and getting a bit louder and bit angrier he said, "Yeah, I know, but you and I talked about this happening. How am I supposed to do my job if I have to worry about somebody else hearing or knowing what takes place in my office. Nobody is supposed to know what takes place in here. This is private! This has to be private! How can they do this? What am I going to do? I just can't believe this!"

As Tim's face began to change to a bright crimson red, Jan thought he might either pass out or have a stroke. Knowing he had successfully pulled another prank which caused undue alarm and distress, he decided that since it worked so well, that he should take a crack at taking it up a notch. So, still just calmly looking at Tim, he quietly stated, "Well, since you feel so strongly about this, I'm going to help you."

And with that, Jan walked over toward the camera, reached up and yanked it out of the ceiling tile, promptly threw it into the trash can and said, "There, now you have your privacy back."

Tim, completely taken by surprise at the action and not one to openly defy authority, exclaimed, "Jan, what the hell did you just do? Oh man, you are going to get me so fired. That was school property. I can't believe you did that. Now we're both dead!"

Jan calmly stated, "Well, you said you didn't want the camera in your office and now it's no longer in your office. Or at least it's no longer functioning in your office. What's the problem now?"

After listening to Tim express how he had no idea of how to explain the camera being ripped down and that they probably had Jan on tape ripping it out, and how he was never going to be able to get another job etc. etc. for the next ten minutes, Jan finally relented and showed Tim that the camera was just a replica.

Tim, turning red, said, "You son of a bitch. Why would you do that? I was ready to call my congressman. Either that or just quit. Why would you do that? Why did you do that?"

Jan said with a relaxed smile, "Mostly because you're gullible, and even more mostly… just because I could."

The next day, after Tim's blood pressure had returned to normal, the two began to discuss what they could do with the bogus camera to cause some discomfort to someone else.

It was decided that the best course of action, short of putting it in the principal's or superintendent's office, would be to temporarily install it into the teachers' ladies' restroom and act just as surprised as everyone else. It was agreed that this would cause the most concern.

Early one morning, prior to the teachers coming in, the camera was installed, and within minutes of the start of the day, virtually every female teacher who utilized the facility brought the camera's installation up in either questionable or accusatory statements to other teachers, and eventually to either Jan or Tim.

Both would act surprised at the reports and then vow to look into the situation, with phone calls to the superintendent as soon as he could be located. As expected, most of the unhappy teachers soon were making additional calls to the superintendent's office themselves. Tim and Jan debated whether to just remove the device but decided to let it ride and see where the train ended up. Within the hour, both were called to report to the superintendent to explain what they knew about the situation.

The superintendent, knowing he hadn't authorized the installation, and with suspicions that a clandestine operation had taken place, was also blessed with a sense of humor and laughed to the point of crying after hearing about all of the different reactions the camera had caused. When he was composed, he advised Jan to remove the camera as soon as possible, to avoid calls to the school board members. He also made both men promise not to reveal how the camera was installed, even though he thought the prank was well-thought-out and executed. It was decided to just go with an explanation that the security camera installers had installed the device by mistake.

Now once in a while, programs for students would involve Jan supplying props to gain the interest of fifth- and sixth-graders whose attention span was usually about three to five minutes. One such program involved discussions about operating vehicles while under the influence of alcohol or drugs.

One Friday, he and Tim had planned a DUI discussion for the sixth-grade students. Jan had recently bought a German Messerschmitt micro car. Because the car was only about six feet long and only two feet wide, he was able to maneuver it into the cafeteria, which also doubled as an auditorium. He thought the little car would help hold their attention for the lesson. The students crowded around the little car and had many questions. It had succeeded in keeping their attention for the entire duration of the lesson.

Jan used it to explain how a classic car could be fun and collectible, but only if they were taken care of, which involved a decision not to consume alcohol while driving. He explained that a mistake while intoxicated could destroy their car, their fun, and their future. The discussion was a popular one and was deemed a success.

The cafeteria floor was tiled, and being the cafeteria, it was kept spotlessly clean by the custodial staff on a daily basis. One of the older custodians, John Morganstein, who was well known as a bit of a sour apple and one who acted as though the school belonged to him alone, made mention that the program was interesting but that the vehicle had left a black tire mark on the floor where the front tires had been turned. In a most condescending tone, he indicated that he hoped in the future that any programs involving *his* cafeteria floor would be less intrusive involving marks to the floors.

Jan and Tim decided that since the superintendent laughed at the security camera incident and knew that the programs they were presenting were having a positive effect, they figured that John and the custodial staff should be indoctrinated into being better sports to programs that reached the students, even though it made a custodian or two unhappy.

That same weekend, Jan again brought his Messerschmitt to the school, and he and Tim maneuvered it again into the cafeteria. However, instead of pushing the vehicle, they had decided to actually drive the vehicle, and when inside the cafeteria, did starts and stops and turns, leaving as many tire marks as possible on the floors.

Monday morning brought the expected concerns of the principal in regard to the cafeteria floors. These concerns were relayed to the superintendent. The superintendent, again with strong suspicions of the real culprits, decided the easiest solution to the problem was to tell the principal he knew all about the floors and to advise John, the sour apple custodian, to bring them up to par prior to the day's lunch.

As lunch time approached, the superintendent met with both Jan and Tim and got the rest of the story. After a laugh, he asked them to give him a heads up the next time they had a plan to piss off half the staff of the school.

All three made it a point to approach John, the custodian, and re-mark just how good the cafeteria floors were looking. A point had been made. Strangely enough, in the future, John Morganstein became the most helpful custodian in setting up areas for youth programs, and Jan and Tim always assisted in the cleanups.

CHAPTER 46

Brotherly Love

Cedar Springs Police Department watched over a modest community which turned into a small metropolis in the summer months after the population tripled and even quadrupled. In the winter months, with the population reduced, the patrolmen sometimes had quite a bit of leisure time. Whenever leisure time became the norm, clever and imaginative members of the department devised irritating ways to aggravate other members.

It was abundantly clear that "everyone" was fair game for condemnation and criticism. As everyone knows, real-life stories are the best and also the easiest to promote jokes and ridicule. In order to be a member of the *Thick Blue Line*, one first had to have *thick blue skin*.

Such is the pensive and thoughtless humor of those who generally become numb to everyday grief or sorrow because they routinely witness to unimaginable acts of outrageous and cruel behavior by the seedy members of the public toward other members of the public.

Stand-up comedians often use their family members as fodder for their acts. They routinely share with the public and add stories to their acts reminiscing about their family members' quirky behavior at get-togethers, holiday dinners, weddings, and funerals.

In contrast, police officers have little or no patience with anyone other than themselves even speaking about their immediate family members. Under-the-breath promises of personal violence and injuries would spew forth whenever veiled threats or insults were remotely implies toward an officer's family from the general public. It was well documented that not unlike the old "Italian Family" business associates, cops felt that if someone had a problem with them, the problem was with them and never with their families.

Knowing their fellow members could at a moment's notice invent some sordid tale about them, all girlfriends and wives were advised as soon as possible never to believe or accept anything as 100% factual if that information was being relayed by another member of their boyfriends or husband's squad.

Of course, this was before individual ownership of cell phones, and the advice was helpful when girlfriends or wives would telephone the station asking to speak to or to have the patrolman call them back.

On most occasions, the caller would be asked if there was some type of emergency taking place just in case a legitimate need was warranted. If told that it was just a routine call, the devious minds of "friends" would take control and the caller would be told with the perfectly practiced bit of hesitation that the patrolman in question had called out sick and was not there or had left early due to an expressed family emergency.

Adding fuel to the fire, the patrolman in question was never told of the call for at least an hour or two, and sometimes not at all, and would then have the pleasure of having to explain the whole and somewhat complex sense of humor of the department members.

Additionally the "after the fact" verification of the patrolman's presence later in the shift or the following day could never be a guarantee to the wife or girlfriend that the reported absence had not really taken place and was not now being covered up. Successes were measured by how much grief was caused in the relationship and how irritated the fellow patrolmen became because of it.

Domestic quarrels as a result of these no-show accounts were always looked upon as victories for the *Thick Blue Line* and ultimately just part of the game. As history invariably repeats itself, victims would always look forward to hiring of new people so that they could also impart a bit of their past misery onto a rookie and their loved one.

CHAPTER 47

The Wedding

Police, not unlike comedians tossing "fat mother" jokes back and forth between themselves, have no qualms about and actually look forward to making fun of other police officers' families. Brothers, sisters, wives, mothers, and of course mothers-in-law are the most often referred to. On the other-other hand, the children of cops would always be completely off-limits, as one could never tell how their own may turn out.

It was not uncommon for an officer, when asked to be the best man at another officer's wedding, to concede that another opportunity to cause some type of embarrassment had probably just presented itself, regardless of personal feelings toward the groom or the bride.

After all, how often does one get the chance to be a part of a group dedicated to completely devastating and embarrassing a fellow employee who has decided to spend the rest of their lives or maybe just the next few years with someone who will never understand the complexities of the fellowship of police officers?

Best of all, although most of the guests and family members at least on the bride's side, would be horrified and appalled by the groom's "friends" behavior, they would probably never utter an objection, as they would know that the appalling procrastinators were all cops, and they would be unsure if they should even complain solely just because of that fact.

One such occasion took place when a fairly new member of the department, Joey Castillano, another transplanted nice Italian boy from a prominently Italian family just outside of Philadelphia, decided he was going to get married. Joey had heard of some of the stories of disruptive behavior at police weddings that had taken place in past years but had convinced himself that they were a thing of the past.

With an alternate plan in mind, and not wanting to insult his fellow employees, Joey explained to everyone that his brother was to be his best man, and all the ushers were going to be friends he had attended college with. He explained that they had all made a pact that they would all attend and participate in each other's weddings.

His prospective bride was a somewhat innocent Irish Catholic girl, not very familiar with the inner workings of a real police department. Joey had given her the impression that all the men down at the station were "good guys" and that even though some might come off as a bit rough, they should all still be invited to the wedding so as to not insult anyone.

Deciding to hold the wedding out of town and in the old neighborhood and in another state would, he hoped, limit the attendance and/ or disruptions, should any be brought on by his buddies and fellow employees--that, and the fact that most of his family and guests were well-respected members of the Italian community whose last names all ended in a vowel. Most importantly, he hoped, was the fact that they probably would not appreciate any police interference or hijinks at his wedding.

"Besides," Joey said to his fiancée, "most of the guys will have to stay in town to work."

Mary, the bride, took this as gospel and planned a typical lavish and expensive Irish Catholic wedding with eight bridesmaids, eight ushers, and a formal catered reception with almost four hundred people invited. At that time, Cedar Springs was only a thirty-man department. Joey figured that at the most, only half that number would attend. Of course, with wedding gifts expected, he cut the half in half again figuring a lot of guys would be too cheap to buy a gift. Joey thought maybe five or six guys.

What could go wrong?

Three weeks before the wedding, preparations were made, invitations had been sent and over three hundred RSVPs were returned--except none were returned by any members of the department. Not even Joey's squad members had bothered to mention whether they had received the original invitations.

Not one member of the department so much as brought up the fact that Joey was supposed to be married. Whatever the plan was, the *Thick Blue Line* was indeed in full bloom, and either a plan was in place, or Joey and/or his bride to be, were really not liked very much.

Two weeks before the wedding, Joey was convinced that no one from the department was going to come to his wedding, and he had spent the better part of the last few days trying to come up with a reason he was being snubbed. Already disappointed, he decided not to even ask any of them for a reason. He was even considering looking for different employment after his honeymoon.

What Joey didn't know was that his friend and fellow squad member, Angelo, now a seasoned department employee, quick-witted and eager to add to his reputation as a folk hero, had contacted Joey's father and uncle, who were acquaintances of Angelo's immediate family, and had suggested some scenarios that they all agreed they wanted to include in the ceremony.

Joey's father, himself a bit of a practical joker, agreed, as long as the priest who was to conduct the ceremony was informed and also agreed. That, and of course that the ceremony was ultimately deemed legitimate and legal.

Joey's uncle Leo, wanting to add to the mêlée, even suggested that Joey be taken out a few nights before the wedding by a couple of his boys and informed that "the family" was concerned about the possibility of a police presence at the wedding and be warned that no unauthorized investigations or interrogations should even remotely take place.

Three days to go. Joey was now completely on edge but somewhat comforted by the fact that no one from the department had indicated they were going to come. The wedding was proceeding on schedule.

It indeed was a beautiful celebration with plenty of flowers and gowns and tuxedos. Organ music accompanied by two violins filled the cathedral as guests were expertly escorted by ushers to their respective seats. The church filled. Joey was nervous, yet relieved that no cops had shown to cause any anguish to his family. The bride was walked down the aisle by her father with pomp and circumstance, and given over to

Joey to be wed.

All wedding procedures were strictly and quite seriously followed, which eventually led to the bride and groom staring each other in the face with expectations of marital bliss, each eager to take the final vows of holy matrimony.

This was probably going to be the most momentous and historical saga to be chronicled in the history of departmental sagas. Just as the priest, Father Anthony was paging through his wedding book and ready to proceed with the final components of the ceremony, the church doors opened, and in walked sixteen members of the department, along with wives and/or girlfriends.

Sixteen members of the department had successfully kept secret not only their plans to attend but had traveled together and entered the church all at the same time, much to the surprise of Joey, the horror of his bride, and to the delight of the department members and Joey's father and uncles.

Actually, the bride's father was informed of the plan by Joey's uncle, and while he did not necessarily agree, he was too uncomfortable to disagree, having been told there would be no discussion about it.

As expected, the proceedings came to a complete halt as the cops filled three rows on the groom's side, each showing as little emotion as possible. After a few minutes of discreet and not-so-discreet murmurings from the other guests, the ceremony continued, with the bride eyeing Joey with disparagement and Joey now just hoping for the best.

Father Anthony, being part of the charade, was doing his best to refrain from laughter and began by asking all in attendance if anyone had reason why these two beautiful, loving individuals should not be joined together as husband and wife and if so, to speak now or forever hold their peace.

Now this is usually followed by an awkward silence or a few whispers, and then the actual wedding vows to follow. This particular wedding was clearly an exception, as all sixteen members, as well as most of their wives and girlfriends, stood up and responded in unison,

"Yes! We do!"

This was followed by a unusually long, awkward silence as the bride alarmingly looked at Joey and a clearly distressed and devastated

Joey looked at his fellow employees, then at his bride, and then at his father and uncles who were now all smiling or laughing, and then at his bride's father, who was also laughing, and finally at Father Anthony, who was also laughing and exclaimed, "What the fu…uu….uu….!"

Yup, Joey almost dropped the F-bomb in church but caught himself at the last moment. Soon after, he began to notice that almost everyone in the church was now laughing as Father Anthony explained that unfortunately he too was part of the prank.

Following Father Anthony's explanation, all sixteen members of the department, along with wives and girlfriends, took a congratulatory bow of thanks, which was followed by the hearty applause of more than three hundred people.

Ten minutes later, the same question was asked again with the sought-after results, and the two were officially wed.

Once outside the church, Joey got the whole story, including the planning by his fellow employees, his father, the bride's father, and Father Anthony. It was decided by all that the prank was well worth the trouble and would be recorded for posterity by the wedding photographer who had captured most of the surprised, confused, angry, and relieved expressions on the couple's faces.

This of course had no useful purpose other than public humiliation toward the groom, or to have something to use as an "I told you so" if the couple should separate or divorce in the future.

Five years later, some of the wedding photos would resurface around the department building walls, complete with added quotes of "Should have listened to the crowd" or "We tried to tell you," and much more, following the announcement that the happy couple had decided to divorce.

CHAPTER 48

Morris, Maggie, and Ma

Cedar Springs in the late 1940s and early 1950s resembled a rural farming area, with two small communities, with borders on both the Atlantic Ocean and the Delaware Bay. Most houses were small bungalows, and most streets were unpaved or coated with oil and stone. While it did have plenty of alcohol-serving establishments, there was no form of public transportation, with the exception of a bus that ran once or twice a day up and down the county road that ran through the middle of the communities. However, in the mid- 1950s, the town got a taxi cab driven by a woman.

The woman, Gertrude Wilson, was a bit of a bar fly in her thirties. Only about four foot eight and 100 pounds, she had the distinction of having breasts which were more suited to a woman twice her size. Always playing up to men in the bars Gertrude became known as "Ma." It was rumored that Ma's popularity became widespread and admired by many men because she welcomed them into the bosom of her personality, and that personality was her actual bosom. Gertrude had married young and divorced young. It was said that she could not seem to concentrate on just one man for any length of time. Her husband left her with a five-year-old baby girl named Maggie, a 1939 Chevy, and not much more.

To earn a living, or at least enough money to pay the rent and have a few drinks, she began to advertise that she would give rides home to some of the more dedicated bar patrons for a small fee. The service became fairly successful, as it was rumored that she provided a bit more than just a ride home.

In time, Gertrude sold the old Chevy and purchased a second-hand cab. The cab was an old checker model purchased from an Atlantic City fleet. Now a legitimate taxi service, Ma provided citizens with a means of transportation for a reasonable fee. It was true that most of her business took place at night, traveling from one bar to the next, but it was a business nonetheless. Not having any relatives in the area to watch the child, when Maggie was not in school, Ma usually brought her along when she drove the cab.

In the early 1950s, it became difficult to keep the Checker running, buy food and clothes, and pay rent. Being an opportunist as well as not much of a mother, Ma began to encourage monetary tips for extra services on the rides. In short time she began to be known as the Wilson bank, as it was reported that for a fee, she regularly received night deposits. Regrettably, she eventually began to allow some of the men to spend time with Maggie. This of course was not advertised but through word of mouth. Maggie began to be quite infamous within the county. By the time she was twelve, she had become a full-fledged child prostitute, usually turning tricks in exchange for money or a free ride or two in the cab when finances were tight and directed to do so by Ma.

Around 1965, Maggie was then seventeen years old. As a frequent visitor to the taverns, she met a local carpenter named Morris Frontier, well known around town as a hard worker but one with a drinking problem. Today Morris would be known as a functioning alcoholic. For years, Morris worked from seven in the morning to four or five at night and was usually drunk by six p.m. Morris was a regular at one of the main taverns that Maggie and Ma visited in business and on a personal level.

Now if truth be told, neither Morris nor Maggie was much to look at, but as the old saying goes, they both looked pretty good to each other around two in the morning and soon began a relationship. It was explained to Morris by Ma that Maggie had specific business ventures that she had to participate in so that she and her mother could survive. Morris never seemed to mind, as long as he got his time with Maggie included.

Over the next few years, Morris moved into the small bungalow with Maggie and Ma. By the late 1960s, they had all become stone-cold alcoholics. Ma had lost her license for drunk driving, and the checker was eventually sold to help pay expenses. Maggie had gained enough weight to signal a severe decline in the demand for her services, so the two women were now dependent on Morris to survive. By the mid-1970s, they had finally figured out that it was much less expensive to drink at home than in the taverns.

The department members had come to know the three "M's" as "regulars" and considered them fairly harmless, with the exception of an occasional domestic argument at the house. No one was thrilled to have to respond to a domestic at the Wilson-Frontiers. It was a given that all three would be intoxicated to the point that they couldn't remember what the police had been called for in the first place and were also unable to comprehend anything the police told them to do or not to do.

The arguments usually centered on either Morris or Ma. Morris, as quiet and respectful as he could be when he was sober, could be an argumentative handful who was also strong as an ox when he was drunk. Ma, now in her in her early sixties but looking to be in her late seventies from years of alcohol, tobacco, and hard living, seemed to continually complain about almost anything and everything. Maggie seemed to be able to ignore both of them, seemingly enjoying drinking and watching television.

It became a rite of passage for every new hire to be indoctrinated into *real* police work by answering one of the many calls for assistance at Ma's. Ma was the usual caller to the police. Her requests could be any number of things but mostly involved telling whatever dispatcher she talked to that Morris was drunk and was being mean to her. The real story usually amounted to all three were drunk, Morris was trying to romance Maggie and Ma, thinking it was twenty-five years earlier, wanted to keep him away from her daughter because she hadn't been paid her fee.

Maggie would typically be attired in a dirty, worn-out, flimsy house dress. Morris would be in whatever he wore to work that day and Ma, shrunk down to around four foot six and no more than eighty pounds, always seemed to wear a washed-out, threadbare, and nearly see-through nightgown for the last ten years. With the now cartoon-like breasts hanging down to her waist and thinning, stringy hair, she had managed to lose most of her teeth, with the exception of one prominent front upper tooth. Besides Ma, she became known as "Ole Snaggletooth."

The house was always in shambles and smelled like a combination of sweat, dirty clothing, fish, leftover food, and urine. This was one home that no matter what had happened, or what the weather, you never, ever entered the front door...at least not more than once. When answering a call at the Wilson-Frontier home, no matter who answered the door, the first thing they did was invite the officer in. New officers usually took the plunge the first visit and swore to repay the favor onto the next new hire. It was not unusual for an officer to stop at a store and spray themselves down with insect spray following a call there.

The usual method of taking care of any problems was to request Morris leave the property for the night. For the first few years, this worked, and he would get a motel room or go to a co-worker's house for the night. As he got older, the functioning part of his alcoholism was diminishing, and daily work became sporadic. With less income, he was also less prone to leave and go to a motel, and co-workers were less accommodating. Occasionally Morris would be arrested after re-fusing to leave the house, but nobody really ever wanted to arrest him. When he was sober, he was a really nice guy. A nice guy who took a really wrong turn in life getting involved with Maggie and Ma, but still a nice guy. Most patrolmen would ultimately speak with the judge and urge that no fines be incurred.

The three M's got to be such regulars they occasionally would call certain dispatchers just for someone to talk to. Maggie, the most fre-quent caller, would ask about the department and inquire if things in general around town were okay. If not too busy, some of the dispatch-ers, especially Dooley, would talk to her for a few minutes. It got to a point that Maggie came to know Dooley's schedule and would call just to say hello about once a week. Most calls were simple conversations, but a few would be cut short by Dooley as it became immediately clear when she was overly intoxicated.

One memorable evening, Dooley and The Crazy Squad were on duty. The day was declared by the calendar as the first day of spring that year. The three "M's" were getting on in age and seemed to have less and less domestics. Ma was bedridden most of the time, and Morris was beginning to have some medical problems. Any holiday or public celebrations were usually heydays for those who enjoyed drinking including the Wilson-Frontiers. This particular evening, a call from Maggie came in to the station. Dooley identified himself and the department and after listening for a moment immediately recognized the caller and said, "Well hi, Maggie. How's it going?

Maggie, clearly intoxicated, slowly said, "Mr. O'Doul, its Maggie. I'm okay. I don't want to bother you, but I just wanted you to know it must be springtime, cause Morris just pissed in my ass!"

Dooley almost used to outburst by any of the three M's, said, "Well, I appreciate the heads up on the weather Maggie. You and Morris take care of things over there. Tell Ma we said hello, and have a good night."

CHAPTER 49

The Blue Crab DUI Patrol

In the mid-1980s, after being barraged by MADD (Mothers Against Drunk Drivers), it was decided that it would be beneficial to the citizens of the entire country to begin a government-sponsored program that would provide DUI (Driving Under the Influence) earmarked monies to municipalities. These grants would cover the costs of overtime pay to police officers to patrol their respective areas and investigate erratic drivers to see if they were driving while under the influence of alcohol or drugs.

This funding would continue as long as the municipality continued to prosecute drivers guilty of driving under the influence of alcohol or drugs. Cedar Springs applied for and was approved for this grant money and began weekend patrols solely for the purpose of arresting suspected impaired drivers.

On a cold, blustery February night with temperatures below freezing and winds gusting up to thirty-five miles per hour, the Saturday night DUI patrol consisted of Sergeant Big Ben Bailey and Patrolman Mike Harding.

Neither man was especially gung-ho on finding drunk drivers, but the overtime pay was a lucrative incentive to volunteer, drive around, and stop a few cars. As long as one of the other patrolmen on duty didn't find somebody driving around intoxicated and call them to take over, it was an easy extra $100 in their next paycheck.

Ben and Mike made the usual drive-a rounds in the neighborhood bar areas, and both had decided that they would stay until 4:00 a.m. and call it a successful night, and one that the good citizens of Cedar Springs had decided to behave themselves in.

At around 2:00 a.m., the dispatcher reported to the cars that an erratically operated vehicle was driving at high speeds in one of the neighboring towns. This information was strictly to alert the town's cars in case the vehicle traveled into Cedar Springs or if they were asked to assist the other jurisdiction's patrols.

One of the roads in town, County Rt. 350, actually passed through three different jurisdictions, one of them being Cedar Springs. The road was approximately three miles long and more or less entirely straight, beginning at an intersection and ending at a dead end. The dead end was actually a beach at the end of the peninsula. The first two miles of roadway were located in two different municipalities. The beach and about the last mile of roadway and lands adjacent to it were located in the jurisdiction of Cedar Springs.

The end of the roadway was equipped with a wooden barrier similar to those on the edges of curves on highways with posts buried in the sand and was located about twenty feet past the end of the paved road. There was also a light post, complete with a blinking yellow light, to notify drivers and make them aware that the road stopped. There was an adjacent parking lot for two gift shops that sold tourists trinkets, hats, coffee cups, and the like.

The beach area located past the barrier was approximately 100 feet of sand and worn gravel leading to the water's edge. This particular area of beach was where the ocean waters met the bay waters. The surf here always displayed great turbulence and sometimes violent waves due to the extended and unyielding ocean and bay currents battling against each other.

Numerous signs stating *no bathing allowed* were posted on the beaches, warning people of the dangerous surf with scientific explanations of water depths, tides, wind directions, velocities, and temperature changes which supposedly described the undertows and the likelihood of drowning in the area. It was often expressed by visitors that plain "Don't go in the Water!" signs would have been easier and more appropriate.

There was permitted swimming several hundred yards to either side of the area, but summer bathers usually steered very clear of this general particular area. Even in the allotted bathing areas, one had to be ever vigilant because the waters dropped off rather dramatically, some after only about ten feet and even good swimmers could easily be pulled away from shore by currents in a short period of time.

Another radio transmission indicated that the erratic driver had been racing through the neighboring towns for the past fifteen to twenty minutes. It was reported that the vehicle was described as a mid-size light-blue or light-green sedan with a white top, driven by a white male. It was also reported that the driver could possibly be headed toward the Cedar Springs jurisdiction.

Thinking that a high-speed chase could be interesting and take up most of the remaining DUI patrol time, Ben and Mike decided to head toward the neighboring town in hopes of possibly seeing and maybe even getting involved in some of the action. Chases usually lasted only a very few minutes. The saying was true, that one could outrun the police car, but one could not outrun the police radio. However, if the chase ended in a car crash or an arrest of a subject who resisted, the time spent watching the events could easily last an hour or two, which would take them to the end of their detail.

Ben had radioed to the dispatcher that he would be changing his radio frequency to that of the neighboring town, in order to get a first-hand account of the speeding vehicle. Being a sergeant, it was assured that no one at 2:00 a.m. was going to advise him that he could not go into another jurisdiction to see what was going on. Secondly, he technically was on the DUI patrol detail, and chances were that the vehicle in question was being operated by someone under the influence of something.

Mike was just happy to have been at the right place at the right time and thought this could turn into a situation that could be talked about for some time. He actually thought that with a bit of coaxing, he could probably get Ben to slap the driver around, grab him by the throat and make him "do the ole John Barleycorn" if he could convince him that the driver had insulted Ben's wife or one of his daughters.

The vehicle was now being chased several blocks away from Ben and Mike's location and seemed to be headed their way. Mike, who was driving, suggested heading to Rt. 350 in case it headed that way. Ben agreed.

Radio transmissions indicated that the suspect vehicle was now being pursued by two patrol cars and had turned onto Rt. 350 and was now headed south toward the dead end in Cedar Springs' jurisdiction. Ben and Mike were now only a couple of blocks away. As they approached Rt. 350, they saw a mid-size light-green vehicle traveling at what seemed to be a high rate of speed, being followed by two patrol cars with lights and sirens blaring.

As they turned onto Rt. 350, they saw the suspect make a sharp right-hand turn onto a side street and head west. The pursuit vehicles reported that the subject had been and was traveling up and down side streets, ignoring stop signs and failing to slow down. Ben suggested that they slow down and get ready to turn around to assist with the pursuit.

Ben said, "He's either going to keep heading west, and travel into Cedar Springs or go around a few blocks and come back onto Rt. 350. Either way, if we stay around the general area, we should be able to get close enough to him, to get in on it."

Just then, the suspect vehicle re-entered Rt. 350, just like Ben had predicted, and headed south directly in front of Ben and Mike. By coincidence and the fact that the suspect was so far ahead of the pursuit patrol cars, Ben and Mike were now directly behind the vehicle, which was now accelerating quickly. Mike told Ben that he thought he recognized the vehicle that belonged to a local youth (Johnny Sullivan), who lived in the area.

Mike said, "If that's who I think it is, he's going to head south and turn right onto Maple Road, where he was last living with his mother."

The suspect accelerated to almost 90 mph and Mike was able to stay fairly close. Ben, with nails digging into the dashboard, warned Mike that they would be in world of shit if the suspect decided to stop quickly.

Just at that moment, the suspect's brake lights came on, and the rear of his car quickly approached the front of the patrol vehicle.

Smoke from the squealing tires of the fast-braking vehicle made it almost impossible to see if they were going to collide. Just as quickly, the suspect re-accelerated.

Ben, with a look of "I almost shit my pants," told Mike, "We better not wreck this car, or The Rude will have both our asses."

After regaining his composure, Mike accelerated to resume the chase when, as they had expected, the suspect made a skidding, sliding right-hand turn onto Maple Road. It was mutually expected that if the suspect was who they thought he was, that he would turn in to his mother's yard, and either try to run or try to hide, or try to do both. When the suspect got near the Sullivan home, he began to slow slightly, but instead of turning into the yard, he quickly accelerated down the road.

Now Ben and Mike had gotten close enough to verify the license number, which after a check, did in fact come back registered to John Sullivan. John had grown up in the area and had been known to drink in excess at times and it was deduced that this was more than likely one of these times with the exception that this night so far, was more exciting than most for both Johnny and the police.

Johnny, or whoever was driving his car, was proving to be a worthy opponent considering his car was a four-door sedan, approximately 15-20 years old, nothing special to look at, but was outperforming all the patrol cars that were in pursuit. Johnny drove to the end of Maple, then around several blocks, heading north and eventually getting back onto Rt. 350 heading south once again.

Mike was still following but at a more respectful distance, mostly to satisfy Ben. The other jurisdiction's patrol cars were still in pursuit, but Ben and Mike were now considered, because of their position, the primary chase vehicle.

Procedures stated the primary chase vehicle was responsible to make decisions to continue or terminate the chase due to the amount of safety that was present or not present. The chase was one which today would have been terminated long ago, after the speed limit was exceeded. In this instance, neither Ben nor Mike had yet even considered calling it off.

Suddenly, Johnny's car lights went out. At first, it was thought that maybe he had suffered some type of electrical problem which would cause him to stop, but he continued to accelerate well past 100 mph.

Ben and Mike knew that the roadway continued only for about another half mile and then it came to the dead-end barrier. Mike could now see the blinking yellow light. Ben begged Mike to slow down, as there were no other roads for Johnny to turn off onto.

Ben said that they and the other patrol vehicles could simply block the roadway near the dead end, preventing the continuation of the chase when Johnny slowed to turn around.

Mike had only a second to consider this, when he realized that Johnny had actually increased his speed and was now pulling away from him.

Mike said, "He's not slowing down."

Ben then said, "He's not slowing down."

Two to three seconds later, Mike and Ben both said, "He's not slowing down."

Fast approaching the end of the road, with the blinking yellow light getting brighter, Mike began to brake. Johnny's lights suddenly came back on again and for a split second, Mike and Ben both thought this was a sign that he also realized the road was coming to an end and he was going to stop.

When his speed continued, and he was reaching the end of the road, Mike said, "He's not fucking stopping."

Ben then said, "He's not... Holy shit!."

Both Ben and Mike watched as Johnny's car continued on, crashing through the wood barrier. Sparks and wood flew in the air from the barrier, which hardly seemed to slow the car.

What it did do was cause it to become airborne. After basically flying for almost 50 feet, the car hit the sandy beach and continued on, with engine racing, straight into the unruly surf. The car finally came to a stop approximately fifteen feet into the water, where it bobbed for a few seconds and then quickly began to sink into the three-to-four-foot waves, with tail lights still on and one turn signal blinking.

Ben and Mike stopped at the smashed barrier and ran to the edge of the water. The winds were especially cold and powerful, causing the sand to blow into small tornado-like shapes, which had the effect of almost sandblasting one's face. Within a matter of three to four minutes after hitting the water, the vehicle was now more than half submerged in the surf. The engine had died shortly after hitting the water, and no movements could be seen inside the car.

They could see the rear window had blown out on impact, but it was impossible to see if any of the other windows were open or were even still intact. Because of the knowledge of the currents combined with the high winds and high waves, it was also unreasonable and irrational to imagine any type of physical rescue.

It was actually universally understood to not only Ben and Mike but to all the cops at the scene that if someone was stupid enough to drive his car through a wooden barrier, across a beach, and into the raging waters of the ocean and bay, in temperatures close to or below freezing, he would have no expectation of a rescue, nor would the witnessing onlookers believe he should deserve or receive one.

Nonetheless, a physical as well as visual search was undertaken in and around the general area and also up and down the beach in both directions without any sign of Johnny or anybody whatsoever. After about twenty minutes with no sign of Johnny or whoever the driver was, it was assumed that they were still inside the vehicle.

A specialized four-wheel-drive tow truck designed to operate on the sand was called; It was driven by a local man who also had been known to have diving experience in the local waters for some time. After rescuing Jan and the Chevy Suburban from the ocean a couple of years earlier, it was decided he was the obvious choice for the job. Dressed in a wet suit, complete with nylon rope tied around his waist, he ventured into the relentless, turbulent surf just far enough to hook a line onto the rear of the partially submerged vehicle, which thankfully was equipped with a tow bar accessory.

The vehicle, after several minutes of hesitation and uncertainty, slowly began to move in reverse and out of the surf and onto the beach. It was pulled approximately 20 feet onto the beach and when approached by Mike and Ben, the first thing they noticed that after only a short time in the surf, there was approximately three feet of gravelly sand inside the entire vehicle.

The front windshield was also missing, but all four doors were still closed, with windows intact. The original thought was that Johnny was under the three feet of sand, but after some initial scooping, it was found that there were no bodies inside the vehicle.

Either Johnny had somehow jumped out of the vehicle at over

100 mph, tuck-n-rolled without getting hurt, and had escaped, or had waited until he hit the water, somehow swam out the windshield into the surf and away from the vehicle without being seen and without leaving footprints in the wet sand after leaving the water.

The other scenario was that the impact of the barrier followed by the impact of the water severely injured or killed Johnny and the turbulence of the waves and currents had forced the body out of the windshield and into the violent unstable waters, where the body was taken out to sea or quickly buried in the surf sand.

The search for Johnny continued for the next few hours, along with confirmation from Mrs. Sullivan, Johnny's mother, that he had left the house earlier in the evening in a bad mood after an argument with his girlfriend.

Experience deduced that a body would surface in a day or two, usually within several miles of the incident, depending on the winds and tide tables. This particular incident was not only bizarre in itself, but the puzzle continued when after several weeks no driver's body ever surfaced. Days turned to weeks and then to months with no sign of any body. Additionally, no indication of a John Sullivan survival was ever produced.

Ben and Mike didn't get a drunk driver that night. They did, however, receive many pictures of submerged vehicles and several fake indictments for conducting an illegal high- speed chase, violating the civil rights of the unknown driver, figuring that whoever it was, they probably had had some type of rights that probably had been violated and the icing on the cake, a fake complaint charging them with vehicular manslaughter, unlawfully disposing of a body without a permit, and pollution of the ocean waters.

It was universally agreed that no one would be eating the local blue crabs the following season, as they were referred to as "Johnny Crabs." Ben and Mike also ended up being responsible to do an actual accident report since the final crash took place in Cedar Springs' jurisdiction.

The final report indicated a "possible fatality" of a "possibly identified driver." The accident report was filed as one of only a very few in existence as an "open" case and one that would be required to remain open until a driver could be produced.

CHAPTER 50

Flash-n-Flush

116

Prior to Pinochle Pete becoming the leader of The Crazy Squad, he spent some time assigned to the detective bureau with his brother Lead Legs, and Angelo Demucchi, who had then returned from the County Task Force.

Upon Angelo's return, it was rumored and circulated by Angelo, that the pretense for his departure from the Task Force was due to the fact that the others on the Force had continually been outshined by him, and they collectively requested his demise. It was probably more accurate to assume that they had all gotten tired of hearing his Woodstock stories and how he was invited to pal around with Arlo Guthrie for two days, which in truth probably never really happened. Of course, Arlo would be the only one to confirm or deny that allegation, and how many people would have the opportunity to personally ask Arlo Guthrie about it? Also, remembering and judging from Arlo's appearance and demeanor in the Woodstock movie, it was assumed he probably wouldn't remember anyway.

At any rate, while in detectives, Pete and Angelo would receive information from informants concerning people who would have drugs for sale in their homes. Of course, this information was offered solely because the informants had somehow been taken advantage of by these so-called dealers, usually by way of purchasing drugs of very low or non- existent potency. The other manner information was received was through a person who had just been arrested and was looking for any way to soften the punishment they knew was coming.

The best way to lessen one's fines or sentence was to supply the police with information about someone else and then hope that the officer who got that information would mention the fact that you had been instrumental in the investigation and arrest of that other individual. In the old days of law enforcement, this procedure was called "being a rat." Today the expression "rat" is looked upon as inconsiderate and politically incorrect. To satisfy those who strive to find fault with anything that takes place in the public domain, a much softer and politically correct phrase that is now utilized is being a "CI," or confidential informant.

The truth was that normally only about one percent of the confidential information that was supplied was solid enough to utilize on its own, and it would have to be investigated and substantiated before it could be used as justification to legally infringe on anyone's rights.

Substantiating the information would normally mean that one had received the same information from several different people. Following that, the police would have to acquire permission from their administrators for manpower to set up surveillance to prove evidence of unusual traffic coming and going from the particular location. When that was done, they would then have to compile all the information into a clear and comprehensible packet and present it to a judge just to see if they agreed that there was enough evidence to obtain a search warrant. All very costly and time-consuming, which was the main reason very few drug arrests were or are made.

Pete, having a motivated and inventive personality, came up with a program that successfully reduced the quantity of illegal drugs in the community and caused many drug dealers to vacate or re-locate their businesses through a technique that came to be called "Flash-n-Flush."

Pete figured that because it was so difficult to actually arrest these individuals, the next best thing to do would be to simply scare them into thinking they were in immediate danger of being arrested. The usual and anticipated result of this fear would be the urgency to flush the contraband down their toilets. The procedure was done on an infrequent basis on various locations and individuals that were known to intentionally sell drugs.

Pete and Angelo would go in one car, Lead Legs in another, and when available, with the right individual who understood the procedure, a uniformed patrolman would participate. With precise timing, and lots of lights, sirens, tire-screeching, and car-door- slamming, they would all converge upon the house in question, quickly covering the doors as though an actual search warrant was being served.

Pete would always go to the front, loudly banging on the door while screaming, "Police!!! Come to the door!"

Now, no television cop show-watching individual would construe this as a prerequisite to a real search warrant, but people who dealt in illegal drug sales were always paranoid, and many later on reportedly stated that it "scared the bejeezus" out of them.

Heavy footsteps inside the house would always follow. Occasionally shades or curtains would be pulled back, followed by more heavy footsteps, mumbled curses, and even more heavy footsteps. The longer it took for someone to come to the door, the better chance there was that they were trying to get rid of their supplies. The sound of toilets flushing was a most satisfying thing.

When someone finally answered the door, Pete would officially say that they had received a report of some type of disturbance in the neighborhood and they were checking the general area. An almost guaranteed response would be that "they" weren't aware of any problems and Pete would say, "Well, we sure are sorry for any inconvenience. If you see or hear anything unusual in the area, please give the station a call."

When his act came to an end, Pete would call for everyone involved to return to their cars. It was reported on many occasions that Flash-n-Flush successfully caused a great deal of drugs to be relocated to the Cedar Springs municipal water treatment plant.

On one particularly extraordinary Flash-n-Flush, Angelo and Lead Legs were stationed at the back door of a well-known residence that was notorious for marijuana sales. While Pete was busy yelling and pounding on the front door awaiting a response, a familiar and renowned individual known to be highly involved in pot sales flung open the rear door and ran straight into the arms of Angelo, carrying a still smoldering glass bong pipe in one hand and almost a half-pound of pot in the other.

CHAPTER 51

Nicky and the Break-ins

As with any group of more than a dozen people, some of them will be a bit more peculiar than others either because they have been raised differently, educated differently, trained differently, or were just different.

Nicky Harlow was one of the patrolmen hired in the early days. Quirky would be a straightforward and simple way to describe Nicky. No one ever knew exactly what his IQ was, but everyone believed that it had to be a very high number. It was probably too high to be a cop, as he always seemed to be thinking about or analyzing the situation prior to taking any action. Whenever new technology was offered to the public, Nicky was the first one to have it or had already constructed something similar to it at home. Nicky was the kind of guy who could make a printer out of a toaster and an adding machine.

All of almost 100 pounds on a 5 foot 7 in frame, he was famous for appearing to be the least able member of the department to be involved in any physical altercation, but also known for never backing down to threats and usually the first to return a punch while making an arrest of an unwilling arrestee.

It was not unusual to see Nicky being literally thrown several feet away from a suspect, by the suspect. Following an Elvis-like lip snarl, a distinct snort and clearing of his throat, Nicky would be quick to return to the mêlée and convince the suspect, using direct finger force on pressure points that were known to cause the most amount of discomfort possible, that they had mistakenly tossed aside the wrong person.

As determined as he was to be respected while in uniform, Nicky was also fond of ingesting large amounts of alcohol when off duty and not in uniform. This didn't seem to have any effect on his policing duties until late in his career, when he decided that he wanted to drink a lot more than he wanted to be a cop and eventually resigned just prior to being asked to leave.

Nicky was assigned to the detective bureau for several years. He would utilize his "equipment allowance" (extra monies given to plain clothes employees to maintain a professional appearance), to buy electronic equipment and then buy his clothing at the local JC Penney's boys' department where he could find cheaper clothes that fit without being altered.

Nicky was instrumental in plotting out some of the more ingenious acts of interdepartmental terrorism through the years. One of the more imaginative acts happened when person or persons unknown apparently made several unauthorized entrances to The Rude's office on numerous occasions.

One would think that an incident such as that would not be too difficult to investigate in a police station. However, the Thick Blue Line was in force, and the actual culprits--and especially the creativeness of how it was accomplished--were not divulged until many years later.

The offices in the police building were outfitted with steel doors hinged to steel door frames installed in solid concrete block walls and were equipped with special locks said to be impenetrable. The keys were specially made and resembled small sword-like pieces of stainless steel with several small indentations on both sides of the shaft.

The indentations corresponded with small spring-loaded ball bearing pins inside the lock; when the key was inserted, the ball bearings in the lock would settle into the indentations of the key, which would then release the locking mechanisms.

Picking these types of locks was said to be impossible, as there were several ball bearings which needed to settle into all of the indentations all at the same time. Added to that, all were in irregular locations and not inline in a row like conventional locks. Copies of the keys could be gotten only through the lock manufacturers, and it was said that other than the custodian, The Rude had the only copy to his office.

It was also a well-known fact that The Rude was a bit anal and liked things placed on his desk in particular places, and no one could remember ever seeing things out of place when being summoned to see him. In fact, no one could remember ever seeing anything on the chief's desk other than a phone, blotter, stapler, pen and pencil set, and of course an ashtray usually half full of cigarette butts, and all of them always in the same spots.

It was decided by the culprits that it would be a good idea to somehow get into the chief's office at night and just slightly move things around on his desk. The culprits decided not to do a full blown rearrangement, but just move the stapler or phone or pen set a few inches to one side or the other.

They knew the chief would assume the custodian had moved the items and would return them to their respective places. This was a reasonable assumption but could account for only one day per week. The plan was to rearrange things more than one day per week.

To add to the experience, it was also decided that this scenario should be repeated for several days, then not take place for a day, and then resume again for a few more days. The arrangements were discussed for a few days and then pretty much forgotten due to the complexity of the locks.

About a month later, it became known that The Rude made it a point to inquire as to whether or not Captain Benny or anyone else had been in his office for any reason.

Because Benny was obviously not privy to the prank, his answer was always negative. This was also prior to security cameras planted everywhere, so there was no evidence to investigate concerning the incidents.

After several weeks, The Rude asked the custodian for his key, stating he no longer wanted his office cleaned. He then instructed the captain to meet with each squad, inquiring as to whether anyone had any information on the intrusions, all with the expected negative results.

It was clear to everyone, including The Rude and now Captain Benny, that someone within the department was probably responsible but had no idea how the entries were being accomplished. Still the disruptions to the desk items continued. A call by Benny to the lock manufacturer resulted in their guarantee that their locks could not be picked and that they had not been contacted to manufacture any additional keys.

After all the hullaballoo, the intrusions came to an abrupt halt for nearly thirty straight days. Just when The Rude thought that possibly he had imagined things being moved on his desk (after all, nothing was ever taken), the movements resumed, and as before, there was no continuity and the disruptions would sometimes not take place for days. Just as quickly as they began for the second time, they again stopped.

The Rude seemed to be on edge for several weeks, which was exactly the effect that was desired. Once the desired effect was reached, it was decided the break-ins were no longer needed or really any fun to continue to do. The method used was discussed for years but was not revealed until after Benny had left, which created the opportunity to spread the rumor that somehow Benny had probably been the culprit.

It was learned that Nicky had actually attempted to pick the lock numerous times without success. He then decided to give it some thought and after several weeks came up with a theory of how the lock could be picked. The plan would require at least two full days, which would mean a weekend, preferably one when the chief and captain were away. Lieutenant Buck was not considered a threat, as he seldom came near the station on weekends, especially when the chief was out of town.

The opportunity came about one Friday afternoon when the two-day clearance window appeared. Nicky, along with Angelo, who were both then assigned to the detective bureau, put the plan into action. It seems that Nicky had deduced the door lock key was similar in size to an ordinary wooden popsicle stick. After some home testing, it was learned that the wood used in the popsicle sticks had a tendency to swell when wet. Nicky had soaked a few sticks in warm water for several hours prior to the test and after approaching the chief's door, inserted one of the sticks into the lock, breaking off the end so that at a quick glance, it appeared untouched. Nicky had also figured it would take two full days at room temperature to dry.

When first inserted into the lock, he hoped the swollen stick would conform, creating indentations in the stick from the spring-loaded ball bearings. Strangely enough, it did, and when removed two days later with a pair of needle nose pliers, Nicky was left with an almost perfect copy of the key needed to unlock the lock. However, it was made of a broken popsicle stick.

Nicky then took the stick and made a wax negative form using some candles and a piece of Tupperware. Now with a negative mold, he then filled it with plaster, using footprint plaster. He now had a somewhat stable solid key blank. In order to make a more durable key, he made another negative form with plaster which he coated and then filled with liquid fiberglass resin. This left him with a hard key. With some sanding, drilling, and small adjustments, the key worked perfectly in the chief's door.

The fiberglass key apparently worked for several months, and neither Nicky nor Angelo bothered to let anyone else know how they were able to make the entrances. It was true that most entrances were made when either Millie or Dooley were working as they were dispatchers, which ensured that nothing was seen, heard, or known. Even after the secret got out years later, to the best of everyone's knowledge, The Rude was never advised how his office was entered.

CHAPTER 52

Pellet the Wonder Dog

One instance of intramural cruelty, or more correctly stated *thick blue* cruelty humor to another co-worker involved Officer Samuel Lakeland. Sam was one of those guys that never quite fit in with the more imaginative and rowdy members of the department. Always a little too sincere and serious to be working at Cedar Springs, he was never one to join in the entertainment when it came to criticizing the actions or misfortunes of another member of the department, which in turn made criticizing him all the more imperative and satisfying.

The state trooper instructors at the police academy were fond of referring to those they personally considered unfit to be involved in law enforcement as individuals who would be better suited to be bank tellers. It was said that Sam could have been the poster child of the type more suited to be a bank employee.

Sam was also reported to have been an army veteran and had often bragged that he had served in Viet Nam as a dog handler. There were many thoughts and conjectures as to how much actual "in country" time Sam had experienced or what exactly he and his dog had "handled," as he really didn't fit the profile of normal veterans that had seen any combat.

According to Sam, his dog, a purebred German Shephard named Corey, had trained together in the States and had become best of friends. They had then been shipped overseas and assigned to guard and patrol duties in Viet Nam. Sam would explain to anyone who would listen that unfortunately, as things sometimes happen, Corey died after suffering a combat injury.

Sam had said that it was speculated by an army veterinarian, who had suggested and ultimately put the dog down, that either an indigenous and poison wild thorn, or one that had been treated with feces by one of the not-so-friendly North Vietnamese, had scratched the dog and a piece of the thorn had lodged under his skin behind his left ear. Apparently the wound went unnoticed for quite some time and later became infected. By the time the infection surfaced, Corey had suffered irreparable damage to his nervous system.

Sam was told that the wound was like that of a dog that had been shot with a dirty BB pellet with the pellet never being removed. The unnoticed infection spread slowly and when finally discovered, the infection had spread so deeply into the dog that it became untreatable. Within weeks of the detection, the dog became lethargic and would have eventually died from the poisoning. It was unilaterally decided it was best to put Corey to sleep.

Of course, this heartfelt personal information was passed on from Sam to those listening with thoughts of forthcoming compassion and empathy. However, when word got out through the department grapevine that dog handler Sam's dog had died while he was being supervised by Sam, and knowing full well that Sam still had quite a bit of emotional attachment to the dog, the thoughtful members of the department immediately renamed Sam's dog "Pellet" or "Pellet the Wonder Dog" and Sam "Lethal Lakeland."

Short yet imaginative stories soon materialized about the heroics of Pellet the Wonder Dog and how he had saved Sam's life on countless occasions in Nam, only to be ignored and suffer the humiliation of a slow and agonizing death due to the lack of attention and care given by his hardhearted and indifferent handler.

Pictures of energetic as well as old and abused dogs soon appeared throughout the building, most of them complete with added drawn-on animal fecal droppings and bandaged heads. With knowledge of the infection being caused by feces-laden thorns that had pierced Corey's head, Pellet was also additionally referred to as "Shit Head." Fortunately PETA was not yet fashionable, and the incessant digs were kept strictly in house.

Sam would react with extreme criticism of the lack of respectability shown by those who participated in the taunts and would often express the total lack of respect for a fellow veteran who, though an animal, gave his life for his country.

Future drawings and pictures of American flag-bandaged dogs then soon appeared, complete with wavy stars and stripes billowing in the background. It was rumored that several members of the department had been heard to respond to Sammy's remarks with, "Now he can never say we weren't patriotic about him killing his shithead dog!"

Additionally, many fictitious but realistic-looking criminal complaints showed up in Sam's mailbox, charging him with animal cruelty and "dogslaughter" of a fellow veteran warrior.

And more

Further brotherhood scrutiny ensued for Sam after it became known that he personally began to experience some unusual soreness under his armpit. He eventually went to a doctor who found a lump that shouldn't have been there. After seeing several specialists and undergoing many tests and biopsies, Sam was advised that the diagnosis was a form of leukemia in his lymph nodes, spleen and liver.

Sam, who was single at the time, underwent leukemia lymphoid surgery followed by many months of chemotherapy and radiation, complete with hair loss and daily bouts of constant nausea and vomiting, aka "talking to or calling Ralph."

Because this was a situation that was not his doing and one that could just as easily happen to any of the other members of the department, no snide or sarcastic comments were made about it, and several members actually helped with Sam's treatments by providing transportation to and from his radiation and chemotherapy treatments. Several members of the department even donated some of their sick days to Sam so that he would continue to receive a paycheck after utilizing all his accrued time.

Following several months of treatments along with several hundred stops to puke on the side of the road while on the way home, Sam was re-examined and told that it appeared he was in remission and no further infections could be found.

After his cure and his return to patrol, Sam took police work even more seriously than before and tried to work only within the exact letter of the law. In addition to this certainly pleasing Benny, he would also try to convince those he arrested that they should try to use the arrest as a sign to start their lives anew.

If Oprah had been around then, Sammy would have been a prime candidate to be on the show. While attempts to alter personalities and criminal behavior seem to work for television evangelists speaking to fairly educated individuals who are genuinely looking for more insight to life, it generally falls on deaf ears when dealing with uneducated career knuckleheads.

Whenever Sam went into his "you can change your life" speeches, department members' eyes would roll, and it soon became apparent that the now-leukemia-free Sam was at least "physically almost normal." However, Sam had seemingly become even more sincere than before his illness and unknowingly had also become even more easy prey for insults and jokes by the department mischief-makers because of it.

It was decided that Sam's sincerity was just way too much sincerity, and something just had to be done about it.

The contributing editors of departmental sarcasms began the task of thinking up tasteful, discerning, yet sophisticated means of ridicule toward a brother member who had avoided a catastrophic end as a result of a disease which affected his spleen and liver and what could have been, and had been, a devastating illness.

Try as they might, after several weeks of frustrating as well as exasperating efforts, the task was found to be extremely difficult and later deemed to be impossible to be sarcastic and polite at the same time.

To make a direct point and to effect an immediate response, whenever Sam was spoken about, he was from then on referred to as "Leukemia Lakeland," "Liver Lakeland," or "Sammy Spleen."

It wasn't long before Sam became aware of his new nicknames. Sam, still too sincere, made it a point whenever possible to express to some of the troops that the offenders obviously had no idea of what he had gone through, which in normal circumstances in a normal work environment would have struck a chord of sympathy and an immediate end to the exploitation.

The *Thick Blue Line* of agitating conspirators again made it clear that in order to gain an advantage over others, be named a department idol or even earn any kind of respect, one had to first have *thick blue skin*.

Immediately they distributed editorials indicating that Pellet the Wonder Dog had not died from an infection but had been infected with cancer from none other than his handler, Leukemia Lakeland, through abnormal and questionable affectionate training tactics.

Too much?

Probably, but the fact that it seemingly was too much seemed to fuel the fires and culminated in a weekend long frenzy of taping logos of two L's (Ll), and two S's (Ss), one large and another small one inside the larger one, indicating a theme name for Liver Lakeland or Sammy Spleen, or as some referred to in a more catchy idiom, "Sergeant Spleen." Not that Sam was a sergeant; it just sounded better.

Following a weekend of taping the double letters on walls, floors, windows, mirrors, urinals, and toilets as well as in the holding cell areas, it was rumored that nearly five thousand combinations of L's and S's were plastered in and around the station.

On Monday morning, The Rude arrived, and seeing a few "Ll's" and "Ss's" on the walls and windows, at first thought it was another harmless prank until inspecting the bathrooms, their toilets and urinals, the Dispatch center, squad room, detectives office, holding cells, fire extinguishers and even his own locked office where he found the double letters on his chair, desk, walls, door, and telephone.

Looking around at his disrespected office while loudly exclaiming, "God damn gang!" and knowing that he would never get a confession as to who the culprits were, he advised Captain Benny to have someone take them down and issued a memo to all the sergeants to cease and desist under penalty of having to do documented property checks for the rest of their careers.

Several years later, someone noticed the wall clock in the patrol room. There, stuck on the second hand rotating around and around as usual, was a small, yellowed but still legible "Ss" logo inside the glass enclosed face.

If nothing else, the culprits were certainly diligent and thorough.

CHAPTER 53

Enough Is Enough

Following Sammy's anticipated complaint to The Rude concerning getting picked on, it was decided by the department legionaries that if any real disciplinary actions were introduced, that something retaliatory would surely have to follow and be carried out.

The Rude, beginning to believe that there was the possibility that things were getting a bit out of hand, put out a verbal order through Captain Benny that the discouraging remarks against Sam should cease and desist.

Captain Benny made it a point to personally speak with each squad sergeant and to as many patrolmen as possible concerning the chief's concerns and orders.

Nothing was ever put on paper, but the directives of The Rude was relayed down through the troops to lay off Officer Lakeland.

True to their promises of retaliation, the famed and as-yet unknown sarcastic special-order authors of instigation quickly struck again, embellishing the theory that more misery is always better misery by releasing the following:

Special Order # 84223

To: All Officers

From: Chief J. R. Dennahee

Subject: Officer Lakeland

It has come to my attention that there have been a considerable number of graffiti- related publications posted on the bulletin boards and elsewhere in the station. While I consider a joke a joke, all things considered, this is still a police station and should function as such.

Be that as it may, and for what it's worth due to the exigent circumstances, I, Jonathan The Rude Dennahee, do hereby declare the week of August 14th through August 21st as within the confines of the police department of the town of Cedar Springs, officially to be "Be nice to Patrolman Lakeland week."

During this brief period, all members of this department will in every conceivable way possible, attempt to treat Patrolman Lakeland as a real police officer and as close to possible as a normal person.

At all times during the week all officers shall:

1. Greet Officer Lakeland with sincere "good mornings, good afternoons, etc" whenever possible.

2. Attempt to treat Officer Lakeland as a normal human being.

3. Open car doors for him whenever possible.

4. Offer condolences whenever possible for what's his name, the bb-ridden, shit headed dog.

5. Speak highly of his spleen, liver, and other body organs.

6. Sit patiently with no eye rolling and listen whenever Patrolman Lakeland talks about his attempts to convince criminals to change their lives.

Additionally, under no circumstance will any officer:

a. Speak in hushed tones or purposely cease to communicate in his presence unless it just can't be helped and becomes absolutely necessary.

b. Make reference to any of his bragged-about philosophical enlightenments toward the public that you and I know are clearly nonexistent.

c. Spit, kick, sucker punch, or urinate upon him or ask him about any possible problems with his health.

d. Refer to Officer Lakeland as Leukemia Lakeland, Liver Lakeland, Sergeant Spleen, Bulimia Leukemia, The Unclean Spleen, LL, SS, The Big L, Wimp, Jerk Off, Dog Killer, or any of the other names used in the past.

Approved and enacted this 10th Day of August.
Jonathan The Rude Dennahee – Chief of Police

P.S. I really mean it this time!

After reading a copy of the correspondence, which had been left on top of his desk of his locked office, The Rude lit a cigarette and mumbled to himself,
"Yup, it's a God damn fucking gang!"
He then actually commented to Captain Benny that he thought the order was pretty funny but threatened Benny with working the midnight shift for six months if he ever told anyone.

CHAPTER 54

A Sarge and Nicky Harlow Story

Captain Benny had called Sergeant Sergeant into his office and advised him that he had some concerns with his squad. It had come to his attention that his squad were in complete noncompliance of one of his memos requiring them to always wear their hats, carry their bullet proof clipboards, portable radios, flashlights, and baton nightsticks whenever responding to a call.

Sarge, never realizing or comprehending that Captain Benny knew nothing about real patrol work, made it a point to have a squad meeting that day. Copies of the captain's memo were redistributed and it was indicated that any further refusals to comply with the memo would result in on the spot disciplinary action. Sarge told them that reports would be written, days off without pay would be implemented, hands would be slapped, children would be sent to bed without dinner, heads would roll, etc., etc., etc., blah, blah, blah.

The squad members, and in particular, Nicky Harlow, who could be as peculiar as Sarge at times, was not pleased with the captain's accusations nor Sarge's rants concerning the accusations. Almost immediately, a plan was formulating in his mind which he decided needed just the right kind of situation in order to convey specific actions with the acceptable results.

It so happened, as these things sometimes do, that on that very evening, Sarge radioed that he was in pursuit of a stolen car out of one of the neighboring municipalities. Nicky was in the north zone and heard Sarge advise that he was behind the vehicle on one of the main roads which coincidentally went through the north zone.

Sarge, with a moment-to-moment litany of his pursuit, then radioed that the pursued vehicle had lost control and had run off the roadway into a lima bean field. He stated that the driver had gotten out of the car and was now on foot, and that he was going to be in foot pursuit.

Nicky arrived at the scene where the car had left the road, within a minute of Sarge's transmission. It was dark, but with an almost full moon, the visibility was respectable. When he got out of his car, he could distinctly hear and then see Sarge screaming at the driver running slightly ahead of him, "I'll get your ass, you son of a bitch."

Nicky stood by his car watching the chase until he could clearly see the runner slowing and Sarge gaining. Deciding that the runner was going to be caught momentarily, he decided then was the perfect occasion and situation to implement his plan for revolt against the captain's unnecessary and unqualified decisions concerning how to respond to an incident.

He methodically began to collect his equipment. First, he put on his hat. Then he slowly gathered his clipboard, portable radio, flashlight, and baton nightstick. By that time, Sarge had caught the runner, utilizing what appeared to be a very ungraceful flying tackle, and was leading the driver out of the field and over to his patrol car.

Sarge was profusely sweating, breathing heavily, and covered in fresh mud from the field. Looking at Nicky, Sarge asked, "What the hell are you doing? I could have used some help!"

Nicky, as was his custom, stated, with a snort and a quick clearing of his throat, "I am truly sorry, but I was getting all of my required equipment together in order to properly be in compliance with the captain's directive in order to appropriately respond to the call."

With another clearing of his throat and visually eyeing Sarge up and down, he added, "And don't worry, Sarge, I won't tell the captain you were obviously in violation of his memo."

Sarge, in an unusual moment of normal clarity, while looking flabbergasted, dirty, and humbled, said, "Get the hell out of here, and don't worry about any of that crap anymore."

CHAPTER 55

Hanging Around

F itting in and being accepted by the senior members of any organization is generally always a priority for those wishing to pursue a constructive and lasting career in their chosen field.

Police work is really not any different, and in most cases it is more difficult to do. In police work, acceptance is comparable to trust. If you can trust who you are working with and depend on them, the job becomes much easier and certainly safer.

Obviously, to be accepted, one had to have substantial self-assurance, while having the ability to shrug off things that cannot be changed. Police are generally the first people called to a scene involving scenarios which result in serious anguish, catastrophic damages, and appalling injuries—and, of course, death.

It is a complete necessity to act genuinely concerned and compassionate yet composed to victims and those closely related to the victims, and still possess graveyard or black humor when discussing the incidents with fellow emergency personnel when the incidents are cleaned up and concluded. Most important is the fact that one should never confuse the two.

Mike Harding had been hired about two years earlier, after working part time in one of the neighboring towns. When hired, he had been told that if he became involved in a situation where he wasn't quite sure what decision to make, that he should ask one of the older guys who had probably made the same decision several times.

Most of the "older guys" had only been on the street for four or five years longer than Mike but were looked upon as unquestionable veterans by the new hires. In the more difficult or complicated cases, one was referred to the detectives for guidance, as they routinely operated within the guidelines of state and federal statutes and could usually give the proper advice for the situation.

Mike had made a decision in the first few months in the department that he was determined to do as good a job as possible and to fit in and be accepted as soon as possible. The goal was to eventually become one of the "older guys" who could give advice to the newer hires. Mike quickly noticed that gutsy behavior, along with humor, carried a lot of weight when discussing situations and eventually being accepted.

It was beneficial never to act squeamish at a grisly accident or criminal scene, even if you were. Most important, you could not take any situation personally as the police were paid to look at all situations objectively.

If you were visibly troubled by other people's unnecessary suffering, you could not ask the proper questions or expect to get the right answers. Immediately following a situation, victims and their families don't need a counselor; they need someone to make intelligent decisions to ensure that the situation is taken care of and that immediate further tragedies do not occur.

Now there were two detectives who had been working together for some time, Angelo Demucchi and Stuart Tarrantino. Both had done well on the job and were known to make the right choices when investigating informational tips of crimes in general and were always eager to assist on physical confrontational calls. They were also well known for their dark sense of humor concerning the day-to-day physical and emotional brutality that would take place.

Angelo, as we have previously said, worked for a time as an undercover agent for the county. That, together with his own past experiences of working as a bartender in one of the local watering holes, famous for regular drug deals, weapon sales, and the occasional sexual encounters in the upstairs lofts, helped him in dealing with the thieves, drug dealers, pimps, and whores that he would encounter in the future.

Stuart, on the other hand, had belonged to a neighborhood gang in Philadelphia. With an extensive and mostly unusable juvenile arrest record, he was lucky enough never to have gotten caught in anything too serious after turning eighteen.

As in most big cities, gang members either grow up to be cops, firemen, or better criminals. Stuart's family moved out of the city to the shore where Stuart decided that he didn't want to be a fireman or a better criminal. With some family help, Stuart was able to get a job as a special or temporary officer during summers in one of the neighboring towns. That experience eventually led to a civil service exam and his hiring in Cedar Springs.

After being hired by Cedar Springs, Stuart, while on patrol, made it a point to befriend the tougher neighborhood kids that other patrolmen often overlooked and was able to gather information that he used to solve many criminal cases. Because of this talent, he eventually was taken off patrol and assigned to the detective division.

Stuart had two things he was known for. The first was meeting each new hire with a firm handshake and to ask them about their religious beliefs, followed by a short synopsis of how they could be washed in the waters of clean and sin-free living. The second was that every few months, Stuart would tire of being saved and slide off the wagon and have a few drinks after work and on weekends with the boys, etc. After a time of personal contrary behavior, several apologies, and an eventual reaffirmation with religion, Stuart would be on the straight and narrow once again.

Both Angelo and Stuart had seen enough in their short lifetimes that black humor and sarcasm were part of their daily routine when discussing incidents they would investigate or had investigated. Feeding off each other and knowing when the other was serious or not also made them somewhat cautious when a new patrolman asked questions or attempted to add information to a case they were investigating.

Stuart would normally not say much at all, while Angelo would listen politely to the whole story, including the patrolman's thoughts on how to proceed. When they finished their statements, Angelo would either just stare and say absolutely nothing or very nonchalantly say, "Yeah. That would probably work.… Whatever, do what ya gotta do."

New employees soon learned that this was Angelo's customary response to almost any questions that were asked of him. His theory was that one had to learn to think and do on his own, and he wasn't about to hold anyone's hand while they did. Whether they had gotten the stare or the "whatever" speech, they usually left confused and dejected. Angelo and Stuart would then critic the patrolman's ideas and either agree to give them more attention the next time around or refer to them as "future bank employees" and completely ignore the next several conversations with them.

Mike listened well and soon realized that Angelo and Stuart only really trusted each other and those whom they had successfully worked with in the past. It seemed that to be accepted by these two guys, a good sense of humor, along with good police work, was needed.

Mike occasionally would work on a case that he thought would, with a bit of extra work, result in several cases being solved. When they were available, he would meet with Angelo and Stuart. After advising them of the situation and what he had found and what he suggested, Angelo would say, and Mike was confident, with worldly certainty and camaraderie in his heart, "Yeah, That would probably work.... Whatever, do what ya gotta do."

At least he wasn't being stared at or ignored.

As things sometimes happen, after several of the heart-to-heart Angelo "whatever" speeches, Mike had the occasion to assert a bit of pent-up sarcasm and humor, which resulted in his finally being accepted as an equal.

Mike had been dispatched to a call in one of the older neighborhoods of converted bungalows for an unknown problem. Upon his arrival, Mike spoke with a highly emotionally and distraught female of about nineteen years of age. She indicated that she had come home from work and had found her grandfather, with whom she lived, in the living room.

After getting to this point, she became even more upset and began to cry uncontrollably. Obviously, Gramps had not welcomed her home with open arms and a smile. Mike got as much information from her as he could and asked her to wait on the front lawn while he entered the residence.

He learned within a few feet into the home that the grandfather had managed to stop breathing utilizing one of the living-room ceiling rafters, a piece of rope, and his neck. The bungalow, being old, and not up to current building code standards, had at the most, seven-foot ceilings that had been stripped to bare wood because they were in the process of being re-sheet rocked.

Clearly the grandfather had succeeded in accomplishing a difficult suicide, because he had only to stand up straight to escape the tightness of the rope. Visually, it was easily determined that it was completely unnecessary to check for any vital signs of life.

The procedure in sudden deaths was to notify the detective division, the county coroner, the local mortuary, and most importantly, not to disturb the body. Mike utilized the home's telephone to contact the dispatcher to alleviate any further unnecessary information over the airwaves.

As luck or fate would have it, Angelo and Stuart happened to be on duty at the time and were in fact a few minutes from the location when they overheard Mike being dispatched for service to the call. Probably either bored or just curious, they radioed that they would be responding to assist at the call.

Because he had given no further information over the radio, when Mike heard that they were going to assist, he assumed that when they arrived, Angelo or Stuart would be asking what was going on. After parking their car, Angelo and Stuart approached Mike.

Angelo said, "What's going on?"

Thinking quickly, Mike said, "I got this young girl who lives with her grandfather. Right now she is very upset with him, as you can see." He nodded slightly in the sobbing girl's direction. "Thinking that this was some type of family argument, I went in to speak with the grandfather to get his side of the story, and he refused to answer any of my questions. He won't even so much as tell me his name."

Acting the innocent rookie, Mike then said, "I really don't know what I should do with him."

Angelo looked at Stuart, then at the girl sobbing, gave a short sigh, and seeing an opportunity to further ridicule a rookie and show how proper questioning should be done said, "Oh yeah?" and with a minor tug on the waist of his pants and a slight re-adjustment of his gun then said, "Where is he?"

With a perplexed and serious look and trying to repress a grin,

Mike said, "He's just hanging around in the living room."

Angelo and Stuart both entered the front door prepared to get some answers while Mike purposely stayed in the front yard thinking to himself that they would either be pissed off and never give him the time of day again or impressed with his ability to cook up the scenario he had given them.

After several minutes went by, Angelo and Stuart came back outside. Angelo was trying not to smile or laugh, as the granddaughter was still in the yard and within hearing distance.

Angelo simply nodded giving Mike the "You have done well, grasshopper" look, walked up close and said, "Good one, Mike."

Because the family and neighbors were at the scene, proper procedures were followed, the situation investigated, the required information gathered, and the call concluded as a simple and unfortunate case of suicide.

Back at the station while doing reports of the incident, Angelo and Stuart advised Mike that they had been completely fooled prior to entering the house.

They told Mike very formally, "We have decided that after careful consideration and analyzing the entire complexity of the situation vs. a perfect opportunity to enter into dark humor completely inappropriate at the scene, you demonstrated a sincere and meaningful originality toward a useless and unnecessary tragedy using skilled language and the performing arts. Therefore we bestow upon you the *Thick Blue Line* thumbs-up."

After this, Mike was given the time of day on a regular basis and often was questioned concerning his thoughts and beliefs about other events in the department showcasing patrolmen and administrative mishaps, misfortunes, and disasters.

CHAPTER 56

Sandy

Not everything police-related that took place on or around the fishing facilities was looked upon as an earth-shattering, serious criminal matter. Presumably not unlike many fishing dock areas in the country, Cedar Springs had its number of calls involving not only thefts, assaults, alcohol, and drugs but some occasional incidents of a sexual nature. Not that these were not considered criminal matters; they were considered more of a nuisance than anything else. There were some sophisticated and some not-so-sophisticated females who would spend an excessive amount of time on the docks making friends, so to speak, with the fishermen and the occasional tourist looking for companionship.

One such individual who always found herself involved with all of the above was a woman named Sandy. By the mid-'70s, Sandy was in her late twenties, an age where most young women are coming to age and making decisions concerning their future. Sandy was by all accounts already over the hill and referred to as being ridden hard and put away wet. Pictures of some of Sandy's earliest arrests taken only seven to eight years earlier, showed a very attractive blonde girl, approximately 5' 4" and listed at 105 pounds. Records indicated arrests from somewhat simple alcohol and drug possession to theft, robbery, and prostitution.

Sandy routinely paid her debts to the courts with short stays in the county jail in lieu of fines. She always exclaimed that "three hots and a cot" referring to a jail bed and three meals a day, was easier and more convenient than having to actually work a real job for money and to give that money to the courts.

Over the years, time and life were not kind to Sandy, who escalated to a 240-pound woman with no teeth who had been severely defeated by a nasty case of acne scarring, most likely due to her hygienic habits or rather the lack of them. Because of her continued use of alcohol and drugs--which over time had escalated to any type of beer, wine, crack, coke, uppers, downers, heroin, and hallucinogenic's. Sandy's arms and legs resembled someone who had been in some type of horrific accident, with open sores, scabs, and scars.

Sandy's womanly talents had also significantly dwindled over the years, and she had regressed to performing oral stimulations to the tune of five dollars per occurrence, which she quickly exchanged for more alcohol or drugs. Sandy had officially gone from a young girl who could have easily won beauty pageants to a full-fledged hard-ridden, put away wet "dock rat."

Sandy exclusively wore very short shorts and cotton tube tops in the summer, and faded elastic lined sweat suits in the colder months. Unfortunately for onlookers or visitors in the dock area who simply wanted to see a *real* fishing boat in the summer months, they also, more times than they wanted to, were able to see Sandy dressed but bulging out of dirty cotton tube tops, "hot pant"-type stained shorts, and flip-flops complete with feet so filthy it was an insult and embarrassment to all the flip-flop-wearing people in the rest of the country.

As unbelievable as it seemed, Sandy continued to solicit and provide sexual favors, and additionally unbelievable as it seemed, many fishermen as well as some dock area visitors continued to utilize her talents.

Shortly before she was mercifully shipped off to a rehab center out west by her parents, who swore this was the last attempt they would make to help her, came one of her more notorious events.

It was on a particularly warm August night that Sandy was attempting to drum up some business on the docks. Adding to her diminished appearance was the fact that she was seriously inebriated, or high, or both. It was reported that she had tried to solicit her only remaining talent on a couple of tourists who promptly complained to the local restaurant located in the dock area, who then promptly called the police as they routinely did on numerous occasions concerning Sandy.

Two patrolmen, Bill Rhodes and Brian Dulkey, got the call and responded knowing that with Sandy's girth, it would take two men to subdue her if necessary without actually hurting her. Armed with thick black leather gloves to avoid actual contact with her, they gathered the information needed from the tourists and then proceeded to the dock area where Sandy had last been seen.

When not totally incapacitated by alcohol or drugs, Sandy usually went along quietly with the police, as she sometimes welcomed the ride home if offered, or if arrested, looked forward to some rest time she would be spending at the county jail. On this particular day, Sandy was extremely out of it and was found on the docks leaning against one of the dock pilings. Of significant interest was the rather large pool of blood by Sandy's feet, and upon closer examination, the somewhat steady flow of blood trickling down Sandy's scarred legs from her dirty and now blood-soaked hot pants.

Brian, who had been on the department for about a year and who had recently graduated from the police academy, had never dealt with Sandy, and with a look of disbelief exclaimed that he was going to call for the rescue squad.

Bill, a veteran of four years who had dealt with Sandy before and was aware of most of her habits, told Brian to hold off on the call. As many strange things that he had witnessed concerning Sandy, including catching her actually performing her talents for money or drugs, which was pretty disgusting in itself, he later admitted that this was a new one even for him.

Sandy did not seem overly concerned that the police had approached her, and she continued to lean against the piling without moving. As calmly as possible, Bill informed Sandy that they had received a complaint about her bothering people, and then just as calmly asked about the blood and if she was feeling okay. As cooperative as Sandy could be, she could also be a handful, and Bill definitely did not want to deal with a handful that was also covered in blood.

Sandy, staring straight ahead, lost in some type of pharmaceutical intoxication, mumbled something unintelligible, and then very slowly, and with a hesitation between words said, "I'm... I'm...I'm just resting...annn...I'm...I'm...I'm not bothering anybody".

Bill once again asked about all the blood. Sandy, again looking lost and far away, slowly looked down at the blood now beginning to coagulate and said again very slowly, "Oh that...oh fuck...I got my fucking period."

A bit shocked even after four years on the job, Bill asked why she wasn't using some type of protection from the obvious effect that was taking place.

Sandy, with a very short-lived clarity, looked directly at Bill and took a deep breath. After exhaling, she hesitated and slowly fell back into her medicinal haze. A few seconds later, in a slurred, just-audible voice she stated, "I ain't got no fucking money...and besides...it's fucking natural."

Even though they both considered it and wanted to, it was decided that it would not be good for tourism to leave her propped up against a piling and bleeding on the docks. Additionally, knowing they were not going to appreciate it, the rescue squad was called in order to transport Sandy to the local hospital.

Bill and Brian followed the rescue squad to the hospital, spoke with the attending doctor, and requested a mental evaluation, which as it turned out was not a difficult thing to convince the doctor to have done.

It was shortly thereafter that her parents sent her out to the West Coast to participate in one last effort in what was advertised as a promising new rehabilitation program. A unique establishment, heavily advertised in magazines and in drug programs, the center resembled a substantial ultra-modern medical facility. It supposedly provided the best care for the money, which was also reported to be a substantial, ultra-modern amount.

Nothing was heard from Sandy for quite some time. Unfortunately, news was received through family members that although Sandy had successfully completed her stay at the rehabilitation center, she had apparently relapsed and died from an overdose of drugs on Hollywood Boulevard about a year later.

CHAPTER 57

A Bridge Over
Very Troubled Water

During WWII, the small airport built by the navy and coast guard was utilized as a training facility for navy bomber pilots. Hundreds if not thousands of unarmed bombs were dropped by pilots in and around the airport area during practice runs. Additionally, armed ordinance was also dropped and exploded so that the pilots could experience the real thing.

As things usually happen, many aerial accidents took place, with plane crashes and unintentional ordinance droppings. It was factual that both unarmed and armed bombs were dropped outside the target areas and into the many wooded areas, some farmlands, and of course the bay and ocean. Additionally, as things also usually happen, many of the armed bombs did not detonate upon hitting the surfaces. The ordinance ranged from small units, which were about the size of a one-liter bottle of soda, to rather large units of about two feet long and twelve to sixteen inches around. Most were recovered shortly after the accidents, but many were never found until years later.

It was not unusual for fishermen, farmers, or building contractors to call the station stating they had netted or uncovered what appeared to be a grenade or a bomb of some sort. During the '50s and '60s, the usual procedure that was followed after receiving one of these calls was one of two things.

One procedure was for the dispatcher to advise the reporting party not to touch the object and then notify the army base several hours away, which would eventually send members of a bomb squad to investigate the find. This usually ended up taking a minimum of four to five hours for their arrival, during all of which a patrolman was required to stand by at the scene and protect the object as well as the public. After their arrival, and after making their determination that the object was indeed a bomb, they would carefully move the object to a clearing as big as could be found. It was then that the army officer's years of expert government bomb squad training would be utilized and put into effect.

Dressed in a heavily padded protective suit, a ballistic-proof helmet, face guard, and Kevlar-type gloves, a government-approved bomb squad member would slowly and carefully attach a government-approved rope, using a government-approved knot, around the previously government-approved bomb. The loose end of the rope would then be attached to the rear end of their government-approved vehicle. After slowly backing away from the object, the bomb officer would then advise his partner to then set in motion the secondary procedure of government military explosive investigation. The bomb would then, not so carefully, be dragged behind the vehicle for an extended period of time in both large circles as well as figure eights at various speeds in order to see if it would explode.

If, after a period of time of being dragged, the object exploded, it was then officially deemed to have been an armed and dangerous ordinance. After several laps with no explosion, the object, depending on its size, would either be placed in the middle of the clearing and blown up using another small explosive, or simply packaged in a cardboard box and taken back to the army base for a more official and probably much less dramatic disposal.

The second way recovered bombs were taken care of was for the responding police officer to take it upon himself to determine that the object was harmless, utilizing nothing more than a hunch, and transport it either in the trunk of his car or sometimes in the passenger's seat, safely secured by a seat belt, to the western canal bridge, where the object was very unceremoniously thrown over the edge into the water below.

For various reasons, this was usually done late at night with few people around. Depending on the officer, it was done either with expectation or at least hope of an enormous explosion upon impact with the water, or with optimism that the object would simply go away without the officer's being tied up for hours awaiting the bomb squad. It was believed that the depth of the water in the area of the bridge was deep enough to make it safe for passing boats.

It was rumored and passed down through the years that Buck Morningston had been the first officer to utilize the canal bridge as an alternative to the wait on the arrival of the army bomb squad. Apparently, he had gotten tied up for six hours for, in his opinion, no good reason on a Friday afternoon, watching a small unearthed ordinance, and had missed a serious appointment with several bottles of beer.

Ingenuity, or the plain urgency to be off duty, led Buck to decide that in the community's best interest to quell the possible overtime pay expenditures along with a decision that better suited his personal agenda, he should simply transport the ordinance a short distance and make a deposit into the waters of the canal.

Along with Buck's promotions to sergeant and then lieutenant, his expertise in dumping unexploded ordinance into the canal was proven to be more and more acceptable as there were fewer and fewer people he had to answer to if something went wrong. As usual, it took no more than 24 hours for the rest of the department to learn of another possible "boat blaster" being placed into the gentle waters beneath the bridge. The procedure was used on a fairly regular basis when numerous unfound bombs were unearthed as housing developments sprouted up in town, replacing wooded areas and farmlands.

Unless the reporting party showed some type of curiosity toward the method of disposal of the bombs, they were usually advised that the bomb was "definitely" a practice unarmed ordinance, and that it would be picked up at the station as soon as possible by the appropriate people.

There were times when a patrolman would actually bring the ordinance to the station, where it was placed into a fenced in area behind the building designated for abandoned bicycles. Sometimes Buck or one of the other officers would take them to the canal for a deposit, and sometimes the army would be called and would advise that the ordinance placed in the bike pen was indeed an armed bomb and should never have been disturbed. Strangely, this never seemed to deter the trips to the bike pen or the canal versus the wait for the bomb squad.

It was rumored through the years that Buck had kept track of the number of objects he and others tossed into the canal with expectations of the proper time to avoid the general area and to begin exclusively utilizing the eastern bridge. Unfortunately, over the years, he could no longer remember the actual number. Around 1985, he began to indicate the total as "enough to take out the bridge and much of the surrounding area."

Curiously, to anyone's knowledge, nothing was ever done about all the canal deposits made; however, the older officers always drove faster over the bridge, and those who owned boats seemed to avoid the western end of the canal, preferring to dock or launch their boats on the eastern end.

CHAPTER 58

Fire Prevention?

There was no paid fire department in Cedar Springs. There were, however, three volunteer fire departments, coincidentally named District numbers One, Two, and Three. Each had their own buildings and entities with chiefs, assistant chiefs, senior fireman, junior fireman, trainees, etc.

Number One and Number Two district departments were located in the more populated areas of Cedar Springs and were run fairly professionally and offered homeowners a feeling of security and protection from the ravages of fire and the damage it can bring. Number Three district department was located in and serviced the rural areas of the town. While the identical training was offered to its members, the end result of that training was vastly different than what was observed in the other two.

For years, fire district Number Three was one that encompassed mostly farmland, the fishing dock areas, and campgrounds. Compared to the other districts, fire calls in Number Three were only half as many as either of the others.

During the 1950s and 1960s and most of the 1970s, they had one pumper truck and one ladder truck, both of which were fairly old and purchased second hand. The chief, Albert Matthewson, was an older gentleman who had been elected fire chief in the 1950s and stayed in the position for more than twenty years. Four of the volunteers were also Mathewson's. They were Carl and Frank, who were Albert's brothers and Al Jr. and Donald, Albert's sons. Most of the other members were local farmers, shop owners or public employees of the town.

Unfortunately, fire district Number Three seemed to be a bungling group of volunteers who routinely seemed to have different degrees of difficulty in extinguishing fires in a reasonable amount of time. In too many cases, they would experience equipment failures, mostly blamed on the age of their trucks, or personal failures, by not performing the correct function at the proper time while fighting a fire. After the water pumps of the pumper truck failed to operate correctly for the third time in as many months, an emergency board of directors meeting took place, and with some financial aid from the town government board, a new truck was purchased in the mid-1970s. Mechanical problems now aside, this left only the individual failures of the volunteers with which to question the performance of the department.

The customary method of operation for a fire department during this time was that a call concerning a fire emergency would be received at the police department. The dispatcher would determine which district the emergency was located in and signal that department. Each fire house had fire sirens reminiscent of World War II air raid or blackout sirens, mounted on top of telephone poles near their buildings. Prior to people having home telephone service, the siren was originally designed to summon the volunteers who lived in the areas of their individual districts, who would then respond to the fire house and then go to the fire.

As technology progressed, department members were issued electric scanners for their homes that would emit a series of loud and distinct tones to notify them of fires, but as things usually happen, old habits die hard, and the telephone-pole-mounted sirens continued to be activated. The howling, wailing sirens, loud enough to hurt your ears if you happened to be within 200 yards of them, would also irritate animals and anyone living within a half mile of their location, especially at night, but were always explained as necessary to warn the general public of speeding firemen trying to reach the firehouse and then for the public to be aware of speeding fire trucks heading to the fire.

There was also a procedure put into practice during the 1980s for only certain members to respond to the firehouses and certain other members to drive directly to the scene of the fire. This procedure was supposed to lessen the time it took for the fire apparatus to reach the scene of the fire and have members waiting at the scene to jump in and take care of the emergency.

Unfortunately, the fire chief in District Three had been the chief for so long, he failed to keep the rotation of who was going to the firehouse and who was going to respond to the fire up to date, and many times it was only by sheer luck that one or two members responded to the fire house to get the trucks. Unfortunately, this particular quirk never seemed to improve until an incident took place which changed the viewpoint concerning the response procedures of the department's members.

On a cold, windy February night in the early '80s (and yes, most unpleasant things seem to happen on cold, windy, wintery nights), a report of a house fire was received by dispatcher Dooley. Sergeant Pete Roberts was in the station when the call came in. The station was approximately five miles from the fire's location, and he immediately told Dooley that he was going to respond. Knowing that the fire's location was only about one half mile from District Three's firehouse, Pete assumed the emergency would be taken care of without too much of a delay.

Dooley rang out District Three fire department and then dispatched patrolmen Mike Harding and Bruce Dailey to the fire, in order to assist with traffic and whatever else might be needed. Both officers were within a couple of miles of the location and arrived at about the same time.

They radioed that there was a single-story ranch-type home located on one of the main roads, with smoke emitting from a window in the rear. A few minutes after arriving, they transmitted that they were speaking with the owner of the home, who stated that he lived alone and had been woken up by a smoke alarm going off in his living room. Thinking that the battery had gone bad, he reluctantly got out of bed to check the unit. When he stepped out of his bedroom, he distinctly smelled smoke and noticed it seeping from the opening at the bottom of the door of his spare bedroom. He immediately called the police, got dressed, and left the house.

After about ten minutes, several firemen began to arrive at the location. Because they did not have all of their fire clothing and equipment, which was kept on the trucks, they too were awaiting the fire trucks' arrival.

Sergeant Pete arrived, found the two patrolmen, and asked, "Where the hell are the fire trucks?"

Bruce Dailey answered, "Well, a few firemen are here." After a moment of hesitation, he added, "I wouldn't be surprised if they all showed up here and nobody gets the truck."

Soon, one of the bedroom windows blew out and flames began to be visible. In a matter of minutes, flames were reaching the roof eaves, and the vinyl siding began to melt from the heat. Fifteen minutes after the patrolmen arrived, they radioed the station and asked Dooley to check to see if the fire truck was en route. No response came from the request. After twenty minutes, several more windows had blown out, and definite flames were engulfing the entire inside of the home.

It had become clear that another small blunder had taken place in the scheduling of who exactly was supposed to go to the fire house and bring the trucks. With no fewer than twelve volunteers, including Chief Mathewson, who had shown up at the location in their personal vehicles, not one had responded to the firehouse. The chief, looking a bit sheepish, began to realize that bad was quickly becoming worse.

Rapidly the flames were now eating their way through parts of the roof, and the entire home was engulfed and undoubtedly would soon be a total loss. Finally, a decision was made at the scene and a couple of the firemen left and went to the firehouse and returned with one of the trucks.

Now, almost fifty minutes after the original call and with the arrival of the fire truck, the volunteer firefighting expertise of District Three sprang into action. Bright yellow and orange rubberized suits and steel hats were put on, radios were turned on with orders being shouted through them, axes and shovels were grabbed from their assigned places, hoses were dragged off the truck, connections made, and with the new hydraulic pumps effortlessly humming, water began to be pumped onto the home.

Within five minutes of the preparation and execution of almost flawless firefighting procedures, another slight difficulty arose. The two main hoses, spraying water onto what was now looking like a home that was going to be a total loss, began to suddenly lose water pressure. The once strong and powerful flow of water was quickly becoming a drizzle. After some quick checks of the hydraulic systems on the truck, it became apparent that one more small error and omission had occurred. Following the last fire call--which incidentally happened to have been the filling of one of the volunteer's new above-ground pool-- it became too apparent that no one had bothered to fill the water tanks on the pumper truck, and it had arrived at the scene with less than 100 gallons of usable water with which to fight the inferno.

Almost 90 minutes had now passed from the time of the initial call, and approximately 90 gallons of water had been sprinkled onto the house fire, which now resembled a few burnt sticks and melted appliances located on a concrete pad.

Sgt. Pete, calmly smoking his pipe, stood with Mike and Bruce, watching the whole calamity. The three had discussed the possibility of the fire being controlled at an early stage if things had gone just a bit differently. The only positive thing he could think of was that a total loss and starting over was probably much better for the homeowner than trying to repair half a disaster. For the next half hour, the frustrated firemen utilized what they could, until the chief ordered that the old ladder truck be brought to the scene, hopefully with water to finalize their battle with what was left of the home.

Chief Mathewson made it a point to advise Sergeant Pete that he was going to go through the remaining areas of the home, closely examine them, separate any debris, and wet it down in order to ensure that no flare-ups would occur. Pete thought to himself that the idea of a flare-up was next to impossible, as there seemed to be nothing combustible left to flare.

As the firemen were rolling up their hoses and getting ready to leave the scene, Sergeant Pete looked at Mike and said with a slight smirk, "And they used to call *us* The Crazy Squad!"

Fortunately, the homeowner was covered by excellent fire insurance and had a pre-fabricated house placed on the concrete pad two months later. Thankfully, this took place prior to relentless media coverage, so the firefighting errors were never made public. It was reported in the weekly paper that although District Three volunteers made a valiant effort at the scene, due to extremely high winds and intense heat, the fire was impossible to control and resulted in a complete loss. Chief Matthewson soon thereafter stepped down as chief, amid rumors of an imminent impeachment.

CHAPTER 59

Dirty Terry and the Stolen Hoagie

Cedar Springs had a patrolman who behaved and performed his duties as close as he possibly could while in the character of a Clint Eastwood movie personality. Terry Adkinson was tall, at about six foot two, lanky, and looked the part of a reasonably attractive young patrolman. While on patrol, he would even look a bit solemn, serious, and somber and usually presented himself as professional and competent. However that's about where the similarities between the actor and the profession ended. Terry had the unmistakable habit of over embellishing anything that he did or claimed that he did.

Most of the other department members considered Terry to be relatively harmless, even though he talked like he was the toughest and the coolest, calm, and collected thing in law enforcement. Terry was known to state that he was going to be the reincarnation of Mr. Eastwood. Even though Clint was still alive, it made no difference to Terry if he was dead or not. No one knew how that was even going to be possible, but Terry seemed to believe it and it was rumored that he had even considered changing his last name to Callahan, a character played by Eastwood.

One of the other patrolmen on his squad stated it was a fact that Terry had the reputation of actually pulling over senior citizens that had been driving a bit erratically. After checking their credentials and explaining that their driving was a precursor to an accident, he would look them straight in the eye and tell them they were lucky they hadn't been involved in one. Then with as much bravado as he could muster, he would ask,

"Do you feel lucky? Well, do you?"

Fortunately, he left out the "punk" part, but the seniors didn't get it or were just too polite to laugh in Terry's face.

Terry's track record in the department was fairly unremarkable, with no real documented life-altering situations under his belt to speak of. Terry would tell anyone who would listen that this was because he handled every situation by utilizing the perfect solutions, along with paralyzing veiled or implied intimidation when necessary.

He would say that as far as he was concerned, he had listened to the "You'll never be as good of a cop as I am" speech from sergeant Sarge Sergeant when he first was hired and believed that he could give him a run for his money as to who the best cop really was. This in itself usually led one to wonder how Terry ever passed the psychological interview when hired.

Following a few of these statements, a rumor circulated that Terry and Sarge might just be related in some way, but thankfully--because it might have upset the entire universe to have two Sarge's or two Terry's-- it was never really even attempted to be proven.

During the reign of "The Legend," as Terry had come to be called, a big transfer of personnel was undertaken by The Rude. During this transfer, a new sergeant, Mike Strong, was assigned to supervise the detective division. The Rude had been convinced that ole Lead Legs had been slacking and not conducting as many investigations that needed to be done and was reassigned to patrol.

Sergeant Strong lasted in the detective division a couple of years, until The Rude was advised that he had decided to share information about most of the department's criminal investigations with the county investigators, which was always one of the chief's pet peeves of things that were never to be done if at all possible.

The Rude's rule of keeping most things in house was being disregarded, and the county detectives were becoming frequent visitors at the station, systematically causing the reputation of the department to become tarnished. Lead Legs would eventually be transferred back to detective, but not until several cases handled by the new sergeant had become an embarrassment. One such investigation involved a case of a police shooting, which concerned and involved Terry The Legend.

In the early-morning hours in mid-August, just a few weeks following the big shakeup and personnel transfers, a local lone male, Tommy Gordon, who was well known in town as a heavy drinker but never much of a problem, decided to enter a convenience store in the north zone, where he ordered an Italian hoagie, or submarine sandwich, complete with a topping of hot peppers. The hot peppers were really not the issue but following the future events involving the hoagie, they became identifiable evidence for the up and coming investigation.

Tommy was clearly intoxicated, which was not unusual. The convenience store clerk, Patty Lovell, who made the sandwich, later stated that Tommy seemed to be acting a little drunk or a little high. Patty said she felt something was amiss, which turned out to be correct when she handed Tommy the sandwich. He quickly grabbed it and took off out the door without paying and began running north.

She would later explain that at first, she was not even going to report the theft, but since Tommy had not even said "thank you," she said that she had decided he should have to pay because of his rude behavior.

Patty made the call to the station and described to the dispatcher the transgression, along with the slighting of common courtesy toward her. She gave a detailed description of the food bandit, the sandwich, and the direction they both had headed.

The dispatcher gave the call to Terry, who was assigned to the north zone and happened to be just a few blocks away. Terry cruised nonchalantly to the area, confident that he could nab the culprit and quell the number of submarine sandwich thefts in the area, even though this was the only one reported to anyone's knowledge. He would later say he was surprised anyone would think about stealing a sandwich while he was on patrol.

Being the crack investigative patrolman that he believed he was, Terry spotted Tommy sitting in front of another closed store about a block away from the convenience store. The difficulty of this was next to nil, as it was 2:15 in the morning and there was no one else in the area sitting down and eating a sandwich. Not to be deterred by statistics, Terry pulled into the store lot, got out of his car, and confronted the young man.

After recognizing Tommy, Terry sauntered over and immediately indicated to him in a slow and precise manner, imitating Mr. Eastwood as closely as he could, that he should drop the evidence and raise his hands up high so that he could see them.

Unfortunately for Terry, Tommy did drop the sandwich, but as he was attempting to stand, he staggered in a half crouch and picked up a red object from the sandwich paper and haphazardly slipped it into his pocket. When he finally stood up, Terry demanded to know what he had put into his pocket. Staggering a bit, Tommy reached into his pocket and after fumbling a bit, was brandishing his soon to be officially documented red Swiss army knife, complete with multiple blades, corkscrew, bottle opener, and screwdrivers.

While chewing the rather large bite of sandwich he had taken and mumbling drunken gibberish, Tommy proceeded to stumble toward Terry holding the Swiss army knife. When Terry backed up, Tommy began to chase a very surprised patrolman around his patrol car, all the while mumbling some gibberish that Terry later stated he believed were threats and curse words, in between spitting bits of lettuce and hot peppers.

Now keeping up with his preferred image, Terry was known to smoke at least two packs of cigarettes during his shift in order to "look cool," and after two trips around the patrol car, panting and coughing, Terry stopped, pulled out his duty weapon, and promptly shot Tommy in the foot.

There was no doubt in anyone's mind that the number of cigarettes Terry smoked per shift greatly diminished his stamina during the two-lap marathon around the patrol car, even though Terry would state that he just decided the culprit had exceeded his limit concerning Terry's lack of using excessive force and so brought forth the wrath of God and Smith & Wesson down upon him, although with genuine compassion, by just shooting him in the foot.

Again, rumors abounded that Terry had actually probably aimed for the heart but was just a wee bit off from a distance of three feet.

Now, along with the detective sergeant changes, the members of the detective division had recently been advised by their new sergeant that he had noticed that overtime hours had been excessive in the past, and he was dedicated to lightening the load on the taxpayer's burden by significantly reducing that number.

In the past, when criminal incidents occurred after hours, two detectives were routinely assigned to most serious calls that had the potential for further investigations that a patrolman could not do, and two detectives would most certainly be called out to investigate a shooting, especially one that involved a patrolman. However, because he was trying to make a name for himself, and keeping the taxpayers' struggles in mind, Sergeant Strong had recently ordered that only one investigator be assigned to *all* calls.

One significant and legitimate improvement Sergeant Strong made to the detective division was that he had convinced The Rude that a new camera was needed for evidential matters. He was permitted to purchase a rather expensive new Nikon with all the bells and whistles. Written directives were given to all the detectives to read and study the operation, use, and care of the new camera.

Stuart Tarrantino, who had finally made enough of an impression dealing with the juvenile crime in the area, had recently been assigned to detectives under Lead Legs. He had been partnered with Angelo Demucchi. Following the personnel changes, the two had managed to remain in plain clothes and were now under the direction of the new detective supervisor, Sergeant Strong.

In six months' time, Stuart and Angelo had become best friends, mostly because they trusted each other and because Stuart could always make Angelo laugh. Stuart hated doing paperwork, so Angelo did the majority of the reports.

Because he figured that Angelo would probably study the new camera directions and take most of the pictures anyway, Stuart had not yet even looked inside the new camera box. Even if he had been assigned to take pictures by the new sergeant, he always thought that Angelo would show him how the camera worked.

Stuart figured--and figured wrong--that since he had been part- nered with Angelo, he would probably never be called out by himself to a call, let alone one that would require the use of the new camera.

Unfortunately for everyone involved, this incident occurred only a few days after Sergeant Strong made the manpower changes, and only one detective was notified for this case. Stuart happened to be next on the list, and he was advised that he would be handling the investigation alone.

When Stuart arrived at the scene, he got the quick account of what had happened from Terry, who naturally omitted the two-lap marathon run around the car, stating basically that he had been viciously attacked by the knife-wielding assailant, who by now was being transported to the local hospital.

Literally the only thing Terry did correctly was that he did not touch anything at the scene. He pointed out the weapon (knife), which was partially under the patrol car, and the spot where Tommy had been shot, complete with a small spot of blood from his injuries, and of course, the partially eaten hoagie with hot peppers.

Stuart, attempting to be the competent professional, took notes and some measurements in relationship to the street, the closed store, and the patrol car. Figuring that the new camera was just a camera, he opened his trunk and removed the new impressive-looking aluminum briefcase type box displaying the Nikon emblem in bold lettering.

As Stuart was removing the camera from the case and trying to figure out how to install the flash, The Rude pulled up to the scene. With his usual sparkling personality, he quickly looked at the scene, took a drag from his cigarette, and said, "Get the scene photographed and evidence bagged and tagged as soon as possible. Do not call the county, as they'll want to find some way to charge Terry with something before the night is over. Don't fuck around with this; just get it done."

Without so much as another word to Stuart or Terry, he promptly got in his car and left.

With a bit of luck, the flash was quickly attached, and with smooth movements and utilizing a small ruler for size comparison, Stuart focused on each item of evidence including the hoagie, its remaining hot peppers now beginning to attract some ants, and the red Swiss army knife, which coincidentally was found with the bottle opener in the open position and all knife blades neatly tucked away.

Shots of these and the surrounding area were taken, with two shots of each, figuring that would be enough pictures to verify the scene was sufficiently investigated and the evidence properly represented.

Stuart said to himself, "New camera, no problemo."

Stuart cleared the scene and returned to the station, where he then officially interviewed Terry. Following Terry's Dirty Harry version for the second time, Stuart looked hard at him and said,

"Okay, we'll put something like that on tape for your formal statement, but why don't you just tell me what really happened so both of us don't potentially go down in flames if something happened out there that shouldn't have."

Terry's Eastwood persona disappeared for approximately thirty minutes while he explained in regular-people language what had taken place, including the race around the car and the exasperated and frightening last effort to stop the chase with a single shot to the heart that went a little low.

Stuart advised Terry as to what should be included and what should be excluded from his report. He then asked the proper and previously discussed questions, which were answered correctly for a formal tape-recorded statement. Terry had not really done anything wrong, but the surrounding circumstances of the event were constructed in the interview, and reports to put Terry in a much better light than what had actually occurred.

Thankfully, no one had called the county, and no one from the county showed up, which would certainly satisfy The Rude.

Bright and early the next morning, and only three hours after he had gotten home, Stuart was called and awoken at home by Sergeant Strong asking where the roll of film from the camera had been stored. Stuart advised that it was still in the camera, as there were probably still a few unexposed shots left on the roll.

This caused some confusion to Sergeant Strong, and he again asked Stuart if possibly Angelo might have removed the roll from the camera and put it away for safekeeping.

Stuart, still thinking two detectives *should* have been on the scene, said to the sergeant that because of his directive to curb the use of overtime, he was the only detective called out.

The sergeant hesitated and then said, "Oh, okay then...where is the film of the shooting that you used last night?"

Stuart quickly answered, "I told you, it's still in the camera."

Seeing that the conversation did not seem to be moving in the right direction, or more importantly not revealing the answers he wanted, the sergeant asked, "Just start at the beginning and tell me what happened from the time you got called in until the time you left."

Now a bit agitated himself thanks to the condescending attitude of the sergeant, Stuart gave him the story as briefly as possible, adding that The Rude had appeared at the scene barking orders to clean it up as fast as possible. In his haste to clean up the scene, he took some measurements, got the camera out, put on the flash attachment and took several pictures, then returned to the station for the interview with Terry.

Stuart, now wide awake, and while relaying the story to the sergeant he was thinking to himself but not yet saying it out loud, and really hoping that he was wrong, that he could not remember if he actually checked to see if the camera had film in it. He just assumed it did.

As luck would have it, apparently it did not. Shortly after confirming that Stuart did not check the camera for film, Sergeant Strong shouted several obscenities, exclaiming how big of a fuck-up had been created, and slammed down the phone.

In his infinite wisdom and desire to keep his new position, Sergeant Strong quickly loaded a fresh roll of film into the new camera and went to the scene taking pictures of the area, what was left of the spot of blood, and the knife, which he placed back on the ground where Stuart had said it was found--and interestingly enough, several pictures of the remainder of the hoagie, now covered with ants feasting on the cold cuts and hot peppers. Stuart, in his haste, not only forgot to load the film in the camera, but also had not thought it necessary to retrieve the sandwich.

To finalize his first major supervised investigation and to begin his future routine procedures, which would soon become unappreciated procedures, when he got back to the station, Sergeant Strong called the county to report the shooting. Thinking that this course of action was imperative, his second undertaking was to go to The Rude's office to advise him that he had called and advised the county of the incident.

Before he could get to the part about the lack of actual crime scene pictures, the chief's face turned red as he shouted, "You called the fucking county? What were you thinking? You moron, they'll try to bury Terry."

Not appreciating these comments, Sergeant Strong came back with, "Yeah, well because you showed up at the scene and hurried Tarrantino to clean up everything as fast as he could, there was a problem with the new camera and none of the pictures came out. I had to go back this morning and take them again."

The Rude then stated, "Oh—okay, brainiac, so now you are going to involve the county and present to them a daytime photo rendition of a nighttime incident. Ya think they'll notice the difference? I did not and don't want the county involved. If Terry takes a hit on this, so will you. Now get the fuck out of my office and straighten it out."

In the end, a very brief post investigation took place, conducted without the county's involvement, with Terry being found to be in the right, mostly because Tommy, the sandwich-stealing, bottle-opener-wielding arrestee indicated in his formal statement that he was so drunk, the only thing he could remember was scraping some of the hot peppers off his sandwich with his pocket knife. Other than that, he couldn't remember what had taken place. His foot wound was not serious, and he advised that as he could not remember anything, he probably deserved the injury. A few weeks later, Tommy pled guilty to petty theft and failure to obey the orders of a police officer. Because of his injuries, he was fined $25 and ordered to reimburse the convenience store for the sandwich.

Shortly thereafter, Sergeant Strong held personal training classes in the use of the new camera, with extra time given to the loading and unloading of film.

Angelo, always known to speak his mind, stated, "Yeah, whatever. If you hadn't been so cheap with the overtime, I would have also been called out and there wouldn't have been any problems."

Shortly thereafter, an unwritten directive was given to all dispatchers that two detectives would again be called out for any incidents which could possibly evolve into serious matters.

CHAPTER 60

Jackie Maloney and the Vomit King

Jackie Maloney had been a member of the department for almost ten years. He was well known to be two things: a proficient investigator with keen law enforcement senses (otherwise known as good gut feelings) and the other, being a bit of a loose cannon.

Although some of his actions could be construed as controversial, Jackie led the department in arrests for several years. Because of his constant enthusiasm toward police work, in today's world, Jackie would probably be diagnosed as being ADD or thought to be doing crack cocaine and sent for random urine testing on a continual basis. Jackie didn't do drugs; he just wanted to be where the action was as much as he could. Jackie was a bona fide cop adrenaline junkie.

He consistently made legitimate criminal arrests through gut instinct, bulldog aggressiveness, and the use of informants, many of whom never knew they were anything more than friends.

One summer midnight to eight shift, at about three in the morning, Jackie had asked for a meeting with one of the new hires, Dave Harrison. Dave had been assigned to the same squad as Jackie for almost a month, and because Jackie had always been on the go, he had really never had the occasion to talk to him.

In fact, the only contact that the two had was when Dave was answering a bar fight call; he was almost run off the road by Jackie, who passed him on a curve, lights and siren blaring, doing about 80 mph. When Dave got to the bar, the fight was over, the participants gone, and there was no cause for any police action. Dave asked Jackie why he drove around him like he did, and Jackie told him, "If you're not going to drive like you want to get there, just get out of my way."

A few weeks later, Jackie asked Dave to meet with him in his zone for some information. When Dave pulled up next to Jackie, a bit of small talk took place, including what passed as something of an apology concerning their last conversation about being almost run off the road, with the explanation that at the time of the call, he was getting some good drug information from an informant and had been a bit aggravated by having to leave.

After a few minutes, Jackie told Dave to turn off his engine. Because it was a hot, muggy August night, Dave was not keen on losing his air conditioning, but being the new guy, did as he was told. Jackie told him that the engines had to be off, as he wanted to be able to hear what was going on in his zone as they talked.

After about ten minutes of chit-chat, a noise caused both men to stop talking and look at the horizon. It became evident that someone in the area had clearly just broken a very large piece of glass. As Dave looked around, Jackie immediately said that it was either the liquor store or the 7-11, both of which were about two blocks away and located within a few hundred feet of one another.

Jackie had his car started and in drive before Dave was able to reach out and turn his key in the ignition. Jackie sped off in the direction of the two buildings, with Dave attempting to catch up. Because it was three in the morning, both businesses were closed (This was when "7-11" actually meant 7 a.m. to 11 p.m.).

When they arrived at the location, a quick check revealed the liquor store looked normal, but one of the glass doors to the 7-11 had been broken out, with tiny bits of safety glass along with what appeared to be a pile of vomit lying both outside and inside the doorway. Jackie was out of his car and almost through the door before Dave got his car in park.

Realizing that a by the book proper and safe search of the building was not going to happen, Dave followed Jackie through the door going to the left as Jackie had gone to the right. The aisles were quickly checked, with negative results. With a quick visual check over the checkout counter, a figure was seen huddled in a corner, his right hand bleeding, with what appeared to be the same vomit that was found by the door covering the front of his shirt.

Seemingly surprised to see two policemen shining flashlights in his eyes and looking at him with drawn weapons ordering him to not move a muscle, and unable to find explainable wordage to explain anything, the young man promptly turned his head and commenced to perform a flawless act of projectile vomiting, covering the floor and stock items on shelves under the counter.

Judging from the odor in the air and in addition to the quantity of liquid leaving his stomach, it was clear that the subject was alcohol-intoxicated. The first vivid thought Dave had of the situation was that he couldn't believe that anyone could vomit that much.

Jackie mumbled, just loud enough for Dave to hear, "Vomit Vernon."

After determining that the young man was not an immediate danger other than the possibility of being hit with flying vomit, he offered information which confirmed Jackie's belief that he was indeed Vernon Johnson. Vernon was a well-known individual who was also well known for being a regularly intoxicated individual who had a penchant for drinking to excess, or in his case, drinking until he vomited. It was clear that he was nearly at the "almost passed out" point of intoxication, and because of his history, which when it happened, didn't surprise Jackie at all, the young man had begun vomiting.

Neither Jackie nor Dave wanted to handcuff Vernon or to put him in either of their patrol cars, so they decided to talk to him outside the store to get his side of the story. While being asked to stand at a safe distance, Vernon very slowly and slurringly advised that while waiting for the late bus to take him a few miles down the road, he had decided he needed a pack of cigarettes. Unfortunately for him and the store owner, the 7-11 was already closed, and rather than wait another four hours for it to open, he had decided the best course of action would be to try to open the store himself.

He stated he pulled on the door handle several times, thinking that someone might have left the store unlocked. Following the realization that the store clerks had successfully closed the store, he had gotten angry and hit the glass door with his fist, which much to his surprise, shattered. He stated that the shattering glass scared him to the point of vomiting at the doorway. After regaining what little composure he had left, he thought that as long as the door was kind of open, he might as well go in and get the cigarettes.

After pocketing a couple of packs from a counter display, he said he could not find matches and was behind the counter looking for some when Jackie and Dave arrived. With two 9-millimeter handguns pointing at him, he said he again became frightened and vomited again onto his shirt and pants, and apparently most of the stock items under the counter.

To finish the lesson for Dave, rather than get involved with a vomit-covered, intoxicated individual, Jackie called for the rescue squad to treat the broken glass injury and then proposed to them that it would be beneficial to Vernon and all concerned for them to make a transport to the hospital to ensure that The Vomit King was saved from possible alcohol poisoning.

When he was released from the hospital the following afternoon, he was rewarded for his intoxicated adventure the previous day by being served complaints charging him with breaking and entering, damage to property, trespassing, theft of two packs of cigarettes, and littering with regards to vomiting all over the store.

The littering was a charge that Jackie had been prepared to drop, as it clearly did not really comply with the wording of the statute; however, Vernon pleaded guilty to all charges without even questioning the wording. It was rumored that after finding out the amount of fines he had to pay, Vernon's face became extremely pale, and he came close to vomiting in court.

CHAPTER 61

Sudden Changes in Jurisdictions

A ngelo Demucchi and Nicky Harlow were pared as detective partners for several years. On a fall morning when the summer bedlam had settled down and the majority of visitors had headed home, the two detectives had left the station en route to a local restaurant in the dock area to have morning coffee and breakfast with the day shift patrol Sergeant Ben Bailey.

When they were almost at the restaurant, they were contacted on the radio by Ben, who advised them that they were needed at a call in the rear of one of the local clam- canning facilities.

They reluctantly diverted from breakfast and met Ben, who was smiling and indicated that they probably wouldn't be making it to breakfast anytime soon. Thinking the problem was probably going to be a break in of the building, they followed Ben.

While walking with Ben toward the back harbor's water's edge in the rear of the building, he advised that one of the buildings workers had flagged him down as he was turning around in the parking lot and told him that he thought that a body had washed up and was floating in the weeds.

When they got to the location, there was clearly and most definitely a body in the water, somewhat half floating in the water and the other half snagged in the weeds and tall salt grass on the shoreline. The body in question appeared to have been in the water for a couple of days, as it had severely bloated, with the extremities missing bits of flesh, no doubt to hungry fish and crabs.

Angelo, usually being the consummate professional in the detective division at the time, started into his investigative mode and indicated he would get the "kit and camera" from the trunk, when Nicky said with a short snort and throat-clearing,

"I believe it would be prudent to slow your response a bit, Ange. I want to peruse the immediate area before we do anything. It would also be wise not to make any radio transmissions as to the status of the incident, as there is a possibility that the status could well change."

He then walked off and disappeared around the corner and toward the other side of the building.

Ben, who had known Nicky for years, wasn't too surprised at his actions or statements, and Angelo simply stood with Ben, wondering what the hell was going on. After several minutes, Nicky reappeared from the rear of the building, carrying an old wooden oar on one shoulder that he had found next to a loading dock. At that point, he put his index finger to his lips in a shushing motion, and again headed into the weeds in the vicinity of the body.

In a few short minutes he exited the weeds, snorted, and advised Ben to radio the dispatcher to contact the marine police and advise them there was a body floating in the middle of the waterway behind the clam-canning building.

Looking at Ben and Angelo and giving another short snort, he said, "Somehow it seems that the body in question apparently floated back into the waterway. According to statute, since it is no longer touching land, it is now in the jurisdiction of the state marine police."

After Nicky returned the oar to its previous location, Ben called for a marked unit to sit at the scene and wait for the marine police to show up and handle the call. The three once again proceeded to coffee and breakfast.

The marine police arrived and conducted a professional investigation and recovery of the floater and ascertained that it had been a vacationing fisherman who had fallen from his pleasure boat and had been missing for the last four or five days.

As much as the department actually assisted the marine police as professionally as possible at almost all times, it was well known that the marine police had performed and utilized the same but reversed investigative procedures toward Cedar Springs and the neighboring municipalities many times in the past.

CHAPTER 62

Car Wash

There were two automatic car washes in the town that were utilized so a patrolman could drive up, sign his name and car identification number, and drive the car through the wash, which aided in keeping the cars respectfully clean. A monthly bill would then be sent to the department. The other alternatives were to wash it manually at the station or at your home, or not wash it at all and pray for rain.

Officially, the cars were supposed to be inspected each Sunday morning using a check-off list to ensure all the equipment was in order and that they were somewhat mechanically sound. This included having the car cleaned. Most patrolmen would drive them through one of the automatic car washes and, when needed, vacuum the insides the same day.

Jan McCord, besides being well known for attempting to drown a new Chevy Suburban in the ocean and driving his car into the cafeteria of the schools, was also one of those guys who would continually wash the patrol car whenever he worked. He would always say that the car was his office for eight hours a day, and he couldn't stand to be in a dirty office.

It was rumored that Jan had suffered a form of PTSD from the sunken Suburban incident and was constantly checking his car to ensure that it was not water damaged or polluted with sea creatures haphazardly stuffed into the bumpers, but no proof of that ever surfaced--and to be honest, it was a pretty far-fetched rumor. It was probably more realistically a fact that he just liked to drive a clean car.

At the end of a shift, a patrolman would pick up their relief at their particular house in the patrol car, then be dropped off at their respective homes. This ensured that no interruptions in patrol would occur, and cars would always be on the road and available to answer calls. It also saved wear and tear on one's private vehicle.

For a period of a few years, Mike Harding worked in the squad preceding Jan's squad and shared the same patrol car. It was common knowledge that Jan had some peculiar ideas about how clean his car should be and simply because of that, it became one of Mike's undertakings to pick up Jan and deliver the car as dirty as possible whenever possible. Routinely Mike would pull up at Jan's house with mud splatters on the car, commenting that he had answered a call earlier in the day where there was mud and he would somewhat attempt to apologize for it.

Mike would always say, "Just leave it and I'll clean it up tomorrow," knowing full well that Jan would not be able to stand the dirt and clean it as soon as possible.

Normally, one would not go out of his way to dirty up a patrol car. The cars, being white, did look better clean, and at times it was just plain hard to find enough dirt in order to really make the car look bad. However, because it caused so much disgruntlement to another patrolman, Mike somehow recognized and understood that the undertaking was just too hard to ignore and considered the chore to be part of his obligation and sense of *thick blue duty.*

As luck would have it, Jan lived in a rural area in an old farmhouse located at the end of a road paved with oil and stone. The roadway was resurfaced with more oil and stone on about a once every ten-year schedule. This in itself meant the roadway was constantly filled with bumps, pot holes, and ruts, which collected dirty water on a constant basis. Traveling through these pot holes at the right speed would certainly splash mud onto the sides of the car, but with rain coming only occasionally, the desired effect was sporadic and infrequent.

Fortunately for Mike and the others who took joy in Mike's vision as well as Jan's disappointment, there was another far less traveled dirt road leading across a field to Jan's house. The road, actually a dedicated municipal road, ran from one street to another, had no homes, had never been paved, and didn't even have a street name.

Once in a great while, the town would send a road grader through to smooth the dirt so that fire fighting vehicles could get through if needed, but that was the extent of road maintenance done. Because of this lack of maintenance, the roadway soon reverted to large holes, ruts, bumps--and of course, mud holes. One in particular stood out from the others and when dry resembled a low spot in the roadway, approximately 15 feet in diameter.

Whenever it rained or snowed, the road became and remained the perfect location in which to acquire the maximum amount of mud on a vehicle and still not get it stuck. Of course, this would require many practice runs whenever the opportunity arose. There were times when it was reported to have taken several runs in a single day through this particular mud hole in order to get the desired effect.

The optimal effect came one day following a heavy rain the day before. The un-named roadway was extremely muddy, and the large mud hole had been turned into the equivalent of the monster tank trap capable of monstrous and unequaled devastation to a white vehicle.

Mike took it upon himself to attempt to offer unto Jan a vehicle so dirty, it would not be able to be identified as a police cruiser. That day, the mud hole was a record- breaking almost one full foot deep in the middle and approximately 12 to 14 feet across, requiring speeds of at least 20 mph to ensure even making it through. With the months of practice and the hopes and dreams of the rest of the audacious, devious, and heartbreaking loving patrolmen resting firmly upon his shoulders, Mike drove through the mud hole three times and successfully covered the patrol vehicle until it was literally difficult to see out the windows.

Mike then nonchalantly drove up to Jan's house, the car literally steaming from the water and mud on the undercarriage and resembling a dirt track racer with overhead lights. Jan, as usual, carrying his overcoat and briefcase, came out of his back door and when actually seeing the car, stopped dead in his tracks. Shoulders dropping a bit, it was as if Jan had just found out he had been adopted or that his dog had just eaten his winning lottery ticket.

After staring at the car for several moments, Jan continued a slow walk to the car, opened the door with two fingers, and got in without a word. No hello, no what happened, nothing. Adding to the experience, Mike never offered an explanation for the condition of the car. About halfway to Mike's home, he considered striking up a conversation but decided it would be better if nothing was said and the entire fifteen-minute ride took place in silence.

It was said that Jan had to take the car through the automatic car wash three times before it began to resemble a police vehicle again. Additionally, Jan used four dollars in quarters to power-wand wash the tires, wheels, wheel wells, and behind the bumpers.

Jan never brought up the condition of the car that day to Mike and Mike knowing that there was no way possible to get more mud on a car than he already had, never again used the field road when it was muddy to pick up Jan.

He did, however, begin to eat shelled sunflower seeds in the car, sporadically spitting some of the empty shells onto the dash and into the defroster vents. This in itself was not a big deal other than being a bit unsanitary. Of course, because the empty shells had fallen down into the defroster vents, no one really knew they were there. That is, until the first cold spell fell over the area and drivers tended to turn on the heat and defroster fan to clear the windows.

Once a year, Mike tried to orchestrate his sunflower shell-spitting into the defrost vents so that Jan could enjoy the full effects and gratification of being the one who was lucky enough to be in the car when the defrost fan was really needed.

When the fan was turned on high, the shells, now sufficiently dried and much lighter, had a tendency to fly out like a meteor shower, causing whoever was driving the car to duck and weave to avoid being hit in the face. First-timers always stated that they didn't know what the hell was flying out at them and would immediately pull over.

Throughout the next several years, Mike would also leave just enough empty shells on the floor to indicate a possible future meteor shower, which would cause Jan to get in the car with a slight eye twitch and heavy sigh.

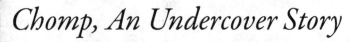

CHAPTER 63

Chomp, An Undercover Story

T hroughout the '70s and '80s, the county investigation department attempted to quell the ever-growing illegal drug infesta-
tion utilizing certain members of the different departments who were
"loaned" to the drug task force to work undercover, usually for six
months and up to a year.

Cedar Springs had several different patrolmen assigned to the task
force over the years. Occasionally a substantial amount of drugs was
confiscated, and significant arrests were made. Also occasionally, arrests were made with accounts of the incidents and methods used in
the arrests that would have made for an unbelievable reality television
show.

Jake Dillon had been assigned to the task force for about eight
months and had, like others before him, grown a beard and let his hair
grow long. He had been making buys of cocaine from a group of people that lived in a rather large and luxurious home on the waterfront
in a neighboring community. Over the course of four months, he had
purchased over three ounces of the drug.

He had worked his way into being a frequent visitor at the house
by hanging at a local tavern nearby and getting to know some of the
people who regularly drank there and stayed at the house. Even after
more than a dozen visits to the house and at least eight purchases, he
had never met the supplier, who was identified as Kevin Spritzer.

About a dozen people reportedly lived at the house, seemingly on
a full-time basis, and there were always that many more partying and
spending the days and nights, which made it seem that people just
came and went as they pleased. It seemed the only real rule was that

Kevin controlled all the sales but had the "live-ins" do all the transfers and deliveries.

When making a buy, Jake had always been told the delivery person was going up to the second floor, which was where Kevin lived. The second floor was a home in itself comprising a bath, kitchen, living room, and bedroom. Along with Kevin, it also housed "Chomp," Kevin's rather large and seemingly untrained and most unpleasant pit-bull dog. The dog usually had the run of the house, and it was fairly evident from its demeanor that it did not seem to like people in general. People likewise generally did not seem to like Chomp, or it could be better described as they were scared to death of him and steered clear of him. It was said that Kevin had trained Chomp to attack on command and that the dog always stayed upstairs at night and early mornings for security purposes.

Following several weeks of hanging out at the house and several drug buys, Jake was introduced to Kevin and had his first real encounter with Chomp. While reaching out to shake Kevin's hand, he came close to losing several fingers, as Chomp apparently took the movement as an attempted assault. The dog lunged with open jaws but was stopped by Kevin at the last moment.

Starting with the next visit, he began to carry dog treats with him every time he went to the house and made it a point always to give Chomp a few on every visit. The first few were simply tossed from a distance. It wasn't long before he could go to the house and whenever he encountered Chomp, the dog would charge toward him but hesitate just prior to contact. Still growling, his head would tilt to one side, seemingly awaiting Jake's next move. A treat would always follow.

Because of the dog treats, after a few weeks, Chomp began to soften his attacks toward Jake. Whenever Jake would visit the house, he would call Chomp, and the dog would charge through the rooms, tail wagging. When he got to Jake, he would stop and wait. Jake would tell him to sit, which he did knowing full well that he would soon be getting some treats.

After several more buys, Jake wrote up his incident report that suggested a date and time for a raid on the house. He also indicated that when the arrest and search warrants were served, if they wanted to seize any drugs, they needed to get to the second floor quickly and quietly to get to Kevin--and more importantly had to be prepared to encounter a badass pit-bull named Chomp, who would definitely mimic his name at the drop of a hat.

It had become well known to the rest of the task force that Jake had an enduring relationship with Chomp due to his ongoing dog friendly gesture of feeding the dog treats with every visit.

Normally the agent that has been making the drug buys is never utilized in the actual raid, as it causes many future problems when those arrested realize who was responsible for their newfound predicaments. However, in this case because of the known demeanor of Chomp and Jake's relationship with Chomp, he was told that he would go and be the first one to hit the second floor.

Because of the number of people usually in the house, ten police personnel were selected to participate in the raid: four members of the task force (including Jake), four state troopers, and two detectives from the municipality where the house was located.

The raid took place in the early-morning hours, which meant Chomp was probably on the second floor with Kevin. As soon as the front door was kicked in, Jake started looking for Chomp. The live-ins were quickly gathered together, and the assault on the second floor began. Halfway up the stairway, Kevin could be heard scurrying around and doors or cabinets being slammed shut.

Jake continued to look for Chomp without results, which meant that he was with Kevin. When the team quickly destroyed another door and entered Kevin's place, Kevin and Chomp were found backed up into the kitchen area. Chomp was straining at his collar with white foam around his mouth, with Kevin screaming that he was going to let the dog go.

With several guns focused on both Kevin and Chomp, who was now fiercely growling and pawing at the floor, Jake called to him. Chomp suddenly recognized Jake's voice and after breaking away from Kevin literally slid across the floor, tail wagging, and immediately sat, expecting to be rewarded with a treat and head pat. Jake complied with the dog's request and added a verbal "good boy," which was quickly followed by a friendly head nudge from the dog to Jake's leg.

Kevin, with an exasperated look on his face, was rewarded by being thrown into a wall by two troopers and then to the floor, where he was roughly cuffed and quite verbally chastised for attempting to sic his dog on a state trooper. State troopers were well known for not appreciating being threatened by people and/or dogs.

Almost a pound of cocaine was found on the kitchen table, complete with scales and hundreds of plastic bags and vials. Kevin, as well as most everyone who was downstairs at the time, was arrested and charged with some type of drug charge. Chomp was escorted to the county kennel and eventually released to one of Kevin's relatives.

About a week later, Jake was advised during a post-investigative meeting that his time with the task force had come to an end. With verbal thanks from the county officials, he was told that he should return to regular patrol work in Cedar Springs, as his cover had obviously been blown. Due to the number of people from the house who now knew his actual occupation, it was determined that it was no longer safe for him to work undercover.

In the next few months, Jake received no fewer than six threats of retaliation by those who were arrested. It was and probably remains true that arrested individuals typically blame their personal misfortunes upon the police who arrest them and not themselves for doing something illegal. In this instance, they all blamed Jake for their problems: all with the exception of Chomp.

CHAPTER 64

Cowboy's in Town

On a fall night in November, dispatcher Timothy O'Doul made an interoffice call to the detective's office and indicated in a lower than average and serious voice that he had two "Texas Ranger" cowboys at the window who wanted to see a detective. Dooley never spoke in hushed tones unless something fairly serious or strange was happening and having two cowboys in Cedar Springs was indeed fairly strange.

Mike Robinson happened to be the detective on duty at the time and took the call, telling Dooley that he would be right up. Mike had been assigned to the detective division for a couple of years and was generally known as being somewhat normal. He was also known as the epitome of a patronizing, egotistical, and bigheaded individual. Not that he was that bad of a guy, but he was always outwardly showing concern for any and all problems while routinely solving virtually none. In his favor and to his credit, his show of great concern was more than enough to accommodate and satisfy most people's anxiety and unease following a traumatic event.

While having a conversation with others, Mike had an uncanny knack of twisting words and grammar into his own vocabulary in an attempt to sound more interesting than he actually was. He was usually harmless, as long as you didn't buy into his philosophy of fantasy law enforcement. However, his one remarkable and respectable trait was his ability to entice--or more likely to confuse--women into spending time with him and what could be lightly construed as romantic interludes.

This reasonably undisruptive yet impressive trait was a part of his well-known forte until a call came into the dispatch center one night of "gunshots fired." The call was received from Mike's home and came directly from Mike. As in any officer assist call, it was met with all available patrolmen responding to the area as soon and as quickly as possible.

Mike offered several frantic allegations about his being a target of some unknown assassin while pointing out the startling indication of two distinct bullet holes in the front of his house.

Twenty minutes later, with a half dozen officers ready to take vengeance upon the unknown attacker, Mike calmed down and with a slight hesitation admitted that the unknown assailant probably was someone he knew. Following another slight hesitation, he admitted that most assuredly the shooter was the jealous and antagonistic husband of one of his latest conquests.

Almost predictably, he added that the man's wife also just happened to have been with Mike at the time of the shooting, and also just happened to be still huddled in a corner in Mike's bedroom.

Mike's ego took a tremendous hit that night, as he reportedly begged the woman to speak with her husband and calm the situation over. He inferred that she should undoubtedly lace the calming with many fabrications of him simply consoling a friend with advice during a trying time in her marriage. Mike's next objective was to then convince the patrol sergeant to not immediately have the woman's husband arrested for attempted murder. Luckily, the sergeant was Billy Durrant, who didn't want to get involved with the call in the first place. Billy told Mike, "Take care of this. Straighten it out, and don't get shot. There's way too much paperwork required if you do.!"

The woman went home and after a couple of hours reported that the fabricated account of her recent actions to her husband was apparently a success. The woman soon reconciled with her husband, reportedly and surely as the safest course of action for her as well as for Mike, and the whole matter was sufficiently swept under the *thick blue rug*. However, many stick-on fake bullet holes routinely were found on Mike's car and mailbox for many weeks thereafter.

Now this particular "cowboy" incident took place a couple of months after the aggrieved husband house-shooting ordeal, and Mike was still feeling the effects of his injured ego as well as his reputation as a player. He had decided that his best course of action in the future would be the straight and narrow and by-the-book routine--at least for a while anyway.

When Mike reached the dispatch center, sure enough, there appeared to be two guys wearing white cowboy hats standing in the vestibule. He opened the door leading to the vestibule and introduced himself. While inviting the two in, he asked how he could help them. Just like on television, they showed him their Texas Ranger identifications. Mike indicated to them to follow him to the detective's office and jokingly asked them if they had tied up their horses outside. This was met with silence and no trace of any facial expression from either man.

Once inside the detective's room, Mike asked what he could do for them. Ranger number one identified himself as Ranger Beau Paxton. Ranger Beau was a strapping six foot two inches tall, wearing a form-fitting, three-piece coffee-colored suit complete with sewn-in brown leather elbow patches, a sky-blue shirt with white string tie, and designer snakeskin boots. He advised that they were looking for a fugitive who lived in the area. Mike wasn't familiar with the name given, but after a quick residence check, the property was identified as being owned by a family from Philadelphia that utilized it during the summer months.

Ranger number two who identified himself as Ranger Morgan Powell, almost as tall as Ranger Beau, and also wearing a three-piece suit. His was pale blue in color with sequins adorning the cuffs and lapels. Footwear was dark-blue designer suede boots complete with stainless-steel toe inserts. He advised that they had good quality information that the guy they were looking for was known to be friends with the property owner and was at the house hiding from the law.

The subject they were looking for apparently was suspected of a string of gas station robberies, and more importantly, they said, was wanted for an assault on a Texas Ranger utilizing a motor vehicle. They indicated that they had already been by the house and that there appeared to be a flickering light, probably from a television, showing through the closed curtains in what was probably the living room.

Mike thought that an assist on a fugitive arrest with Texas Rangers could certainly quell the recent "angry husband shooting up his house" ridicule. He stated that he could have the zone car drive by the residence to double check for movements and be available for back-up, but advised the two Rangers that without an arrest warrant or a search warrant, an entry could not take place.

Ranger Beau said, "We don't need a warrant. He'll let us in without a problem. We're just telling y'all in case the neighbors call in with any questions or complaints."

Ranger Morgan added in a deadpan voice, "We won't need any back-up!"

With a flood of questions flickering through his brain at an alarming rate, Mike stated that he would go with them just to be sure there were no problems with any of the neighbors. Rangers Beau and Morgan reluctantly agreed, and Mike followed them to the location.

When they all got out of their cars, Ranger Beau came up to Mike and told him, "Why don't you stand by the cars and watch out for any unruly neighbors."

Ranger Morgan immediately went to the rear of the house. When Ranger Beau loudly banged on the front door, Mike distinctly heard Ranger Morgan holler from the rear, "Come on in."

Ranger Beau then ever so slightly nudged the front door with his shoulder, complete with the distinct sounds of splintering wood and screws being pulled out of the doorway, and quickly entered the home.

A few minutes later the two Rangers, still wearing their hats, came out the front door, each holding an arm of a guy handcuffed at the wrists and at the ankles, wearing a look of disbelief on his face.

For every two steps the Rangers took, the suspect was forced to hop. He was quickly taken and put in the rear of their Ford Crown Victoria and secured in a seat belt.

Mike, not completely confident that the arrest had not in fact been an abduction, approached the Rangers and said, "All right, we have a holding cell at the station. We can go back to my office and work on the arrest and extradition papers. Our county prosecutor can probably help get the papers through to a judge as soon as possible."

Ranger Beau then very calmly said, "Hey partner, we appreciate all you did. We don't really worry about extradition papers. The fact is, this guy fucked with a Ranger. That's all the information we need. We're taking him back to Texas."

Ranger Morgan nodded in agreement as the sequins from his suit glittered under the streetlight. Both Ranger Beau and Ranger Morgan shook Mike's hand, again saying thanks, and with a tip of their hats, got into the Crown Vic and drove away.

Mike returned to the station, now glad he hadn't notified the zone car or the shift supervisor, and advised Dooley what had taken place.

Dooley, said, "Hummm, remind me to never fuck with a Texas Ranger."

No mention of the incident was relayed to the shift sergeant, and no record of the event was ever recorded.

CHAPTER 65

A Simple "Thanks"
Would Have Done

Because of a large influx of visitors in the summer months, Cedar Springs hired temporary police officers to assist the full-time members with patrol duties. In the 1960s and 1970s, the hiring process was fairly simple. All one had to do was be recommended by one of the full-time officers, pass a simple criminal history examination, and qualify with a firearm at the range. The temps, or "specials" as they were called, were given a couple of uniforms, complete with the mandatory hat to comply with Captain Benny's wishes, a gun, a badge, and were paid a tad more than minimum wage. Most specials would work 20 to 30 hours per week directing traffic or riding along with a "full-timer" in the busier areas.

Mike Harding, a full-time officer, not unlike the other patrolmen, worked part time on his off days and half days on the night shifts and midnight shifts. Mike's second job was with a construction contractor. The company built new homes and constructed additions to existing ones.

On one of the home additions, he met the homeowner Al "The Animal" Meadows. Al was a history teacher at the local high school and also an avid weight lifter. Al had bartered part of the cost of his addition by doing his own painting and volunteering his labor at the site after school and on weekends. Being six foot three, 220 pounds, with 21- inch biceps automatically meant that Al was deemed to be two things: the "HL" and the "ERT." The "HL" was the heavy lifter who got to move the lumber from where it was delivered to where it was needed. The "ERT" was the environmental refuse technician or what was commonly known as the trash clean-up person.

Mike, being part time with the builder, was sometimes also designated as the ERT at sites and welcomed Al to the world of being low man on the totem pole. In a short time, the two became good friends.

Al was interested in most of the police stories that Mike would talk about and Mike became interested in Al's suggestions on how to gain inches to his physique by lifting weights. Mike also continually inquired about Al's nickname of The Animal but never got a definitive answer.

It was soon thereafter that Mike and Al began to go to a neighborhood gym at five o'clock in the morning three to four days per week. Following the first visit, Mike found out why Al was called The Animal.

It seemed that whenever Al worked out, he would always utilize massive amounts of weights, routinely bench pressing 400 pounds and doing one arm curls with 110-pound dumbbells, all while grunting and shouting. At times this seemed rather comical, and others at the gym would stop and stare but no one even thought to question Al, as he was usually lifting several hundred pounds more than they were.

The gym was owned by a man named Gino Rossi, a transplant from southern California who qualified for the "Mr. Universe" body-building competition but had to pull out after ripping his left bicep muscle from the bone, requiring major surgery and months of rehabilitation.

Following rehab, Gino was warned by doctors to only lift about 75 percent of what he had grown accustomed to. With those limitations, the results needed to tone his body for competitive presentation was no longer possible. He retired from competition, moved to the East Coast, and started a construction business. He bought several acres of land and made a gym out of some old chicken coops that were on the grounds. He affectionately named the gym "The Coop World Gym" and it was thereafter simply referred to around the county as "The Coop."

Gino was a quiet sort and still possessed a well-defined physique. In his early forties and a bit over six feet tall, he still looked able to compete. He took gym workouts seriously. Trying to influence youth, he routinely let high school students in for next to nothing, so long as they didn't play around. If and when they did, they got one warning. The next time they were asked to leave and not return.

Each morning Gino would open the gym at four a.m., work out for an hour or so, then go home, eat breakfast, and go to work at his construction company. He had a gym manager who would re-open The Coop at seven a.m. and run things the rest of the day.

Al had known Gino for several years and had been lifting at The Coop for the last five years. Because of his dedication to lifting, Gino had stopped charging Al to lift, as many days he would stay at the gym and look after things until the manager showed up.

It took no more than a few weeks of going to the gym to convince Mike that he really did feel better during the day, even though there were some days that it was hard to lift his arms for a few hours after trying to keep up with Al's routine.

As these things sometimes happen, Mike mentioned to Al that the department was again getting ready to hire specials for the summer months. Because as a teacher with summers off, Al said that he would be interested and filled out an application at the station. A few days later, Al was interviewed by The Rude, and following probably one of the shortest background investigations in Cedar Springs history, he was offered a job. The Rude, after coming face to face with Al, thought just his size would be advantageous at some of the bar fights and significantly reduce most of the confrontations.

For several months, Al worked alongside the regulars and convinced many of them that lifting weights at the gym was a good thing to include in their daily routines. Soon at least a half dozen members of Cedar Springs PD were working out at Gino's gym. Many, including Mike, saw significant gains in their muscle mass, which more than helped when faced with those who did not wish to be arrested after being advised that they were under arrest.

Now all of that leads us into the following.

Late in the summer on a Sunday day work shift, Mike was on patrol with Al as a partner. Trying to mind their own business, they were driving around a slight curve in the road when another car, a convertible Corvette with what looked like two occupants, traveling in the opposite direction, crossed the middle line and forced Mike to veer off the roadway to avoid a collision.

Al said, "Whew… that was different." Mike said, "What the fuck… what an asshole."

Mike slowed and began to turn around, thinking that he would at least stop the car and give the driver a piece of his mind. As he completed the turn, he saw that the car did not completely make it through the curve. Instead, it drove straight ahead, off the roadway, through a row of low hedges and struck a large tree, causing it to overturn, spin around in a complete circle and finally come to a stop, on its top, smoldering in the front yard of a home.

Mike then said, "Ah shit," now knowing that they would have to do an accident report.

Mike called in the accident, and when he and Al pulled up in front of the house, a disheveled man with blood dripping down his face staggered across the lawn toward the patrol car.

"What the fuck just happened?" said the man in a slow, drunken slur. "Look at my fucking car."

Mike's first question was, "Are you all right?"

Al added, "Was there anybody else in the car with you?"

The man looked around at the upturned car and answered in a slow slur, "What the fuck happened? Look at my fucking car!"

Now within a foot of the man, Mike could detect a strong odor of alcoholic beverage emitting from him. What a nice way to ruin a perfectly peaceful day work shift. Mike was now a bit angry that he not only had to do an accident report, they now had to deal with a drunk driver who was obviously more interested in his car than the police or any passengers he may have had.

The man, later identified as Joey Simone, visibly not seriously injured, was told to sit down and take it easy. Mike called for a rescue squad and a back-up to respond to the scene and walked toward the overturned, still-running car. Reaching into the open upside- down driver's door, Mike was able to reach in and turn the key off. With a quick look toward the interior of the vehicle, it was then that he formally met the driver's passenger, Joey's girlfriend Sherrie. The inside of the vehicle smelled like the back room of a brewery. Mike caught site of a body crammed between the area behind the front seats and the trunk area. The body twitched as the engine stopped, and then it spoke. "Hey, asshole! How about getting me the fuck out of here," came the charming and obviously female voice, spoken in a slow drunken slur.

Mike, instinctively acting on the assumption of having an injured person in the car, asked, "Are you all right?"

Answering in a coarse and antagonistic tone, Sherrie said, "No... I'm not. Are you fucking blind? I'm stuck under the fucking car. Now get me the fuck out!"

By this time the driver, Joey, had stood up and wandered over to the car and had heard Sherrie yelling. Adding nothing useful to the situation in a short period of time, he too began to demand in a long, drunken rhetoric that she be rescued.

"What the fuck are you waiting for? Get her the fuck out of the fucking car. I pay taxes.... It's okay, Sherr.... He'll get you out.... I pay your fucking salary.... Do something, you assholes!"

Mike, sensing that due to the fact that the Joey's suggestions were being offered with such pensive finesse and understanding, he thought that the best way to accommodate Joeys brooding lack of charm was with an urgent, yet thoughtful and attentive response.

Mike looked at Al and nodded, and as Al moved toward Joey, Mike then promptly advised Joey that he was under arrest.

With that, Joey stopped talking. By the look on his face he was obviously slowly processing that statement and he began to say, "What the fuck fo--?"

Mike quickly grabbed an arm and AL a leg, as they upended the man immediately to the ground. Mike swiftly placed handcuffs on him then helping him to his feet, he was escorted to the patrol car to be placed in the back seat.

Joey, now at the patrol car and realizing that he had crossed the *blue line*, decided that he would not go without a fight and began to struggle and kick while loudly cursing both Mike and Al.

While Mike had a firm hold on Joey's wrists, Al promptly and powerfully assisted with the arrest by grabbing the man's feet causing him to again fall to the ground. As Mike inserted Joey's upper body into the back seat, Al pushed the lower half in and closed the door.

As these things sometimes happen, no doubt because of the alcohol involved, Joey did not seem to comprehend or understand that after being arrested, he should sit quietly and contemplate his rude and unlawful behavior. Adding to his immediate faltering and now very uncertain situation, he promptly raised his legs up and kicked out the back door window of the patrol car.

Mike looked at Al, who smiled and asked, "Attitude adjustment time?"

Mike said, "Yup."

For his effort, Joey was immediately removed from the car, and his ankles were then handcuffed. Those cuffs were then attached to the cuffs on his wrists, effectively hog- tying him. Now unable to cause any more damage, he was then not necessarily gently reinserted into the rear of the patrol car.

The homeowner was 76-year-old Riley Smith who was a retired fire fighter from Philadelphia. He was also now the owner of the severely damaged front lawn, bushes, and his stately 30-foot red oak tree. He had patiently watched the entire arrest and vehicle window damage proceedings from the front stoop of his house. Looking at Joey now hog-tied in the back of the patrol car, he shook his head and said, "What an asshole!"

During this time, the still-trapped Sherrie continued to yell that she wanted to be out from under the car. A careful examination of her position showed that the entire car was pinning her to the ground. It was only the so called "luck of the drunk" that saved her from being crushed by the weight. Apparently not all of the weight of the car was completely on her torso, but because of her location, almost the entire vehicle would have to be lifted in order for her to be released.

The rescue squad had arrived at the scene by this time. One medic was asking Sherrie questions which were being answered by verbal threats and promises of lawsuits and farm-like removal of his testicles. The other one was attempting to give some aid to hog-tied Joey in the patrol car. It was a brief and fleeting bit of aid when it was decided that it was not worth the effort, considering how Joey was verbally not appreciative of his efforts, stating he would sue him, their department, have their jobs, and retaliate his misfortune upon them, their families, and whoever else got in the way.

Fortunately for this particular situation, Smalls, the rescue chief, had arrived at the scene and quickly formulated his opinion of Joey's threats toward the rescue squad. He made his opinion known by introducing himself to Joey and then rubbing a rather large dose of iodine onto his forehead wound, which caused a shriek of a scream not unlike that of a young girl.

Smalls also did not bother to be careful that it did not drip into Joey's eyes. This effectively caused him to immediately change his demeanor and beg for relief. After several minutes of apologetic begging, a few squirts of saline solution seemed to help, along with a stiff undocumented warning from Smalls to never threaten a rescue squad member again.

It seemed that the only way to remove Sherrie from under the car was to have a tow truck attach a cable to one end and lift the car up. The problem became more immediate when it appeared that she seemingly had passed out and was probably going into shock. It was unknown whether it was because of the weight of the car or her continued complaining about not being helped.

Al told Mike that he thought that the two of them could probably lift the car far enough to release the woman. Grabbing the bumpers and door handles, an attempt was made that resulted in lifting the car about an inch but not far enough to release the woman. When the weight was released, Sherrie seemed to recover from shock and screamed and cursed even louder than before, which at that point was hard to imagine even possible.

Mike then crawled under the car, telling Al that they might be able to lift the car with their backs, and told Al to crawl under the other side. There seemed to be just the right amount of room where the two could be on their hands and knees and be able to possibly lift the car. Of course, Mike would have never even considered this action prior to meeting Al and going to the gym.

Unfortunately for their hearing, crawling under the car started a new litany of rants, threats, and curses from Sherrie, not to mention the odor associated with an overly inebriated individual who added to the mêlée and stench by inadvertently emptying her bladder. After listening to the rant for a minute, both Mike and Al, both at about the same time said, "Sherrie....Shut the fuck up."

This seemed to startle her momentarily, and Mike and Al began a three count and lifted. With the second attempt, Smalls and the other rescue members were able to pull Sherrie from under the car.

Miraculously, she seemed to be unhurt, with the exception of a few abrasions on her arms and face. After a thorough check, with no apparent broken bones or major injuries, Sherrie asked, "Where the fuck's my old man?"

When advised that he was under arrest for drunken driving, Mike, Al and the rescue members were rewarded and showered with sweetness and gratitude as Sherrie said, "You mother fuckers! You arrest him and then take your good ole sweet time getting me out from under the fucking car. Look at me. I got cuts all over the fucking place. Just look at his fucking car!"

Sherrie paused for a bit as she stared at the heavily damaged car and then added, "I could have been killed! You fuckers should have gotten me out a long time ago. Fuck you, you lazy bastards! You'll be hearing from my lawyer!"

Mike and Al just looked at each other and rolled their eyes in disbelief. Mike, thinking about rule #10 said, "Aahhh...a simple thanks would have done!"

Sherrie was transported to the hospital to be checked out. Joey was transported to the station where he refused to submit to a breathalyzer test, which added yet another charge to his DUI and patrol car damage summonses.

Because he apparently knew no one other than Sherrie who liked him or was willing to take responsibility for him, and also because he had been so cooperative and helpful, he was kept overnight in a holding cell in an attempt to reaffirm in him a belief in the local justice system.

Hours later and somewhat sober, he was released in the morning pending a court appearance. Hoping that he was now sober enough to comprehend what was being said to him, he was cordially advised that his prized 1966 427/435hp fully restored and pristine Corvette had been towed to one of the area's collision shops. He was also advised the owner of the body shop who towed it assured them that it was also totaled beyond repair.

CHAPTER 66

Methods of Construction and Dealing with Ghosts

Joe Minor had been hired in the mid-1960s and quietly went about his business as a patrolman without much ado. Joe was quite sociable and affable to everyone and never openly disagreed with decisions made by anyone. Because he seemed to stay in the background, some were under the impression that Joe wasn't the brightest bulb in the pack, and he generally never did anything to prove it otherwise. However, Joe would go on to prove that acting and/or giving the impression that "I didn't know," sometimes has its rewards.

Joe lived in an old early 1900s farmhouse with his wife and three children. The house was the only thing left of a once large parcel of land where lima beans and corn once flourished. Now it was just a large old two-story home backed up to a housing development, with a church property and parking lot next door.

Like most of the patrolmen at that time, Joe also worked second jobs for extra money. One of his part-time jobs was an employee at the local lumber yard, assisting with sales and delivering building supplies. Little by little, Joe had been fixing up the old farm house, adding a new central heating unit, new windows, and a roof. Soon to follow were cedar clapboard siding and a rather large A-frame open porch over the front door.

Most of this sounds pretty mundane and normal for most folks. However, in a fitting manner suited to some of the peculiarities of the town, Joe conducted the improvements to his home just a bit differently than most.

Take, for instance, his new roof.

With his old roof showing definite signs of wear, Joe went to a building supply yard, (coincidentally not the one he worked at), and bought enough roofing material to cover his home. When asked which brand and quality he wanted, Joe advised the salesman that he wanted the least expensive, as he was on a budget. This in itself was not necessarily anything out of the ordinary. He also inquired as to the best way to install it. This also was not an unusual question for a homeowner to ask.

The salesman indicated that it was simple and said anyone could do it. Candidly speaking like he had spoken to a hundred other homeowners he said, "Throw on some tar paper, lay out the shingles, put a few nails in them, and you're good to go. It's all in the directions on the roofing packages."

Unfortunately for the salesman, he assumed that Joe would at least read the directions on the packaging or take heed of how the shingles he was going to cover up had been installed.

Now it's always been a rumor that Joe had planned this scenario for quite some time and asked the salesman how to install the roofing hoping for just such an answer as he was given. Joe proceeded to put the tar paper down and lay out the shingles and put a few nails in them. The trouble was, Joe had run the tar paper with virtually no overlapping, as he had decided he would use less this way. He'd only bought one-inch nails, which were a few cents cheaper, with which to nail down the shingles. As the box they came in said "roofing nails," he figured, or so he later stated and wanted everyone to believe, that that was what he was supposed to use.

Product directions as well as common sense to most people would indicate that the tar paper should be put on with one layer overlapping the layer below by at least a few inches to ward off water getting past the singles. Additionally, there was no way one-inch nails were going to hold shingles laid over tar paper and the original old shingles that were dried up and cupping. A second layer of roofing (which is really not recommended in the first place) requires at least a two-inch nail or longer to penetrate the layering and hit the sub roof of wood under those shingles. But as they say about common sense: "If it was so common, everyone would have it!"

About a month and a half after reroofing the house, a fairly heavy rainstorm approached the area, along with some relatively high winds. Sure enough, the majority of the new shingles Joe had installed, containing virtually no straight rows and no nails long enough to make a difference, were now found to be in Joe's front and side yards and the church parking lot next door.

Joe made his displeasure known by notifying the building supply that his roof had blown off. Following their first question, along with his explanation of the installation process used, he was promptly advised that his problem was his and not with the product. Joe's next few calls were to attorneys and the manufactures of the shingles and nails.

It took several weeks, but Joe was finally able to find an attorney to handle his complaint. His claim was that the building supply employees had supplied him with fraudulent information concerning the correct method of installation. Strangely enough, rather than go to court, the manufacturers of the shingles and nails, along with the building supply company, agreed to pay the expense of having Joe's roof properly installed, which included the removal of the old roof and the disposal and clean-up of the area.

No one at the police station could believe that Joe had been smart enough to plan this incident and just attributed it to the fact that the other parties had gotten tired of Joe's whining and didn't want to be characterized as companies that would turn their backs on a young police officer with three small children and a leaky roof. The truth was that Joe had in fact planned the incident, playing the "I didn't know, I asked and wasn't told the right thing, somebody should have warned me" game, and as things sometimes happen, was rewarded for his supposed gullibility and/or stupidity.

The most impressive part of the "Joe I didn't know" story is that Joe, finding that his roof plan was successful, decided to try it again. Joe decided that the old wooden clapboard siding of his house had seen better days and needed to be replaced. With a bit of research, he found that cedar siding was a preferred wood to use in the seashore area due to its durability and resistance to rot.

Off to another building supply company Joe went, being cognizant not to utilize the same one as before, figuring, and figuring correctly, that they would be hesitant to sell him anything ever again. With measurements from his house, Joe purchased more than enough siding to finish the job. Now when it came to buying nails, Joe asked what *size* nails were recommended and was advised of the many different-sized choices. What Joe didn't ask, and purposely so, was: what *type* of nail was recommended?

If the cedar was to be painted, then a regular steel (most inexpensive) or galvanized flat-headed nail would be perfectly acceptable, as they would be covered with paint. If the cedar was to be left unpainted or even stained, the correct choice would be either a galvanized or stainless-steel round-headed or dome-headed nail that, once nailed in, would prevent water from getting behind it and one that would also not rust.

As one could guess, Joe got the regular flat-headed steel nails. He installed the brand-new cedar siding which to passers-by appeared very nice and stylish. Joe also decided that he would not paint the siding, as he liked the natural look. However, after a month or two and a few rainstorms, the steel nails began to rust, and tiny drips of reddish brown rust began to appear under each and every nail on the house.

History repeated itself again, with accusations and proposed lawsuits resulting in the second building supply company footing the bill to remove all the new siding, and replace it utilizing stainless steel dome-headed nails to ensure that there would be no rust in the future.

Now if that weren't enough, a couple of years later, Joe decided to go for a "hat trick" (three in a row) and constructed the large overhead porch on the front of his house. The porch later became known as the 50-foot porch because it appeared to be well constructed from that distance and continued to look that way for several months. As luck or pre-planning would have it, one of the area's famed northeastern storms struck, and the next morning Joe's porch was found located in the front yard, completely ripped from the front of the house. Also, as one would expect, the storm's removal of the porch from the house was quite loud and terrifying to Joe's wife and children.

One would think that this would become a simple homeowner's

insurance claim; however, with Joe, nothing was simple. After the insurance adjuster examined the porch and house, he determined that the porch, all of about three tons of wood and shingles, had been improperly constructed and was attached to the house with nothing more than a few nails instead of large lag-type bolts which would have been required by the building inspectors. With this information, Joe's claim for reimbursement of the damages was denied. Joe's reaction was that one would have thought the heavens caved in and the weight of the entire world had fallen upon his shoulders.

Not to be outdone, Joe appealed the insurance company's decision with the assertion that the town's building inspection office was to blame due to the fact that no one inspected his work or even advised him that a proper building permit was required. After six months of debate, daily phone calls, and numerous letters, the insurance company relented and paid for a new porch to be installed properly. Following the installation, their company president wrote a scathing letter of disgust to the town fathers concerning the lack of observance and regulatory neighborhood inspections for unlawful and unlicensed construction. They also cancelled Joe's homeowner's policy, which was fine by Joe, as the claim had already been paid. The town council admonished the part-time building inspector and after much debate decided to make the position a full-time appointment so that incidents such as this never happened again.

Now, as it has occasionally been in the past, all of the above was a prerequisite to the real adventure story involving Joe and his farmhouse.

The real story was that the old farmhouse reportedly had a ghost. All of Joe's family had seen it at one time or another, and Joe reportedly saw it regularly. The ghost was a female of approximately 16-20 years of age, dressed in clothing appropriate to the late 1800s to early 1900s, or close to the time the house was constructed.

Folklore in the area indicated that the original owners of the farm had had either lost a daughter or possibly a friend of their daughter's, who died suddenly in one of the upstairs rooms of the house. Another story was of a sudden death of a female acquaintance of the owner of the property. The apparent unsubstantiated and unreported mysterious death had occurred in the upstairs section of the home and reportedly included some type of scandalous situation which today would certainly be considered unlawful.

Being a small rural farming community a hundred years ago, some embarrassing situations and even crimes or unfortunate criminal situations were not spoken of and forgotten through the years. Forensic science was not an integral part of law enforcement then, and it was not unusual for incidents, some of which today would be easily considered homicides, to be recorded as unfortunate accidents, with the particulars forgotten and lost to time. The strange thing about the ghost, besides being a ghost in the first place, was that the apparition was seen only on the second floor of the house, usually at the top of the stairs.

Joe also had a pet black Labrador retriever. The dog was a typical Labrador and was gentle and friendly with the children and guests in the house. However, for the two years it had been in the home, it had steadfastly refused to go up the steps to the second floor and would sometimes be heard whimpering during the night time hours. When investigated, it would always be found huddled near the back door, which was coincidentally the furthest area from the steps leading upstairs.

The ghost would appear on a regular basis but generally only to Joe, who reported that while a bit of an annoyance, she really didn't do anything but stand at the top of the stairs, wait until someone saw her, and then disappear. Joe routinely stated that the ghost seemed to be harmless and would make a fairly regular visit on the stairs after midnight when Joe had finished a 4 p.m. to 12 a.m. evening shift. As he would be heading up the steps to go to bed, the girl would appear. Joe had gotten somewhat used to the appearances and got into the habit when she showed up to say, "Aww, crap…what do you want now?"

The apparition would just stare, never giving an answer. With a wave of his hand, Joe would then say, "Go away! Get out of here! Go wherever it is you go!"

Strangely enough, this always resulted in the disappearance of the girl until the next time.

Joe's wife, however, had a much different opinion of the visits. It seemed that the girl was in the habit of appearing to her just at the last second as she reached the top step, scaring the bejeezus out of her time and time again. The children, with the oldest being only eight at the time, had told their mother stories of a lady who visited them sometimes in their rooms at night but would not speak. Much too young to realize the girl was not real, they assumed she was a friend of the family who just didn't say much.

As time went by, Joe's wife became more and more concerned that the children were getting to the age where they would recognize some potential dangers of having an apparition in the house that was not a real person and become frightened and possibly hurt themselves or that the ghost would become jealous and attempt to harm them.

Joe's wife finally presented Joe with an ultimatum. Either the ghost had to go, or she and the children would. Faced with bachelorhood, or possibly more importantly, the threat of spousal and child support for many years, Joe decided that since the ghost was only on the second floor of the house, the best way to rid the home of it was to rid the home of the second floor.

Joe's wife and children went to stay with relatives while the work was being done. With help from a local contractor who hesitantly agreed to work with Joe, knowing his reputation, they disassembled the second floor of the home with hammers, pry bars, and the occasional use of a chain saw, and converted the home into a one-story building.

Three months after the first nail was removed, the home was now a much shorter rancher and did not resemble the old farmhouse at all. Strangely enough, following the reconstruction, the young girl ghost was never seen again and apparently left with the removal of the top of the house.

CHAPTER 67

What Goes Around

Through the years, there were many people--or clientele, if you will--who were constant problems, in that not a week's time went by that they did not have some type of involvement with the police. Every community has a few, and Cedar Springs was no different--and in some respects had more than their share.

Admittedly, most were a byproduct of their own environment because their parents had been, and usually continued to be, constant problems themselves. It was truly unfortunate and also very clear from the time most of them were in elementary school that they didn't have a chance to grow up and become productive, non-irritating at the least, members of society, as they were witness to nonconforming and sometimes criminal elements from the day they were born.

Without even knowing why, most grew up to despise the police for no other reason than because they were told to despise them nearly every day of their lives.

One such young man was Carl Buddy Smith, the son of Bob and Judy Smith, who together had amassed an estimated forty to fifty combined arrests and at least seventy-five thousand dollars in fines over a twenty-year period. It was rumored that the Smiths were attempting a Guinness book of records award for number of arrests, but that was never proven.

Buddy's first run-in with the department took place at the local hardware store when he was a mere eight years old. The family was having a backyard barbecue, and Bob had sent his son down the street to get some supplies. It seems that Buddy had attempted to stuff a can of charcoal lighter fluid upside down in his pants without paying for it. Buddy was caught by the store owner, who cautiously watched him every time he came into the store.

Unfortunately for Buddy, this was prior to almost everything being shrink-wrapped in plastic, and the can had one of the little flip-top spouts on it, which had slightly opened up, spilling almost the entire contents onto Buddy's genitals. It goes without saying to anyone who has spilled gasoline or paint thinner on their skin that this had a disquieting and troubling effect on eight-year-old Buddy.

Because the store owner as well as the police genuinely felt sorry for him and his now-burning genitals, Buddy was taken home, where his father and mother were advised that everyone had agreed the discomfort that Buddy was currently experiencing was a sufficient punishment for the theft and hopefully a deterrent to any future unlawful behavior.

However, as things sometime play out, mostly due to the fact that Bob and Judy were the top-notch parental guidance system that had advised Buddy to steal the lighter fluid to begin with, he was chastised and punished by his father for not being more careful. Additionally, he was convinced that the consequence of the second-degree burns he was rewarded with were not the result of doing wrong but simply the result of not doing wrong right.

With this type of guidance, Buddy grew into a fairly competent yet incompetent thief who routinely was caught approximately thirty percent of the time. Being a juvenile for a better part of his indoctrination into a life of petty crime, Buddy, when adjudicated, was usually given probation or community service duties as punishments.

One of the noteworthy things Buddy was known for was every "Mischief Night" or the night before Halloween, at least one but usually two or three patrol cars would be egged and/or water ballooned in close proximity to Buddy's home. Then, on Halloween, several youngsters would be robbed of their candy usually within one hundred feet of Buddy's house.

Of course, Bob and Judy would cover for him every year, personally vouching for his whereabouts while enjoying the fact that in their opinion the cops were getting what they deserved and the added fact that they got some free candy.

When Buddy finally reached the age of eighteen, he had become the neighborhood "pain in the ass"--not smart enough to stay out of trouble but smart enough to know the police couldn't really do what they wanted to do to him in public and get away with it, although at least a half dozen patrolmen had sworn to do just that should the opportunity ever arise.

On the second week following his eighteenth birthday, Buddy was arrested for simple assault in one of the neighboring towns after he got into a fist fight over an argument concerning the actual meaning of the word cunnilingus. The other boy involved advised Buddy that it was a name for oral sex performed on a woman, but Buddy insisted that the term was a name given to someone who specialized in speech therapy. His vocabulary obviously lacking, verbal jousts escalated to pushing and shoving and then into an old-fashioned mêlée which resulted in the eventual arrival of the police.

This particular jurisdiction's police were routinely faced with hundreds of daily complaints such as this, due to their being a central young adult entertainment area, which attracted hundreds of thousands of people during the tourist season. Solutions to simple assault calls were swift, with virtually no time taken to listen to explanations or theories of who was right and who was wrong.

Buddy, expecting only the usual angry looks and manageable threats from the police, was certainly surprised when both combatants were thrashed to within an inch of their young lives by the responding officers. When Buddy reached the point of numbness, he was then promptly advised he was under arrest and taken directly to a jail cell which he shared with six other similarly thrashed individuals until 8:00 the next morning. When released, Buddy was given a summons to appear in court, where two weeks later the officers testified about how very uncooperative and combative he was, and was found to be very-very guilty and fined $500 dollars. A fitting welcome to adulthood.

After chasing Buddy for the better part of eleven years, admittedly with Buddy having the better record for who harassed whom, many of the patrolmen who had vowed to repay some future misery to Buddy were certainly elated after hearing of his indoctrination into the adult world by the other department.

The two biggest problems with Buddy were his parents, Bob and Judy, who would continually stick up for him, swearing he was home at the time of an incident even though he may have even been caught in the act. Their attempts to convince Buddy that the cops were simply out to get the whole family seemed to somehow make sense to Buddy. Buddy's first adult arrest was no different, with Bob and Judy insisting that the cops in the neighboring town had simply picked their little boy out of a crowd and assaulted him.

Buddy, however, began to doubt how much sense his parents' excuses made when Bob advised Buddy that the fine and the adult arrest record were his responsibility.

Buddy told himself that he would be more cautious in the future, not wanting a repeat of his arrest altercation or a repeat of the outcome that he had received in court.

After using all of his savings to pay his fines, Buddy finally found a girlfriend who apparently didn't know or care about his sorted past. He even got a job at the local lumber company and managed to stay off the police radar for almost a year.

On a hot summer night in July at approximately 3:30 in the morning, a call came in of a traffic accident that had occurred involving one car that reportedly had overturned and had come to a rest after breaking a telephone pole in two. It just so happened that the patrolman who received the call, Tommy Sutliff, was one of the patrolmen who had taken the oath to inflict some emotional or physical payback on Buddy years ago, if the right occasion ever came to pass.

When Tommy arrived at the scene, he found that a sedan had apparently lost control, slid across the roadway and struck a curb, causing it to overturn once and then strike a utility pole, which was now broken in half and lying across the hood of the car. Tommy observed one occupant in the driver's seat, bleeding from lacerations around his forehead and slightly pinned inside the vehicle due to the damage the telephone pole had caused.

The dashboard had been pushed back toward the driver about ten inches and the driver's door pushed in, effectively pinning the driver in where he was slumped in the seat. It was apparent that the driver had also sustained a compound fracture of his left leg, with the femur bone now sticking out of his skin. The driver, who was surprisingly awake, recognized Tommy and begged the patrolman for help.

It took Tommy several looks to finally recognize Buddy due to the amount of blood on his face. Buddy, now in intense pain, was crying when Tommy finally recognized him and said, "Oh...hey, Buddy. It's gonna be okay. Just hold on."

A back-up patrol car arrived driven by Mike Harding, who was another on the list of those who had taken the oath of administering some sort of justice to Buddy.

Tommy immediately advised Mike, "You'll never guess who the driver is."

"Who?" Mike said.

When informed that it was Buddy Smith, Mike's first question was, "How is the little darling?"

Or, in other words, was he dead, or were they going to have to help him? Tommy advised Mike that he was pretty banged up but conscious. It was his opinion that Buddy had suffered no real life-threatening injuries.

Tommy, being one of the more imaginative members of the department, came up with a plan that if implemented quickly, before the rescue squad or a supervisor arrived, would install some much-needed payback and give some satisfaction to them both for all the years of anguish and aggravation Buddy had caused.

Tommy and Mike approached the passenger's side of the damaged car, which now was smoking but in no real danger of catching fire. The cooling system had burst, and coolant was dripping onto the hot engine. Opening the passenger's door, they leaned in.

Buddy, now probably going into shock, looked up with blood running down his face, groaned, and tried to speak. Tommy, putting on his most serious face and with a glint of imaginary compassion in his eye, leaned in close to Buddy, looked him square in the eye and said, "Buddy...I gotta be straight with you.... You're in pretty bad shape, and I'm pretty sure that nothing is going to help."

Mike then took center stage, and with as much sadness as he could muster in his voice advised Buddy, after a full five seconds of silence, "the bottom line is we're pretty sure you're not gonna make it!"

Tommy, quickly stepping up to the plate while it was hot, added,

"And we're also pretty sure that we're not gonna do a damn thing to help." He added, "You remember all those years of you fuckin with us? Well, now it looks like today's the day that what went around is coming back around... or you could just say... it's your judgment day."

Mike, then looking at Tommy flatly said, "I'm gonna call for the coroner cause it's gonna take him a while to get out here. Of course, the way this thing is smoking, it may just catch fire and then I'll have to call in the fire department.... But then again, maybe we'll just let it burn for a while?"

Buddy, hearing all of this and fearing the worst, openly wept and continued to beg for help. Within a few seconds, he began to hyperventilate and then suddenly passed out.

Tommy looked at Mike and said, "Oh, crap! you don't think he's really gonna fuck us again and die on us, do you?"

Mike took a long look at Buddy, noticing that there was some chest movement indicating he was still breathing, and said, "Nah, I don't think so, but if you think about it, it might be a nice to have to wake up Bob and Judy with the sad news, wouldn't it?"

Even with a seemingly perfect scenario taking place, Mike and Tommy had already done what was expected and had called for the rescue squad, along with a fire truck, just in case a blaze did appear shortly after the first examination of the car. Pain in the ass or not, certain lines were never crossed. Bumped into, and ridden real close to, but never crossed.

A short time later, the rescue squad arrived, cut Buddy out of the car with the Jaws of Life, and transported him to the hospital... (via the back route) as requested by Tommy and Mike, and was later rewarded for surviving the crash by several traffic tickets including a DUI arrest, using the blood taken at the hospital which was just below borderline under the influence--but Tommy and Mike figured, and figured right, that the accident itself would be enough evidence to sway the judge into a guilty verdict.

Buddy was fined a few thousand dollars, lost his license for a year, and because of his broken leg, gained a noticeable limp for the rest of his life. Tommy and Mike were rewarded with the gratification of knowing that with just a few well-chosen words, sometimes, even though it takes a long time, what goes around does come around.

CHAPTER 68

Can-u-Canoe, or
Just One of the Regulars
Trying to Get Home

I t's not unusual to see two marked patrol cars parked next to each other. The impression that this is to convey to the public is the exchange of vital information between two officers. That impression is only somewhat and sometimes accurate.

The actual truth is that the information exchanged is seldom related to police work but merely an opportunity to talk about almost anything but police work. Two patrol cars parked next to one another is kind of like what hanging around the water cooler is to office employees.

Some patrolmen actually had codes or certain sayings to use for meetings in particular areas and locations. Occasionally, when the meetings would become a bit too long and frequent, citizens would make mention of them at town meetings, and the chief or captain would send word down the ranks that meetings should take place only in emergency situations and not last more than the time it took to convey the information.

Whenever this took place, a lot of patrolmen would resort to a code of clicks using the police radio microphone. A number of clicks would represent a request for a meet. A series or clicks or a certain pattern of clicks would represent the place and/or time. This was done similar to the secret coding done in WWII and frequently changed to keep the administrators from catching on. All very avant-garde, but effective, especially on day work shifts when cars were much more visible.

On one summer midnight shift, Stuart Tarrantino and Joey Castillano were working. Stuart was working the north end and Joey was assigned to the south end. Being in an administrative "no meeting unless necessary" period of time, Stuart requested, by means of several consistently inconsistent taps on the microphone, a meet with Joey around 3 a.m. They decided, by another series of taps, to meet at the Highlander Restaurant parking lot, as it had closed a couple of hours earlier. This particular restaurant was located near the bay and down the street from an out-of-business fishing boat rental business, which used to rent small aluminum boats to the public for fishing in the bay.

They sat talking in the lot for about a half hour with absolutely no calls being recorded anywhere in town. Thankfully, it seemed that even the neighborhood dogs were asleep. The sky was clear, a half moon was bright, and millions of stars were visible over the bay. They had both turned their engines off, as the night air was warm, with an easy breeze blowing off the bay waters.

As they were talking about wives, children, bills, and such, Joey noticed some type of movement about 75 yards away and about a half block from where they were sitting. A more concentrated and detailed look revealed the movement to be an upside-down canoe, complete with legs, making its way down the street.

After telling Stuart about it, they both watched the canoe. They could see the two sturdy yet short legs moving fairly steadily beneath it. The more they watched the moving canoe, the more they noticed that it appeared that there was a very good chance that the canoe, or at least the legs beneath it, were probably inebriated, as it was not moving in a straight line but was weaving to and fro.

Stuart and Joey could not help but laugh at the sight, knowing that something was not right, but neither was able to watch the weaving canoe and be serious, either. Joey said, "Let's see what happens when we turn on the ole spotlight."

Joey turned on his car's spotlight and shined it on the legs under the canoe, which caused it to immediately come to a complete stop and then begin to move much faster. They laughed again as they watched it zigzag down the road.

Since it was now 3:30 in the morning, it didn't take a lot of police savvy to surmise that the canoe was no doubt in the process of probably being stolen. Because canoes are generally light in weight, it was also assumed it was being carried by an individual who was trying to get the canoe from one place to another but was having difficulty because they were obviously inebriated.

They decided to give pursuit to the zigzagging canoe by way of a slow vehicle pursuit, all the while shining a bright spotlight beam at the legs. The two patrol cars fell into a side-by-side position behind the slow-traveling canoe. After about a block and a half, the canoe began to slow and to teeter from the front to rear, with obvious indications that the legs were getting very tired. Stuart finally pulled in front of the canoe, and as he got out of his car, he could hear a lot of panting and coughing from the exhausted set of legs and whoever they were attached to.

When the canoe was finally lifted, Stuart and Joey were confronted by one of the town's regulars, Larry Spalding, who frequently overindulged in alcoholic beverages. Larry was usually calm when he drank, but at times, had a bad habit of doing unconventional things when he drank. Apparently, he had decided to keep up with his reputation this night by trying to walk with a canoe on his head. Needless to say, the canoe was rescued.

Stuart, trying hard not to laugh, asked very condescendingly, "Larry, what the hell are you doing?"

Answering with a heavy slur, Larry first attempted to convince Stuart that he was going fishing. Because of the time of day along with his condition, he was advised that his story really didn't make sense and was not going to work.

After slowly nodding in agreement, he then tried to say that his friend had borrowed the canoe a few weeks ago and had never returned it. Believing that he had waited long enough, and considering a fishing trip in the next day or two, he had decided to get it back.

Joey and Stuart looked at each other, shook their heads, and told Larry that this story was also just not believable. He was then asked if the canoe actually even belonged to him. Larry, after a few seconds of closed-eyed contemplation, or more likely trying to come up with a better story, finally admitted in a slow slur, "Ah…no, it does not."

Larry was then officially advised that he was probably going to be placed under arrest. Just prior to being handcuffed, he tried to offer up another excuse for his actions.

He said, "Okay, okay…I was out drinking tonight and while on my way home, I noticed the canoe sitting alongside a fence by the roadway and thought that it had been put out for the trash man. I thought that with some work, I could fix it up and either use it or re-cycle it to someone who could. So, I decided to take the canoe home before someone else got it."

Unfortunately for Larry, after some closer looks at the canoe and simple follow-up questions, it was apparent that the canoe appeared to be almost new. After checking a few yards in the area, Joey found a fenced yard with a one-car garage, with two saw horses on the side of it. Near the saw horses, he found two new wooden oars. The canoe had actually been located inside a fenced yard and not out by the street awaiting trash pickup.

Larry was told this story was the best of the three but that it still wasn't good enough. The culmination and high point of the question-ing came when Larry was asked why he started to run with the canoe when the spotlight was shined on him. Larry advised them that he fig-ured he should start running because whoever it was shining the light would think that he stole it.

Although Larry was placed under arrest for the theft, both Stuart and Joey congratulated him on his athleticism and the great job he did while running and carrying the canoe. He was told they were impressed that he never tripped or fell while running, even though he was unable to see anything other than the pavement at his feet.

Larry accepted the praise with a smile and advised Stuart that he tried to stay healthy and took vitamins every day. Additionally im-pressed that he had eventually admitted the truth and added some laughter to an otherwise long night, they told Larry that they would let the judge know that he had been very cooperative.

Believing that a judge or at least a prosecutor would also appreci-ate the lively and energetic feat, they both included their observations of Larry's ability to run carrying an upside-down canoe on his head in their reports.

As they had presumed, when Larry appeared in court, the judge, after hearing the testimony concerning the theft and recovery of the canoe, chuckled and gave Larry community service with no fine and advised him not to drink and drive a boat in the future.

CHAPTER 69

Maxwell

In the mid-'60s, the State made it mandatory that all full-time policemen must attend and complete accredited law enforcement training. Most small municipalities relied on the state police training academy for this. Along with training for state troopers, municipal police training programs were also offered. Basically, it was the same training the state troopers received but in a shorter period of time. What started in the early 1960s as a six-week course eventually lengthened to a fourteen-week course by the mid-to-late 1970s.

The academy was a state police and national guard facility, centrally located in the state, on a multi-acre site located on the ocean front. It was a live-in Monday through Friday school where trainees stayed in old Army WWII barracks sleeping twenty to a room. Belongings had to be removed on Fridays, as the base was used for national guard training on weekends.

Being located on the ocean front, there was hot, humid weather in spring and summer, and freezing cold weather in the fall and winter. Outdoor range practice in the winter months would sometimes be cancelled due to temperatures being so low that guns refused to fire.

The National Weather Bureau was known to advise the instructors to cancel outdoor events because the life expectancy due to cold and wind was twenty to thirty minutes. Somewhat reluctantly, the trooper instructors would comply, but only after twenty to thirty minutes outside. They perceived this as a method to evaluate anyone not serious about being in law enforcement.

The first two to three weeks were filled with physical and mental exploitation and challenges which would normally weed out 10 to 15% of the trainees. All trainees would be indoctrinated into the world of state trooper "witticisms" in the first few days by way of early morning (usually 3 a.m.) fire drills, in which trainees were roused with shouts, sirens, whistles, clanging of trash can lids, and cheerful yet humorless threats of bodily harm if they didn't leave the barracks within the very few minutes they were given. To solidify the exercises, all trainees were required to carry their mattresses out of the buildings. It was said that because the State was so generous in providing the mattresses, the trainees should return the favor and remove them from the building so that if there were an actual fire, they wouldn't burn.

All trainees eventually got their turn at personal, up-front, in-your-face belittlement by all of the instructors at one time or another, with some getting less and some getting more.

In the many years that Cedar Springs participated in training by the state police, only two individuals failed to complete the instruction. One, Cedrick Heathcliff, did not pass the academic requirements and was given some options by The Rude to resign from the department in order to save some face. Cedrick resigned utilizing family problems as the reason. As usual, within 24 hours, the entire department became aware of the real reason he had left the academy, and beginning the 25th hour, he was forever and always affectionately known by the remaining department members as "dumbass." It was always said that Cedrick would probably never have lasted for any amount of time anyway solely because of his name.

The other, Maxwell Adams, was able to pass almost effortlessly in all academic matters and did well enough in the physical fitness classes to get by, but could not hit the preverbal broad side of a barn with a gun. Prior to going to the academy, department members had given Max about a 2% chance of completion, for a multitude of reasons.

As some people are born with individual talents or genes that naturally help to guarantee success in their chosen fields, Max was born with absolutely no physical assistance that would make anyone consider him as a police officer.

Max stood 5' 8" and weighed around 110 pounds, absolutely none of which appeared to be muscle mass. With a wisp of a mustache, and a receding hairline, he additionally had the unfortunate misfortune of a well-pronounced lisp. Max had as much chance of being a successful cop as he had of being a heavyweight boxing champion.

Max was hired when patrolmen were permitted to work on the street for a period of time prior to accreditation from the academy, provided the department accepted the responsibility. Max's family had some political clout used to ensure his initial hiring, but he was viewed as a distinct liability to anyone having to work with him. On the street, Max would usually be assigned to ride with a full-time patrolman to assist, if possible, with complaint calls.

After a period of time Max had not made any big mistakes, mostly because he was told to wait in or by the car or because he always let the regular patrolman do all the talking. This continued until his squad was short on personnel a few nights, and he was reluctantly allowed to patrol by himself.

Max had virtually never received a solo call and was normally dispatched as a back-up unit, as he was not exactly a foreboding presence or much of a crisis negotiator due to his physical appearance and his lisp.

On a fairly busy night when all other cars were tied up at calls, Max was dispatched to a strip store location that historically always had juveniles loitering around. A routine request from one of the business owners was received, asking that the juveniles be dispersed.

Max accepted the call. Approximately ten minutes after he radioed that he had reached the area, Max requested the patrol sergeant to respond to the scene. Everyone who heard the request initially assumed that either Max had accidently shot someone or the juveniles had taken Max's car or his gun and would not give them back.

Big Ben Bailey was the sergeant on duty and responded along with another patrolman, Rick Ginessie. Upon arriving they noticed Max sitting in his patrol vehicle with several juveniles standing around the car with several more just lounging in front of the stores. All were local kids that routinely were chased away without incident.

Ben pulled up, got out of his car and said to the juveniles, "Yo.... Get the hell out of here."

In seconds, the kids disappeared, but Max had yet to get out of his car. Ben walked over to the car and asked what was going on. Max sheepishly advised him that he had gotten out of his car and informed the juveniles that they had to leave the area. Then with a nervous heavy lisp, he added that several of them had politely told him to go fuck himself and that if he didn't leave, they would take his nightstick and gun and shove them up his ass.

Max stated that not knowing exactly what he should do, he returned to his car and called for the sergeant. Ben just shook his head and said, "Ooooo-kay." Not knowing what else to say, he left it at that.

It was split-second reactions like these that caused the department members to estimate the remaining time that Max had in law enforcement to days instead of years.

Max somehow survived a few more weeks on the street, collecting dozens of splattered eggs and water balloons on his patrol car, until he received his paperwork assigning him to the training academy.

Max went to the academy with two other hires. It took no more than the first day when each trainee had to introduce themselves and indicate which department they were from for the instructors to get a first impressionable sense of Maxwell.

It seems that the first directive of conduct that was installed in the cadets was the rule that when spoken to, after hearing their name called, they would immediately respond, standing at attention, with "Sir-Yes-Sir". Unfortunately for Max, because of his lisp, when called to introduce himself, his response sounded more like "Thirr-Yeth-Thirr."

When the other two unfortunate men from Cedar Springs identified themselves as being from the same department as Maxwell, this information brought forth many added "witticisms'" from the trooper instructors who apparently believed that they may have somehow been genetically related because they worked in the same town. Witticisms and insults, etc. continued upon the two until such beliefs were determined to be unsupported.

Cedar Springs had always utilized automatic hand guns well before automatics became popular and the norm for police. Automatics were designed for only one double- action firing. They required a full pull on the trigger for the first shot which sometimes caused the shooter to inadvertently pull the gun down resulting in a low aimed shot.

However after automatically ejecting the spent shell, the gun would be half cocked, requiring only a slight pull on the trigger to fire the subsequent rounds. Utilizing the gases from the powder explosion to eject the empty cartridge also meant that there was very little recoil action after the first shot, making it extremely easy to aim and fire several accurate shots in a row. Because of this, automatics had a distinct advantage over the revolvers, which had a double-action pull on the trigger for each shot and the additional recoil action, requiring the shooter to carefully re-aim before firing each shot.

Somewhat unexpectedly, because he used an automatic, Max could not seem to get the hang of firing his gun. Not only were his first shots found to be feet below the targets, Max was lucky to hit the target at all, after firing fifty rounds from various distances. It became unsettling to the other trainees that Max could have even been considered for the academy when he was not hitting the target from 15 yards away.

With a strong resemblance to Don Knotts, who played *Barney Fife* from *The Andy Griffith Show* and the movie *The Shakiest Gun in the West*, Max was handed the moniker of both "Barney" and/or "Shaky" by his classmates. These were two nicknames that he kept in future years whenever his name was mentioned.

Max was even afforded hours of practice on weekends with the department range master, shooting up thousands of rounds of ammunition to no avail. After ten weeks of tragic and disastrous range performance, it became crystal clear that Max was never going to be able to catch any bad guys, at least not with a gun, guts, or a silver tongue, and rather than be dismissed from the academy, it was suggested by the trooper instructors and The Rude that he resign.

Max somehow explained his resignation to his wife and took a part-time job collecting quarters at a toll booth on the weekends while he sold life insurance during the week. Because of his pronounced lisp, Max realized that insurance was not his calling after he realized that selling involved speaking. With no commissions in his near future, he ironically relocated to a neighboring town and settled down into a career of a teller at one of the local banks.

CHAPTER 70

A Nicky Harlow "Floater" Story

Nicky Harlow and Angelo Demucchi had been working in the detective division for several years. After many months of working with Nicky, Angelo had begun to get used to and was beginning to become accustomed to some of the odd behavior of Nicky but was also learning to believe it when he said something was, used to be, or would be. Ironically, things almost always turned out to be whatever he said it was, used to be, or would be.

One day a call was dispatched to the cars around 10:30 in the morning of a report of a possible missing boater. It was reported that a woman had called to say that her husband had gone fishing in the bay the day before and had not returned. Another fisherman had called to report he had seen an empty 16-foot aluminum boat floating about 300 yards out in the bay around the area of one of the rock jetties in the South end of town.

Sergeant Michael Strong, who had taken over for Lead Legs as head of the detective division, and contrary to The Rude's wishes, had advised or allowed the county to know everything that took place in the town. As The Rude had predicted, the county prosecutor's office had begun to monitor cases throughout the county and had no qualms about getting involved, whether they had been requested to or not. Their office had a couple of investigators who were becoming well known for worming their way into local investigations and then taking credit for any favorable outcomes. Because they had the ability to monitor the Cedar Springs radio frequency, along with the continued information from Sergeant Strong, it wasn't long before Mathis and Buell, the two infiltrators from the county, showed up in the area to declare they were going to take over the search for the missing boater. The patrol unit that received the initial call really had no complaints about the move, as there was really not much he could do other than try to find out if the boat belonged to the missing man and if so, where he had started out with it.

Mathis and Buell had requested and were utilizing the marine police, the coast guard, and the local fire departments to assist in searching the shoreline of the bay. Nicky and Angelo decided that because the incident had probably originated in Cedar Springs, they would drive out to the improvised command post, which was the end of a dirt road leading to one of the rock jetties.

Actually, Nicky and Angelo were also not disappointed when the county investigators decided to take over the search, as it meant less for them to do, as the investigation would have eventually been passed on to them. Curt pleasantries took place with Mathis and Buell, along with absolutely no information as to what they had already done or were considering doing being offered.

After taking in the scene for a few minutes, Nicky strode over to Mathis, and with his signature short snort and throat-clearing, advised him that they were wasting their time searching that area, as the boat found had undoubtedly drifted to that location without anyone in it.

As was customarily the case with Mathis and Buell, they again didn't disappoint and advised Nicky that they knew exactly what they were doing. They stated they didn't want to hear any of his ideas and that they didn't need his or Cedar Springs' assistance.

Of course, and as expected, Nicky took the retort by Mathis as a personal affront to his own abilities and disrespectful to the entire Cedar Springs Police Department. He answered, "Oh…all righty then, you just keep looking. I'm sure you'll find something someday."

Nicky then turned around, and while he and Angelo were walking back to their car, Nicky had decided and advised Angelo that both of them would locate the body.

About an hour later, when the empty boat was towed in to the beach area by the marine police, Nicky quickly ascertained from the logo on the side that it was one of the rental boats from a rental business in the north end of town, about five miles up shore from where they now were. A quick telephone call check determined that the missing man had indeed rented the boat the day before.

Leaving the scene, Nicky told Angelo, who was driving, to head across the town to the ocean side of the district. He told Nicky that they were going to pay a visit to the coast guard electronics station located on the ocean front on the southeastern side of town.

The station supplied "Loran" technology for fishing, pleasure, and commercial as well as government vessels in the area. Loran, short for long range navigation systems, used radio waves to determine locations of ships up to 1500 miles away and could pinpoint them within a ten-mile area.

When they arrived, Nicky spoke with one of the employees he knew and obtained a copy of a local waterway current chart, daily wind speeds and directions, and a tide time table, which encompassed the ocean and bay waters in the area.

Angelo had no idea what Nicky was up to but decided to ride the train and see where it ended up. After studying the charts, making notes, using a calculator, and drawing lines across the charts for about two hours, Nicky advised Angelo that if the weather held, the body would turn up the following morning around dawn, floating in the bay about ten miles north of the boat rental business in the neighboring jurisdiction and almost six miles from where Mathis and Buell were now looking.

Attempting to be the consummate professional, he then called Mathis and again advised him that they were wasting their time looking where they had been and told him exactly where he would be able to find the body the following day. Again, Mathis in his best condescending tone told Nicky he didn't know what he was talking about and to stop bothering him while he was conducting a real police investigation.

The county continued their search throughout the day and into the night, to no avail. As Nicky expected, at around eight p.m., the county called off the search until daylight the following day.

The next morning, as they had agreed, Nicky and Angelo came in early and immediately went to the area about ten miles north of the boat rental business. There was a dirt roadway located there that led to the bay. When they reached the end of this roadway, there was a larger turnaround area. Parking here, they then walked to the waterline. Nicky grabbed his binoculars and after looking at the water for about two minutes, snorted, cleared his throat and said to Angelo, "Take a look around the 11 o'clock area and about 80 yards out. Does that look like a floater out there to you?"

Angelo took a quick look and simply said, "Yup."

A few minutes later, Nicky radioed the dispatcher to make the necessary notifications of the find to the coast guard, and the marine police. After some consideration, and hoping that they would be listening in, he also advised the dispatcher, as sarcastically as he could, to give the county a call and tell Mathis and Buell that a bill for his maritime and real investigative services would be in the mail.

The Rude, who had been monitoring the progress of the initial call through the previous day and night, had also been up early and monitoring the transmissions that Nicky had just made and took a ride up to their location. He pulled up alongside Nicky's car, got out and walked down to the waterline with his ever-present cigarette. He walked over to Nicky and Angelo and said, "Heard the county mounties were trying to be the heroes again."

Angelo handed him the binoculars and pointed to a spot on the water. The chief took a long look, chuckled and said to Nicky, "I've been trying to tell um for years, the county oughta start listening to us." With that he turned, went back to his car, and left.

Mathis and Buell never showed up when the marine police recovered the body. Nicky and Angelo stayed until the body was removed. They both decided that their reports should be and ultimately were possibly the shortest in history.

"While on patrol, observed what appeared to be a body in the water. Advised marine police. Body recovered and removed. All other information concerning this investigation should be found in the county investigator's reports."

CHAPTER 71

The Crib

Constructed in the early 1960s, The Crib was a 3100-seat auditorium located a block from the ocean beachfront in the southeastern part of Cedar Springs. Originally called The Crestview Auditorium, it was the venue of hundreds of well-known as well as many up-and-coming performers such as Johnny Mathis, Liberace, Fabian, and Frankie Avalon.

The Crestview was a respectable and popular auditorium. It was also the only building on an entire city block surrounded by a sandy and dirt gravel parking lot. It was said to have been the inspiration and start of an entire area devoted solely to high-priced housing and entertainment. Three major motels, two restaurants, and of course a liquor store were constructed in the vicinity. Added a few years later were a giant water slide and miniature golf course.

Then came the late 1960s and full blown rock-n-roll. The Crestview was purchased by a well-known East Coast entrepreneur, who also owned large entertainment venues in New York and Miami. After changing the name to The Crib, he transformed the auditorium into one of the most popular and busy rock clubs on the East Coast. It was routinely visited by thousands of young music enthusiasts from New York and Philadelphia.

This was due to two distinct things. One, it showcased some of the most famous individuals and groups of the 1970s; and two, the drinking age in the state at the time was eighteen and in the neighboring states twenty-one.

The Crib withstood the test of time, hosting hundreds of big-name acts from country rockers The Allman Brothers and Arlo Guthrie to heavy metal bands such as Johnny Winter, Blue Oyster Cult, Meatloaf, and The Ramones. The building, during the late 1970s and early 1980s, consisted of four separate nightclubs, a delicatessen, and as many as eight different areas located on two floor levels where alcohol was available. On weekend nights and the occasional weekday night, they would sometimes have crowds nearing four to five thousand people and fill ten large trash dumpsters with empty beer bottles and anybody's guess as to how many plastic cups, which were utilized for mixed drinks. The local electric company had to install more power to the building in the early 1970s to handle the bands' multiple amplifiers and light shows.

Because the building was situated on an entire block of land, with the additional parking lot encompassing another block, they certainly entertained many problems with crowds, alcohol, fights, and traffic. Most of these or the ramifications from them overflowed into the responsibility of the Cedar Springs police department.

The Crib employed about 50 to 100 attendants or what was more commonly known as "bouncers," depending on the night of the week and the events or performers playing. The majority of the calls for assistance came from patrons complaining about being quickly escorted out of the building in a not-so-pleasant manner. However, because 99% of these people were obnoxious, intoxicated individuals, not too much attention was paid to their complaints. Those wanting to sign complaints against the attendants were advised that they first had to sober up, and second, they needed to acquire the name of the individual who they wanted to sign a complaint against. As this was next to impossible, virtually no complaints were ever taken.

Another frequent call was because of automobile accidents. The lot surrounding the building, along with the entire lot north of the club, was dirt and gravel. No concrete, no macadam, just dirt, sand, and gravel. When accidents occurred, which happened frequently, and there were no injuries, the drivers were advised that if the accident took place in or around the parking lot, the incident was considered to be a non-reportable, private property accident and one for which no police report would be filed. They were advised that vehicle damages would have to be reported personally to their particular insurance companies just as though the damages took place in any private lot.

Back in that day, bars in Cedar Springs were allowed by ordinance to stay open until five in the morning. The neighboring towns had ordinances requiring their bars to close by two a.m., so most all of their remaining patrons who didn't want the night to end made the short drive to The Crib for another three hours of drinking, dancing, and supposedly having fun.

In the late 1970s, problem incidents became so common that the producers of the shows and the owners of the property asked for and paid an overtime rate of pay for off- duty members of the department to patrol the parking lot on foot from the hours of 11 p.m. to 5 a.m.

The squad that was scheduled to be off duty on the "extra patrol nights" were offered the overtime detail. The specials or part-time police officers were also utilized for this duty. It was not unusual to have a group of eight to ten officers walking or walking and driving around the two-block area with the sole intention of just being seen by the patrons, and of course to quell any problems that took place.

When dealing with the average of approximately two-to-three thousand mostly intoxicated young people, there was an almost 100% chance that something was going to happen that would be noteworthy.

It was estimated that about half of those three thousand people would be females, and at least half of that half would be particularly attractive, and half of that half would be scantily dressed; therefore the overtime details usually amounted to observing an average of three to four hundred scantily clad attractive and quite possibly intoxicated women who were easy to talk to and easy to look at. Bikinis, short skirts, elastic tube tops and a lack of brassieres made this detail, strictly from an observational point of view, a success from the department members' standpoint.

Of course there was a fair share of fights, brawls, disagreements, traffic problems, and injuries, which required more than observation, but the assessment and viewing of the half of the half of the half more than evened the score.

One of the more popular time-consuming things to do usually oc- curred directly after a heavy rainfall. The management erected a post and rail fence around the entire parking lot with only one entrance and one exit, in order to quell the many vehicles all pulling onto the roadway at the same time at closing.

There was an area in one of the lots that was significantly lower than the rest of the lot. This was not a problem when the lot was dry but was turned into a small lake after a rain. The puddle, approximately 12 feet across, appeared to be only a few inches deep when in fact it was more than a foot deep in the middle. The best part of the mini lake was that it was located right in the center of the travel portion of the parking lot and close to one of the exits. Patrons had to either travel through the lake to leave, or turn around and drive through the majority of the lot to leave through the entrance.

It was not unusual to see several patrolmen standing by the rail fence awaiting the next victim of the lake. Some drivers would approach cautiously and enter the lake slowly. Other spirited drivers would enter the lake like it was the puddle it resembled, and others, seeing the water, would increase their speed, thinking they would power through it with a splash, like children walking through a puddle in the street.

Virtually all drivers would try to stop once they realized the puddle continued to get deeper. The main problem with that was that most of the time there were several other cars following right behind, which prevented them from backing up. There was really nowhere to go except forward.

Normally about one of every fifty cars attempting to go through the water got stuck in the middle of the lake, or made it through and coughed and sputtered and stalled out after going through. The ones that got stuck were always a treat, as the sometimes intoxicated occupants would exit their vehicles and almost immediately fall into the water. As the water became mixed with the surrounding dirt, the lake would become a large mud hole with the same appearance of being only a few inches deep. With intoxicated or even slightly intoxicated people, this was always entertaining to watch. Even though many times people would watch others get stuck, they would continue to try and outsmart the lake or mud, with the expected dismal results. There were nights that as many as fifteen or twenty cars became stuck or broke down because of a mud puddle. The management must have enjoyed it, as they never seemed to fill in the low spot.

When traffic through the lake was minimal, the police would

sometimes drive their four-wheel-drive vehicle through the puddle, but keeping to one high side or the other, causing people to believe they too could make it through. This was usually followed quickly by someone driving through it and getting stuck.

Sadly, by the mid-1980's, the drinking age had been raised again to twenty-one, and the crowds diminished. The rock and roll bands were being replaced by heavy metal bands that attracted more serious and angry-minded individuals rather than the laid-back culture community of the 1960s and 1970s, and The Crib eventually closed, reportedly due mostly to the large number of civil lawsuits against their employees. About a year after the closing, it burnt to the ground, with the cause being established as probable arson.

With the times changing and memories of the intoxicated thousands still fresh in most of the adjoining property owners' minds, a decision to rebuild was objected to by the town and later dismissed. Shortly after that decision was made, the remaining debris was bulldozed and removed. One of the original motels, the restaurants, and the giant water slide were also sold and demolished, and the land soon began to fill up with high-priced luxury condo units. In ten short years, most people who resided there had never heard of The Crib.

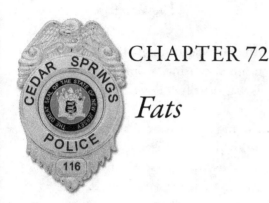

CHAPTER 72

Fats

Burt Mooney was a licensed electrician in the area and was also a special officer or what they refer to today as a Class II officer. Specials were paid minimum wage by the hour with no other benefits and were utilized to supplement the full-time officers, mostly as back-ups or traffic control at incident or accident scenes. They were given uniforms, badges, and guns, providing they were able to qualify twice a year at the shooting range the same as full-time officers. Back in the day, these men were a lot like volunteer firemen and were in it mostly because they either wanted to be or were waiting to be full-time police officers or just wanted to provide some service and support for their community.

Bert was the kind of individual who never had a bad thing to say about anyone. The officers' opinions about Bert were the same. Everyone liked him and had no problem ever having him ride along as a partner. An added attraction was the probability of getting free advice about electrical problems or a substantial discount for any work done. Bert was a knowledgeable electrician who also happened to be best friends with the town's electrical inspector. Unless major construction work was being done, this also meant that there was a good chance that those pesky time-consuming and costly electrical permits would usually not be required, as both the requesting officer and the electrical inspector knew that any work done by Bert was done correctly and up to the current code.

Now because Bert was a highly regarded contractor in the area, he was recommended by many people through word of mouth and also by the town officials, who shared the opinion that Bert was a qualified electrician and also a genuine good person. Next to Big Ben Bailey, Bert similarly seemed to be liked by everyone and also seemed to know everyone in town.

In addition to his likable personality, Bert had a knack of being in the right place at the right time and speaking to the right person when it came to food. It seemed that no matter where Bert and/or his partner were stationed, he always knew where free food could be found. No one was really sure if the free food was offered because of prior work that Bert had done at the establishment or if the shop owners liked the police and wanted to show their support for all the fine work that they did. It was universally agreed, in the long run, that it was probably prior work that Bert had done, but the food was appreciated anyway. Hoagies, cheese steaks, pizza, sodas, and the like were the usual treats, but Bert was also adept at getting the more exotic or extravagant foods from the better restaurants. It was not unusual for Bert to be offered orders of shrimp cocktail, broiled scallops, and on a few significant occasions, lobster tails with all the trimmings.

One memorable summer in the early 1980s, Bert was in high demand as rumors of pizzas and seafood were running through the squads as the customary and routine giveaways on the evening shifts. There was a respectable Italian restaurant called Louise's Lounge located in the area of The Crib. It was one of the businesses erected in the area designed for entertainment which was expected to flourish and expand and to support the more affluent members of the community. Known for quality food at somewhat reasonable prices, it also hosted some first-rate entertainment, with night club acts from New York, Philadelphia, and Las Vegas.

During the month of August, and also at the peak of the tourist season, The Crib area was bursting at the seams with visitors. The Crib was rocking nightly with rock and roll with as many as two to three thousand young people crowded into the auditorium and its many bars. The beachfront hotels were routinely sold out, with almost permanent "No Vacancy" signs in their windows, and the restaurants and convenience stores were doing large amounts of business. Louise's had waiting times of up to two hours.

Bert, not surprisingly, knew Louise and her husband Carlo very well, having done some kitchen rewiring at the restaurant after the addition of larger ovens and storage coolers. Carlo always welcomed Bert and the police at the restaurant. Arrogant or intoxicated patrons were handled discreetly whenever possible, with Carlo and Louise routinely treated as politely as possible. At Louise's, the free shrimp, steamed or fried, scallops, and desserts were readily available to Bert and whoever he happened to be paired with.

One Saturday night, or technically Sunday morning, at around one a.m., The Crib was in full swing but somewhat subdued for the amount of people crammed into the building. Louise's dinner crowd was done for the night, and the late-night entertainment crowd had filled every table. The memorable draw for the crowd was none other than the legendary Fats Domino, who had been booked for an entire week and was entertaining for the third night of his engagement.

As luck would have it, Sergeant Pete Roberts' Crazy Squad was scheduled and working the overtime detail to walk and patrol The Crib parking lots. And also as luck would have it, Bert was also scheduled and working. At around 1:15 a.m., Bert made mention that he was hungry and asked Pete and two other members of his squad, Danny Green and Mike Harding, if they were interested in some shrimp cocktail. Because Bert had not mentioned pizza, everyone knew he was referring to Louise's. Pete reminded Bert that Fats Domino was playing at the lounge and figured that it would be packed and busy, and there was no possible way that Carlo would be giving out free samples.

Bert, with a grin, said, "Well, let's go see. The worst he can say is no. Besides, my buddy Fats is playing."

Now everyone was aware of how many people Bert knew and were appreciative of the free food that was given to all those associated with Bert, but not even Pete, who had known Bert for more than twenty years, expected that it was possible for Bert to get any gratuities on such a busy night while a famous entertainer was on stage.

Pete, smoking the usual cherry blend tobacco in his pipe, chuckled and said, "So you're saying you're tight with Fats? I guess we'll find out if you're as illustrious as you want everyone to believe you are. Heck, I'd settle for some french fries."

Danny, with his usual sarcastic flair said, "Yeah, let's go see Fats.

Maybe Bert will introduce us."

Mike Harding, being fairly new, looked at Bert with a new found awe and asked, "You mean to tell me that if we walk into Louise's with Fats Domino playing and singing, that Carlo is still gonna offer us some free food?"

Bert answered, "Carlo loves us. The other day, Fats sat down with us at a table and talked about New Orleans and about how nice he thought people here are. So let's go get some shrimp."

The four of them entered the restaurant through the kitchen door so the patrons would not get upset or concerned with an unannounced police presence.

Carlo, doing one of his usual walk-arounds, noticed Bert and the others and made a point to come over, giving Bert a man half-hug, and then shook hands with Sergeant Pete, recognizing the stripes on his uniform and realizing he was probably the ranking officer. With quick handshakes to Danny and Mike, Carlo asked with a concerned look if everything was all right. Pete smiled and said that Bert had mentioned that he wanted to stop in and say hello, and that he and the others had just tagged along.

Carlo visibly relaxed gave a big sigh and told the group that they were always welcome to stop in anytime. He said, "How about some shrimp cocktails or some chicken wings? You guys hungry?"

As politely as possible, and trying not to give the impression that free food at one in the morning was exactly what they were thinking about, they muttered acceptance in tones hoping to convey the acceptance as nothing more than good public relations.

Carlo said to follow him, as the shrimp and chicken wings were located in a corner of the lounge room. The group walked out of the kitchen and headed toward the lounge area where several tables were set up filled with patrons intently listening to, tapping their feet and singing along with the entertainment, Fats Domino, who was located on the small stage playing a pearl-white grand piano and singing "Blue Monday."

Coincidentally, Fats had just completed the song as the group tried to walk nonchalantly past the stage. Fats, who had turned away from the piano and toward the audience, was politely thanking the crowd for their applause. Then suddenly he rose off the piano stool and said, "Hey, Bert. How's it goin', my man? Good to see you again."

As expected, this stopped Pete and the others in their tracks. One by one, Fats shook hands with all the officers saying he appreciated them stopping in to see him.

After the brief interruption in his show, Fats returned to his piano and indicated to the crowd that he was always pleased to see the boys in blue, which resulted in a round of applause for the group.

Carlo spoke quietly to the hostess, and chicken wings, shrimp, and steamed clams were packaged up by a waitress in four carry-out containers. Carlo again thanked the group for stopping in, patting Bert on the cheek just like in the Italian movies, and with appreciative thanks, the small group left and returned to the parking lot and their cars to feast on the donations.

Not much was said during the walk to the cars but upon reaching them, Pete was the first to exclaim, "Holy shit, Bert. How the hell do you know Fats Domino? I about shit my pants when he got up from his piano and called your name."

Bert calmly grabbed a chicken wing took a bite and said, "I was fixing a broken outlet in the lounge for Carlo the other day when a big van pulled in and delivered that big white grand piano. Right after the piano was set up, in walks Fat's who wanted to make sure the piano was in tune. Carlo introduced me, and we sat and talked for about an hour. He's a really nice guy."

Pete, Danny, and Mike just looked at Bert, shook their heads, smiled, and ate some shrimp cocktail.

Sometimes, being a cop is just plain good.

CHAPTER 73

Callous Conway

By the mid-1970s, Cedar Springs had begun to utilize part-time or "special" officers during the summer months. A few would be retained to work on weekends during the rest of the year. Most of those retained had either taken a civil service exam for police and were waiting for the opportunity to be hired full time or just wanted to volunteer their services to the community. One such individual was Thomas Conway.

Tom's family owned a contracting business in town and had been instrumental in the construction of homes and buildings in the area for many years. Tom had been born in town, gone to the schools and had worked for the family since he was twelve. While he always said he didn't mind doing the work, he also said that he wanted to do something different for a living. He was hired as a special, and after one summer decided police work was much more enjoyable and a lot cleaner than construction.

Tom took a civil service exam and waited on the list for almost three years before being hired full time. Tom also had the misfortune to attend the police academy with Maxwell Adams and was awarded a full complement of state police insults, exploitation and verbal abuse or what became known as "training witticisms" on many occasions after they became aware that he had come from the same town.

Most of the witticisms were purely and almost certainly intended to find out if Tom's character was even remotely similar to Maxwell's. While Tom's personal attributes in relation to law enforcement were deemed to be much more developed than Max's, there was one incident involving Tom which took place at the academy that brought many "witticisms" which were also well deserved.

On one unforgettable early Monday morning of the fourth week of training, following the two-and-a-half-hour drive to the academy, Tom, along with the rest of the recruits, was awaiting the arrival of the day's drill instructor. As directed, the nearly seventy recruits from around the state were standing at attention in front of the barracks. The day's drill instructor was no doubt watching the group's reaction to standing still in formation, with each man attempting to ignore the morning's cold winds.

Once allowed to break formation, the first task the recruits were required to do was to secure their weapons in the academy's armory. Each recruit would hand over their weapon and receive a "chit" used to retrieve the weapon for range training during the week.

All proceedings came to a complete halt when Tom was forced to admit to the armory assistant that he could not produce his weapon, as he had left it at home.

This admission was immediately met with a repeat of that information by the assistant, loud enough for every recruit as well as the day's drill instructor to hear. Instantly all recruits were ordered to return to the parking lot and again stand in formation. This was done solely to direct as much criticism and grief to Tom as possible and to install a distinct memory to the other trainees to never repeat Tom's inattentive achievement. Forgetting one's gun and going to work--or in this case the training academy --without it was without a doubt the worst or dumbest mistake a police officer could make.

Maxwell Adams had been on the instructor's radar since the first day that he introduced himself and confirmed the instructor's first impressions of him with the emergence and presentation of his unfortunate heavy lisp. With Tom's no-gun exploit, he had successfully taken the attention off Maxwell for the entire week, becoming the focus of many comical remarks and questions during meals and in classes. Because of the slight miscalculation of the location of his gun, Tom also succeeded in adding the always much- appreciated extra miles and calisthenics to the recruits' physical education activities.

In addition, Tom was required to call the station and have someone go to his house, get his weapon, and bring it to the academy. To make sure that the situation never happened again, it became compulsory that Tom stand in front of the trainees every Monday morning for the remaining ten weeks and advise them in a loud, clear, and concise manner that he had indeed remembered to bring his weapon. He then would always have to be the first in line to secure his weapon in the armory.

Following Maxwell's demise from the academy and the department, Tom graduated from the academy. His career started out like most, and Tom went about his police work without much ado until he became the arresting officer of a drunk driver. Now this in itself is not really a big issue, as sooner or later patrolmen are faced with the task. With Tom, it became something of an epiphany.

Most new patrolmen, equipped with their newfound power, tend to overdo some type of enforcement for the first few months of duty. For some it may be illegal parking, or people who don't come to a complete stop at stop signs. For Tom, it was impaired drivers.

In a small town with well over twenty-five alcohol-serving establishments, finding drivers who decided to drive after drinking was not difficult. Most of the veterans would either ignore most of what they saw or at least pull the erratic ones over, make them park their cars, and drive them home with stern warnings. For whatever reason, Tom had decided that warnings were not proper and that the drivers needed some form of punishment for their illegal actions.

In the big police picture, almost every department has a Tom--a patrolman dedicated--or better described as resolved--to persistently enforce the law when encountering any and every violator. With Tom, his determination was geared toward drivers on the streets after midnight, in particular those who had just left one of the neighborhood taverns. Tom's arrests were completely lawful and legitimate, and one could safely say that the recipients were in a way rightly deserving of the penalties.

Following his run of about three years on impaired drivers, the majority of the town's regulars had become aware that the preferred or at least lesser treatment that they had become accustomed to in past years was slowly becoming difficult to expect. Whenever Tom happened to stop someone who had been only warned in the past, or those who maybe had dropped a name of another patrolman, they were straight-away advised that no favoritisms would be forthcoming in their immediate future.

Tom's enthusiasm for the letter of the law in particular motor vehicle violations soon culminated into his becoming well known for never giving a break to anyone. This included old business acquaintances and former school colleagues, as well as distant and not so distant family members.

It was well documented and admitted by Tom that one of the only people he did not write a traffic summons to was his own brother...to whom he gave a written warning instead.

Tom's style was his own. In many instances, a police officer had and still has discretion to either write a ticket or not to write a ticket and in some cases to arrest or to not arrest. Tom had decided that for him, discretion would be a sign of weakness and decided against it. For all his efforts to install law and order, Tom acquired a nickname fitting to his ego and personality.

Judges were becoming accustomed to defendants complaining that they had been pulled over for nothing more than a slight weave in their driving and had passed the roadside tests but had just barely registered in the red when administered a breathalyzer test and were issued a summons for driving while impaired. While sometimes sympathetic to their complaints, he would explain that the law instructed him to find them guilty because of the test results.

One particular driver thought it unfair that Tom had followed him home the entire way and did not turn on his overhead emergency lights until he was parked in his driveway, engine off and ready to enter his home. After clearly admitting that he had been driving the car, Tom administered roadside sobriety tests and arrested the man for impaired driving. In court the man indicated that the arresting officer, Tom, had been cold, calculating, and callous. The judge, looking at Tom said, "Officer Conway, do you disagree with anything this gentleman has said?"

Tom said, "No sir, your honor. He was exactly correct."

From then on, Tom became known as "Callous Conway." No one really wanted to work with him, and no one really understood why he was as unreasonable as he was.

In later years, Tom became a sergeant. It was speculated that the particular civil service promotional test he had taken must have been predominantly associated with motor vehicle traffic laws and "by the book and nothing but the book" police protocol and nothing about human sensitivity or ethics.

Soon after retirement from the department, Tom and his wife moved into a newly constructed custom home in a nice neighborhood. The house was a two-story home with a pyramid or hip type roof. Interestingly, Tom had planted no trees or shrubbery around the house. Many of the patrolmen Tom had worked with, and many people he had been unsympathetic and callous toward, amusingly all came to the same conclusion whenever the house was identified as Tom's.

It was often referred to as being a cold, rigid, and callous-looking design, devoid of any style. One particular individual looked at it for a few moments, and after giving it some thought said, "Well, it certainly fits the personality of its owner. To me, it looks like a giant penis."

CHAPTER 74

Fire from Above

For those who have experienced the situation, they already know what happens when the police catch someone with fireworks. It usually happens during the Fourth of July week but can also occur most anytime. A noise complaint is received, a patrol vehicle is dispatched, and if the noisemakers are found to have an unexploded reserve of sparkly and loud entertainment, the remaining load is routinely confiscated. Generally, there are not many arguments with such confiscations, as the fireworks are, in some states, generally unlawful to possess. Cedar Springs happened to be located in one of those states.

As one might have always expected, the confiscated items are virtually never turned in at the police station for legal destruction. The norm was that they were usually used to provide some holiday entertainment for the summer picnics given or attended by the officers who had confiscated them.

One of the optional scenarios in which illegal fireworks were destroyed, in particular firecrackers and bottle rockets, would take place when a meeting was requested by a fellow patrol officer. When pulling up close to another car, it was not unusual to be confronted by a patrolman's arm holding a recently lit firecracker (either one or a pack of twenty or more) moving quickly and tossing the pack into the open window of the visiting patrol car.

If the ordinance was a standard small firecracker, there was not much damage done other than the noise, the smoke, and the cleanup of the blown-up paper that the powder had been wrapped in. However, if the pitching patrolman utilized an entire pack or quite possibly an M-80 or its equivalent, then just the noise and percussion were usually enough to affect the rest of the recipients shift and cause patrolmen to reconsider the meaning of police camaraderie and friendships. On the other hand, the attacker was usually paid back in triplicate in the near future.

The absolute epitome of this prank would also come shortly after an arrest had been made, when an officer would request a quick meet with the arresting officer regarding information. The semi-normal part of this was that the requesting officer knew that the arresting officer had just made an arrest and had the subject handcuffed in the car and was on their way to the station. The ruse was that the requesting officer had some important information concerning the recent arrest that they wanted to pass along prior to the subject getting to the station.

This prank took place when and only when the requesting officer personally knew that the arrested individual was a "regular" or "usual pain in the ass arrested person." In such instances, the meet for important information could possibly turn into a lit firecracker or two being thrown into the car holding the arrested "pain in the ass."

In today's world, this incident could never be explained, but back in the day, it was utilized simply for the enjoyment of the patrolmen and at times to make a lasting impression upon those individuals whose constant arrests for trivial matters were becoming chronic and time-consuming irritations. More times than not, the arrested individual would believe that their lives had come to an abrupt end and change their future behavior. For others, it was sometimes a relief, as they knew that they would be *un-arrested* and the charges against them would disappear, as it would be difficult to explain to a judge that the explosions were meant to be a training exercise.

Another solution to the elimination of these illegal fireworks sometimes took place on midnight shift weekends in the parking lot of The Crib, with hundreds of people at any one time being in the parking lot, coming and going or arguing and fighting or getting stuck in the mud.

Patrolmen at the time utilized three D cell or four C cell aluminum flashlights that reportedly could, because of their elongated size, if necessary, be used as nightsticks, but of course that was simply a rumor and absolutely never ever happened in Cedar Springs. It was found that they could also be utilized as handy launching tubes for bottle rockets with no concerns of accidental burns and were surprisingly accurate aiming devices for the rockets. One simply unscrewed the end cap, emptied the battery pack, and the tube was ready.

When crowds at The Crib became disruptive and overactive, there were several ways to disperse them. One ploy involved in dispersing a group without actual physical interference was to drive to an adjoining parking lot approximately two to three hundred yards away. While parked, it was easy to unload a battery pack and aim a couple of bottle rockets into the air, which would swoosh and soar through the night, exploding slightly overhead of the group and/or occasionally landing in the crowd prior to exploding.

This always had the effect of dispersing a crowd in a hurry with absolutely no one suspecting the flying ordinance to be coming from the innocent-looking police cars parked hundreds of yards away and barely visible.

Many times, members of the unruly crowd would see the patrol cars and report to the police that they were being attacked by someone shooting fireworks at them. The police would always do their best to look appalled and concerned and indicate to them that they would do their best to investigate the complaints, all the while kicking the remaining rockets under the front seat and out of sight.

CHAPTER 75

Alienating the Aliens

In the late 1970s, and coincidentally during the surge of UFO popularity brought on by the influx of available information supplied by television, magazines, and the new-fangled computers, came a situation and the explanation for that situation that still does not completely satisfy most of those who were eye witnesses to it.

On a warm summer cloudless night with bright moonlight and a sky filled with millions of stars, a somewhat routine call was received by Dudley Sergeant's dispatcher, Raymond Burry. The caller reported unusual lights shining out in the water in the south area of the town in the vicinity of where the ocean meets the bay.

The caller had told Ray that there didn't seem to be any type of immediate problem with the lights but that they were just curious as to what they might be and thought that the police might know. Ray, (Mr. Imagination), unexpectedly and not like him at all, somehow gave the caller a reasonable explanation and told them that the lights were probably fishing boats but that he would have a patrolman check it out.

However, after contemplating that the call could have hundreds of explanations more interesting than plain old fishing boats, Ray dispatched to the cars that he had received a report of "numerous suspicious and unusual lights hovering approximately one to two miles out in the water." Of course, because it was not unlike Ray to under embellish an already over-embellished report, he also added that there was a distinct probability of a "maritime distress or a major disaster" involving a ship or an airplane.

Knowing Ray's penchant for exaggeration, both Nicky Harlow and Joe Cornwell rolled their eyes and figured that some tourist had probably seen a fishing trawler complete with outrigger lights, which during the summer months was not an unusual sight in that area.

Sarge Sergeant, true to form, seeing nothing wrong with the way the call was dispatched, advised Nicky and Joe to let him know what they found when they got to the location.

After arriving at the end of the roadway, which would become somewhat legendary as Johnny Sullivan's high-speed car chase lift-off point and entrance into the cold wintery surf, Nicky indicated that there were indeed lights in the sky. His second broadcast was that the situation was definitely not a ship or a conventional plane in distress, as he believed the lights he was observing were somewhat stationary and approximately 500 feet above the water.

Joe arrived at the location shortly thereafter and when pulling up alongside Nicky's car, he looked at the sky and said, "What the hell?"

Nicky, with a short snort and a clearing of his throat, said in typical Nicky fashion, "What you have here is a definite anomaly deviating from what we normally consider to be typical light behavior."

Joe said, "Yeah, right. So what the hell are those things?"

The so-called anomaly was actually five anomalies, which appeared to hover in the sky in perfect formation, each displaying several bright lights of which a definite shape could not be distinguished; however, the lights made them appear to be of a triangular shape.

Sarge Sergeant, who had been traveling toward the area, asked Nicky over the radio what he had. He said, "Nicky, whaddya got up there?"

Nicky and Joe had by this time exited their patrol cars and were standing in the middle of the roadway alongside another officer from a neighboring department, looking into the sky at the objects and discussing their possible identifications.

Sarge arrived and saw three officers and now several civilians, who had apparently heard the call on police scanners, staring at the horizon. Initially he was ready to chastise Nicky for not answering him on the radio when he noticed what the crowd was witnessing. Sarge gingerly got out of his car, donning his hat, and with a now-quivering hand slightly resting on his gun, joined the group and began to silently stare. It was rumored to be the only time to anyone's knowledge that Sarge was at a loss for words.

For the next ten minutes, the crowd watched the lights in the sky hovering in the exact same spot. Suddenly, the lights began to move slowly north-westward toward land, still in perfect formation. After moving for what appeared to be approximately one-half mile, the objects again stopped. Additionally, with only a slight breeze coming off the ocean, no discernible noise could be heard.

The object or set of lights that was in the middle of the formation began to move forward again toward land, while the others stayed in position. As the object moved closer, it also grew in size and lost altitude until it appeared that it was only slightly above the waterline.

Nicky asked Ray to call the coast guard base to inquire if any of their helicopters were on maneuvers in the area. After getting a negative result, he then instructed Ray to contact the nearest military base to inquire if they were involved in any exercises in the area. Another negative answer was received, along with confirmation of no known commercial or private planes being airborne in the area.

Sarge continued to stare at the sky while the object continued to move slowly toward land, getting larger and larger. Nicky, calm as usual, began to theorize his opinion to the officer from the neighboring jurisdiction of this being a case of visiting extraterrestrial aliens. He stated that he was disappointed that he had left his camera at home, stating that he could have gotten a better idea of what method they were using for propulsion and also that he probably could have sold the photos to *Newsweek* or at least the *National Inquirer* magazine.

Joe, thinking about the space monster B movies which showcased all types of body testing and anal probing, began to inch his way toward his patrol car and wondered if anyone would notice if he left, thinking that if aliens were landing, he didn't really want to be one of the first humans they literally came into contact with or wanted to probe.

Sarge, finally realizing that he was the ranking officer at the scene, began to think that if he prevented or even survived an alien invasion, he might become famous. He was also thinking that if Elvis were still alive, he would be his first choice to portray him in a movie about the aliens. He tried to sound relaxed and in charge as he stated, "I, Ahhh, think you're gonna find that it's a secret part of the government and they're testing secret aircraft and conducting secret practice runs of some sort."

Nicky snorted and said, "Sarge, if it's so secret, then why would they be showing all their secrets right in front of us?"

At about this time, the forwarding craft came to a complete halt approximately one- half mile offshore. No sound of any kind could be heard, and a definite shape resembling a triangle or possibly a pentagon seemed to be visible.

Sarge then said, "Well, then maybe they're some sort of secret government helicopters!"

Following another short snort, Nicky added, "Helicopters make noise and rotors churn up the water beneath them. You hear any noise or see any white water beneath that thing, Sarge?"

Sarge was about to speak again when just as quickly as it had stopped, the object then began to reverse without turning, still showing the same lighting as before but moving at a much faster speed until it reached the area of the other lights.

The five sets of lights then slightly separated and began to gain altitude straight up. Gaining what appeared to be incredible speed, they seemed to head east and upward, and within less than a minute were soon out of eyesight.

The small crowd dispersed after about fifteen minutes of waiting to see if they would return. Sarge, Nicky, Joe, and the officer from the neighboring department all pretty much agreed on what they had seen. They all figured that if what they saw was what they thought they saw, their reports would probably be confiscated by some government agency.

Reports were written and absolutely nothing was said, and nothing out of the ordinary happened. However, as usual, the following day pictures of flying saucers and little green men appeared around the station.

Joe was the recipient of several hand-drawn pictures of aliens performing anal probing on bodies dressed like policemen.

Nicky got a photo copy of a *National Inquirer* cover with an old picture of Sarge Sergeant taped on its cover. The headlines were proclaiming "Local Cop Saves World after Telling Alien Visitors: You Will

Never Be As Good As I Am."

Sarge got a photo of Elvis with several little green men peeking out from behind him that had been signed "To Dudley...There's no such thing as aliens. What were you thinking?"

About four nights later, another report of unusual lights was received in the same area. Big Ben Bailey's squad was working and reported a somewhat similar occurrence but with only one object in the sky. The other difference was that the object headed toward land, emitting motor noise and churning water and flew over the land, and it was definitely identified as a coast guard helicopter.

Almost immediately, the previous call witnessed by four police officers and as many as twenty civilians was now being explained as having been a group of helicopters misidentified as something else.

Sarge's chance at a legitimate claim to fame of witnessing aliens or government secret aircraft was now being explained as nothing more than a few helicopters out for an evening stroll.

Joe was more than satisfied with the new explanation, stating that he was just happy that no anal probing had taken place.

Nicky still insisted the call was a definite unexplained encounter with aliens. He persisted that the "visitors" had probably conducted some sort of mind meld à la Mr. Spock with Sarge Sergeant and had established there was a definite lack of substantial intellect and diverted their visitation to another location, if not another planet.

Sarge continued to convince himself that he had formulated the closest determination to the now-reported explanation and once again decided that he was as smart and as good a cop as he thought he was.

No strange lights in any kind of configuration, or even low-flying helicopters, were reported in the early-morning hours again. Future helicopters or aircraft sightings were easily identified within minutes. It was never clearly or sufficiently explained how the witnessed hovering vehicles seen by the patrolmen made no noise or churned any water beneath them.

Additionally, it was never explained why, if the vehicles in fact were otherworldly, they had quickly decided to come so close to land and then had just as quickly decided to retreat and leave the area.

Maybe…just maybe…if one was to consider Nicky's theory of an alien *mind meld* with Sarge concept, which would surely have been done in order to measure the intelligence and intellect of the earth's populace …. Well then, maybe Sarge really did save the world.

CHAPTER 76

One That Almost Got Away

One day during the early 1980s, a citizen, 58-year-old Wilbur Morrow, arrived at the station and asked to sign a complaint against one of the town's regular pains in the ass, Randy Dugan. Randy was about twenty-five years of age and had been a general trouble-maker for the better part of ten years in Cedar Springs.

He had been arrested as an adult more than a dozen times since turning eighteen. His approach toward life seemed to always involve drinking or doing some type of drug, followed by some type of disruptive behavior. Obviously a slow learner, Randy's technique and approach toward an encounter with the police, because of his ill thought actions more times than not, resulted in an arrest for the misbehavior or due to his comments and threats toward the police after their arrival. Without fail, following being told that he was under arrest, a short scuffle would ensue. Randy would always lose, as he wasn't much of a fighter, but he was persistent in his goal to be a major problem to the police no matter what the final outcome.

Mr. Morrow, who lived a few houses down from Randy, apparently had a confrontation with him earlier in the day. The confrontation concerned loud music and ultimately involved shouting, accusations, threats, a few shoves, and a couple of thrown punches which culminated with a beer bottle being thrown through Mr. Morrow's kitchen window. This all happened within a ten-minute time frame, with the police not being notified until Wilbur walked into the station to explain the incident.

Mr. Morrow, complete with bruising on his chin and left eye slightly closed, shared the complete story with Mike Harding, who happened to be assigned to that zone. It was impossible to substantiate because the police were not involved, but judging from the bruising on his face, Mr. Morrow was encouraged to sign a citizen complaint for assault against Randy.

Mike, never one to shy away from a potential scuffle, was actually elated by the signing of the complaint, as he had endured several incidents involving Randy in the past several years. Due to Randy's alluring personality, he looked forward to another opportunity to explain to him what society's theories of proper behavior should be.

Once the paperwork was completed, Mr. Morrow was assured that the situation would be taken care of quickly and that he would be notified as soon as the complaint was served.

Randy lived with his girlfriend, Julie. When she was eighteen, Julie was one really good-looking young lady--brunette, big brown eyes, five foot two, about one hundred pounds, and built like the proverbial brick outhouse. Now she was twenty-five years old and while she used to be a rather attractive girl, she was now often referred to as one that had aged way beyond her years. Julie had proven to be the perfect mate for Randy. Her years of drinking, smoking, and drug abuse not only caused her looks to decline, they also helped to create a personality that could sometimes be as antagonistic as Randy's at the drop of a hat.

When Mike arrived at their house, Julie answered the door in a pair or very short cut-off jeans and a worn and very tight white tee-shirt. Her facial looks may have deteriorated, but her physical characteristics continued to be in top form. In the most sincere sweet innocent little-girl voice she could muster through her alcohol-and-tobacco-impaired vocal cords, Julie indicated that Randy was in the bedroom asleep. Just like in the movies, Julie asked, "What's this all about, Officer?"

Mike gave Julie the reported short version, even though he assumed that she had probably been an eyewitness to the entire incident. Julie indicated to Mike that Randy had told her what happened. After listening, and as predicted, her story turned out to be the complete opposite of Mr. Morrow's.

Mike said that he understood, but since a complaint had been signed, Randy would have to be taken to the station to complete the paperwork involved, and when completed, he would be released on his own recognizance. Of course, right on cue, this was followed by a short and vulgarity-laced rant about how much grief and suffering they had endured since moving near Mr. Morrow and how they were perfect citizens and never caused a problem.

Julie culminated her rant by saying, "Old man Morrow is a no-good, trouble- causing son of a bitch. Ever since we moved in here, he's just out to get me and Randy."

Mike, frustrated by having to listen to the "poor us" rant, then said, "Julie, just go in and wake up Randy and tell him I need to talk to him. Don't make me have to go in and get him."

Julie agreed, and while walking toward the bedroom door stated as sweetly as she could and with her usual all-American charm, "You cock-sucking motherfuckers are always picking on us."

Ahhh…rule number 10 strikes again.

Julie went into the bedroom, and eventually Randy made his appearance and was informed of the charges. He was also advised that following the paperwork, he would be released on his own recognizance. For the first time in recent history, Randy kept his mouth shut, and for the first time in anyone's memory, was peacefully taken from his house and brought back to the station. Mike thought maybe he had finally realized that his wayward behavior was not conducive to a high-quality and significantly bruise-free lifestyle. Either that, or Mr. Morrow had gotten in a couple of good head shots.

While Mike was at Randy's house, the dispatcher had been doing a standard records check of the up-and coming-arrestee. It was found that Randy had an outstanding warrant out against him for failure to appear for a court appearance in a neighboring town. After arriving at the station, Mike was advised of the information and realized that knowledge of the warrant was no doubt the real reason he didn't cause a scene at his home. He more than likely was hoping that if he cooperated, nobody would bother to check for other warrants. Inevitably, Randy's calm demeanor had no reflection on any life-changing standard of living or behavior.

After securing his gun in a weapons locker, which was department policy when dealing with an arrest inside the station, Mike advised Randy that in addition to a mandatory appearance in court for the Morrow assault, he would have to produce $500 cash bail for the outstanding warrant if he wanted to go home.

Julie had arrived at the station by this time inquiring when her little darling would be released. Mike met with her in the front entrance vestibule where she was informed of the extra warrant and the bail.

Julie, still in short shorts, had changed into a skimpy light-colored, low-cut tank top with no brassiere, which certainly accentuated her physical characteristics. With as much of an innocent look as she could muster, along with a considerable amount of cleavage, she informed Mike that there was no way she could produce the bail.

After being informed that Randy would probably be transferred to the county jail, she asked if she could at least see and speak with him before he was transferred.

With the idea that the other offense was really not too serious, and with the knowledge that the usual procedure in such cases was that he would probably be released the following day after speaking with a public defender, Mike agreed to let the two speak.

The vestibule at the station was an area about eight feet by ten feet with a bulletproof window facing the dispatcher's office, an exterior door leading to the street side of the building, and an electronically operated door leading to the inside of the police station. Julie was patiently waiting in the vestibule for the meeting. Mike led Randy to the vestibule and then stood in the open doorway.

Randy and Julie embraced and seemingly whispered sweet nothings to each other. In fact, and for reasons that were never learned or understood, Julie had been advising him to make a run for it if the opportunity arose. Randy, with visions of freedom and the possibility of seeing a bit more of Julie's cleavage dancing through his brain, thought that maybe he would go for it and advised Julie to try and block Mike's further entry into the vestibule if and when he made a break for it out the front door.

Just like in the movies, in three short steps, Randy became a certified, bona fide, legalized, okay to shoot um if need be-ized, U.S. Prime, A-1, star-studded and now officially authorized fugitive and proceeded to high tail it out the front door toward the vacant lot next to the station.

The surrounding area of the police station was somewhat rural, with a large field south of the building. Just past the field, there was a wooded area which encompassed the town's water treatment plant amid about 100 acres of dense brush and trees. If Randy made it to the woods, there was a good chance that he could make it to the big time with what would surely be well-documented and advertised, more than likely by Randy himself, as the escape of the century.

Mike had other plans. As irritating as it is when a suspect runs from a scene after being told they should stay, running away from inside the police station was a situation that should never happen and was one which, if successful, would bring substantial ridicule as well as substantial disciplinary actions.

This was a situation that Mike was not willing to accept, especially since it pertained to a decision that he had made. As quickly as Randy had made it through the exterior door, Mike followed, pushing Julie aside and was only about six steps behind.

Now additionally to all this, The Rude had recently performed one of his interdepartmental transfers and Mike had only two days earlier been reassigned to Dudley Sergeant's squad. Mike had heard all the Sarge stories but had never had to work with or for him. He knew that an escape from the station was no way to start things off. Sarge would undoubtedly lecture him for hours and weeks on end about how good a cop he used to be, still was, and shall ever be, and also how bad a cop Mike had been and would forever be by letting a dangerous criminal (even if it was only Randy Duggan) escape from custody.

Sarge had coincidentally been pulling into the station's rear car port area when Randy, with Mike in pursuit, ran quickly into the open field and toward the woods. Sarge entered the station and was quickly informed of the recent incident and returned to the rear of the station to assist in the chase.

Angelo Demucchi, now in the detective bureau, had been at the station when Randy had been brought in and had been talking with the dispatcher when Randy made his move. He too ran out the front door to assist and was just a few yards behind Mike.

Mike, being in fair shape, managed to keep within a few feet of Randy. Actually, the thought of just shooting him crossed his mind until he remembered that his service weapon was in fact still nestled safely in the weapons locker at the station. Mike quickly came to the realization that he would have to run faster and harder than he had in years in order to save face and to rule out the possibility of being dismissed from the force. An escaped prisoner was a bit more serious than getting cars stuck in the sand or having the chief take your unlocked car from the station.

About three-fourths of the way across the open field, Mike managed to pour on a bit of momentum and caught up with Randy just on the edge of the field, utilizing a picture- perfect flying tackle that Knute Rockne or Dick Butkus would have been proud to witness. With a few choice words concerning Randy's decision to run, and with threats and promises to him if he dared to move a muscle, along with a few well-aimed body shots, Randy the fugitive was handcuffed and once again in custody.

Angelo easily beat Sarge to the capture site, where Mike was finalizing his lecture to Randy on what it meant to be under arrest. Randy's face was pointed into the soft sandy soil and mumbling something that sounded to Angelo sort of like, "Oh, you cocksucker, you're going to be sorry. I'm gonna get you for this."

On the other hand, there was the small possibility that he actually was saying, "Okay, sorry, sorry, okay, okay, I'm sorry. You got me."

Either way, Angelo decided that the dirt that Randy was now eating was justified and deserved. He added in typical Angelo fashion,

"Yeah, whatever, you dumbass. You shouldn't have run."

Mike, with a decision that he never regretted, pulled Randy to his feet with a well- chosen handful of hair. Because that seemed to work so well, he decided to escort him all the way back to the station, which was now about 100 yards away, by the hair. About halfway there, Randy tripped and was effectively dragged back to his feet while pleading for leniency.

Sarge finally made it to that point and made an attempt to assist. Mike quickly and firmly stated, "I got this," and continued to drag Randy most of the way back to the building before letting him walk with just an arm hold the last 20 feet.

Sarge, not really knowing exactly what had taken place and now looking somewhat astonished and concerned at Mike's aggressive behavior, looked at Angelo and asked, "Does he always act like that?"

Angelo, who had shared some experiences with Mike on The Crazy Squad and also knew how Sarge operated toward any new squad members, answered, "Only if someone runs on him," then thinking quickly, added, "or if he's working with someone he doesn't like."

Sarge started to ask for a better explanation but hesitated. He let the last part sink in for a moment and then simply said, "Oh."

It became factual that Mike was the only patrolman in memory that did not have to go through the Sarge Sergeant theory of making the new guy on his squad answer all the crap calls. The alleged escape was never mentioned or recorded in any reports. Randy was never charged with the incident, as he reportedly profusely apologized for the better part of twenty minutes and it was thought the hair drag was sufficient punishment for the lack of proper judgment on his part.

Two weeks later, Randy made his appearance in court for the Morrow incident. Without so much as a whimper, he pled guilty, publicly apologized to Mr. Morrow in court, paid his fines, and never complained to anyone about the hair-dragging incident.

In addition, for years whenever Randy and Mike ran into each other, whether job- related or not, Randy was heard to address Mike as Mr. Harding.

CHAPTER 77

Tires That Go Thump in the Night

During the winter months when calls for service were at a minimum and a midnight shift seemed to last much longer than acceptable, patrolmen had a list of "games" they would play to pass the time.

On one particular night, Tommy Setliff and Mike Harding were working. Tommy had called Mike on the radio to meet him in front of the entrance to a local park. The park really wasn't a park but rather a patch of woods that fronted the entrance to the municipal water treatment plant. It had a couple of swing sets and slides, so according to political dignitaries looking to promote recreation for town elections, it was deemed a park.

There were a few houses located down the street from the park and a small business located across the street, so it was fairly remote from people, and a good place to meet with another patrolman and chat without having to worry about passing motorists or other civilians complaining about two police cars being at the same location for any length of time.

Because it was fairly remote, it was also a good spot to do things with a patrol car that one would normally not do anywhere else. Doughnuts in the dirt, squealing of tires on takeoff, and seeing just how close you could get to the other car without scratching it were some of the amusements.

On this particular occasion, Tommy had parked his car in the vicinity of the park's children's slides and was awaiting Mike with his engine running but with his lights off. Mike decided to try to make a grand entrance and while approaching the park area, he turned off his lights, sped up to about 50 mph, and when in the vicinity of the slides slammed on the brakes of the patrol car, leaving a rather long and somewhat permanent tire impression mark on the roadway, which also scared the crap out of Tommy--which of course was the desired effect. The tire mark in the roadway was simply an additional accomplishment added to the imposing entrance.

Once parked alongside Tommy and basking in the success of his efforts to put a bit of panic on Tommy's plate, Mike indicated, "That skid mark was pretty cool, huh?"

Tommy, not to be put off, quickly replied that he thought that he could have done better. With that small bit of competitive counter, a contest was invented, and it was decided that each driver would have three tries to make the longest skid mark on the roadway.

Starting and braking locations were decided. As each car was an identical make and model, it was deemed that vehicle performance should be equal and that only the driver's skill in so-called emergency braking would prevail.

As each man attempted to outdo the other, leaving more and more marks in the road, the end result was that Tommy had indeed won the competition. He credited his victory with applying only the emergency brake and not the brake pedal, which resulted in working only the rear brakes. His stopping distance was greatly increased but that really didn't matter, as there was no real emergency to stop for.

After tiring of the new game and thinking that they should probably leave the area after making so much noise, the boys went about their patrols as usual. In the morning, they picked up their reliefs and basically forgot about the competition.

Unfortunately, Tommy's relief happened to be Sammy Lakeland. Yes, Mr. Serious and Sincere Leukemia Lakeland. After driving around in the patrol car for a while, Sammy thought there was some type of mechanical problem, as the car continually made a small thumping noise. Sammy, not mechanically inclined, advised his sergeant, Billy Durrant, about the noise. Billy told Sam that he should probably take the car to the town garage and have one of the town mechanics take a look at it.

A few minutes after arriving at the garage, Sam called Billy and advised him that the garage wanted to keep the car as it needed tires. Nothing out of the ordinary was indicated at that time, as tires do wear and need to be replaced. When Billy picked up Sammy at the garage, things began to get a little more complicated. Sammy told Billy the mechanics told him that the tires were ruined and had large flat spots on them. Billy said, "Yeah… so what?" Sammy said, "The tires were only two weeks old."

Well with a set of tires costing a sizable amount of cash from the municipal budget after only two weeks' wear, the mechanics decided to advise the chief of the matter. When The Rude heard the news, he grumbled some and drove to the garage. Of course, en route to the garage, he drove past numerous black tire marks in the roadway but at that time really didn't think much about them.

The Rude talked to the mechanics, looked at the tires, grumbled some more, and while returning to the station, again passed the numerous black tire marks in the roadway. Thinking to himself that nah, couldn't be, but also thinking that there was a better than sixty percent chance the marks were in fact the remains of the tires in question, he mumbled, "God damn knuckleheaded gang."

He returned to the station and promptly found out what squad had worked the night before and called the squad's sergeant, Big Ben Bailey. He explained what he found and told him to find out what the hell happened and who did the happening and make sure it never happened again.

That night, Ben got the squad together and passed on the information. In true blue fashion, it had been 24 hours since the competition, so everyone knew who made the tire marks on the roadway and how they were made, but each and every patrolman questioned stated that either they knew nothing about it or had not noticed anything unusual about the cars they had been driving. Tommy did add that he thought he noticed a slight thumping noise under his car the last few nights but thought he had picked up some mud in the treads.

Ben who had also seen the numerous tire marks in the roadway near the park that mysteriously had not been there a few days earlier, looked sternly at Tommy and Mike and said, "Yeah, right, You guys are killin me!"

Needless to say, there were no further tire mark competitions.

CHAPTER 78

The Last Nicky Harlow Story

I n the late 1980s it became common knowledge that Nicky had a serious problem with alcohol. This is not uncommon in police departments, but with Nicky seemingly able to do whatever he wanted to and do it well, it was a bit unnerving to the rest of the department that he would be transforming himself into a hapless individual who didn't seem to want anything more than to be intoxicated.

Nicky had been assigned back onto patrol and out of detectives following his rather embarrassing display of alcohol-induced unorthodox methods of evidence-handling at a homicide scene. The scene was the result of a bludgeoning murder that took place on the beach, with the victim being discovered the following morning by early beachgoers. It seemed that a young lady was beaten to death with a piece of driftwood following some type of domestic argument.

Nicky's peculiar investigation of the scene included showing up for work intoxicated and then walking through the crime location indiscriminately prior to it being properly photographed and diagrammed, and wildly and haphazardly swinging a three-foot-long two-by-four around and over his head, which coincidentally turned out to be the actual murder weapon.

Fortunately, he was removed from the scene rather quickly and transported home before all of the rubberneckers at the scene or the press who showed up later realized he was actually one of the investigators. Fortunately for him and the department, his re-creation of events at the scene was kept under the *thick blue rug* and the suspect, after his arrest, made a full confession.

The whole incident drew a bit of prominence throughout the

remaining summer months at the local bars after a popular bartender thought up a clever concoction of different alcohols and named it "The Two by Four." Those specialty drinks in the beach area were popular the rest of the summer, and with the bludgeoning story being frequently spoken about, very few domestic arguments took place.

Nicky's new patrol assignment was coincidentally in the same general area where he had attempted to re-create what he envisioned took place concerning the bludgeoning murder.

His re-creation also sealed his fate of being permanently assigned back to uniform patrol, with the stipulation that he was operating on his last chance to continue in police work. The zone he was assigned to was known for the fewest number of calls for service during the winter months. This was the area with beachfront hotels and condos that were owned by mostly summer visitors. It was thought that Nicky would be better suited to performing property checks than actually dealing with people's problems, especially since it was fairly clear he had a problem dealing with his own.

By this time, Angelo and Lead Legs were partnered in the detective bureau. One night at about 1:00 a.m. they happened to be returning to Cedar Springs from a neighboring jurisdiction where they had been speaking with a suspect in several robberies involving missing electronics from pleasure boats. Typically, when a suspect was arrested for thefts from pleasure boats, they were ultimately responsible for numerous thefts from numerous boat docking locations in the area.

While passing some of the beach motels, Lead Legs mentioned to Angelo that he thought he had seen one of the town's SUV's out on the beach. Knowing the particular squad that was working, Angelo said that it was probably Nicky and that they should drive over and say hello and see how he was doing.

Lead said in his usual mumble, "Let's try to sneak up on him and scare the crap out of him."

Angelo, in typical Angelo fashion, said, "Yeah, whatever."

They drove around the block, circling another hotel, until they found an area to park and walked down the beach toward the town's SUV that was now parked about 30 feet from the water's edge. The motor was running, the windows were down, and the radio was playing country-western music.

Knowing the recent personal complications he was going through and secretly hoping that Nicky had not decided to try and drown himself, Angelo looked toward the water, which revealed Nicky, in full uniform plus knee-high orange rubber boots and a white boat captain's hat. He had two lines from surf poles in the water and was relaxing in a folding aluminum chair, sipping a beer from a freshly opened six-pack.

When he spotted Angelo and Lead Legs approaching, Nicky snorted, cleared his throat, and hollered in a somewhat alcohol-induced slur,

"No bites yet, but I just got here!"

Both Angelo and Lead assumed that the best thing that they could do for their own futures was to act like they had never been there, and seeing that they could be of no real assistance, offered curt exchanges, advised they had to get back to the station, then returned to their car and left.

It wasn't long after this that Nicky's fishing expedition became public knowledge around the department. It was learned that the fishing excursions had been taking place almost every midnight shift and most of the evening shifts since being transferred from the detective division to patrol. It became clear that Nicky was really no longer interested in police business and on the advice of his wife and as a last-ditch effort by The Rude, entered and tried his third attempt at a 28-day rehab program. Unfortunately, the "third time's the charm" adage did not apply, as his rehab endeavor was unsuccessful and unfinished, as Nicky walked away and returned home on the seventeenth day.

Shortly thereafter, upon The Rude's *request*, which came one day before what was an anticipated *demand*, he voluntarily resigned from the department. Able to collect only a small pension, within six months his house was sold and he and his wife moved to Florida.

Sadly, as these things usually happen, Nicky passed away reportedly due to complications from acute kidney and liver damage only a few years later.

CHAPTER 79

Training for the Changes

Official state-mandated police training was accomplished in the 1960s, 1970s, and 1980s through the state police academy, utilizing their "been there, done that" instructors. Mandated information was offered and written tests were given, which were required to be passed in order to graduate. The trooper instructors also offered many stories with very few embellishments about cases that they had worked on concerning how police work *really* was and how people *really* acted.

The state police patrols covered all the rural areas of the state that did not have their own police departments. They also patrolled and had jurisdiction over all the state highways. They were routinely called in for assistance in some of the larger cities and handled most of the major social and sporting events as security. Due to being involved in these activities throughout the state, there was an abundance of incidental stories to relate to the recruits.

These factual stories were instrumental in differentiating how things worked in the real world vs. how they were described in the books and training manuals. The trooper instructors helped to solidify the fact that there should definitely be and definitely are gray areas in the black and white of law enforcement.

When the 1990s rolled around, the town fathers of Cedar Springs and several other municipalities decided that they could and should offer the mandated training to police by starting their own accredited academy. It was rumored and probably true that this decision had nothing to do with cost vs. savings, but more with plain old political ego and bragging rights that the county was able to provide the same service the state did.

The different departments decided to send some of their employ-ees to additional training to be certified as instructors. To soften the financial part of the endeavor and to make it more of a desirable idea to the taxpayers, they decided to also utilize the location of the academy as a fire fighting training facility.

A plot of land was appropriated, two small buildings were erected, one to be used as an instructional classroom and the other as training for fire fighting.

The land was complete with an outdoor shooting range, and in ad-dition to most of the county's police departments, several in the south-ern end of the state began to utilize the county academy for initial training and subsequent supplementary training in specific areas.

The individual departments involved agreed that any newly ap-pointed instructors would be given time off from their regular duties in order to train the new recruits. The calculated practicality of this action was the fact that the majority of the new instructors were mostly handpicked favored or preferred individuals who ironically, had been recently promoted to administrative positions through the wonders of civil service examinations.

Unfortunately, the painful reality was that with the exception of a very few, most of the new instructors were from dry towns (no alcohol licensed establishments), where personnel spent almost eight months of the year doing physical property checks in affluent neighborhoods, leaving 3X5 index cards in the doors indicating their name, the date, time, and condition of the property when the check was done. The remaining months were spent regulating parking meters, beach and traffic safety, and the occasional loud party complaint.

In towns like this, it could be years where the most controversial police action was the arrest of a burglary suspect, a drunken driver, or a dispute between a business owner and an unhappy customer over the price or the taste of a meal.

It was hard to imagine how someone with little or no experience in aggressive and hostile problematic situations could give guidance and advice to those who might be assigned to areas where there were noth-ing but aggressive and hostile problematic situations. Unfortunately for those attending the new academy, the answers to aggressive and hostile problematic situational questions from rookie recruits soon began to start with, "Well, the book says...."

It was rumored that Stuart Tarrantino was interviewed in the selection process of possible instructors and was initially accepted because of his work with the juveniles, as well as his years in the detective division in Cedar Springs. However, during a quick tour of the sparse facility, Stuart made an instructor career misstep by sarcastically indicating to a county freeholder that an ice cream dispensing machine had to be installed somewhere in the building before he could possibly be comfortable teaching at the academy. Stuart was advised by mail a few days later that due to an over selection of instructors, his anticipated services were no longer required. Years later, following the election of a new freeholder, Stuart was again selected to instruct at the academy bringing more semblance of actual investigative situations and procedures to the new recruits.

Because no dormitories were included in the original plans, the new recruits began attending the county training academy Mondays through Fridays from 8 a.m. to 4 p.m. and were at home sleeping or out partying at night. Patrolmen who went to this academy were somewhat like aeronautical bio-molecular engineers who went to a community college instead of MIT. You get the book education, but unless you're taught by someone who has "been there, done that," it's not quite the same.

New recruits were being taught by the book and nothing but the book. No gray areas, just the black and white in any and all situations. Most damaging was the theory that if it wasn't by the book, then somebody did something wrong, and if you knew about it and didn't say something to someone about it, then you were also wrong.

A new era was beginning to emerge where patrolman who called for backup no longer were assured that whoever showed up would, more times than not, support their actions and protect their back. It was slowly and surely evolving into an era where if assistance showed up, they would critique what was taking place and what actions took place or did not take place and report any gray area decisions to the administration.

The "touchy feely, tell me how you feel, nothing's your fault" teachings of the 1980s and 1990s were catching up to those in law enforcement. It was never uncommon for the police to be criticized by an arrestee or other disgruntled members of the public. However, in the 1990s, after making an arrest, it was not uncommon to be openly criticized or become part of an internal investigation due to statements made by your own department co-employee for the way you spoke to or handcuffed an offender while advising them that they were under arrest. The *Thick Blue Line* was becoming a thin, very light-blue remembrance.

At around the time when The Rude retired, old-fashioned creativity was denounced as not by the book, or something that could be taken as personally offensive. Knowing, working with, or past contacts with those accused of wrongdoings were no longer distinguishing characteristics to be considered when reflecting on how the situation should or could be handled. Recommendations from the county level, who seemed to want to be involved in or just plain be in control of everything, were to follow the letter of the law. Soon the recommendations were no longer recommendations but perceived to be compulsory and mandatory.

The new perception of law enforcement was one where only black and white areas would be permitted, and no venturing into gray areas was to be considered. If the books suggested that someone should be charged if they followed a particular course of action, then it didn't matter what the circumstances were or who the particular person was who had followed that action. Personalities and past behavior, good or bad, were no longer to be considered. Friends, relatives, and/or specific personal problems didn't matter anymore.

Cedar Springs, along with the rest of the country's police, embraced advanced technology with the addition of pagers, mobile telephones, personal protection equipment, and of course computers, but the personal interaction with the community digressed to the point that there was no longer any real meaningful personal communication or contact.

Even the addition of a community policing unit failed to reach any common goals, as they were utilized primarily to patrol so-called problem areas and to write traffic tickets. This always succeeded in making people so much more satisfied and comfortable with their police department when handed a $35 seat belt ticket or a $100 speeding ticket for going five miles over the limit while making a milk run for the baby to the local convenience store.

As patrolmen were promoted through the ranks, they were being sent to officers' training courses, which stressed that individual decisions not sanctioned by the letter of the law or by an administrator would not be the suggested means of handling a situation. It seems that occupational liabilities and attorneys trained to sue for anything and everything had even reached police work and its employees.

The new department became very black and white, and personnel were advised to leave any personal feelings, or ideas of doing something another way, at home. No deals for information from suspects were tolerated unless first approved by the county prosecutor's office or one of their law advisors. Even when approved, it was sometimes suggested that the individual supplying the information be charged with conspiracy, which could be dropped at a later time should the information lead to a conviction, just to be sure they had covered all the bases and could not be chastised at a later time for showing any type of favoritism.

Patrol units were advised not to make any decisions unless they were absolutely certain they could not be challenged. They were told it was better to ask their sergeant for advice, who themselves were told to ask the lieutenant or captain for advice or to call the county for their advice.

Today The Rude would probably be demoted or disciplined for not answering the questions of the town fathers in more detail other than "I'll look into it" and certainly chastised for smoking in a public building.

Captain Benny would probably be under scrutiny by the county prosecutor for adding his "spin doctor" wisdom to an internal affairs investigation concerning some indiscretion by one of the patrolmen.

Pappy Buck would definitely be fired for any number of reasons, most of which would have involved alcohol.

Billy Durant would probably be given days off without pay for spending too much time in his garden and out of uniform while on duty.

Pinochle Pete would probably be banned from law enforcement for betting on court decisions, even though he would have probably lost every bet.

Lead Legs Roberts would probably be ordered by a judge to go to a speech therapist to find out exactly what he was mumbling about.

Big Ben Bailey would probably be civilly sued by his neighbor for property damage or indicted for keeping perishable evidence which he shared with other cops.

Sergeant Dudley Sergeant would probably be sent to a psychiatrist to find out exactly what he was thinking.

Dispatcher Dooley would probably be given a Nobel Peace award after quelling his 1000th bar fight call utilizing only the threat of sending out some of his boys.

Jim Burry would probably be civilly sued by some petty criminal who pocketed a candy bar at a convenience store after being hog-tied by the police following Jim's explanation to the responders that the suspect was an extremely dangerous martial arts expert with homicidal tendencies.

Harriet Slater would be charged with animal cruelty by PETA after repeatedly smashing a box containing endangered salamanders left in the dispatch center, which were scheduled to be picked up by state wildlife authorities.

Millie Townson would be charged with harassment in a class action proceeding by over one hundred former arrestees who never got their breakfasts.

And virtually every member of The Gang would end up resigning after being told they could no longer use their own discretion or ideas when dealing with local matters.

Personalities and eccentric peculiarities aside, the *Thick Blue Line* group of the 1960s, 1970s, and 1980s would be missed more they ever realized.

CHAPTER 80

Changes and Retirement

In the 1990s many changes took place, not only in Cedar Springs but in the county, the state, and the entire country.

Reminiscent of Henry Ford introducing the affordable automobile to the public making travel, exploration, and new experiences possible to everyone, the 1980s and 1990s technology made available any and every circumstance or event that took place in public or private to everyone through television, radio, computers, and personal cellular telephones. This availability also reduced the possibility that one could conduct their lives without being chastised for decisions they made that were contrary to the popular norm.

It seemed as though the more that people embraced advanced technology, the smaller one's private world became. With so much information now available to the public, police were analyzed more closely than ever before.

Too often, perceptions of situations began to be and still seem to be stated as factual by members of the media and the so-called advocates for social change before investigations are remotely started, much less completed. Statements, both incomplete and taken out of context, also seem to add misconceptions concerning events that either took place, or were reported to have taken place.

In short, the end result of too much available information has resulted in what has become known as:

"People who make decisions about the actions of others must live in glass houses that everyone is permitted to throw stones at."

After so many years of dodging the stones, it eventually becomes something that you don't look forward to anymore.

Now anyone who has worked any type of job usually looks forward to the time that they no longer have to. Police officers are no different. In fact, most cops look forward to this a lot more than the average person does.

The vast majority of police officers who worked in areas of high crime and even those who worked in relatively low-crime areas will tell you that twenty to twenty-five years in police work is more than enough. They all hate to admit the fact that police work, somewhat like parenting or being in the military, is a young man's--or being politically correct, a young person's--game.

There are only so many times a person can genuinely show empathy toward other human beings' misfortunes and hardships. After a while one begins to lose the concept of being compassionate, impartial, and nonjudgmental. When witnessed tragedy becomes "ho-hum," it's time to move on and do something else.

Spouses and children also become involved in the retirement process--either because you haven't spent enough time with them or haven't spent enough time with them without thinking about the job.

Good cops are like adrenalin junkies. They want to be on the job solely because they don't want to miss what just might happen or the chance to be involved in the conclusion or what has happened, whether that conclusion is good or bad.

Even this curiosity runs its course, and one day they realize that they just don't want to know, and just don't care what happens. Once again, this genuinely is the formidable clue for one to move on.

Those who actually attempted to be of assistance on the job rather than another hindrance in people's lives usually merged back into society without many disparaging events along the way and generally found life after law enforcement enjoyable.

The cops of the 1950s through the 1980s were unique. The times and the solutions to problems were also unique. Admittedly, sometimes the solutions worked and sometimes they did not, but the unique attempt was there, and those that benefited from them appreciated them.

Nowadays the overabundance of media coverage toward any type of controversial police actions by the "one in a thousand" knuckleheaded cop, who probably shouldn't have been a cop to begin with, also undermines any respect or appreciation toward the profession. The daily heroic or kind-hearted actions of the hundreds of thousands of good cops largely go unreported, unnoticed, and unappreciated.

Unfortunately, the media has yet to realize that their push for what they perceive to be equality or diversity for anyone who sought to be in law enforcement not only lowered the standards by which those in law enforcement were chosen but also lowered the personal ethical standards of the profession.

Times may have changed and inevitably will continue to change. Law enforcement situations have and will become more complicated and even more open to suggestion. The truth is that law enforcement hasn't changed. The laws have changed. The police are still the ones who are entrusted with the resolve to determine whether infractions of the laws have taken place, and to what extent. They then need the fortitude to deal with them equitably but with realistic options that will satisfy the complaint without discrimination.

Whether you're in support of or in opposition toward law enforcement, for whatever reasons you may have, when faced with any type of crisis or emergency, you still want to call the police for assistance.

Using conservative numbers, there are approximately well over one million sworn police officers or those with powers of arrest in the United States. With any type of occupation comprised of this many people; there will be instances of errors and/or mistakes mostly made by those who probably shouldn't have been in that line of work to begin with.

The press and media are quick to converge on the mistakes made by police, usually prior to a definite determination being made as to whether their actions were justified or not justified. Meanwhile, the countless millions of good, hard-working, civic-minded police officers do their jobs and do them well, without so much as a thank you for being the referees between a peaceful existence and lawlessness.

Even with new personnel seemingly being trained to shy away from doing anything other than what the law says, as well as to seek an administrator's advice prior to making a decision in the field, most cops are still just regular people who for some reason chose a sometimes dangerous, sometimes boring, sometimes exciting, sometimes depressing, and sometimes even fun occupation.

Hopefully there will always be those who choose to make the best decisions based upon the particular circumstances and not just what a book says.

The End

Printed in the USA
CPSIA information can be obtained
at www.ICGtesting.com
LVHW041253151023
761121LV00001BB/101